The Unlikely Gunwharf Rats

Carla Kelly

Kenmore, WA

Camel Press books published by Epicenter Press

Epicenter Press
6524 NE 181st St. Suite 2
Kenmore, WA 98028.
www.Epicenterpress.com
www.Coffeetownpress.com
www.Camelpress.com

For more information go to: www.Epicenterpress.com
Author's website: www.carlakellyauthor.com

The Unlikely Gunwharf Rats
Copyright © 2024 by Carla Kelly

ISBN: 9781684921430 (trade paper)
ISBN: 9781684921447 (ebook)

LOC: 2023945702

Printed in the United States of America

Dedication

To Euclid.
I wish I had paid more attention in plane geometry class
at A.C. Jones High School in Beeville, Texas.

Books by Carla Kelly

Fiction

Things which are equal to the same thing are also equal to one another. If equals be added to equals, the wholes are equal. If equals be subtracted from equals, the remainders are equal. Things which coincide with one another are equal to one another.

An Axiom of Euclid (around 300 B.C.)

Prologue

To say that Davey Ten, Gunwharf Rat and former workhouse boy, understood dismal days was no exaggeration. In the workhouse he learned that he was nothing but a blight upon the economy of England and fit for nothing but the meanest labor. As a Gunwharf Rat in Portsmouth's St. Brendan the Navigator School, he learned that not only his skills, but he, himself, were worth much more to the Royal Navy and a nation at war.

This was the reality he took to the University of Edinburgh's exalted College of Medicine. To his dismay, he learned by degrees that in the eyes of his professors and peers, he was still a workhouse boy, now inflicted on the college and worthy of no one's notice.

This dismay didn't come all at once. He was a member of the Royal Navy, he wore the black uniform of St. Brendan's proudly, and he had no vulgar habits. He was never one to put himself forward. After Trafalgar, he knew, with hard-earned confidence, that he had nothing to prove to anyone.

Maybe not, but Davey soon became aware of scrutiny of the meanest sort, however subtle at first. When he raised his hand to answer a question, he was never selected. At first, he put it down to the other sea of hands that generally went up, along with his, because this was not an ignorant set of prospective physicians.

The matter was confirmed to him on a more sophisticated question concerning the circulation of blood. His was the only hand raised this time, and the professor ignored him. Maybe Davey could joke with the other students about that later, and laugh that his blood ran in chunks when he was so blatantly overlooked. Blood in chunks? Haha.

He had no friends there, no one to confide in or gripe with. In his early zeal and fear that he needed to do some monumental catching up to fit in with this sterling bunch, he hadn't sought friends. It was soon obvious to him that he had none. No one sought him out, no one with whom to share notes and ideas, no professor who even slightly resembled a mentor. Nothing but silence.

Davey remembered his beloved teacher Master Able Six reminiscing with the Gunwharf Rats on one of their ship-to-shore jaunts to the blockaded French coast and back, bearing dispatches to – in his own mind certainly – a vastly superior sloop captain who knew of the Rats' mean origins. "He's rude to us Rats, so we'll kill him with kindness," Master Able advised. And so they had, perplexing the captain, to their real satisfaction.

Master Six had jokingly warned them that this was only the revenge of the powerless. "I wonder if anyone not raised in a workhouse – I include myself – truly understands genuine kindness as well as we do," he told them on another night.

By the end of that endless term, Davey Ten had learned a different, more terrible truth: *They're killing me with silence.*

Chapter One

The silence finally moved Davey Ten to tears, no matter how much he wanted to spare Master Six from what he had endured for a year and more at the University of Edinburgh's College of Medicine. Silence both profound in its judgment upon his status as a workhouse bastard, and cruel in its treatment of a Royal Navy surgeon's assistant, bona fide Gunwharf Rat.

There was also the matter of serving with valor at Trafalgar aboard a small messenger craft with no guns or cannon, only stalwart lads and a master of fierce resolve.

On this return journey from Edinburgh to Portsmouth for a longer-then-usual Christmas break, Davey decided he would say nothing about the silence to anyone. Mrs. Six – the Rats called her Mam – had insisted he write monthly letters, which meant there was plenty to say about the classes, the hours spent in the Royal Infirmary's indigent ward, and the grind of book study. He could tell her of surgeries attended, along with curious onlookers off the street, some of whom fainted at the gruesome sight. Before Edinburgh, Davey had never considered surgery a spectator sport.

From Captain Dutton of the scrappy *Mars* and his exploding head, to men on fire and leaping in the water, he had seen worse at Trafalgar than in the operating bays at the College of Medicine. A Gunwharf Rat prided himself on remaining calm in all surgeries and medical emergencies. He decided he needn't trouble Mam about the silence, this strange sort of bullying that ground him down worse that a schoolyard pummeling

1

would have. He had plenty of stories. She would never suspect what he was leaving out, what coldness he faced daily in a place of medical education.

He knew it wasn't supposed to be like this. What had he done to deserve veiled looks, lads laughing together as he passed them in the halls, the turning away when he worked up the nerve to question someone. He had found the cellar privies on his own because he had no choice but to search.

After Trafalgar, his immediate plans to travel north to the University of Edinburgh at Mrs. Mary Munro's recommendation – she was a lady of influence – had been thwarted by war for a year. Although the Admiralty had promised Master Six that the *Mercury* would be released from duty, the demands of war claimed her due in weeks of carrying messages to and from the blockade. Arguably, what the Rats learned aboard the *Mercury* eclipsed anything found even in Master Six's classroom, since he taught his Rats on land and sea.

The only one among them who suffered was Master Six, who missed his son and daughter, and the gentleness that was Mam to them, but Meri to him, her husband and lover. This meant Mam welcomed them inside their home on the lee side of St. Brendan's and held out her arms to her husband.

Mrs. Perry, that big, black cook who frightened younger Rats, took them in hand then for food while the Sixes went upstairs and closed their door. It was at sea where Master Six answered their questions about life and love and told them not to hang around the docks for "poxy hoors," as he called them. Master Six, whose genius probably allowed him to instantly adopt any lingual inflection he chose, had never abandoned his Dumfries Scot voice. Not for him the cultured sound of Captain Sir Belvedere St. Anthony – gone almost three years now. "I'm a Scot," Master Six said simply.

The sea beckoned them all, and war suited the Gunwharf Rats right down to the deck. The bright spot in the tedium of ship-to-shore messaging on the blockade had been the chance to hove to alongside the *Dauntless*, a 28-gun frigate, and see Smitty – silent, no smiles, but something in his eyes of pride and duty – serving as the sailing master's assistant, a rating lower than mate, but a living, breathing sign of the worth of Gunwharf Rats to the fleet.

Messages delivered, they had returned to the *Mercury* and laughed over Master Six's story of four captains and masters nearly coming to gentlemanlike blows over who would get Smitty. Like Davey in the sickbay, Smitty had proved his worth on deck at Trafalgar.

Still unarmed, the *Mercury* had come upon several ship-to-ship skirmishes off the Barbary Coast and Spain, where blood was spilled, and Davey's services required. He had sutured and cauterized – this under Master Six's tutelage – and set bones, plying his rough trade in Channel chop and those greasy swells before a storm that sent many Rats to the railing to puke. Davey would have followed them, but his hands were busy with suturing needles or capital knives, on Able Six's watch. Davey learned to master himself, much like the quiet teacher beside him.

That was war. A promising surgeon's assistant, Davey continued his education at Haslar Hospital because now and then, the *Mercury* did not require his services. Not until the following autumn, did he make his way to Edinburgh and formal education, as promised earlier by Mary Munro, Master Six's newly discovered grandmama.

It had been on the tip of his tongue to ask Master Six to let him continue at Haslar and learn naval surgery from men who practiced it. With tutelage from the staff of the busy naval and Royal Marine hospital, he knew he could eventually pass the rigorous exams to qualify him as a surgeon to the fleet, a warranted officer.

There was no overlooking Master Six's eagerness to send a Rat to that distinguished repository of medical knowledge in Edinburgh. "We Rats" – for so Master Six included himself – "are earning renown for excellence in the fleet," he had assured Davey. "Your matriculation will further burnish our reputation. Both Sir B and Headmaster Croker, bless their memories, wanted this, too."

Davey acquiesced, arriving in Edinburgh with money waiting for him at Mrs. Munro's counting house, where her more-than-comfortable fortune nestled. With money, credit, and a letter to Silsby's Room and Board close by the grey stone walls of the university, he had been assigned a clean but spartan suite on the first floor.

Mrs. Munro must have written a highly convincing letter requesting Davey's admission to the chancellor of the university. The summons waited for Davey in Mrs. Silsby's apartment on the ground floor, with the admonition to not waste a minute in appearing before the chancellor, a stern-looking Scot name of Winston McLeish.

Davey had arrived in uniform, of course, wearing the black coat and trousers of St. Brendan the Navigator School, with the school's patch over his heart. Headmaster Ferrier had informed Davey before he took the mail coach north that he would remain in uniform because St. Brendan's had recently come under the supervision – irregular, but there you are – of the Royal Navy. "Besides all that, Mr. Ten, you are already a surgeon's assistant," Headmaster Ferrier had reminded him, as if he needed reminding.

Here he was in Edinburgh, seventeen now. Chancellor McLeish sat him down with tea and biscuits in front of a welcome fireplace and asked about his history at St. Brendan's. Davey made his first mistake: He thought the chancellor was actually interested in him as a human being. Davey's description of years in a workhouse, with a bastard last name of Ten, because he was the tenth wretched foundling in that year, made the chancellor frown.

The dignified man in his black robes of scholarship seemed to understand. He sighed when Davey told him about his change of fortune from a London workhouse to St. Brendan the Navigator School. He leaned forward with apparent interest as Davey described this new school where England's castoffs might receive an education to set them on a path to leadership in the Royal Navy, in this time of grave national emergency.

Sitting on the mail coach now on his return to Portsmouth, determined not to disappoint Master Six, Davey knew he had no total recall of all conversation, as Master Genius did. But even now, he cringed to think of what he had told the chancellor. "Sir, Master Six informed us that St. Brendan's headmaster then, Mr. Croker, had found us when he asked workhouse masters to give him their most troublesome boys for his new school."

Why did he say that, even if it was true? Headmaster Croker, gone these three years, had come to realize that the troublesome boys might be bored because they were bright and needed the challenge of a place like St. Brendan's, and not the bleak misery of a workhouse. "He knew you," Master Six had told the Gunwharf Rats simply. "I was the same way. I wanted more, and so do you."

Davey looked out the mail coach window at the rain dribbling down the pane, some of it seeping inside. *And then I told the chancellor about the Gunwharf Rats*, he thought. *Why did I do that?*

How was he to know, or even suspect, that Chancellor McLeish loved a good tale? Like most Gunwharf Rats, Davey knew how to read a room, as Master Six put it. "I suppose we Rats are naturally suspicious," Master Six had told them early, when they were all shivering in their smallclothes, learning to swim in the stone-lined pool next to the old monastery-now-school. "Don't make a career of suspicion, lads, but make sure you know who to trust."

God help him, he had forgotten that lesson. Chancellor McLeish shared his story with the faculty of the medical school, something Davey learned too late from one of the students who broke that vow of silence imposed since Day One in anatomy class. "We know who you are," the student said, when Davey gathered the courage to ask why he was ignored when he raised his hand to answer a question, or ignored by students his own age who turned away when he approached. "You don't belong in polite society."

"But who…"

The student, more patient than the others, or possibly more cruel, had continued Davey's rough education at the University of Edinburgh, the education St. Brendan's and Mrs. Munro weren't paying for. "Chancellor McLeish warned all of us to stay away from you because you are a joke foisted on us and our scholarship. Go away."

Davey endured in silence, taking his usual careful notes, watching with envy, then despair, the easy camaraderie of the others, probably sons from comfortable homes, if not august ones, because nobody in higher social spheres would have considered medicine as a vehicle for advancement. No, *those* sons might be law students eventually, called to the bar and serving in courts, bewigged and gowned. Medicine remained a rung down, even if it was respectable, and money could be made.

These were lads from good homes, lads with mother and father and siblings, not babies found in hedgerows or on church steps like Master Six, who had survived a rough beginning of his own. No, these were lads educated in church and chapel to be good Christians and assist the deserving poor, within limits. Toss money in a collection box and let others do the dirty work. These were students seeking the advanced degree of physician. Not for them a surgeon's sick bay in a heaving frigate's underbelly during a noisy fleet action.

Why am I here? Davey asked himself as he studied, took notes, and made superlative grades that seemed to startle his professors, who had predestined him to fail. His best moment was the assignment to attend in the Royal Infirmary for the Poor and Indigent, Ward B. He understood these patients, who came to the wards usually too late to receive any real medical care.

He ward-walked with a few volunteer physicians, men in general practice who provided this free service to teach students. Some students fainted at the sight of entrails, or babies half born and women dying after days of dry labor.

Not Davey; he understood. Long after the others left, gagging and retching for show, he sat beside terrified children, smelly vagrants, and women used cruelly since childhood. He wiped faces and held hands and felt the nobility of the profession he wanted, but which seemed to be receding from his view because of the studied neglect forced upon him by faculty and students.

To his chagrin, he discovered he was the only student assigned to the indigent ward. The other, more favored classmates ward-walked in the Royal Infirmary's ward for the middle-class and "deserving" poor, Ward A.

When he did not think he could take another moment of others' derision, good fortune smiled upon him. Well, smiled upon them all, if he had felt inclined to charity toward his tormentors.

He had been dreading the advent of Christmas, a mere two weeks of respite from school, and not enough time to travel to the opposite end of the island to Portsmouth and St. Brendan's. He had already decided to spend most of those weeks in Edinburgh in Indigent Ward B.

His good fortune was an outbreak of erysipelas in those selfsame wards, of such magnitude that patients died, and even three of the older students. The professors, worried and upset, had importuned the chancellor to close the school for a month. Davey's *materia medica* professor had explained it this way. "Now we know that ill humors and bad air spread such ailments with amazing rapidity," he told them all. "We will suspend classes after tomorrow's examinations, and dismiss you. We will not risk your lives."

Davey smiled at that, wondering how such hot house flowers would fare among the bad air found in the average Royal Navy vessel. Of itself, bad air didn't carry disease from patient to patient. It couldn't – or so he suspected – but that was his little secret apparently. Still, a month!

He could go home. He could rethink this painful, silent education and decide if it was worth it. Mam would understand. Surely a Haslar surgeon would take him in hand and teach him in the wards full of Marines and sailors fresh from battle.

Would Master Six understand? Oh, please let him.

Chapter Two

"**M**r. Ten, will you be returning when school begins again?"

Davey started, embarrassed, because he so seldom heard his name on anyone's lips. For Christ's sake, it was his landlady, not some bully trying to corner him. He looked into wary eyes. Amazing how someone's background could come to everyone's attention, even in a city the size of Edinburgh.

I sincerely doubt I am returning, he wanted to tell her. Once he admitted - if he did - to Master Six and Mam what he had endured, he didn't know what would happen. Better not say no, though. "Aye, Mrs. Silsby, I'll be back," he told her. "No need to do anything to my room. I will see you in one month."

"Very well," she said.

She was a thin woman and a busy one. The lodging housed twenty students and he knew the widow ran from morning to night, tending to minutiae that he never dreamed of troubling anyone about. After all, he was perfectly capable of getting his own slops down to the backhouse in the yard, rinsing out his chamber pot and taking it up two flights of stairs. He knew how to sweep out a room, too. Hell, he could swab it out and holystone the floor, if she wished. Excepting St. Brendan's when Mam and Master Six took him in, he had been well trained in subservience in the workhouse and in the rough and tumble of fleet actions.

Therein lay the problem, even with a busy landlady. None of the others carried out their nighttime leavings or mopped their floors, or tidied up in any way, if the sight of her mopping and hauling at all hours was any indication. She must have observed how her other boarders ignored him, and how he did the work of a workhouse lad with no complaint, and in the seeing, slighted him, too.

"I'll return," he repeated, even though he knew he lied. He would write the landlady from the safety of St. Brendan's and mail back the room key. He imagined her going inside his room, irritated that now she had to forward his belongings, until she saw that he had taken everything with him. The floor was swept. The sheets and blanket folded neatly at the foot of the bed. It would be as though he had never suffered the abuse of silence for one and a half terms.

A Gunwharf Rat travels light. He had first come to St. Brendan's from London's Pancras Workhouse with the clothes on his back, and nothing more except a comb with teeth missing. He went north to Edinburgh with two St. Brendan's uniforms, blouses and changes of linen, plus books, capital knives and surgeon's kit, and shaving supplies. Ever the teacher, Master Six, towel around his middle, had taught him to shave after a good look at Davey during their return from Trafalgar.

"What a pair we make," Master Six had teased him in the washroom of the Six's house across the street from St. Brendan. "We go through an unnerving battle. Your face sprouts whiskers and my hair turns gray."

Eager to leave Edinburgh, Davey added textbooks to his duffel – one of Master Six's – and his treasured, beloved sextant. No, only the velvet-lined case now. The sextant was a gift from Ezekiel Bartleby, baker and former gunner's mate whose bakery supplied Mrs. Six with her favorite sugar-sided petit fours – he always made more when she was with child. He often gifted the Rats with dinnerplate-sized cinnamon buns.

Mr. Bartleby's gift of a sextant puzzled him at first, since he was destined for the sickbay below deck, and not fighting above board. However, in the strange environment of a medical school, the sextant quickly became his lifeline to the Royal Navy he was already missing, and the people who cared for him. The sextant had come with advice. "Listen to me, Davey Ten," Bartleby said, making no attempt to hide his emotion. "Above and beyond its actual use, this sextant will remind you who you are, a member of the Royal Navy. Take it out and look at it as often as you need to."

He must have looked at it one time too many. He set the beautiful thing on top of the case and placed it in a prominent spot on his bureau, where he could see it after each trying, soul-sapping, silent day in class.

One day he dragged himself upstairs to find it gone. The sight brought him to his knees in disbelief.

He told Mrs. Silsby, who shrugged and said to keep his door locked. He assured her he did, and she fixed him with a scowl. "Blaming me, you pup?" she asked.

"No, Mrs. Silsby." What else was there to say? He knew he would mourn the loss of Mr. Bartleby's sextant forever, this first gift. Well, it made the duffel lighter, he decided. One had to be philosophical about misfortune, which probably made workhouse bastards the most philosophical creatures on England's sceptered isle. He packed the velvet-lined case, along with his medical kit and Master Six's treasured capital knives, which he had prudently kept hidden under his mattress.

Davey knew he could turn his back on Edinburgh with few qualms. He dreaded facing Headmaster Ferrier at St. Brendan's, a quiet man who could speak commandingly loud when volume was needed. Master Ferrier had a way of fixing a blood-freezing stare that had probably terrorized any number of midshipmen, when confronted by a navigation expert determined to teach his skills aboard many a ship of the line. As headmaster, Mr. Ferrier had also become unflinching in his loyalty to the Rats of St. Brendan's.

Davey knew Mrs. Six would welcome him with open arms, she being a generous sort and fond of her Rats. Hadn't she and Davey and Nick, now serving as assistant secretary to Admiral Lord Collingwood himself, cleaned those rat bones that were now mounted on a plaque at St. Brendan's? He had no doubt of her love.

Master Six was the mystery. There was no finer man, but what would he do? Davey knew he must face his mentor and find out, unless he left the mail coach between Edinburgh and Portsmouth and melted into the English countryside. Perhaps Canada's great interior would call his name. The last person in the world he ever wanted to disappoint was Durable Six.

So, he settled aboard a mail coach, money in his purse for inns and meals, and misery in his heart.

The misery only lasted until the mail coach thundered out of Edinburgh. Davey leaned back, closed his eyes, and felt his shoulders relax as tension poured from his body. He was free of the medical school, and he knew it. What a relief. Not even two farm wives carrying baskets, one with a noisy goose inside; a parson, probably of the Presbyterian faith, contentedly reading the Bible despite the noise; and two children of middling age carrying protesting goslings, disturbed his peace.

Or so he thought. He ended up staring out the fogging window, wondering about ambition, and the acquisition of knowledge, and the sheer folly of trying to turn from a sow's ear into a silk purse. The odd image made him smile, but it didn't last long. He knew he would have worried less, had he any idea of the reception that awaited him in Portsmouth. Thank God scurrilous, raffish Pompey was two days away.

He took a book from his satchel that went with him everywhere, containing a bistoury, those capital knives, and bandages and ointments that all students carried, or at least those few who listened to and benefited from lectures in *materia medica*, as taught by someone almost as quiet as he was, Josiah Coffin.

Davey put the text back in his satchel, content to think of the one pleasant memory of the college of medicine. Hardly could a man be more inappropriately named, unless one thought too long about Ten as a surname to rejoice in. Mr. Coffin was different from the other professors. No one ever told Davey, because no one spoke to him, but he overhead gleanings from the others about Coffin the Quaker, which made some of them convulse into laughter of the mean kind usually leveled at Davey. The meaner among them would shake as though they had palsy. "Look, I'm quaking," made those idiots laugh.

Coffin the Quaker dressed soberly in black, which made Davey give him another look, since he wore black, too, the St. Brendan's uniform with the patch of St. Brendan holding tight to a vessel out of the Dark Ages. Outdoors, the quiet instructor wore a flat black hat. To Davey's surprise, Mr. Coffin did not bow when the chancellor of the university entered a classroom or was encountered during daily obligatory prayer. Mr. Coffin also did not bow the time Lord Sinclair, a wealthy peer, donated one thousand pounds to the college. Mr. Coffin remained upright when others bowed to the marquess. Davey decided Quakers bowed to nobody. No wonder many of them had been hounded throughout England in the past century. He also heard they did not swear oaths.

During Mr. Coffin's first lecture, the matter explained itself, if Davey had any doubts. "Gentlemen, thee are to be prepared at all times to alleviate suffering, no matter who amongst the many on earth crosses thy path," Mr. Coffin announced. He spoke softly, requiring the students to pay attention. "Thee will make no exceptions, on pain of angering Deity, who loves all his children equally."

Mr. Coffin wrote on the board what he wanted each of them to carry in a satchel, from smelling salts to tightly wound bandages. He looked at the satchel Davey already carried as a matter of course, a battered leather carryall that had seen hard duty at Trafalgar. The glance earned Davey a smile and a slight nod, reassuring him as nothing else could have. His only comment, "Thee already knows what to do," also warmed Davey.

The professors took turns teaching *materia medica* to the first-year students. Davey had braced himself for the worst in his initial encounter with higher education, he who had no education really, except at St. Brendan the Navigator School, located on quiet All Saints Way. A week of lectures made Davey realize he already knew what was being taught. He had learned it under fire in the fleet. He took dutiful notes anyway, even when the others joked around and wrote precious little.

His next encounter with Mr. Coffin came during a painful time when Mr. Alistair Grundy, chief professor of first-year students, assigned everyone duty in the Royal Infirmary, the teaching wards directly next to the university. Master Six had told him that the Royal Infirmary alone was what set apart Edinburgh's medical school from other institutions of medical learning.

"Even beginning students ward-walk there," Master Six explained. "The poor will be your workshop."

Mr. Grundy made this duty clear when he explained the Royal Infirmary, reminding the students that the university's enlightened attitude toward treatment of all, even those who could not pay, reflected the best of Christianity. "It is your duty to attend," he thundered, and glared at them all. "Clean a wound, hold a hand, wipe a fevered brow. The infirmary is your medical Valley of the Shadow of Death."

Davey looked at the shocked expressions of his fellow students, reminding himself that none of them were at Trafalgar to see men clutching their entrails, burned gunners staring at unrecognizable hands, now stumps, or sailors regarding with the odd complacency of the dying, that place where a missing leg shot a stream of blood across the slippery deck. To them it might seem like a rung of hell. To him, it was merely Tuesday, and a long one.

Mr. Alistair made the assignments. Davey knew he would be named last, already resigned to being the afterthought. A mere two weeks at the college had already cured him of the notion that he was only one of many, and not a leper with bells to shake and warn away others.

The assignments were four nights a week for two hours. Mr. Alistair assured the classmates when he handed out the assignments, "You'll work amongst the deserving poor."

To Davey's everlasting shame, he turned last to him. "You, Mr. Ten, will be more at home among the undeserving poor: the bastards, the drunken sots, the whores, the homeless. They have their own ward. Gentlemen, you are dismissed."

There it was. He, Davey Ten, was the butt of a carefully designed joke in humiliation, perhaps to shame him into leaving this august place. He would have left, except he had nowhere to go. To return in defeat to Portsmouth so soon was unthinkable.

Head high, eyes straight ahead, Davey ward-walked alone. To the Royal Infirmary's credit, even the undeserving poor were daily well-tended and clean, bandages in place. He checked their bandages, sniffed them for gangrene, and kept the patients warm. No one instructed him, but he read the physicians' scrawled instructions at the foot of each bed, and administered what medications had been prescribed, because whether anyone knew or cared, he was a Royal Navy surgeon's assistant and knew his business.

He had seen to the admission of a prostitute, rough-handled and who knew what else by two watchmen of the precinct, her eyes rolling in her head. "Befuddled by opium," the constable told him with a wink.

He cleaned her as best he could as she moaned and grabbed at him, all the while talking fast, her eyes dilated, her mind wandering in some place that he hoped was better than her usual cold street corner in this drafty, damp town. She slept finally, snoring loudly and whimpering.

He fled the ward with all the dignity he could muster, when the orderly relieved him at midnight, then shivered in bed nearly until dawn, marveling as his own inadequacies. Where was the mentoring physician on *his* shift?

They want me to fail, he thought.

Chapter Three

The mail coach slowed for an inn and the coachman blew on his yard of tin. Unnerved even now, the school miles away, Davey Ten forced himself to drink porter and swallow a stale sandwich as the horses were changed and the coach readied for the distance to Carlisle.

The farm wives with their geese and goslings left the mail coach, to be replaced by salesmen with sample cases and a timid-looking female who might be a governess, a fate possibly worse than his. At least he could ship out on a Royal Navy vessel because he was a surgeon's assistant. What could a governess do except endure the slights and jibes, count her small salary, and wonder if she could support herself until death?

No one spoke to him in the public house, but he was used to that. Better to sit in the corner again, close his eyes and think of what had happened that next night in the Royal Infirmary. It began the same as the one two days before. He would much rather have been studying for another bones examination in Anatomy, this one on the feet. Who knew feet could have so many bones? As he left his room at the boarding house, he watched the other students studying in a group, testing each other, and envied them.

The night was raw, even for September, but the infirmary close. At least he could be thankful for his Royal Navy boat cloak, and watch cap, not nearly as dignified as Master Six's fore and aft hat, but definitely warmer.

As soon as he arrived, the orderly on duty left for his meal. Hoping for no problems that he could not solve, he walked the men's ward. He sat with a one-armed man feeding another one-armed man, and enjoyed their quiet banter. He knew one was homeless and the other a hopeless drunkard who had fallen down a well, of all things, nearly drowned and dislocated his shoulder. Infection set in with this result, but here he was, eating gruel and feeling good enough to smile.

The women's ward was also quiet. He sat beside the opium-addled woman, shaking his head over the deep scratches on her arms. He recognized the itch, seeing it on a frigate in the Mediterranean, where the *Mercury* had delivered dispatches. The captain had cajoled Captain Six – for such was the master's rank aboard their little yacht – to take the man to the infirmary in the Azores, run as a satellite aid station.

"I warned the crew about what they could find in the *souks* of Algeria," the captain said. "He's useless to me now."

He saw the same futile scratching as he watched the woman dig at the ants moving just under her skin, or so she insisted. He took a moment to prepare plasters of calomel for her forearms and left her feeling somewhat relieved. He knew it would not last long.

A woman two beds down burned with fever. Her chart told the tale of a failed birthing and a placenta that would not budge until a physician pulled it out. *And why did you not find a surgeon*, Davey thought in anger as he read the words again. *Physicians know nothing about surgery*.

She was too far gone to know anything, so Davey pulled back the coverlets and stared at her swollen belly and inflamed private parts. What could he possibly do? *I am inadequate*, he thought, something he already suspected.

"Mr. Ten, thee is seeing what happens when a physician, well-intentioned or not, never bothers to wash his hands."

There stood Mr. Coffin, watching so quietly behind him. "It's that simple?" Davey asked, when he recovered from the sudden fright. His next emotion was relief; he was not alone.

"I think it is, though my colleagues laugh at me behind my back," the man in black replied.

"Can we do anything for this lady, sir?"

"We're too late, lad. If thee remembers anything from this evening's work, remember to wash your hands, preferably in hot water, as you move from bed to bed and touch people. Physicians except me will laugh at you; ignore them." He looked at Davey, and his eyes seemed to bore inside his skull. "Do this even for the undeserving poor, because we are all equal in the sight of God."

In silence, the two of them sat on either side of the bed, holding the woman's hands, wiping her fever-red face, until she died. "Don't let them die alone, if thee can help it," Mr. Coffin said. He pulled out his timepiece. "Time of death, eleven in the evening. Write that on her chart and initial it." His smile was bitter. "Cause of death, medical malpractice. No, no. Don't write that, even if it is true."

When they parted company that night, Davy expected nothing, which always brought him forcefully back to his workhouse days at St. Pancras, when nothing equaled nothing and always would, until the late Headmaster Croker reeled him in and delivered him to something better.

What he got as they parted company was more unforgettable education. Mr. Coffin took his arm and looked him in the eyes again, that same probing glance. "Thee knows something the others don't," he said. "Always wash thy hands. I do believe thee already knows there isn't anything that a man cannot wash off his hands." He looked toward the college where he taught, teased by some, and in Davey's situation, ignored by others. "Until they learn that, it will not go well for their patients."

Mr. Coffin released his arm. "As my equally despised Catholic surgeon colleagues might say, 'Here endeth the lesson.' Good night and God speed thee."

The memory warmed Davey as the mail coach continued its steady, swaying way south. How could he ever forget, no matter whether he returned or not, that Mr. Coffin was there every night that Davey ward-walked the undeserving poor beds, walking with him, sitting at bedsides with him, quietly teaching him.

Even their brief breaks for dinner continued the education, at least for Mr. Coffin, who asked questions of Davey and probably learned far more about St. Brendan's than he ever wanted to know. "A school for workhouse bastards? My word," had been his comment. Other nights, the good man teased out more information about the wall of silence thrown up around him here in Edinburgh. At least someone else knew, even if that someone else had his own trials at the hands of students and faculty. "I am allowed to fill in when professors are drunk or ill," was how Mr. Coffin put it.

He furthered Davey's education in bone-setting after a public house brawl brought in two drunken combatants to the undeserving poor ward, or UPW, as Davey sometimes called Ward B. Master Six had taught him the rudiments of bone work on *Mercury* patrols of the blockade off the French coast. Mr. Coffin continued the schooling.

Davey considered the matter now, grateful down to his stockings that Mr. Coffin had not left him alone. If he was honest, and he generally was, Davey felt himself waver in his determination to quit the college of medicine. He knew he could learn much from Mr. Coffin, but he also knew he could learn practical medicine by attending to the Royal Navy surgeons at Haslar.

To Davey's real dismay, the ward-walking finished before the end of the term, so the students could look over their notes and prepare for final examinations, some written, some oral. Davey treasured those moments because he knew his notes were meticulous and far easier to read than the notes he took at sea, with the pitch and yaw of the *Mercury*. He was not troubled by group study which, from the number of bottles outside the doors of the other students' chambers, indicated more liquor than knowledge flowed. He studied alone.

He sat for the written exams, almost late because the other students had altered the message on the board to change the date and foil him. Mr. Coffin had saved his bacon then by telling him of the change. "That happened to me once at college in London," was all he said, which stuffed the heart back in Davey's chest.

The orals gave him no fears. He knew bones and blood circulation. The sight of his four professors sitting close together in their own fraternity and looking at him as if he did not measure up might have frightened him, had he not sailed at Trafalgar in the unarmed *Mercury* and conquered real fear. He answered his black-robed professors quietly and competently, feeling, somehow, Master Six's firm hand on his shoulder. Someone's hand, anyway; he felt it.

His reward was posted two days later on the board outside the classroom. He stood at the top of his twenty-four-man class, he, Davey Ten, bastard born in an indigent ward to a dying drab much like the ones he tended here in Edinburgh. He expected no word of praise from his professors and got none. The greater reward was a smile and a nod from Mr. Coffin, when they passed in the hall before that final class.

That would have been the sugar on the rout cake, if Mr. Coffin hadn't paused and asked pointblank, "Mr. Ten, I trust thee is returning when this month is gone."

He had to be truthful. "I honestly cannot say, sir."

"Is it a matter of money?" It was a kind question and Davey knew it.

"No, sir."

Did nothing faze Mr. Coffin? "Then it must be a matter of courage. Think thee on that, David Ten."

Try as he might, he could not forget Mr. Coffin's quiet statement as the mail coach approached Lancaster. Davey felt himself waver in his resolve to quit the school. He argued with himself, certain he did not lack in bravery. Why be miserable for a possible two more years? He argued with himself that no one deserved the treatment meted out to him, solely through fault of his birth. He decided to face Able Six's probable wrath and withdraw from torment.

The resolve strengthened, especially when they stopped at Lancaster. The public house was a large one, and other riders waited, the more modest for a mail coach, and the better-heeled for their postmen to change horses on their chaise. He breathed deep of sausage and beans, common fare, but always welcome to a former workhouse boy, who remembered beans but no sausage, until St. Brendan's freed him from hunger.

There also waited Edwin Hamilton, fellow student, and member of that odious fraternity determined to put him down and keep him silent.

Chapter Four

Davey sidestepped out of the doorway, hoping not to be spotted by Edwin, who likely waited for his post chaise. Davey patted his hip, well aware that he had sufficient funds to bespeak a post chaise for himself. He owed this largess to Mrs. Mary Munro, who had pledged a not-immodest sum for his education. "I believe it is her atonement for the treatment her beloved grandson Able Six endured, even though she had no way of knowing his early circumstances," Mrs. Six had explained to him, before he left for school, and it was just the two of them alone.

The mail coach suits me, Davey thought, as he tried to calm his nerves, set humming again, just when he thought he was done with medical school. He sidled along the wall. So far Edwin Hamilton had not seen him. He would wait until the student left, before braving the counter where the publican's wife stood, hands on hips, ready for orders in a hurry.

The mail coachmen came in and walked directly to the counter. He turned around. "Those of you bound south, ten minutes."

Ten minutes? Davey looked at Edwin, who sat alone with food in front of him. His back was to the counter. Maybe if the other travelers stayed tight around the counter, he wouldn't be detected. Maybe...

Davey couldn't have explained what happened next, but he felt a distinct snap of forefinger to his temple. He looked around and saw no one. He hung back, and felt the same snap, harder this time, as if it could tell him some home truth in no other way.

Maybe it jostled his brains. The invisible jab reminded him that he was hungry, he had money, and he was quitting school anyway, so what did Edwin Hamilton even matter? He went to the counter, and firmly placed his order.

The only place to sit was at the same table with Edwin Hamilton, and Davey chose not to. Sausage and beans taste just as good standing up. He knew Edwin Hamilton was aware of him now, but the jolt to his brains must have done something else. He didn't care.

He had asked for an extra order of sausage, and that came his way, too, with the publican's wife pointing out that he could sit at Edwin Hamilton's table. "No, thank you," he said distinctly. "I'd rather stand. Been sitting a while, don't you know."

She laughed and returned to the counter. As he ate Davey remembered an incident during anatomy class – commonly called Bones – an incident that involved Edwin, who now seemed to eat faster so he could get away, too.

Their professor was a stickler for bones. Davey heard the other students laughing about that and making fun. Since no one was speaking to him, he never had to explain his own love of bones. He could have told them about the rat bones Mrs. Six had allowed the new St. Brendan's boys to simmer in her kitchen until they were clean. He could have told them how that kind, but squeamish lady even helped them search in the grass outside for the tiny bones, trying not to miss a single one for the pot.

There was Mrs. Perry, cook and former slave, who looked mean enough to knock heads and take no prisoners, until a boy realized he had no better ally. She had found the perfect bit of board, which she allowed them to smooth with the sanding paper from her late carpenter-husband's stash. Even Mrs. Six had watched as the boys, needy in ways that had nothing to do with money, mounted the rat bones on the board. She gave them their own nickname of Gunwharf Rats. Yes, he liked bones.

It was a weekly test, where the professor numbered each bone of a human foot and ordered the boys one at a time to label them, then take their seat. Davey waited to follow Edwin, who labeled the bones, then stepped back.

Davey looked over Edwin's shoulder and saw the error, a simple one. "Switch your final answer with number five," he whispered.

Edwin turned and glared at him. Davey shrugged, past caring. "Suit yourself," he whispered, and stepped back to wait his turn. Edwin hesitated, then made the change. No one noticed what took place, because the professor chatted with two of his favorites. When he checked Edwin's work, he nodded. "Good lad," he praised, then stepped back for Davey's turn, which was also correct, but did not elicit a good lad.

That would have been that, but after Davey left the classroom, alone as always, Edwin surprised him with a slight nod, then joined his friends. That was it, minus any eye contact. Maybe it was Davey's imagination, but the brief inclination of Edwin's head warmed him for weeks.

I did the right thing, Davey thought, as he finished his hurried meal and followed the mail coachman from the inn. He smiled at the two weird snaps to his head and realized that he never had to deal with Edwin Hamilton again.

Edwin Hamilton followed him out the door and Davey stepped back deferentially, thinking of years ahead in the fleet where he would do that because of rank, not low birth. Commissioned officers outranked warrant officers, which he would become as a surgeon. That was a fact, and not unpleasant. Maybe his mistreatment at medical school wasn't really important, not in the world at war where he lived. Maybe he *could* quit with a clear conscience. He had done no harm and he intended to keep learning. That thought warmed him, too. He started for the mail coach, fed and content, and happy not to think of Edwin Hamilton.

"Ten."

He stopped. His contentment fled, until he willed himself to remember Master Able's hand on his shoulder, and the love and kindness in Mrs. Six's eyes. He was a Gunwharf Rat who had stood firm at Trafalgar. "Aye?"

"I should have thanked you."

Davey shrugged. "I didn't expect it then, and I don't expect it now. Good day." He turned on his heel and left Edwin standing there.

They traveled all night, getting the royal mail through on roads less traveled after dark. Davey listened to a salesman snore, and a mother whisper to her whimpering child until both were silent. He wondered if he was mentally doing what Master Six did at sea, as his mentor walked about the *Mercury*, standing the watch.

As for the college of medicine, he knew Mr. Coffin would soon forget him and Edwin Hamilton could label his own bones. Napoleon still troubled the Continent, and that was the larger issue.

One thing troubled Davey – explaining all this to Master Able Six.

Able Six seldom had trouble sleeping. Before his marriage to Meri-delectable, he tossed and turned for lengthy periods, simply because his brain never shut down. Even after Euclid, Harvey, Galen, Lavoisier *et al.* retreated to wherever cranial specters go, he could ponder until daylight. He wondered how it would be to have a mind at rest.

Able Six – christened Durable because he survived those church steps and Six because he was the sixth bastard that year in Dumfries – sometimes wondered what it would have been like to know anyone like him. He understood now that his mind had been busy forever, but he was a naked, squalling foundling, retrieved from cold church steps and trundled to a workhouse to live or die.

He lived, at first assuming that all little ones must have soothing voices that offered encouragement. Able assumed that other children could read by merely glancing at words. Enough beatings when he questioned the workhouse teachers taught him to be silent and look within for solace. He stole books when he could, and came to understand those voices, Euclid first among them. In a silent language of the mind he could explain to no one, not even Meri, Able found other voices who answered his questions, mentored him, challenged him, teased him, loved him.

When Euclid suggested that he run away to the ocean and the Royal Navy, Able found work, and he found Captain Sir Belvedere St. Anthony, who dug a little deeper and discovered the genius. One thing led to another, and he became a sailing master at a young age, and then a teacher of workhouse boys like him.

Then he found Meridee Bonfort, who proved to be his keeper. She loved him. What she didn't understand about him, she accepted on faith. Able knew she had reached some sort of commonality with Euclid, which she tried to explain, then shrugged and gave up. "I believe you, Able," she told him. "That's enough for me. Go be a genius. I will always love you."

Marriage to the woman who captured his heart soothed him in ways he never could have fathomed. Through his single years, he had found respite from stress in lovemaking, but it never lasted. Meridee's love, the love of a wife, was wide and deep. It was married love, the kind that ranged from wildly passionate moments after too long away at sea (ahem, or maybe only three days in London), to something he could only describe as warmly comfortable, because he knew this woman's body and mind inside and out. Whether Meri even tried to know his unfathomable mind scarcely mattered. She knew what soothed him. Oh, did she ever. Only then did his brain grind to a halt, as he happily turned into putty.

Trafalgar changed Able Six; so did fatherhood. Once he knew who he was, and who his parents were, his cranial companions seemed to pop in only now and then. After Ben's birth, Meri took the lead at first, assuring him in her practical, endearing way that yes, babies were tender little morsels, but also resilient in odd ways. She told him he didn't need celibate Isaac Newton's advice or a nudge from Copernicus to flop on the sofa, raise his knees, and rest a daughter against them.

Little Mary Munro, two now, had been a solemn infant with kind eyes much like her mother's. Able soon learned how loud she could laugh when he made outrageous faces and growled against her fat belly. Once or twice, he thought he heard Euclid chuckling, but that was all. The polymaths and genii who sometimes fought each other for his attention let him be a father.

The newest daughter, christened Ella because Meri had firmly objected to Minerva, was only four months old and still more the property of her mother, although Meri did turn over Ella to him for burps and what not. Mostly he found Ella vastly amusing when she had been nursed to the limit and collapsed against him in a boneless milk coma. He also found himself assuring Mary Munro, now a big sister, that in time, this lump of baby would become a trusted and dear companion. "Give her a few years, and you two can gang up on Ben," he told her.

Ah, Ben. Nearly five, he was comfortably at home in three languages and a fourth one that escaped Able's understanding. It seemed to consist of zeroes and ones sung softly. The zeros and ones changed patterns, so Able knew it was a code of some sort, obviously binary, and perhaps from the future.

He took great delight in Ben, seeing himself in the handsome child with curly hair and brown eyes. Able saw something more, because no one stifled Ben, or starved him, or punished him for answering other students' questions for them. A cheerful child, he had wrapped baker Ezekiel Bartleby around his finger, which meant Ben overindulged in his mother's favorite rout cakes, and also crème buns from another source.

The crème buns were supplied by his great grandmama, Mrs. Munro, who lived not far from Grace Croker, former Lady St. Anthony. Grace was now the wife of Angus Ogilvie, Trinity House's chief dogsbody and assassin, and – to the amazement of all except Grace – a doting husband, whenever he was in town.

At first, Mrs. Munro created all manner of excuses to visit the Sixes and stoke Ben's crème bun habit. Meridee understood the woman's almost visceral need to see Able and Ben, and gently told her to drop by whenever she felt like it, no reasons necessary. Mrs. Munro soon found herself adept at handling the babies that followed, as well. In some small way, the two girls seemed to ease the still-mourned loss of Mrs. Munro's own genius daughter, Able's mother.

As much as he loved to eat – quite the contrast to his workhouse-raised father, who looked on food with indifference – Ben shone when by himself in the tiny spare bedroom kept for visiting Gunwharf Rat alumni. It became his private study, with books everywhere, all of them read at that same rapid rate as his father used. Able had found a small armchair at a jumble sale. "Prodigiously fine, Papa," Ben had assured him as he settled in with a sigh and picked up Newton's *Mathematica*, his favorite book.

So it went. St. Brendan's had added two more teachers, in addition to Grace and himself. Headmaster Ferrier willingly stepped in to fill Able's classes when the demands of the Royal Navy dictated that the *Mercury* sail with its crew of Rats to deliver mail and urgent reports to Admiral Lord Collingwood himself in the Mediterranean, or to the blockade.

In essence, whose head needed spectral mathematicians, physicists, and philosophers when St. Brendan's ran so efficiently, and Able Six so perfectly capable of everything else? Life was smooth, well-ordered, efficient and…. wrong. Able knew something was not right.

Able knew it wasn't Meridee nudging him that night. She did nudge him now and then, but her nudges were caresses and back rubs culminating in what they called General Merrymaking. This was different. Able sat up and looked around.

Same old room; he closed his eyes, pretty sure his brain wouldn't fail him, and somehow in his mind saw Ben sound asleep across the hall in the room that used to belong to Davey Ten and Nick Bonfort-Six. Mary Munro slumbered in the next chamber. He knew Ella slept in the well-used crib on Meri's side of their bed. She was still a tender babe.

Able lay down again and Meri slid closer, seeking his warmth because it was early December, after all. He gently pulled the blanket higher on her shoulder. God, she was a pretty woman. He thought of her complaint only that morning which he naturally remembered word for word, because he was Able Six. "'My love, please slap my hand when I reach for another rout cake,'" she said. "'I can't continue blaming Baby Number Three because my bodices don't fit.'"

She didn't wake up now, which was also fine with Able, for a change. Someone lurking in his brain had nudged him. Perhaps it was time to actually summon Euclid.

All right. You have me, Euclid. What is going on that I don't know about?

Silence. Ah, Euclid was going to pout, and probably call him out because Meridee had told Able several years ago that she did not want Euclid in their bedroom, no matter the emergency. Still, Able knew he had been nudged.

I know you're there.

Silence.

Able knew he hadn't lost the touch. Strength in numbers. *Mr. Harvey, would you please tell our mutual friend Euclid that I need to know what troubles him?* William Harvey was an exacting man of science, not much given to pouting.

Silence. Able heard a whispered conversation, which was joined by a third voice, louder than the others, and probably with hand gestures: Galileo, an Italian.

Very well!

Able put his hands behind his head, which meant Meri rested her head on his chest. He felt her eyelids flicker. Her breathing slowed again, though she did put her hand on his stomach.

Keep your mind on business, Master Six.

Aye, Mr. Harvey. Euclid? Are you hereabouts?

I am. You have a problem.

Meri's hand drifted lower, and Able laughed to himself. This was going to be a race to the finish line. *Better tell me quickly, sir. Someone is competing for my attention.*

It's Davey Ten. He's coming home.

I know, I know. It's the winter break.

Coming home for good. They have broken him.

Chapter Five

"How do you know that, Able?"

Meridee wasn't sure why she woke up. Ella didn't need a feeding yet. Able was warm and comfortable but he was sitting up in their bed. The faint glow of the street lantern showed her man with his head bowed, as though in defeat. In that odd world between awake and asleep, someone had distinctly said Davey was broken. It must have been Able.

She reconsidered. The last few years of relief from Able's cranial companions had spoiled her. She didn't miss them, and he seemed not to. Since Trafalgar, Meri had noticed a calm assurance in her unlikely genius of a husband. But now, this man who sat with his head bowed was not the confident fellow who had jollied her a few hours earlier.

She put her hand on his back and drew him closer. It was probably silly of her, but she said it anyway. "Euclid, I will take care of him from here, please."

She convinced Able to lie down and kept him there with her leg thrown over his body, something she knew he liked. Leaning on one elbow, she looked into his face.

"Able, my love, something is wrong with Davey. Did…did Euclid give you any indication what it was?"

"They must have found out he was a workhouse boy," Able replied, after a long silence, which gave her time to slowly rub his chest. His heart was beating too fast, which worried her. This had happened before, though not in six years at least.

"But why would that… He's so smart and already knows more than most students, I would wager," she said.

"He doesn't know his place, and I suppose they mean to remind him," Able said. She heard the bitterness. "I wonder what they have done to him. He should be here later today. He's been riding on the mail coach.

No sleep, I imagine. Um, Euclid just told me he even felt obliged to give Davey a smack to his head. Oh, Meri!"

She could have asked how he knew that much, but she knew better than to question what went on inside his ever-churning brain. She had no doubt about her role in his life. She was his lover, his keeper, his chief consoler, the mother of his lovely children, and the manager of family finances, because his brain was too large for simple adding and subtracting. She was the woman he turned to in good times and bad because he knew the depths of her heart.

"We'll find out soon enough and deal with it," she whispered. "Go to sleep, dearest." She held him close, loving him with every fiber of her heart, matching her breathing to his. To her infinite relief, she felt him relax and sleep. She lay back herself, and then did her own foolish thing. *Euclid, I don't mind a little help now and then, not when it's Able and the Rats. Or our babies.*

Nothing changed in her mind, but she knew nothing would. Time to snuggle close and close her eyes. To her breathless amazement, she felt a gentle hand on her shoulder - Euclid's? – then nothing more.

Morning brought the usual scramble of a baby demanding a good suck and a dry nappie. Breakfast meant cheerful Avon March dropped by to "escort" his mentor across the street to St. Brendan's, where Avon now lived with the other Rats. Avon had begun the escort habit not long after Trafalgar. "He was indefatigable and untiring during the battle," Able observed to her once. "I think he still believes I could require his services at any moment."

"If you ask me, he likes breakfast here," Mrs. Perry said in the kitchen. Her put-upon glower never proved effective because everyone liked Avon.

"We all do," Meri reminded her, and patted her less trim middle. "If I weren't so famished, I could resist your cinnamon buns."

"Missy, you are nursing another baby," Mrs. Perry reminded her, and gave Meri a little swat with the wooden spoon when she turned to carry in the scrambled eggs.

Meri laughed when she set down the bowl in the dining room. Someone else had materialized with Avon. She held out her arms and hugged Nick Bonfort-Six to her, the boy – no, young man – Able had adopted. "Nick! What in the world? Avon, please tell Mrs. Perry we need more eggs and toast."

Able was still shaving with Ben watching, and Avon briefly out of the room. She kissed Nick, the boy with no last name who had taken her maiden name, and then became their adopted child. He was far taller than she now, and filled out in the way of a man in the making. With wind and sun lines around his eyes already, she gazed at a mariner.

"My goodness, why are you even here? Did Lord Collingwood decide he was tired of the Mediterranean?"

Oh, and a deep voice, too? Her Rats were growing up. The mischief and wonder that was Nick remained Nick, to her delight. "Mum, the admiral expressly sent me here to deliver private messages to the Admiralty! I've only just come from London."

"An audience with the First Lord?"

He nodded. She motioned him to the sideboard for bacon and eggs and he did not hesitate. He looked splendid in his uniform, just a simple dark coat and pants, because he served as one of the secretaries to the man who had assumed Lord Nelson's command after the little admiral's death at Trafalgar. A closer look suggested that the trouser legs could be let out. Nick was still growing. Maybe there would be time to tackle that bit of hemming before he left.

His plate full, Nick ate a few hurried bites to take the edge off his hunger. With a pang, Meri remembered that all the Rats did that even now, as if they would always fear the food might disappear. Better to get a mouthful in immediately. He leaned back. "The First Lord even offered me rum as I waited while he read the dispatch," he said, as if he couldn't quite believe his good fortune.

"Only a small tot?" she asked, because she thought he expected her to comment.

"A small one," he assured her, then turned into the boy she remembered. "Mum, that room! The maps, the gilt chairs! Such a place." He grinned and picked up his fork again.

Avon returned with toast and jam, and Able himself brought in more eggs. Meri watched her husband, pleased to see the delight in his eyes. Nick sprang to his feet, and they embraced.

"This is a rare pleasure," Able said. "Who's minding the shop?"

Nick grinned at the teasing. "I think Admiral Collingwood knows his business." His face grew serious then. "Da, he has been trying to wangle some shore leave, but no. It's been years."

"He's not well?"

"His dog Bounce looks better than he does. He's been at sea for six years now." Nick looked from Meri to Able. "Could you two stand that?"

Meri felt tears well in her eyes. She shook her head, unable to speak. Able drew her into his generous embrace. Her tears spilled over when Able gestured for Avon to join them. "We're all part of this family, Avon," he said simply.

Meri blew her nose on the handkerchief Able gave her and looked around for Ben, who generally tagged along with his father, after they "shaved" together, Able applying soap to his son's face and scraping it off with the flat side of the razor.

"Our scamp of a son is trying to wheedle an extra cinnamon bun from Mrs. Perry," Able said. "My heir and offspring is far ahead of me. I'm still a little afraid of Mrs. Perry, but Ben simply forges ahead." They all laughed and settled at the table.

Ben joined them, holding two cinnamon buns. He saw Nick and his eyes brightened. To Meri's delight, he took his extra prize to Nick. "You probably don't get these on the *HMS Ocean*," he told Nick. "I can wait a bit and try Mrs. Perry later." He leaned closer. "She's getting forgetful."

"Same old Ben," Nick said to Able.

"The same. After breakfast, would you care to join Avon and me across the street? Ben, too, of course."

"I would like that, sir. *Ben*?"

"He's rather enjoying the calculus," Able said. "He'll join my second hour class once he finishes diagramming sentences with Mrs. Ogilvie."

Nick rolled his eyes and returned to the eggs.

"We'll leave Mum with my girls. Ah, and here is Mary Munro, no early riser she."

Still in her nightgown, their daughter climbed onto Meri's lap and turned her face into her mother's breast. "My love, you remember Nick," Meri said.

Mary Munro nodded, but still didn't look. Meri cuddled her, breathing deep of sleep-tousled hair, and the tender warmth of little ones.

She smiled at her husband. In return, his gaze was long and deep. She reminded herself that he was only going across the street for the day, even if he did suck out some of the air from the room when he left. She had been married to him for seven years, long enough, surely, to take him for granted a little. It never happened. She rested her cheek against Mary Munro's curls, too shy to look at the man who knew her inside and out.

The sweet moment passed. They continued eating. Soon she heard Ella begin her morning demands upstairs and felt the familiar tightening in her breasts. She set Mary Munro in her own chair with the two books on it to bring her to table height. "As soon as you are done, my little love, come upstairs and we will cuddle some more," she said. "Luncheon here for all of you, or must you leave, Nick?"

"I sail on the afternoon tide, so yes, lunch with Mum and my...my sisters," the young man said.

Meri kissed them all, even Avon, then left the room to tend Ella. At the door she looked back, pleased with what she saw of order, good food, no harsh voices ever. Before his death three years ago, Captain Sir Belvedere St. Anthony had told her, "Mrs. Six, I know you wonder how on earth you can manage our unlikely master genius, but here you are, and all around is your gift of serenity. Bravo, little girl. The First Lord of the Admiralty could not have planned this better."

She thought of that as Ella nursed, and Mary Munro joined them after reminders to dress and tidy her room. Ella dozed and dreamed of milk as Meri Six pointed to numbers on what Able called flash cards. To her vast relief, Mary Munro, while obviously bright, was no Ben. She looked down at Ella. What about this child? Time would tell.

She left Ella to slumber a little more, with Mary Munro reviewing her number cards and sitting cross-legged on the bed beside her sister. After a fresh dress and quick brush of her hair – Able had whispered over scrambled eggs that he wanted to brush it tonight, which usually preceded General Merriment – she hurried downstairs as someone knocked on the door.

Pegeen was busy in the kitchen, so Meridee opened it, wondering what baked treat Ezekiel Barnaby was bringing by so early in the morning.

Davey Ten stood there, his duffel slung over his shoulder. He opened his mouth and closed it, then bowed his head and wept.

Chapter Six

If you can't be anything else, at least be brave and don't cry, Davey had told himself on the last leg of the journey. If he put up a good front, he could manage this whole miserable business, and pick a good time to announce his decision never to return to the hell of medical school. He could knock on the door of his favorite place in the world, and fool everyone.

Oh, really? One look at Mrs. Six, who had the uncanny ability to see right through his best plans, undid him entirely. Why couldn't Mrs. Perry have opened the door? He and the other Rats held *her* in vast awe that edged on terror. Or failing that, Pegeen, who would have joked with him.

But no, here was this kindly lady, the mother every Rat wished he could have. Why did she have to simply hold her arms open wide and call him by name? He hadn't heard his name in months, because with one exception – Mr. Coffin – no one spoke to Davey. No one.

As he cried into her shoulder, he wondered how many Rats had done the same thing. This was his first time, and he felt the shame; seventeen and weeping like a baby.

"Davey, we knew something was wrong," she whispered to him as she held him tight. "Master Six did for certain, and I felt his discomfort."

She pulled him inside and closed the door. Her arm in his, she took him into the kitchen, where Mrs. Perry peeled potatoes. "Look who we have here," Mrs. Six said. "Davey's hungry, I would imagine. I'm sure he has been riding the mail coach, so I know he is tired."

"Hand him over," the redoubtable Mrs. Perry said. "You're too early for potato soup, but I have eggs." She whisked the lid off a pasteboard box of eclairs. "Mr. Bartleby's already been by." The cook laughed, a great

33

rumble that seemed to come from somewhere deep inside. Davey began to think he was as hungry for that sound as he was for scrambled eggs. "Cheeky man, Mrs. Six! He seemed to think I'd believe him that these were yesterday's leave-behinds."

"I know," Mrs. Six said. "Maybe he thought we needed them this morning." She touched Davey's shoulder. "I'll brush aside Ben's books and make a bed for you in the little room."

He sat at the kitchen table, surrounded by wonderful aromas and not alone at the table in Mrs. Silsby's lodging. Once he discovered that none of the other student-boarders were going to speak to him, it was easier to eat first. This was different. Pegeen sat at the table, too, picking up Mrs. Perry's knife and continuing with the potatoes. He knew she wasn't talkative. She hummed and peeled, and he felt a layer of hurt peel away, too.

Scrambled eggs and eclairs: Such a combination of delights and a far cry from food snatched at public houses and inns along the mail coach route. He felt his eyes growing heavy. He was aware when Mrs. Six whispered for Pegeen to take a wee note across the street, but even the thought of Master Six's upcoming irritation at his dereliction of duty struck no fear. All he wanted now was to sleep in a place where people knew his name and his background and loved him anyway.

Through party closed eyes, he nodded when Mrs. Six sent him into the bathing room for a quick scrub of his face. He took only a moment to shuck his clothes in the small bedchamber, pat the pillow and sink into slumber.

He was aware of kitchen smells a few hours later and then a steady tread up the stairs of someone heavier than Mrs. Six. The door opened and he knew Master Six stood there looking down at him. He braced himself, then sighed as Able Six touched his shoulder, and drew the coverlets higher.

"Sir, I..."

"It'll keep, Davey. Rest yourself."

Would he? Aye, he did. A kiss on his cheek.

Davey woke hours later. Through the room's small window he saw that afternoon shadows were soon to bow before the dark. He had slept the day away, his first peaceful sleep since he left, so full of hope and eagerness for the challenge of not only medical school, but the best medical school anywhere.

Master Six, his long legs splayed out in front of him, sat in the little chair where Ben usually sat as he pored over books that would leave anyone but his genius father dumbfounded. Davey peered closer. The master's eyes were closed, but he didn't seem to be sleeping. Nick had whispered to him once that the master's eyes remained in motion behind closed lids, and Davey, ever skeptical, hadn't believed him.

There they were, racing along. Davey felt sudden pity for a person who could never entirely rest. Or did he? Surely there was a time he could relax, amid war and tumult, and teaching students, and trying to enjoy his own growing family. Maybe there wasn't. Shoving aside his own troubles, Davey felt a sudden, fervent desire to never add to the master's burden. He would say nothing and return to school.

Then those restless eyes opened. Master Six didn't sit up any straighter, but he regarded Davey in a long moment of silence, his face entirely neutral. *I can do this*, Davey thought.

"We've been given a month holiday, sir, because of illness among the staff and patients," he said, striving to sound matter-of-fact. "I thought I would come back for a visit."

"That's not the information I am receiving," Able Six said. "You're telling me only a partial truth." There was nothing in his tone of anger or recrimination. Davey knew he was not being scolded, but how…

Those eyes. Davey knew he would never willingly remember the terrible afternoon of Trafalgar, but suddenly, briefly, he was there again, guns around them firing, masts falling, wounded rigging shrieking before it toppled, clouds of smoke obscuring the nearest ships like deadly fog, and men screaming. After Avon March raised the flags signaling that *Mercury* had a surgeon on board, Davey knelt beside the master as they pulled injured friend and foe alike on deck.

With stunning clarity, Davey remembered looking into Able Six's eyes, and seeing strange depths, as though his mentor and master saw far more than a battle at sea. Was it humanly possible for a person to see *everything*? The sight unnerved Davey and he never understood it. To his relief, the moment passed quickly, and then the man beside him became the usual Master Six, which in itself was a contradiction in terms.

Davey looked away. When he looked back, he saw only compassion and deep understanding. Whoever else lived behind those eyes had retreated, but Able Six knew the truth.

"I am not being honest," Davey said, knowing he could not fool this man, who had sources of information that none of them would understand. He doubted even Mrs. Six knew. He also knew he had been given a glimpse of something beyond the realm of mortal reality. "Medical school is a living hell, and I cannot endure it."

He thought he was too frightened to cry, but he cried anyway, which brought Master Six to his side, his arms tight around Davey. "The punishment of silence," the master said. "To some we will always be workhouse boys, but not to all, Davey, I promise you."

"Who told…" Davey stopped. He knew. Of all the Gunwharf Rats, he finally understood. He also realized that this was his knowledge alone. "No one speaks to me, sir, not even the professors, except for one. It is as though I do not exist. I am ignored by all the students. I cannot bear it."

Master Six released him. "Nor should you, but tell me: Are your grades good? Surely, they were posted before you left."

Davey wiped his eyes on the sheet. "Aye, sir. I rated best in anatomy and *materia medica*. A few steps down in Latin, however."

"Pharmacoepia?"

Davey grinned. He couldn't help himself. He felt his ship right itself. "Tops. I had harder tests at Haslar under that dragon of a pharmacist mate." They laughed together.

"How about dissection?"

"That is in the upcoming term, sir."

"The one you won't be attending, eh?"

"I…I…suppose I will not."

"A pity, that. After Trafalgar, you already know what insides look like when they're on the outside."

He did. He threw up the first time, but not the second. "I could manage a dissection at school." He smiled in spite of himself.

"Possibly you might return?"

Davey felt his resolve dwindling, but he yanked it back, remembering his terror at the mere sight of Edwin Hamilton, fellow student, in the public house. Still, Edwin had thanked him there outside the public house, and the earth's foundation hadn't quivered. "No. I'd rather learn from the surgeons at Haslar, sir."

"I understand." Able patted his leg. "Get yourself up." He held up one finger. "Oh, wait. You can't go anywhere yet. After you stripped and slumbered, Mrs. Six grabbed your trousers and let out the hem in the legs. I'll send Ben in with them. Join us for dinner? We have a guest."

Master Six went to the door and stood there. "You have almost a month to think. Tell me one thing: Was there someone who showed even a spark of interest in you?"

Davey thought of Mr. Josiah Coffin, assistant in *materia medica* to the august professor, Sir Lionel Henderson. "There's a physician who is an assistant. The students make fun of him because he is a Quaker."

"He speaks to you?"

"Yes, sir, in the indigent ward where I am assigned by myself four evenings a week. I was all by myself in the ward at first, then Mr. Coffin showed up. It was the two of us. Josiah Coffin."

"Good Quaker name. I would imagine students who twit you would laugh about such a fellow, too."

"I've heard them. It's not kind."

"Something to think about. I'll send in Ben with your trousers."

Oh, that Ben. He brought in Davey's trousers draped over his arm like a footman. "For you, sir," he said most formally, then giggled. "My Great Grandmama Munro has a footman and a butler, and they are most proper."

Trust Ben to take the stone off Davey's heart. He was a confident little boy, four years old and already studying the calculus. He knew his parents adored him and he tolerated his sisters. He was in all ways totally normal except he was not. Never mind. He was surrounded by more love than most mortals, and it made all the difference.

"Thank you, kind sir," Davey said, and pulled on his trousers. "Your mother very sweetly let out the legs for me."

"She is nice to everyone," Ben said, as if every woman were just like his mother. "Do you have a mother?"

"No, I don't."

"You do here, Davey. We'll share."

Chapter Seven

What a strange day this had become. For reasons known only to … someone, David Ten knew he had been privileged to see farther into Master Six's mind than any of his fellow Gunwharf Rats. Now Ben, that generous little fellow, informed him that he would share his mother with Davey. Maybe he had learned more in a few hours than he had ever known in his life. He already knew that people could be cruel. It was also possible that they were kind.

Davey knew he still didn't want to return to Edinburgh, but as he dressed for dinner, he felt the door start to open, that door he had slammed shut and bolted from the inside years and years ago, and not solely in Edinburgh.

A tap on the door, and Nick Bonfort-Six stuck his head in. He opened the door wider and grabbed Davey in a bear hug. "I have to hurry," he apologized. "I'm sailing with the tide back to the Mediterranean, but Mum said you were here."

Have I changed as much as Nick? Davey asked himself as they sat on his bed and Nick hurriedly went over his duties as assistant scribe to Admiral Collingwood's secretary. "So far, I'm merely copying orders and letters." He laughed, and Davey heard the confidence that *he* lacked. Nick was obviously in the right place at the right time. "It is my duty, when the admiral is otherwise engaged, to take his dog Bounce on a trot around the deck." His face turned serious. "I hear you're having a hard time of it in Edinburgh."

"Aye, Nick. I told Master Six I didn't want to return."

Nick was silent a long moment, for Nick. "I've always thought of you as the bravest amongst us Rats," he said finally.

"You never told me that," Davey said, startled.

Nick shrugged. "We figured you already knew it." He stood up and held out his hand. "I have to leave. Time and tide and all that, don't you know."

They shook hands. "Don't give up, Davey," Nick said softly.

"What would you do in my place?" Davey asked, hoping he didn't sound belligerent, because he sincerely wanted to know.

Trust Nick. "If I were a medical student, I'd probably imagine all the ways I could poison, purge or otherwise incapacitate those damned students and your professors." He struck a pose. "I'd let them writhe on the deck, maybe even froth at the mouth if I truly despised them, and walk on by."

They both laughed. Nick touched Davey's sleeve, his eyes serious now, all joking done. "Then I would get back to work and save them, because that's what Gunwharf Rats do."

A brief embrace and he was gone. Davey realized he was the wiser for Nick's advice. The thought remained with him through dinner. He had little to say, as he wondered what Master Six was thinking. When calm, rational thought took over, probably thanks to Nick, Davey knew he would return to Edinburgh. The thought made him shudder inside and he made a massive attempt to keep his fears there.

Oh, futile effort; he knew Able Six was well aware of what was in his heart. Still, he could put on a good show for Mrs. Six, who was nothing but kindness and good intent. He ate heartily – no issue there; he was hungry – admired Ella, the bright-eyed little newcomer – again no issue; she was all that – and sincerely enjoyed Ben's amazing interaction with his parents, as sophisticated as discussing Newton's theories with his father, and as childlike as leaving a ring of food around his plate, so intent was he on discussion. *How strange is genius*, Davey thought. *But I already knew that.*

The time had come. Pegeen came from the kitchen to clear the table. Master Six looked at him. "Do you mind if we discuss in the sitting room what is weighing on your mind? I'd prefer right here, but Meri and the little ones will be more comfortable in there." He drew what looked like a Greek letter on the tablecloth with the blunt side of his knife. "I also believe that you need all five of us Sixes. Thirties?"

Why did the tears have to come? At least Davey remembered in time to let them course down his cheeks in utter silence, as he would have done at the workhouse so many years ago. Able reached over and clasped his hand. "We are your bulwark, lad. Never forget that."

They went into the sitting room, Master Six's hand steady on his shoulder now, as Davey had seen that same hand so steady on Smitty's shoulder as he directed him through the flaming path that was Trafalgar, ever the teacher. Davey felt himself relax.

Meri handed off their youngest to her husband and turned to her older children. Within minutes, Ben was occupied with his beloved Newton and Mary Munro sprawled close by, creating a building of blocks. They were different colored blocks, and she had a sure hand with color. So much for his thought that perhaps Mary Munro was an ordinary child. *My God, what a family*, he thought, with admiration.

He became aware that this extraordinary bunch of mortals had taken him right out of his own misery. When Mrs. Six retrieved the baby and gazed into Ella's eyes, he was suddenly so grateful for a glimpse into what could be his future some day: a family of his own.

"Tell me what is going on," Master Six said. "You have already told me the issue – No one is speaking to you. You have no one you could remotely call a mentor, except perhaps a quiet Quaker who has his own problems with ridicule." Able leaned back. "You say the teasing goes on behind his back. I assure you he is aware of it."

"I suppose he is," Davey said, wondering where *his* mentor was going with this conversation.

"I could tell you right now that *not* returning to the college of medicine would defeat everything we are trying to do here at St. Brendan's," Master Six said. "You have been given a rare opportunity."

"I know," Davey mumbled. "I am certain there is not another workhouse lad in all of Great Britain so lucky." He hadn't meant to sound bitter, but there you are. He was.

"True enough," Master Six said. "And that is where I have erred." He leaned forward and clasped his hands together. "I think differently than everyone I know." He glanced at Mrs. Six, and she at him, giving Davey the smallest glimpse into what deep love looked like. He sighed. "In this great honor, I thought of me, and not of you. If you truly wish to remain at Haslar and move up the ranks that way, I won't stop you. To do so would be cruel. I see that now."

The tears came again. "Master Six, I have stood in front of my mirror and wondered if I am invisible."

A sniff, and then another; Mrs. Six wiped her eyes. Her husband gave her a handkerchief. He returned his intense gaze to Davey. "And I wondered for years why I knew everything, forgot nothing, and had a brain full of noisy people." He smiled and reached out his hand to Davey. "Such is the cosmic hand we have *all* been dealt. Dear lad, spend the next few weeks at Haslar filling your pharmacopeia and surgical duties, and also doing some ward-walking."

"You…you won't mind, sir? I mean, whatever I decide?"

"Not at all." He leaned back and wagged his finger. "But mind you, I'm going to be thinking, too, of how to make Edinburgh more palatable. What's the worst thing troubling you?"

"No one to talk to, who will answer me," Davey said promptly. He stared down at his feet. "I don't like being alone. I hate it, in fact."

"Join the human race, lad," Master Six said. "Neither do I, although I didn't always know that. Even now, I doubt I could cross the street every morning to teach if there wasn't someone here to arrange my neck cloth, remind me to get a haircut, scold me about something, and give me a kiss whether I deserve it or not."

Davey had another thought, a new one that seemed to crowd itself into his brain and plump down in plain sight. "I also worry whether I will ever really know enough."

"Ah, yes, Meri, he *is* human."

Davey looked up, startled. He watched the Sixes smile at each other. It dawned on him that perhaps, just perhaps, even these two paragons struggled with that very matter. Did *everyone*? "Sir, Mrs. Six, are you trying to tell me that you have serious doubts? You always seem to know what to do."

They laughed. "You or me?" Master Six asked his wife.

"Oh, me first!" she said. Ella went to her shoulder. "Davey, the first time the midwife laid Ben in my arms, I nearly went into shock, wondering why *anyone* in the universe would trust me to raise a child!"

"But you have such a sure touch," Davey said in protest.

"I learned," she said simply. She nudged her husband with her shoulder. "*This* man learns extraordinarily fast, I will give you that, but he learns, too. So will you if you trust yourself."

This began to make sense. "When the four of us original Rats came here to live…" He almost couldn't say it. "You truly didn't know how to manage us?"

Meridee Six laughed. "Davey, don't let me embarrass you, but I had been a wife for mere days, and I was still learning how to be that!" He saw the tenderness in her eyes. "Still am. But that very first night when Able turned the key in the lock and carried me inside our first home, you and Jamie MacGregor showed up shortly after on the doorstep. Remember?"

He did. Jamie, now at sea, had seen the fear in his eyes at even the idea of St. Brendan's and marched him across the street to knock on the door. Mrs. Six had opened it, and Master Six assured him that he was welcome and that no one would ever thrash him if he had the wrong answer. What to say? "So…so you were going along and figuring things out on the fly?"

"The same as you."

Davey considered. "I'm being too hasty?"

Master Six shrugged. "I don't know. Give yourself a few weeks here." He snapped his fingers. "I nearly forgot. Meri, would you measure this friend of ours for a new uniform?"

"Uniform?"

"You're probably not aware of this, Davey, but the Navy Board has finally approved a uniform for the Royal Navy's medical personnel. You'll have to surrender the black of St. Brendan's for navy blue, and green piping at the collar. You are a member of the Royal Navy, and a veteran, after all. Let's remind those sanctimonious stuffed shirts in the college of medicine of that."

"If I go back," Davey said cautiously.

"Aye, indeed. Whether you do or not, the uniform must be worn. We are a nation at war."

Master Six snapped his fingers again and stood up. He went to the writing desk, rummaged about and took out a small pasteboard box.

"Yes," Mrs. Six said. She set the now-slumbering Ella on the sofa and joined her husband. "I believe you're the last one of the *Mercury*'s crew to receive his."

Master Six held up a small medal. "Several years ago, a Trafalgar medal was struck and given to all participants. See here? Lord Nelson, of course, and on the reverse, our battle. *Our* battle, Mr. Ten. You can credit Nick with reminding Admiral Collingwood himself that the crew of *Mercury* had been overlooked for the Trafalgar medal. Come here."

Davey had to remind himself to breathe as he joined his two favorite people in the world at the desk. He touched the medal in Master Six's hand, seeing again the little admiral who visited St. Brendan's once, and gave his life for his country. He turned it over to see the ships and the inscription, "England expects that every man will do his duty."

"Stand at attention, dear lad."

Davey did. The captain of the *Mercury*, his patient instructor, friend and mentor, pinned on the medal just above the patch of St. Brendan the Navigator.

"You are to wear this on your Royal Navy uniform at all times, Mr. Ten. Start now."

"Aye, sir."

Davey found himself in the middle of a strong embrace, made all the sweeter when Ben and Mary Munro joined their parents.

"We'll get through this together, Davey," Master Six told him. "Report to Haslar tomorrow and trust us." He ruffled Davey's hair. "Trust is the hardest thing for a workhouse lad, maybe even for a Gunwharf Rat and a veteran of England's greatest sea battle. What say you?"

"Aye aye, sir."

Chapter Eight

A day passed and another, spent now at Haslar Royal Navy Hospital, where Davey was needed and spoken to. It was almost as though he hadn't been away, living in cramped quarters next to the apothecary on the ground floor, eating in the infirmary mess with other lads bound to the Royal Navy, as personified by a dragon of a pharmacy mate who didn't frighten Davey anymore.

In fact, he realized that nothing and no one had really frightened him since Trafalgar. *Except the college of medicine*, he reminded himself that first night, and then wondered if perhaps he had turned tail too soon. Suppose Admiral Horatio Nelson had not charged pell mell into the Combined Fleet at Trafalgar? Mrs. Six would probably still be wearing widow's weeds.

It was food for thought, and he had nearly a month to chew it over. Davey rolled pills, ground compounds, and spread bandages with ointment that caused more than one burn patient to close his eyes in relief. He wondered briefly what Mr. Coffin would think of such a place, and decided that the quiet Quaker physician would understand Haslar.

By unspoken words, Davey knew to present himself on Wednesday nights at the Sixes' home. Every Wednesday for years, the door was open to any Rat from across the street. The food was Navy plain, but plentiful. Some of the newer boys did little more than eat and stare at the noise and camaraderie around them, unable to understand how a family did things. They gawked in amazement when the Sixes teased each other, perhaps wondering why the master didn't smack his wife into the next room, because that was all they knew, if they even knew that.

Davey had watched other Rats come to terms with the love around them. Most did, but not all, and he wondered how they would fare. He had personally never known anything but the bleak reality of the workhouse, so there was never a mother or father to either mourn or regret. He had come to the Sixes as a clean slate, more or less, which they wrote upon with love.

He had permission from Haslar's apothecary dragon to stay overnight at the home, and he did, enjoying relaxing in the sitting room after the other Rats trooped back across the street. Little Mary Munro had taken a shine to him, bringing one of her books to him and crawling into his lap for a read. He decided she was a bit of a martinet, but he liked the way her curly hair tickled his nose, and enjoyed the book as much as she did.

Mary Munro, a three-year-old, gave him hope, an odd little thing that flitted about him after he arrived at St. Brendan's for the first time. Once he recognized hope, he embraced it, but only cautiously. Certain hope had deserted him in Edinburgh, he discovered it again. Perhaps hope had only been driven into a corner in Edinburgh. Then came the harder thought: Perhaps he had put hope there himself.

He faced the reality that first Wednesday, when Mrs. Six had gone upstairs with their children and Master Six still sat in his chair thinking. Halting at first, stopping and then starting again, he told Master Six that perhaps he had only made matters worse for himself by retreating into a quiet shell and avoiding the others.

"That's what bullies want you to do," Master Six told Davey.

"It's hard though, when no one talks to me. Hard not to think that maybe I truly don't measure up."

"Your grades would indicate otherwise," Master Six gently reminded him.

Davey heard laughter upstairs. "You have someone to help you through those moments when you doubt," he said, wondering if he was being too cheeky.

"Aye. I am the most fortunate bastard I know," Master Six said. "You'll find your anchor when you're old enough, Davey. I am certain of it. Until then, it's on you."

"How do I manage, sir?"

Master Six sighed. "I am not precisely certain. I think I would ignore their behavior, but never shrink from asking questions of your professors."

"Even if they don't respond?" Davey asked, unable to keep his voice from rising.

"Even then. You have to be stronger than everyone in the room. Is that fair? No."

"Then I leave for my lodging, and all is still silent. I…I… don't do well in silence."

Master Able gave him that measured look, the look of intense concentration that warmed Davey inexplicably, as he realized the genius who sat before him was marshalling all his forces on his behalf. How did he know that? He couldn't have said, but it seemed as though the room was full of listening ears.

"Perhaps we can change that part of the equation, Davey. I'm not done with this. I've only started." He looked around with a smile. "And there are others helping me, as I think you know."

*

Time was passing. Able always heard a clock ticking somewhere in his crowded brain, so it was generally a minor nuisance. When time began to matter, the sound increased. The clangor never seemed to bother his bed partner, who had her own interior timepiece, one that operated regarding the needs of babies. He felt his face grow warm…and his needs, too. Meri did have an instinct.

Baby Ella had apparently reached that stage when she filled up sufficiently to sleep longer at night. "I have no argument with that," Meri informed him. She liked to sleep as well as the next woman, except there was that time when full breasts hadn't yet synchronized themselves to Ella's changing demands. The matter resolved itself in a few days, which made Able envious. Why couldn't his interior clock work that way? No, it had to bang about until…

That was it. Until it woke up someone else slumbering, and not Meri. *Oh, for Jove's sake. Can't it wait? You go for months and never seem to need any of us, then here you are, making demands.*

Euclid, you know you and your cohorts have spent years banging about in my brain. I need to know what to do about Davey Ten. He's reluctant to return to Edinburgh, but I know he wants to. It's the silence there that disturbs him. Ahem, something I know very little about.

Able swore he heard someone moving about and glanced at Meridee, who was a silent and pleasantly soft body nestled close to his. *Euclid, I need your help. You're dead. You don't sleep.*

And now you're the expert on what happens after death?

Have it your way, Euclid.

He listened, and heard the faintest sound of someone rolling over and perhaps reshaping a pillow for more slumber. His heart sank. Then, *My boy, think of the first five axioms. It's elementary. Goodnight.*

Hmm. Able moved slightly away from Meri and put his hands behind his head. He thought through the five axioms, forcing himself to think slowly this time, and savor the simplicity. Oh my word, that was it. He smiled up at the ceiling. *Thank you, but leave us, Euclid. You promised Meri you wouldn't come into our bedroom.* His answer was a monumental snore from somewhere inside his brain, where the clock ticked more quietly.

He glanced at his wife, now awake, who watched him. "You're awfully pleased about something, my love," she said as she reached for him.

"Who wouldn't be?" he whispered back, pulling her closer, and then onto him. "Euclid just solved my problem and I'm at the mercy right now of the most wonderful wife a man could have."

"I warned you about Euclid in here," she said, her lips on his ear now, and then her tongue doing marvelous things to his external auditory canal.

"He's asleep," he said, as he raised her nightgown and ran his hands over her hips. He glanced to his right. "So is Ella."

"I'm not," his wife said, as she tugged her nightgown higher. Her breath came faster, but she asked, "What did Euclid tell you?"

"The first axiom answered my question, but the fifth one is currently engaging me."

"Which is…" My, but she was having trouble forming words.

So was he. "Dearest love, according to Euclid, and me right now, the whole is greater than the part."

That was that for a lengthy time. Hopefully Euclid slept through it.

Chapter Nine

Able knew he was too long married to cross the street next morning with a stupid smile on his face. He looked back and there was Meri in the window, her hair tousled, with the same stupid smile. *We may never grow up*, he thought, and smiled all the wider.

He had informed her as he dressed that he knew he could get one of the new instructors to take his afternoon class on shipboard mathematics if he hurried across the street before classes began. "We are paying a visit to my Grandmama Munro after lunch," he told her. "Send her a quick warning if you wish. Ben will insist upon joining us, and he will be sorely disappointed if there are no crème buns."

"Aye, aye, sir," she said from their bed, then sat up. "Tell me: did Euclid ever say anything wiser than that sensational fifth axiom which I trust you will never forget?" She spread her arms and flopped back. "As if you forget anything."

My word, but he loved this woman. "Probably not," he joked. "That has to be the wisest thing Euclid ever said." He laughed as he felt that spectral thumb and forefinger ping against the inside of his brain. "Nothing wiser for *us*, anyway. Send Davey on his way back to Haslar. The rest of Euclid's axiom is for him. Tell him I'll pay him a visit soon, depending on what we learn from Grandmama."

In the street, he blew another kiss to her, which meant that a passing carter laughed and blew one back. *There's a high level of lunacy in Portsmouth*, he thought, then was realistic enough to admit that he and Meri contributed their fair share.

It was a matter of moments to ask the younger instructor to take his afternoon class. Able wondered if he would ever get over the surprise he still felt when those younger instructors seemed so eager to please him. Too bad the professors in Edinburgh had little regard for workhouse scum. St. Brendan's staff was far more enlightened. *We need to change that, Euclid*, he thought, and wasn't surprised when that brought back a prompt rejoinder from his interior mentor. *We? We? Able, do you have mice in your pockets?*

He had a moment before the calculus class to acquaint Headmaster Ferrier with Davey's woes and then joke a bit – but only a little, because even after all these years, Able Six still held his own living mentor in considerable awe. "Master Ferrier, I think the stiff rumps among those Scottish Presbyterians have no notion what we workhouse types are capable of."

"Little by little, Able," Master Ferrier said. "What's that Spanish saying you quote to me now and then? 'Patience, and shuffle the cards.'"

Able nodded and watched for his son to cross the street with the redoubtable Mrs. Perry, for whom all carters stopped for at a respectable distance, and never ever thought of blowing a kiss. Hmmm. Mrs. Perry. *What say you to her, Euclid?* No answer. Apparently even Euclid was careful around the tall and formidable African woman.

Calculus was solid and educational, as usual. Able wondered if he would ever get over the delight at the sight of six students (he included Ben, sitting on two large books) applying themselves. He remembered with a pang that earliest class with Jamie MacGregor, now a seasoned third luff on Admiral Collingwood's flagship, and Janus, dead these many years, and his most promising student. These students were prepared and unafraid. *If only you could see them, Jan*, he thought.

How to change the prejudiced minds in Edinburgh? Since Mary Munro wouldn't be left behind on a visit to her great grandmama, Ben knew he was a favored child, and Ella had to go where Meri went, Able was prepared to happily squash them all into a conveyance after luncheon for the brief journey to Mrs. Munro's residence.

No need, it turned out. Meri sent that early message of warning about the crème buns, which meant Mrs. Munro's larger carriage conveyed to them to Jasper Street. As much as each trip delighted him – he loved having an actual grandmother – Able never could quite avoid a moment of sadness as they passed the imposing residence of the late Captain Sir Belvedere St. Anthony, only four doors down from the Munro mansion. *I will always miss you*, he thought, even though Grace Croker Lady St. Anthony Ogilvie lived there happily now with her newish husband.

Trust Meri to notice his lingering glance. She kissed his cheek, which meant she also had to kiss Mary Munro, who sat on Able's lap. A quiet "Ahem," from Ben meant another kiss. What a family he had.

Once inside, Ben and Mary Munro were both easily distracted with crème buns at their own little table, built just for them in the sitting room. Able seated himself in his usual place next to his grandmother, restored to him after years of his own loneliness, and her own sad search for the whereabouts of her genius daughter. Here they were, family again and always.

It took mere minutes to acquaint this lady with the matter at hand. "Davey isn't happy and doesn't want to return," he concluded. "He has been subjected to total silence from professors and students alike. I don't know how this happened, dear lady."

It was Mrs. Munro's turn to pace the room in agitation. She stopped her circuit in front of her grandson. "I suppose I am to blame for that, Able," she admitted. "I am on close terms with the chancellor. Perhaps I was wrong to tell him of Davey's origins." Her face hardened. "Perhaps Winston McLeish is not the kind educator I thought he was. Perhaps he is a bigot and a snob."

"Please don't blame yourself, Grandmama. I don't blame you for your enthusiasm for the Gunwharf Rats. Anyone who bothers to become acquainted with them generally has your same willingness to champion their cause. I wish everyone were as enlightened as you are, but sadly, all are not. Let us sit down again." He smiled at his grandmother. "I like to cuddle you, dear lady."

She flashed him a smile that made Meri clap her hands. "Mrs. Munro, I do believe Able has your smile," she said, which somehow calmed everyone in the room. *How does Meri do that?* Able asked himself. He felt Mrs. Munro relax in his arms.

Simple, he heard from somewhere inside his brain. *Mrs. Six only states what she sees. I cannot understand why she thought you were such a prize.*

It was Able's turn to smile, but only on the inside. Now *this* was more like the Euclid who had followed him around for a lifetime. Perhaps

Euclid had been bored for the last few years when he wasn't so needed. *Help me now, sir*, he thought, and hoped.

"There now, Grandmama," he said. "You probably know enough about academicians to know that they are proud and too often petty."

"I suppose," Mrs. Munro said. "What can I do for Davey to right this wrong?"

What, indeed? Able looked at Meri, a question in his eyes. He would try her before Euclid.

"He needs people to talk to," Meri said promptly. She dipped a napkin in a jug of water by the crème buns and wiped Mary Munro's fingers. "We cannot depend upon the people at the college itself. What about his boarding house?"

Able reminded her. "They're no help either."

"He needs to live somewhere else with friendly folk," Meri said. "Mrs. Munro, you mentioned a house in Edinburgh..."

"Aye, I did. My older brother, Strachan, gave it to me, plus enough income to keep it." Mrs. Munro laughed. "Strachan always insisted that he might come to visit Edinburgh someday, even though his estate near Dumfries was sufficient unto the day. I let him maintain that little fiction about an Edinburgh visit." She sighed, then raised her head with pride. "I think he did that to ensure I would always have a place to live, if things fell out between me and my now-late, and alas, somewhat unlamented husband."

Even a teasing tone couldn't disguise the pain of a wife and mother unable to help a beyond-brilliant daughter whose own father never understood her, or tried to. No wonder the woman had rejected her married name of Carmichael and resumed Munro, after her husband's death. No woman did that, except one strong enough to ignore raised eyebrows and whispers.

"Does anyone caretake it for you while you are here, Grandmama?" Able asked.

"Yes, indeed. A spinster sister-in-law of my younger brother Lachlan tends the house now, after too many years – according to her - as a sort of nanny to Lachlan's two sons."

"That was nearly my fate," Meri said. "No dowry. It's a good thing I found someone as impoverished as I was, eh? Thank goodness Durable Six is at least handsome."

Mrs. Munro laughed, breaking all the tension. "Meridee, my niece doesn't have your pretty face and charming manner, but she isn't homely by any means." She pursed her lips, as if contemplating the right touch and tone. "Let us say she is opinionated, and considers herself quite the equal of any man."

"You mean she doesn't know how to lose gracefully at cards, or simper about and look helpless?" Meri asked.

"Clueless," Mrs. Munro stated, with a shake of her head. She lowered her voice. "She is all of twenty-eight."

"Horrors," Able said. "More to the point, what would she think of a lad like Davey Ten?"

Mrs. Munro walked to the window again, but this time without her earlier agitation. She put her hands behind her back and gazed down at the street. "Miss Twig will be honest and fair with him," she said at last. "I know that."

"Miss Twig?" Meri asked.

"She's a trifle thin," Mrs. Munro said.

"I trust she has another name," he commented.

"Esther Teague," Mrs. Munro said. Her expression turned thoughtful. "In her last letter, she chafed about the solitude. Also that she was getting tired of her cook, who never ventured much beyond porridge and meat pies. Can Davey cook?"

"No, but Mrs. Perry can," Meri said, completely serious. She picked up Ella, who was starting to root about, and unbuttoned her bodice, soon occupying Ella.

"But what about *us*?" Able asked, diverted.

"We will do quite well with Molly, an undercook at St. Brendan's. Like Mrs. Perry, she is of African persuasion and West Indies-trained in the kitchen."

"How did you meet Molly?" he asked, wondering at this wife of his.

"She accompanies Mrs. Perry and me to the market. We talk."

"Meri, would Mrs. Perry agree to this?"

"Perhaps, if we limited the experiment to six months. You know, long enough for Davey to decide if Edinburgh is truly for him. If it isn't, they will return to us together. Davey will train at Haslar as a surgeon, and not an exalted physician, which, I suspect, never was his real aim."

THE UNLIKELY GUNWHARF RATS • 53

"Hmm. Mrs. Perry can organize a kitchen, and Davey would certainly talk to her," Able said, warming to the idea.

"I am also thinking of a friend more his age. Make it a special assignment for another Gunwharf Rat." She smiled at him. "Who is the eternal optimist amongst our Rats?"

"Avon March," he said, with no hesitation. "Meri, you amaze me."

She gave him a look that came near to scorching his smallclothes. She glanced at Mrs. Munro, who was minding Ben, and lowered her voice. "And you, dear man, may brush my hair tonight. As long as you wish."

Chapter 10

Lord love the Scots. By the time Able and Meri pried the children away from their great grandmama's bounteous table, Mrs. Munro was already seated at her writing desk, informing Miss Twig – a.k.a. Esther Teague – that a cook was coming her way, along with an all-around useful and abidingly cheerful lad, plus a gifted medical student who had been cruelly used by those who should have known better.

"I will inform Esther that she will be vastly entertained, and that Mrs. Perry wouldn't dream of porridge in any form," she said, looking up after Able kissed the top of her head. "Oh, you dear boy!"

"Mrs. Perry does make excellent baked oatmeal, but Miss Tw – Teague – can be the judge of that," Meri said. She kissed Mrs. Munro's cheek. "I fear we are riding roughshod over Miss Teague."

"Don't give it a thought," said the redoubtable Mrs. Munro. "I provide her with pleasant surroundings, a servant or two, and a comfortable income to stay there. Davey might do *her* good."

"I do hope she's right, Able," Meri said as they started home. "I will suffer vast remorse if Miss Twig ignores Davey, too." She leaned against her husband. "Please tell me you weren't ever ignored."

Should he or not? Why not? "I fell madly in love with the hot-blooded daughter of a rich Italian merchant, when berthed at Livorno. This was years ago, I might add. She was beautiful, until that unfortunate moment when she wanted to know something about my parents. When I told her, she couldn't usher me out of her bed fast enough."

Meri gasped, then laughed, until he began to fear that her stays were laced too tight, and she might faint from merriment. "Should I loosen your stays? Like I did to that merchant's daughter?" he whispered, *sotto voce*, which only set her off again. Ben shook his head and returned to his well-read copy of Plato's *Apologia*. Mary Munro laughed, too, because she was a jolly girl even though – hopefully – she didn't get the joke (Able hadn't yet decided just how much she understood). Ella slumbered on his shoulder.

"You're a rascal," Meri said.

"I know," he replied modestly. "But in all seriousness, it happened to me, too. Obviously, I survived, and made wiser bedroom choices."

She laughed some more, and Able never felt better. He directed the coachman to drop him off at the dock for the ferry to Royal Haslar Hospital, and sent Meri and the children on. He handed her the still-sleeping Ella.

"Able, there are days when I wonder what I did to deserve you."

He knew she was teasing him, but his simple reply brought tears to her eyes. "You're my keeper, dear wife. I am continually amazed that I wandered into your orbit. God is good." He couldn't resist and rubbed his hands together. "And now I will leave you to explain to Mrs. Perry what we have in store for her. She might veto our idea, you know, shoot it right down."

"I can convince her," Meri said. She settled Ella on her lap as he opened the door. "She was telling me only yesterday about one of the under-cooks at St. Brendan's who was recently widowed and needs a change of scenery. I believe that is Molly."

They let him off with a wave. He was familiar with Royal Haslar Hospital, the sprawling facility and largest brick building in Europe, or so someone claimed. He found Chief Surgeon David Haysberry seated behind a desk piled with papers.

They knew each other from the Battle of the Nile. Able knocked on the doorframe, and Haysberry looked up from the papers threatening to spill off his desk and onto a floor already littered with papers. Able saw relief in his eyes.

"Please tell me you are here to offer distraction from the problem that higher command causes," he said, holding out his hand. "Give me a heaving deck and a leg to amputate any day. I hate invoices and complaints and all this damned paperwork."

"You could use one of my Gunwharf Rats," Able said, clearing paper off a chair and seating himself.

"Send me one."

"I wish I could. My most effective secretary and bean-counter is serving in the Mediterranean aboard Admiral Collingwood's flagship."

"At least I have your clever surgeon assistant, even if I suspect he is temporary," Haysberry said. He leaned back in his chair. "I suppose you are here to tell me he is returning to Edinburgh. Damn you, Able, if you weren't such a useful, pleasant fellow, I could dislike you."

Haysberry's unshaven face grew solemn as Able explained what was going on with Davey Ten. "I assured him he could choose to return for more uncertainty in Edinburgh, or stay here, perhaps with you and the other surgeons to teach him what he knows to be of use in the fleet."

"Do you mean it?" Haysberry asked quietly.

"I do," Able replied. "He'll get no recrimination from me. I know what it's like to be an unwanted bastard, lower than a worm in anyone's social sphere." He sighed. "I just don't want him to feel defeated. I want him to choose from a position of strength, not failure, because that is where he is now."

"He's in Block Four. Take him for a walk," Haysberry said. "Lord knows we can use him here, but I understand what you're saying. When is he due to head north?"

"Two weeks."

"You know that with an apprenticeship here, we can teach him everything practical that he needs."

"I do. I also know that you surgeons need a certain spark to do your hard and dirty work. I don't see that in Davey right now. He's a sad young man."

"Can you help him?"

"I think so." Able almost added, *according to my best friend, Euclid.* He resisted.

Haysberry picked up what looked like invoices. "Then go to it, Able. Block Four."

Davey was spreading ointment on a stack of bandages to roll and appeared not to mind liberation, although his expression was cautious.

"Mrs. Six and I paid a visit to my grandmama and your benefactor this afternoon," Able said. "I have news."

They sat on a bench in the courtyard, after Davey took a moment to visit with some of the patients well enough to ambulate outside, even though the breeze off the Solent was chill. Able watched the Rat's sure touch, and his camaraderie among the wounded sailors and marines. *You were born for this*, he thought. *Euclid, please.*

I told you what you need, he heard in response. *You busily applied part of it to Meridee Six just this morning.* As he watched Davey, Euclid's words reminded him forcefully of the time Euclid himself had come to Meri's aid when bad men threw her into the water not far from here. *I will always be in your debt for your kindness to her*, he thought. *And here I petition you again.*

You know what to do, Master Six, he heard in reply, quiet words with no needling or bombast. It gave him confidence.

Davey sat beside him, their shoulders touching, which told him all he needed to know about the boy's silent plea for comfort.

"I acquainted my grandmama with your dilemma," he began.

Davey nodded. "I…I suppose she is disappointed in me," he managed to say.

"Not at all. She is merely sorry that you had no recourse," he said. "She has offered to let you stay at her Edinburgh house with Esther Teague, her niece who caretakes the place." He chuckled. "She assured me that Miss Teague is fond of conversation. Point of fact: you wouldn't be alone in the evenings."

"That would be nice," Davey said. Able heard all the caution and wariness, as if the next thing he expected was for that small consolation to be yanked away.

"As we speak, Mrs. Six is right now petitioning Mrs. Perry to accompany you there and remain as a cook for the next term."

"*Really?*" Able listened close and thought he heard the tiniest bit of enthusiasm. "Oh, but she won't succeed."

"I think she will. My wife is remarkably persistent in her quiet way, or haven't you noticed?"

"She does get things done," Davey agreed.

"So does Euclid," Able said, casting his lot on a good toss of the dice. "I was thinking about him last night, and his five axioms."

"Pardon me sir, but only you would do that," Davey joked.

It was only a modest tease, but it gave Able cause to hope. "Too right. Do you remember them?"

Davey shook his head.

"'Things which are equal to the same thing are also equal to one another,'" Able recited, thinking of the comfort Euclid's treatise had given him. "'If equals are added to equals, the wholes are equal. If equals be subtracted from equals, the remainders are equal. If...'"

"I know where you're going with this, sir." Davey's comment was quiet, but Able heard a firmness, perhaps confidence coming out from a hiding place.

"And where might that be, my dear lad?"

Davey swallowed at the endearment, and leaned closer. Able's arm went to his shoulders. "I am as good as they are. I am equal."

"Then what is your challenge?"

"They don't know it yet, do they?"

"Someone does. You mentioned a Quaker physician."

"Mr. Coffin. He fills in for anatomy and *materia medica*."

Able felt a stirring in his brain. Euclid was paying attention, down to the hot breath on his neck.

"A friend, do you think?"

Davey nodded, but warily.

"Then consider the fifth axion: 'The whole is greater than the part.'"

"That smacks of cooperation," Davey said. This time, Able heard the humor and felt his own shoulders relax. This was the courageous, certainly too-young surgeon on the *Mercury* at Trafalgar, calmly doing as Able directed as they tended the wounded. "Sir, do you think the students will cooperate, too?"

"They might. They might not," Able replied. He didn't know how those superior-in-their-own-eyes students would treat Davey, the workhouse lad. "Will you give it one term? Mrs. Six is attempting Mrs. Perry's assistance. She'll go with you. I am going to advise Avon March to go along, too."

"As a friend," David said. Able heard all the satisfaction. "I don't want him to waste his time, though. They won't let him in the school with me."

"Have you ever known Avon to waste time?" Able asked, and they both laughed.

"But my professors… So far, it has been silence, even when I raise my hand."

"I went through that, too, in Dumfries, when I was beaten for knowing too much," Able said. Even though years had passed since such indignities, he heard his own voice harden.

Able sat up suddenly as he saw the scroll of his mind unroll with a snap, something that had not happened since his early days at St. Brendan's before the war began again. At that time, His mental scroll revealed the shocking sight of the Solent turn to blood. *Please not that*, he thought.

This was different and far more benign – the sight of a wagon with *McAdam's Brewery* painted in elaborate gold lettering on the side. As he watched in that split second, the wagon lumbered down Frazer Street and slammed into a round little man with a hook nose as he crossed the street. The man went flying, and that was that. The scroll snapped shut. Hmmm.

"Davey, tell me what your…your anatomy professor looked, um, looks like?"

"He's no taller than a minute and fat. The exalted Sir Lionel Henderson."

Able heard all the scorn. "You …you say Mr. Coffin is Sir Lionel's assistant? He teaches when Sir Lionel is…um…unavailable?"

Davey nodded. "Yes. Mr. Coffin is kind to me."

"I doubt that will change. You'll return then?"

Davey considered the matter. "Aye, sir, for a term. If I decide it isn't for me, I will leave."

"That is fair. I talked to Chief Surgeon Haysberry before I kidnapped you from Block Four. He said he and his fellow surgeons will gladly teach you here." He eyed one of his favorite Rats. Oh, hang it all, they were all his favorites. "You are perhaps wondering why you have to return at all?"

Davey looked him in the eye. "Sir, I need to prove something to myself, don't I? That I am equal to anyone and anything."

Here endeth the lesson, Able thought, humbled by Davey's courage.

Able walked Davey back to Block Four, then sat on a stone bench close to the entrance, needing another word with Euclid. *Sir, let's not be rash about that anatomy professor*, went through his mind.

I don't like him, Able heard in reply. *He is cruel to Davey Ten.*

I don't like him, either, but would you, could you, merely make him too uncomfortable to teach for, let us say, a term at the College of Medicine?

You're getting soft, Durable Six. I'd rather he were squashed flat by that brewery wagon.

Au contraire, Euclid. I am getting kind. He thought of Meri Six. *It's the company I keep.*

Chapter Eleven

Mrs. Munro had no objection to paying for a post chaise to return Davey Six to Edinburgh, accompanied this time by Mrs. Perry and Avon March. "I would not care for someone to treat Mrs. Perry unkindly on the mail coach," Meri Six added, when the wealthy Scotswoman seemed to be toting up a sum in her head.

"I hardly think anyone would dare mistreat your cook. She scares *me* a little," Mrs. Munro said. "But I see your point. Aye, a post chaise." She peered over her spectacles at Meri. "But Avon March, too? Another Gunwharf Rat?"

"He is cheerful and already Davey's friend." Meri smiled. "And he was *my* idea." She glanced at her husband, who picked up the conversation.

"Avon didn't hesitate when I asked him to drop his studies and spend the next six months in Edinburgh, for the good of Davey Ten. He'll be a friend. That is enough."

Sitting there in Mrs. Munro's elegant parlor, Meri didn't mention what happened when Grace Ogilvie let drop the news of Avon's inclusion to her newish husband, recently returned from a continent on fire with Napoleon's bloody ambitions. Grace told Meri that Angus Ogilvie modestly owned up to the silencing of two government turncoats. "Dear Angus named no names, except to say they wouldn't be missed much, probably not even by their wives." Grace shuddered. "On rare occasions, I wonder why I married Captain Ogilvie."

"You love him," Meri pointed out. "And I married a genius. Love is blind."

Their conversation led to a late-night visit with Avon to the Ogilvie's residence, the former home of Grace's first husband, Captain

Sir Belvedere St. Anthony. Beyond raised eyebrows, Able offered no objections when Meri asked to accompany him and Avon.

Perhaps she should explain herself. "Dearest, Avon is almost fifteen. Truth to tell, I am not entirely certain I trust Captain Ogilvie's devotion to mayhem of the skulking sort. What can he have in mind for Avon?"

"Wise of you. Come along. Let's both hear this."

Oh goodness, Avon, but you're not very big, Meri thought as they rode to the Ogilvie residence, Avon sitting between them. It saddened her, thinking of other Rats who would always be short, because their early years in desperate homes or equally bleak workhouses had deprived them of proper nourishment at critical times. There sat Avon, always eager to please and ready for whatever awaited him, no matter his stature. He was as game as a rat terrier.

After refreshments, Captain Ogilvie wasted not a moment. He pulled two sheets of paper from the inner lining of a coat where most coats had no such pockets, and handed them first to Able, who took a second per page to read the tiny writing. Able frowned, but handed them to Avon. "Your turn."

Angus Ogilvie drummed his fingers on his chair until Grace put her hand on his arm and gave him The Look she usually reserved for a classroom of younger Rats who needed reminders.

Avon took his time; he was a thorough lad. When he handed the sheets back to Ogilvie, Meri saw something else in him, a mature gaze that belied his years and reminded her forcefully that Avon was also capable, loyal, and understood danger.

"What would you have me do?" he asked simply.

"Are you good at skulking? Blending into crowds?" Ogilvie asked.

Avon nodded. "None better, sir," he said. Meri heard a certain quiet pride. "I could probably still lift a gentleman's purse."

"You, too, Avon?" Able asked, with that lurking smile of his.

"Aye, sir. Were you good?"

Able nodded, and that was that, the camaraderie of Rats, one a student, and one a teacher. It was a world belonging to no one else in the room. Meri understood. There were times when she woke at night and watched Able sleep, because he could be so calm in repose. Sometimes she noticed that he slept with his thumbs curled under his fingers, the way infants slept. She wondered if he had somehow transported himself back to his early workhouse childhood. She had not the courage to ask, because he was usually sad of expression when he woke up after a night of curled fingers.

"I need a skulker," Ogilvie said. He turned his attention to his wife and Meri and winced theatrically. "Avon, I'd better explain this directive. Dear ladies, during my last visit to Trinity House, I was tasked to look into the disappearance of a Royal Navy man and a Royal Marine."

"Jumping ship is scarcely new," Grace reminded her husband. "I imagine there is somewhere a clay tablet from Hammurabi describing such an event."

"Except these were men from a frigate in Oban, on Scotland's west coast. They took ill and were sent across country to Edinburgh's Royal Infirmary." *Deep breath*. "And never seen alive again."

"No word of death or burial?" Meri asked. She felt a little prickle of fear and took Able's hand. He squeezed it.

"None. The captain sent his first luff to Edinburgh to inquire, and this letter is the result. Their deaths were recorded in the dead book in the Infirmary, but there was no indication of burial." He gave them all a significant look. "What do medical schools need to educate students?"

"Corpses for dissection," Grace said. "But did these unfortunates have families?"

"Indeed they did, wives – now widows, sadly – living right here in Portsmouth. One man was the *Trenchant*'s carpenter's mate, and the other a sergeant of Royal Marines. They were men of note and skill, not orphans or indigents, with no one to miss them. Dissection is the fate of indigents, but not men of the Royal Navy."

"Body snatchers, sir," Avon said quietly. "Master Six, did such men lurk around your workhouse, too?"

"Aye, they did." Able put a hand on his student's shoulder. "Captain Ogilvie, I must take exception to your scheme, whatever it is. Avon is too young to be involved in such skullduggery."

"I agree," Ogilvie said. He looked at Avon. "I'm asking, just the same. Lad, maybe you can do a little nosing about. Maybe see if such rumors are true. No danger there."

"And nothing more," Meri said firmly.

Captain Ogilvie gave her a look of innocence. Grace intercepted it and cleared her throat with more force than usual. "Certainly, ladies," he said smoothly. "Avon, see if you find out what, if anything, is happening to bodies unclaimed. That's all. The Royal Navy is interested."

Avon considered the matter. "I'll find a way, sir." He turned his charming smile on Meri. "Mam, I can do this for the Navy." His voice softened. "After all the Navy has done for me."

Still working at Haslar, Davey had been privy to none of this, until he joined them on the last Wednesday night when Rats gathered at the Six house, before his return to Edinburgh. "Avon, you're coming with me?" he asked with real delight, as the little Rat made it known, and Able looked on approvingly.

Avon nodded. "Master Six said you might need a friend." Davy nodded. "Headmaster Ferrier has given me leave of absence." Avon looked around, as if the cheerful sitting room had ears. "I am to do a little skulking." Avon had a whispered question for Davey.

"I am not signed up for dissection yet, but I know a little," Davey answered. "Some of the corpses come from the instructors, who have legal sources. Others are indigents in the Royal Infirmary."

"Did you see any Royal Navy men there?" Able asked.

"No, Master Six." Meri saw Davey's inward look again, but it didn't seem so hard this time, not after the news that not only Mrs. Perry was to accompany him, but also another Gunwharf Rat. "I was only allowed on the ward with the truly desperate." He managed a faint smile. "Navy men and Marines would have been on a ward for ordinary people, I imagine. Ward A."

He touched his Trafalgar medal then, and Meri became aware that Davey wore his new Royal Navy uniform, the navy blue of the service with green piping and caduceus, symbol of the fleet's medical corps. No longer were surgeons, pharmacist mates and stewards an afterthought. They were a uniformed class now, and high time.

"Looking smart, lad," Able said. "Be sure to take along your surgeon's aprons."

"I can't scrub the bloodstains off them, master."

"Even better. Let your unkind peers and so-superior professors see you as *we* see you – a tested veteran." He held open his arms and embraced Davey Ten. "Stay in touch with me. Let me know how you get on. If at any point it is too much, come home to us."

The embrace ended, Davey stepped back. "I do worry about my anatomy professor, Sir Lionel Henderson." He made a face. "I wish Mr. Coffin had the teaching of that instead. We're allowed to watch some dissection, but not participate yet." He shook his head. "Sir Lionel is a windbag. He's a cross to bear for many, I think, and not just me."

Meri knew better than to glance at her husband, and firmly stifled a laugh. Able had told her about his memorable view, probably courtesy of that scoundrel Euclid, of the round little man hit by a brewery wagon on an Edinburgh street.

Able didn't look at her either. "Davey, you never know what'll happen in this crazy world of ours," he said. "Remember that you're equal to them all. Equal. It is enough."

Still, Meridee had her doubts, and didn't mind expressing them later in the quiet of their bedchamber. She played with the hair on her husband's chest. "Able, Davey came from Edinburgh so sad. You yourself have told him and me that Haslar's own surgeons are perfectly willing to teach him all they know, and it is a lot. You know it is."

"No argument there," Able said. "Davey would be in excellent hands at Haslar." He pulled her closer. "It's more than that. Like it or not, each Rat must prove himself *to* himself."

"Do you feel that way personally?" Meri asked shyly, feeling like an interloper into the workhouse world she had never known, not with her social status and gentle rearing. "Your accomplishments carry their own weight." She thought of her husband's thumb under curled fingers as he slept, and touched his hand, which opened to clasp hers. "Do you still doubt yourself a little?"

"Less and less," he replied, which suggested that he was taking his own council and doing it with deliberation, no jostling from his cranial companions necessary. He raised her hand and kissed it. "My cerebral specters do not visit me as often. Do I need them less? Perhaps. And there is you." He laughed. "At times, I am almost normal."

What could she do except kiss him? "Meri, it's your generous love and the everyday living with you that makes me more content than I ever thought possible." He sighed. "And the knowledge of my parents now, both of them. Davey doesn't have that yet." He patted her. "Would you think me a terrible fellow if I told you" – he lowered his voice and spoke into her ear, a pleasant sensation. "…that I have petitioned Euclid to find ways to help our Davey?"

She laughed softly. "Dearest, I would be more surprised if you had *not* done that. Besides, your cover is blown. You told me about the brewery wagon. I remain skeptical."

"Euclid's getting bored with me." He yawned. "Let's see what he can do for Davey and Avon."

Chapter Twelve

The Society of Friends favored frugal, temperate living. Josiah Coffin knew that. When he made the journey three years ago to teach at the University of Edinburgh's College of Medicine, his father had reminded him, which made Josiah smile inside – only inside – during his father's current and similar admonitions during his last night in London.

I wonder if I will always appear to my father as a twelve-year-old child, he thought, as his father waxed on about virtue, perspicacity and adherence to the Society's precepts. *He told me this several years ago and I am thirty-four now.*

Josiah decided that the only way to test this theory was to apply it to himself someday, were he ever to marry and father children of his own. He could assume he would act the same, so he listened charitably to the man who loved him, even when Josiah had insisted upon medicine instead of joining his father's prosperous counting house in London's commercial district.

"Lad" – there it was: lad – "If thee ever tires of ill treatment meted upon thee, and those slights and snubs we know well, thee is always welcome here."

His father gave him a blessing – gentle hands on his head – which soothed Josiah's heart, even as he wished his father could somehow give a similar blessing to Davey Ten, who suffered the silent treatment, as well. Davey had no one to talk to, no one to listen with a sympathetic ear, because in some eyes, he was less than nobody.

As Josiah left the house that morning, his father did one thing more. He walked his son to the waiting chaise, the door already held open by the post boy. "I will pray for thee and this lad thee mentioned. Stay the course, son.

Thee always has a sympathetic ear."

Do I? he asked himself, as the post chaise blended into London traffic then headed for the familiar Great North Road. There were times when the loneliness of his position took its toll. He knew he was introspective, but he didn't want to be a hermit.

He knew the sympathetic ear his father referred to was Deity, that Light Within. *I wish I could see thee, thou God of the Universe,* he thought. *More to the point, am I changing into someone I shouldn't be?*

Dissatisfied with himself, he closed his eyes and settled back, only to feel a distinct thumb and forefinger to his temple and the words from somewhere: "Reconsider your route," with a second tap for emphasis. "Now!"

That couldn't be, but it was, and Josiah was too smart to ignore it. He opened his eyes and looked around. They were just passing Smithfield Market on the edge of the City. His smile grew, as he wondered for one moment of levity if that gentle Light Within bludgeoned him to get his attention. It seemed out of character. He rolled down the window and leaned out. "Mr. Coachman, take me instead to Portsmouth. The Great North Road can wait. Can thee have me there by nightfall?"

"It'll be late, sir. Let's see how much I can spring'um, with your permission."

"Thee has it."

Dusk was coming on when the post chaise pulled into Portsmouth, traveling toward the center of town, which consisted of the usual narrow streets and was further amplified by wharves and ships at anchor. Out in the bay, Josiah saw four hulks floating at anchor. He knew they were prison ships, probably full of unhappy Frenchmen. He shook his head at the folly of war, as any good Quaker would.

The coachman spoke to his horses. Josiah felt the chaise shift as the man climbed down. He stretched, then opened the door. "Where to now, sir?"

"All I know is All Saints Way, and Saint Brendan," Josiah said, suddenly regretting his spontaneous decision.

"I'll ask around."

The man vanished into a nearby grogshop, one of many lining the street. *I am a babe in the woods*, Josiah noted with some regret. He considered the matter, then joined his coachman inside a well-lit place rejoicing in the name of Cleopatra's Nipples. Josiah couldn't help his smile, as he imagined how shocked his father would be to see his son there.

The place was crowded, noisy, and smoky, with a strong smell of sausages which made Josiah's mouth water. Their stops from London had been long enough to change horses and snatch a bit of bread and meat. He made his way to the counter and ordered three plates of sausage.

The woman behind the counter rejoiced in hair a color not found nature. She leaned across the counter and leered at him, exposing a generous portion of breast and tit. He nearly went into a fit of the giggles, thinking to himself, *And Cleopatra's nipples before me. Julius Caesar would be appalled.*

The woman handed over the food, took his money, and decided to appraise him a little more. "A handsome feller like you, sir…would you be interested in a quick one in the back room? I have some time…"

"No, no thank thee," he said, suddenly feeling all of fourteen and decidedly out of his element.

"So you're a handsome feller," his coachman joked, taking his plate and sitting down. "Thank ye, sir."

"This other plate is for thy post boy," Josiah said, his face warm.

"My son. I thank'ee," the coachman replied. "I'll take it to him. Back in a moment."

They ate in an odd sort of companionable silence, as life and noise and booze swirled around them. When the edge of his hunger subsided, Josiah leaned closer. "Find out anything?"

The coachman shrugged. "People say there is an old monastery just beyond what they call the Gunwharf. I have directions." He chuckled. "Or what passes for directions from a tar a sheet or two to the wind. Colorful lot, eh, sir?"

"Indeed."

Outside, Josiah did another spontaneous thing. "Let me sit with thee up there," he said. "The view is better."

The view was better, if a man didn't mind staring at women barely clothed, even in January cold. He looked away to avoid gawking at a couple engaging in stand-up copulation in an alley.

"Rough town," the coachman commented, and shook his head. He looked over his shoulder to the post boy hanging on behind. "Eyes to the front, son," he admonished.

So this is the Gunwharf, Josiah thought, as they passed a wharf with piles of cannon stacked there and guarded by Marines. The wind blew cold off the bay, and he felt sorry for them. "Gunwharf Rats," he said softly.

One side street yielded nothing beyond more women and men finding some sort of solace, even in the cold. The next street boasted a bakery and then up ahead, he saw the unmistakable shape of an old church, close to the water's edge. Josiah sighed, relieved not to take a coachman and his impressionable son past too many more working girls.

Now where? "Wait here a moment," he said. "The monastery is well-lit. Someone in there can direct me."

The coachman tipped his hat. "Can my boy sit inside the chaise?" he asked. "It's a raw night."

"Certainly," Josiah said, flogging himself mentally for not suggesting that hours ago. *There are times I am no Friend*, he thought. "Thee as well, sir."

"I'm fine."

"I insist."

Josiah went inside, admiring the tidiness of that drafty place, which must have seen centuries of monks gliding up and down the magnificent stairs. He saw boys of all sizes instead, dressing in the selfsame black uniform Davey wore. He stopped one of them, a bright-eyed lad whose parentage must have included an African.

"I say, friend, can thee direct me to the home of Master Six?" he asked.

The boy executed a charming bow. "This way, sir," he said and led Josiah to the entrance again. He pointed across the street to the terraced row and a two-storied house with blue shutters. "Up there."

"I hope they do not mind unexpected visitors," Josiah said.

The boy shrugged. "They're used to what Master Six calls organized chaos."

Josiah laughed and thanked him. He crossed the street, which angled slightly uphill, giving the occupants a marvelous view of the bay below. One knock, then another, brought a pretty lady to the door. She carried a baby on her hip, a little one in the process of teasing out her mam's curls from under a lacy matron's cap.

"Come in, sir," she said and held the door open wider. "Able, we have visitors."

She was joined by a tall man in stockinged feet, and obviously the author of his baby's wonderful curls. Josiah saw a handsome man with dark eyes and an open, welcome face, his hair liberally speckled with grey. His eyes, though – they seemed to see deep into his own. So this was what genius looked like.

"Come, come. It's cold out," the man said and ushered him in. "Meri, please ask Molly to set another place."

"Oh, I…"

Mrs. Six peered out the door to the post chaise across the street. "They may come in, too. We have plenty."

"Oh, but…"

Master Six called to a small boy looking much like him. "Ben, bring in the coachman and post boy. He can blanket his horses for now. There you go." Off he went with a wave.

"Sir, thee doesn't even know who I am," Josiah said in mild protest, touched by their spontaneous hospitality. He could tell the Sixes were accustomed to nearly anything.

"You are Josiah Coffin, are you not, sir? Davey has mentioned you as his lifeline at the College of Medicine. He said you were of the Friendly persuasion. You're in time for dinner." He glanced toward the kitchen and lowered his voice. "I told Molly to make another pan of rolls."

Josiah tried not to stare, he really did. "How did thee know…"

Able Six waved his hand. "I have ways. Come into the dining room. Mary Munro is already there, and she does not like to wait for meals."

That was that. The coachman and his son ate in the kitchen, and Josiah joined the Sixes and their three children at the dining table, one end of which was stacked with books. Mrs. Six followed his gaze. "We have a lot of books here, Mr. Coffin," she confided. "Aren't we lucky?"

To call them all charming was to miss the mark entirely, even though that was obviously true. He had never experienced anything like this before. It was as if he had been caught in a net of kindness. No wonder

Davey wanted to return here. Better eat and savor the whole experience, before rigorous duty – unwelcome, admit it – summoned him again.

Josiah ate with real pleasure, enjoying this little family he had just met, simply because he had followed an impulse, which, if he was not so logical and rational, didn't seem like an impulse at all, but well-planned by.... someone.

After dessert of plum duff, a favorite of Ben Six – if his sigh of sheer pleasure was any sign – Able pushed back his plate. "Mr. Coffin, I thought I might see you today," he said. "Davey left this morning. He was not alone. He has allies this time."

For some reason, Josiah felt no skepticism at Able Six's comment beyond, "Thee knew more than I did about my change of plans today," he said. "I am glad Davey is returning to us, as onerous as it is for him."

"Davey agreed, but only on my guarantee that he can leave at any time and continue his surgical education at Haslar with no shame or recrimination," Able replied. "Why should he suffer from my prideful folly at wanting to see a workhouse lad at the best medical school in Europe? Our Navy surgeons right here are amply qualified to instruct. We also sent along Mrs. Perry, a cook and most formidable woman, and another Gunwharf Rat by the name of Avon March."

"Such an odd name."

"Not if you're an infant found by the River Avon in March," his host said. Josiah could have sworn he heard a touch of bitterness. "Avon is friendly but fearless." He chuckled, the rancor gone quickly. "He was formerly a noted thief and pickpocket and has a knack for blending into any crowd. You'll never know he's around."

What could Josiah say to that? *I am a babe in the woods*, he thought.

"You're not as naïve as you think," Able replied, which jolted Josiah further. *God Almighty, does this man read minds?* Wisely, he did not comment. Better not to be thought an idiot.

Able looked at him expectantly. Josiah obliged. "I was heading north back to Edinburgh and acted on an impulse." He leaned forward and rested his elbows on the table. "I wanted thee to know that David Ten is not friendless. I hold him in high regard."

"Among his peers, he is friendless," Able said, and there was no overlooking his concern. "Davey is a sociable sort. It chafes him raw to be reminded every minute of his lower than low status, especially since he and other Rats have proved themselves adept and helpful to our nation at war. No one at the College of Medicine can make such a claim."

"Why is he even there?"

Able glanced at his wife and leaned back. "I alluded to my prideful ways," he admitted. "Like a fool, I thought all would see his battle-won esteem and treat him as an equal. He has the intelligence and commitment to be a great physician."

"Of this I have no doubt," Josiah said.

"I was wrong, though. All most of the faculty and students see is a bastard foisted upon them," Able continued. "This is harsh treatment for a lad who has already served king and country in ways most his age wouldn't dream of." He fastened that deep gaze on Josiah, who knew better than to squirm. "Can you help him?"

"As thee can imagine, as a member of the Society of Friends, I am at the College of Medicine on sufferance, too. I cannot show favoritism," he said, almost cringing inside because it sounded so cowardly.

"You don't bow to kings or magistrates or preening academics, either," Able said. "Many of your sect have paid for this with their lives in painful ways. I do not doubt your courage."

The man understands me, Josiah thought with relief and humility. "Thee knows," he said simply.

"Aye. Besides that, Davey wouldn't accept help at your expense. I know my lads," Able said. His expression turned wistful. "I thought I knew them before Trafalgar, but I know them better now. We have been through our own furnace."

"I will do all I can," Josiah assured Able. Perhaps he assured them both, because Mrs. Six nodded, her eyes serious. He couldn't help himself, even though he knew better than to speak against even an enemy. "Sadly, sir – and madam – a great obstacle is Sir Lionel Henderson, old, esteemed and set in his ways. He plays favorites. If I may indulge in a sinful wish, it is my fervent desire to have someone besides Sir Lionel teach anatomy and elementary dissection."

To his surprise, the Sixes exchanged a potent glance. "Let's see how things play out this term," Able said. There was no overlooking the humor in his eyes. "Meri, please ask Pegeen to swamp out that extra room tonight for our guest. Sir, Molly will prepare a room off the kitchen for your posting crew. They will be comfortable. I will send Ben with a note to take the horse and chaise off the street and into St. Brendan's stables."

"Thank thee, Mr. Six. I know better than to argue about thy kind hospitality."

"Wise of you, sir. We'll send you off in the morning with a fine breakfast and our best wishes that much good will be accomplished this term." Master Six stood up and took Ben aside. After a brief conversation, the boy shot off on his errand across the street. Mrs. Six was even now talking to a bright-eyed maid, who hurried upstairs.

When they were alone, Able leaned closer. "This is for your ears only. Avon March is more than company for Davey. He's been tasked with learning what he can about the disappearance of a Royal Navy warranted officer and a Royal Marine sergeant. They were sent from Oban to your Royal Infirmary in Edinburgh because of illness." He looked around again. "They were eventually declared dead, but their bodies never returned to their loved ones."

Josiah let the startling words sink in. He was no man to rush a comment, even though he occasionally wondered where bodies for dissection came from. It was never his business to ask or accuse, but everything changed with Master Six's statement. "Thee seems to be placing a great deal of trust is someone so young as Avon March."

Again he was captured by the depth in Master Six's eyes. It wasn't hypnotic, but…he couldn't explain it. "Mr. Coffin, you have no idea about these lads. Avon is almost fifteen, aye, but there is not a Gunwharf Rat – I include myself – who isn't much older than he seems." He sat back, as if relieved to have this conversation over. "I wanted you to know. Avon will be discreet and observe only. Hopefully, the disappearance of the men's bodies has a logical explanation."

"Aye, sir," Josiah said, touched to his heart's core.

Able went to the sideboard and poured them each a glass of rum. They sipped in silence. A rap on the door, and the maid of all work opened it and stuck her head in. "All's ready upstairs, sir."

"Thank you, Pegeen. All's well with the men of the post chaise?"

"Aye, sir, bedded down off the kitchen. The horses are stabled."

"I am putting thee to much trouble," Josiah said after Pegeen left.

"I was expecting you," Able said.

"I don't doubt that." Josiah didn't. There was far more afoot here than he was used to, and oddly enough, it seemed to energize him. Maybe his life had been too boring, up to now.

They finished their rum in silence, then, "Let me show you upstairs, Mr. Coffin." Master Six paused at the top of the landing. "I like this," he said quietly. "I never had a lullaby sung to me."

Josiah listened, touched to hear Mrs. Six singing softly. "Thee is a lucky man," he whispered.

"You will be, too. Stay the course, sir. Help Davey if you can, without trouble for yourself, and don't worry overmuch about Avon March. I think we've barely tapped Avon's abilities here at St. Brendan's." He opened a door. "Ben keeps his favorite books in here. I like to read them, too."

Josiah's eyes went to a copy of Newton's *Principia*, the English edition of which he had labored over for too long, then given up. "This one's in Latin," he said.

"Aye. It's nice to read the real thing. Wouldn't you agree?"

Josiah nodded. *My God, what a family*, he thought.

"Goodnight then. Breakfast is at seven." Able chuckled. "Mary Munro is particular about *all* her meals."

The door closed. Josiah Coffin looked around with real pleasure. *These people!* he thought. *I do not know when I have been so adroitly managed. I like it.*

He felt no chagrin, no fear of what lay ahead. He felt something far better. He felt hopeful.

Chapter Thirteen

Davey was not a pretentious fellow by any means; no Gunwharf Rat was. Still, by the end of a nearly pleasant three-day journey via post chaise from Portsmouth to Edinburgh, he decided that traveling in style was far from onerous.

It didn't hurt that he had a fine uniform now. Mrs. Six's parting gift was an equally handsome Royal Navy cloak. She cried when the three of them left – he included Mrs. Perry of course – but Master Six kept his arm tight around her and Davey knew all would be well.

The journey began awkwardly enough, with Mrs. Perry on one side of the chaise, and Davey and Avon on the other, no one knowing what to do or say.

Avon broke the silence. "Mrs. Perry, I really hope the lady filling in for you knows how to keep Rats in line," he said, with all the earnest appeal that made him a favorite at St. Brendan's.

Mrs. Perry chuckled, to Davey's relief. "It's mostly just the Six children and you Rats on Wednesdays."

"Do you miss us?" Avon asked simply.

Davey was astounded to see tears gather in the formidable woman's eyes. "Like a fiber gone from my heart, you scamp," she said.

That broke every barrier, and Davey had to give little Avon credit for rare courage. The three of them talked and read and spent time with their own thoughts as the chaise smoothly traveled to a place Davey didn't want to be.

The first night took them to Presley and the Regent's Arms, per Master Six's instructions. "All you need to do is hand over this paper, which comes all stiff and formal with seals and furbelows from Admiralty,"

Master Six told him. "Mrs. Munro gave you plenty of money for food and lodging."

He had to ask. "What will the inn do about Mrs. Perry?"

Master Six's reply was quick and firm. "That is for you and Avon to settle. I will say this: Whatever happens to her should be what happens to you. If they think to relegate her to a barn, you will go there, too."

Before the three of them went into the Regent's Arms, Mrs. Perry took Davey's arm. "I can sleep anywhere," she told him in an unexpected kindly voice.

"Mrs. Perry, we will never desert you," Davey said, even as he feared the worst.

To his continuing surprise, Avon March took matters in hand when Davey hesitated. He walked to the high desk where the innkeeper stood polishing silver, and handed him the Admiralty letter and spoke in a clear voice, the kind of voice that sounded like firm command.

"Sir, we are requesting lodging for the three of us, per these orders from Admiralty House." He gestured to Davey. "Mr. Ten here has the fee for two rooms. If there is an adjoining parlor, we three will eat there."

"I've never housed a black woman," the keep said. "At least, not upstairs. It isn't done."

"It will be this time," Avon said, his voice crisp with command. "The three of us are going to Edinburgh on Royal Navy business."

The keep looked them over. Davey wondered what he saw. Was it two lads and a black woman, or was it something more, that something they were learning at St. Brendan the Navigator's School, the something called command and purpose, during these fraught times of national emergency?

The keep stared at Avon March, who did not wilt under his gaze. He looked closer, then looked at Davey, who could only hope he looked as stalwart as Avon.

The innkeeper glanced from one to another again. "Is that a Trafalgar medal?" he asked finally.

"Aye, sir," Davey said, taking heart from his traveling companion's oddly affecting air of control, the sort of spirit found on quarterdecks. "We served aboard the *Mercury*."

"Well, I'll be damned," the keep said, his skepticism gone.

"Mr. Ten is returning to the University of Edinburgh Medical School," Avon said. "I am under special orders, and Mrs. Perry has been named head matron of the Royal Infirmary."

It was a whopper of vast proportions, delivered with nearly ministerial aplomb. "What say you, sir?" Avon concluded.

Without a word, the keep handed Avon two keys. "There is a sitting room between," he said. "Up the stairs to the left, second door. Five shillings. I will send up a maid with the table of fare, and you will eat there."

"All of us?" Avon asked.

"Aye, lad, all."

Davey handed him the money, hoping he could get into the room before he split himself with laughter. And here he thought he knew everything about the unfailingly cheerful Rat who did not flinch at Trafalgar, even as he ran up signal flags without a thought to the fire and mayhem all around.

When they got to the rooms and shut the door, Mrs. Perry spoke for the first time. "That was a monumental lie about me, Avon," she said.

"Only a little," he returned. "I have no doubts that were this a fair world, you would be precisely that – head matron of the finest infirmary in Scotland." Avon grinned, returning to the fourteen-year-old Gunwharf Rat. "Wouldn't you, Mrs. Perry?"

"You're a scamp," she said, but Davey heard the pride.

You're all equal, came to Davey out of the blue, almost as if someone were intruding on his thoughts. That couldn't be. Whoever bothered much about Rats? "You're on Royal Navy business, too, Mrs. Perry," he added.

"I suppose I am," she said, then shook her finger at Avon. "You're still a scamp, but I'll overlook it." Her voice mellowed. "And, I might admit, a cool liar."

Avon nodded, as if she had showered him with great praise. "It comes in handy, now and then, doesn't it, Davey?"

He nodded, then glanced to the door, where someone had just slid the bill of fare. "Let's eat."

They didn't succeed the next night at the Bird's Nest. Even Avon March at his best was unable to convince the innkeeper to let Mrs. Perry stay in good quarters with them. Because he would not yield, neither would they, choosing instead to follow the post boy and driver to far less distinguished quarters behind the stables, where they made themselves comfortable.

Mrs. Perry objected at first, reminding them that she would be fine and it was warm. "No, ma'am, we won't do it," Avon said. Davey echoed his sentiments, and they prepared to bed down in clean straw.

The innkeeper didn't mind seeing the color and heft of their coins. Avon polished off his usual prodigious amount of dinner, reminding Davey of Mrs. Six shaking her head and wondering how someone so slight could eat so much and remain small.

Davey ordered the same for Mrs. Perry and took it to her. She tucked in, her eyes – those eyes that could look so stern at some infraction from a Gunwharf Rat – expressing her gratitude this time. "You know you didn't have to go to this trouble," she reminded them.

"Aye, we did," was Avon's prompt retort, which only made their cook and disciplinarian look away, as if she suddenly found the horses lipping down their oats fascinating.

Something puzzling happened a little later, when Avon returned to the inn for cider for the three of them. He came back quickly, his expression purposeful. "Davey, the strangest thing happened. The innkeeper had hardly started to polish a glass when it broke in his hand. He's bleeding prodigiously. I said you'd be right in to patch him up."

Davey grabbed for the leather satchel he carried everywhere, a practice Mr. Josiah Coffin had advised him to continue. He looped the strap over his head through force of habit, as if he expected the deck to start heaving.

He paused at the door. "I could leave him be," he said. "I'm no surgeon yet. What good has he done us?"

Avon shrugged, his expression cheerful as usual. "Mrs. Six was forever reminding us to be kind. That's enough for me."

"Me, too," Davey said, and knew he was on the right side of the angels. "I was just teasing." Was he?

The slice was a clean one, the kind that bled freely, but presented no difficulty to a surgeon's assistant who had seen far worse at Trafalgar. He spent a moment washing his hands, something Master Six – and also

Mr. Coffin – insisted upon without fail before he touched anyone. He threaded a needle with cat gut and stitched the innkeeper's forearm as he sweated and moaned. (Davey knew he could have been more gentle, but why?)

The man's wife rolled her eyes. "That's what you get for being careless," she scolded her husband. "Don't know how this happened though." She looked toward Davey as he merrily stitched away, mindful that he was inflicting misery on a miserable man. "It's like the glass just leaped out of his hand with a mind of its own." She shook her head. "I never saw nothing like it." She looked around and whispered. "Lad, do you believe in ghosts?"

"No, ma'am," he assured her. He resisted the urge to add, "Serves him right." He wrapped the innkeeper's arm in what he hoped was a clean dishtowel and made a firm knot over the bound-together wound with its neat row of stitches. "That should hold you, sir. I wouldn't get that wet for a while."

"Thank'ee lad," the man said. He looked away, as if trying to decide, then, "You and the other lad can stay for free tonight upstairs, if you'd like."

"No thank you, sir," Davey said. "We'd rather stay where we are."

"Free breakfast then?"

"Only if you include Mrs. Perry."

"I can't do that."

You could, Davey thought. He waited for anger to cloud his mind, but all he felt was pity for someone so narrow of purpose. As he repacked his supplies, he thought of the silent days ahead, the whispered scorn, the deliberate rudeness, and something turned over in his mind and heart. Maybe this was a teaching moment. Some people would never be wise or kind, but he didn't have to count himself among that number who retaliated.

"Goodnight, sir," he said. "You'll feel better in the morning."

"Take five shillings."

"No, sir. You probably need it more than I do," Davey continued. For the first time in his life, he felt rich beyond measure.

The next evening's stop resembled the first night. The three of them were warm and comfortable. Avon was still shaking his head over their last view of the bandaged innkeeper at the Bird's Nest, who, when he stepped outside to bid farewell to the more well-heeled travelers in the coach with a crest on the door, slipped and landed against the beautifully cloaked lady in the party, knocking her down, too. Their last view has been the poor man being struck over the head with a cane.

Avon craned his neck to follow the drama as Davey heard laughter from the post boy hanging on behind them. "Gor, it's like someone gave him a push!" Avon declared to Davey. "Strange doings."

Davey felt himself growing more distant for the final leg of their journey; he couldn't help it. *Why did I agree to return?* he asked himself, as the post chaise bowled along through clouds and rain that seemed to say Scotland. *Master Six said I could stay at Haslar.*

He forced himself to pay attention to the others in the chaise, not wishing to inflict his own fears on them. Hadn't they come along to help him? Just how many people did he wish to disappoint? He started to listen to Mrs. Perry, and decided they were kinder to him than he deserved.

"You came to St. Brendan's later, Avon," she was saying. "I have not told you my story. I am Ibo," she said, her voice low and sorrowful. "I was captured along with my family and taken in chains to the coast by slavers. I was fourteen years old, as near as I can tell."

Davey shoved his own misery aside and listened to her quiet tale of shackles, and dancing on deck for exercise as the sailors leered and touched. He had heard her story before, but this time, he began to compare his own early years of hunger and shame because he was a bastard and no favorite of God or man. His own years included no Middle Passage where the dying were thrown overboard to sharks that followed slave ships. No one ever fingered him or fondled him as he stood and shivered, naked, on an auction block in Georgia.

He listened for it, perhaps to justify his ill usage, but Davey heard no personal pity in Mrs. Perry's voice. She told her story to Avon, his eyes wide and sad, of what happened to her, which also included her purchase by Mr. Perry, a Welshman who was a carpenter's mate on the *HMS Marlebone*, docked in Savannah not long after the Treaty of Paris that turned the colonies into a nation. "My life changed, and I was happy again," she concluded, her generous gaze including Davey this time. "I made the best of things."

And you can, too, was her implied message. He understood. He was not alone.

Chapter Fourteen

For the umpteenth time – she was a careful lady – Miss Esther Teague smoothed down her second-best dress and looked out the window. Rain beat against the panes, but that was Edinburgh. Before he died many years ago, a seafaring uncle had told her of warm sun, blue skies waiting to be painted, sand nearly yellow and squishing through his toes as he walked barefoot along a beach on Barbados.

And here I stay in Edinburgh, when I know there are better places, she thought. She knew her address would never change, but at least she was not living entirely on charity yet, thanks to Aunt Munro, her father's sister. Well….. Auntie Ro had perhaps too easily convinced her three years ago that she was needed to manage the Munro house in Edinburgh. Auntie wrote that someone, preferably a trusted relative, could at no discomfort keep the place tidy against the day when she would probably return.

As for now, Auntie Ro had discovered a grandson rejoicing in the improbable name of Durable Six, and a great-grandson name of Ben, followed by little Mary Munro, and now the almost new Ella – my, but those Sixes were prolific. "I expect I will return someday," she had written, "but meanwhile, I need you in my house, Esther. I will, of course, include a generous stipend to run the place, provide for sufficient servants, and pay you for your sacrifice of home and hearth in Fife with your brother and his darling sons," Mrs. Munro had written, and that was that.

In truth, Esther's removal to Edinburgh from Fife was no sacrifice. She saw it as a summons to duty. She was happy, nae relieved, to assume the management of this house on Wilmer Street, a posh enough address and far above what could have so easily been her fate – life as a governess – since she had neither beauty, money nor prospects. She rejoiced to remove from Fife and away from the temporary sufferance of her brother, and more particularly, his wife and sons.

Her brother was charming in his absent-minded way, much like their father, but Edmund's wife enjoyed needling her about her unmarried state and dropping lofty comments (out of Edmund's hearing) that *some people* (substitute Esther Teague) were put on earth to remind Christians to be charitable.

That stung, but there was truth in the statement. Esther knew she was underendowed both in appearance and fortune, and opinionated, qualities that would never find her a husband. She was more than relieved to move her clothes and books to 158 Wilmer Street in Edinburgh. The house was two-storied, ivied, built well against the damp and quite to her liking.

There was one problem, which, in the world of twenty-eight-year-old spinsters, was not a big one. Esther Teague found few people to talk to besides her housekeeper, a woman who could rattle on about nothing for hours. At least she wasn't ignored.

Still, Esther had admitted to some disappointment when her housekeeper/cook rushed in only weeks ago to announce that a cousin of *hers* needed her culinary skills on Prince Edward Island, a remote spot in Canada. "I am sorry to abandon you, Miss Teague, but needs must and family comes first," her cook had informed her. "It won't be too soon," she added. "My cousin says the money to get me there might take a month to arrive."

The whole affair turned slightly strange only days later, when, addressed to the cook, a sizeable draft on a prominent counting house appeared. In fact, the parcel was tied to the wrought iron railing that led below to the servants' entrance, out of sight. Esther marveled that a well-known counting house would ever deliver funds that way. Still, what did she know of the transmission of money? She had so little of it herself.

Cook was gone within the week, still shaking her head over the amazing speed that such a thing could happen, right down to finding passage on a ship bound for Canada and sailing in mere days.

"Miss Teague, he must be desperate," Cook had said, as she packed. "I don't understand how such matters happen." She tittered (something Esther knew she would *never* miss). "'Tis almost magical, except that we Scots don't believe in such things."

No, we only believe in judgment, righteousness, and oatmeal, Esther thought as she waved goodbye to her chatty cook, wondered how long it would take to find another cook, and thought it might be a good time to sharpen her own culinary skills.

She had her own surprise a day later, with a letter from Aunt Munro, announcing that soon she would soon be in charge of something dubiously called a Gunwharf Rat. In fact two Rats, according to the hasty scrawl of a postscript. The letter had been propped up against that same iron railing. That was odd enough, but it rained hard all night, and the letter was dry as a sermon. She looked up and down Wilmer Street, wondering if she had just missed the courier. Odd, that. Perhaps it had been misdirected and a neighbor dropped it by.

Another letter from Mrs. Munro followed, explaining the Gunwharf Rats in detail. It elicited considerable sympathy from Esther, who had a generous and sympathetic heart beating inside her mostly flat chest. She read the letter twice, dabbing at tears for a poor lad ignored by one and all at the College of Medicine. Mrs. Munro stated that Davey Ten was a talented fellow blighted by his illegitimate birth and shunted off to a workhouse until he was sent to St. Brendan the Navigator School, where Mrs. Munro's grandson, Master Able Six, taught. Apparently the oddly named Davey Ten was also a surgeon's assistant, a veteran of Trafalgar, and all of seventeen.

The second letter referred to Avon March, another Gunwharf Rat. "'He is monumentally cheerful,'" Mrs. Munro had written. "'He is to keep Davey company.'"

To her further surprise, the Rats were to be accompanied by Mrs. Perry, whom Mrs. Munro described as an African woman, black as ink, with a gold ring in her nose. "She is a most excellent cook and organizer," Mrs. Munro had added in a postscript. "If you do not currently have a cook and housekeeper, your worries are over."

How in the world….. "Aye to this," Esther informed the letter. Mercy, did the letter move a bit in her hand, as though in approval? Surely not. She set the letter down quickly, hoping she was not turning into a barmy old maid, talking out loud to letters. At least she did not have cats…yet.

The additional occupants at Wilmer Street arrived early in the evening. After downing a highly unsatisfactory supper of bread and cheese and something unknown that didn't smell rancid, Esther paced the sitting room, wondering at herself. She had no indication when the Gunwharf Rats would arrive – today, tomorrow, next week – but some odd imperative suggested it would be soon.

A letter had arrived that morning from the University of Edinburgh, College of Medicine, handed to her by a courier, and at least not tied to a railing. It was addressed to David Ten, RN, 158 Wilmer Street and so forth, and bore the address of Chancellor Winston McLeish.

This was strange. How did the College of Medicine know that Davey Ten would be living here? Maybe the courier would know. She hurried out the front door. No one was in sight. Shaking her head, she bolted the door against...what? For the first time in her life, she wished there was a bottle of whiskey in the house. The strongest thing she had was vanilla extract. She downed a small cup of the extract, which rewarded her with nothing but a fervent desire to never do that again.

At dusk, she heard a vehicle stop on her quiet street. Before her stood a Black woman of formidable proportion, her expression inscrutable. This must be Mrs. Perry, who was flanked by two young men in navy blue with calm demeanor in one pair of eyes, lively interest in the other, and above and beyond that, a certain wariness in both. Esther gazed back, keeping her expression neutral, even as she felt her natural sympathy bubble up. Did they expect her to judge them on a moment's notice? Another glance told her they were used to dismissal.

Not from me, she thought suddenly. *Never from me.*

Chapter Fifteen

Esther's only previous experience with boys had been those wretched nephews in Fife, unmanageable spawn probably destined for either Newgate or the clergy, depending. She could tell at a glance that these two were different.

In her previous letter, Mrs. Munro had given her a little to work with, writing that Davey Ten was seventeen and already a Royal Navy surgeon's assistant. Also Royal Navy, Avon March was almost fifteen, interested in everything, and yes, possessed of an odd name. Who would name a boy Avon, after all? Even Mrs. Munro's comment that he was born in the month of March and abandoned along the bank of Bath's Avon River, left Esther wondering what to expect.

The younger one must be that Avon of interesting name. A quick glance at him suggested he had an air of good cheer about him. Behind that smile were eyes that probably missed nothing. After all, what else could a powerless workhouse boy do except understand his surroundings immediately? It might mean survival.

Beyond that good cheer was an utterly nondescript appearance – brown hair, brown eyes, lacking in height, no distinguishing features. She thought Avon March could blend into any situation where he found himself. She found herself smiling, knowing she was probably observing the ultimate skulker. Thank God he was here as a friend to Davey only. No need for him to skulk about in Edinburgh.

She spoke to the African woman. "You must be Mrs. Perry," Esther said, "And I think you are Avon March."

That earned her a smile from the younger and smaller fellow. He pointed to the quiet lad beside him. "Here's Davey Ten, Miss Teague."

Again, brown hair, brown eyes, but the possessor of a deep dimple in his right cheek that rendered Davey Ten charming. She only knew about the dimple because Avon had whispered something to Davey that made the older lad's eyes grown smaller as he smiled. When he smiled, she also saw the smallest relaxation as his shoulders lowered.

There was something else, an awareness that soon to be housed under her roof was someone with considerable intelligence mingled with a practical air. She knew without anyone telling her that to become Davey Ten's friend would be to have a great and loyal defender.

Where was this coming from, this split-second delineation of character and ability? Esther had no idea. She liked it, though. This understanding of two workhouse boys put her at ease. She felt her shoulders relax, too.

First, she needed to get them sorted out. She had never seen anyone like Mrs. Perry either, so tall and black. Something else, Esther Teague knew kind eyes when she saw them.

"I've been expecting you," she said, then remember Aunt Munro's letters. "She called you Gunwharf Rats."

"Aye, mum," said Davey. "That we are."

They were more. She could tell that with another glance. They were battle-tested veterans of a nautical engagement that, according to Mrs. Munro, would be on everyone's lips forever. She looked at their plain uniforms and saw a medal on each chest. She doubted Admiralty handed those out with reckless abandon.

"Let's do this, gentlemen," she said, which meant the two lads exchanged amused glances. "Go up the stairs and you'll see two rooms to your right. You two are welcome to quarter together, if you choose, or separately. It's your choice. Come down when you've unpacked. We'll eat in…"

The dining room? Too intimidating. She didn't like eating there in solitary splendor and knew they wouldn't care for it either. That was about to end. "We'll eat in the kitchen," she said and smiled at Mrs. Perry, who seemed to look on with approval. Please let it be approval. "I think the food tastes better there. Very well?"

"Aye, Miss Teague," Davey replied. He was the leader and Esther knew it. He didn't stop there. "Mrs. Perry, if it's just cheese and bread, you already know how we like it."

The big African woman nodded. "Torn up bread and melted cheese." She laughed. "And if there is any ale to be had, I'll tuck that in, too."

Avon gave Esther a small salute, hand to forehead, then followed Davey up the stairs. She was left with Mrs. Perry, who regarded her with what Esther hoped was calm acceptance.

"Mrs. Perry, you know them pretty well, don't you?"

"Aye, miss, I do. I love them," Mrs. Perry said. "Back in St. Brendan's, we call them men, too." She laughed, a hearty sound in a quiet house. "And we call them Rats."

"I'm glad you came along," Esther said.

"I was Master Six's idea, even before we added little Avon to the mix," the housekeeper said. "T'master doesn't know you, as much as he loves and respects his grandmother Munro. He wanted to make sure Davey had conversation at morning and night, since there appears to be none during the day. Let's find that kitchen, Miss Teague."

Esther felt an apology was needed. "There's a small servants' dining room, but really, no servants." She opened a door on a small chamber. "This is for you. My former housekeeper took her scullery maid along to Canada, so there is no staff."

"The Rats will help," Mrs. Perry said, unperturbed.

"You really call them Rats?" Esther asked, amused.

"Rats suits us all," was the reply. "When we're formal, it's Gunwharf Rats."

They laughed together, and it felt surprisingly good. That was when Esther realized that no one had talked to her much, either. The realization made her pause, and then look at Mrs. Perry with even more appreciation. *I have been wanting*, she thought. *Maybe I didn't know how much.* The notion made her shy. "I hope your room will do," she said.

"Quite well, I think," came Mrs. Perry's reply, after a look around. She felt the mattress, nodded her approval, and set her satchel beside the bed. "Let me at that pantry now and give me twenty minutes."

"Here's the pantry," Esther said, relieved at the mere idea of a cook. "And there is the latest word in cooking ranges. Um, there isn't much food about, but we'll go to the market tomorrow," she added, already wondering what her usual grocers would think of someone as intimidating as Mrs. Perry. The thought occurred to her that she was perhaps unlikely to be cheated or bullied ever again.

"Indeed, we will go to the market." Mrs. Perry eyed Esther, but not unkindly. "Skinny thing like you, what have *you* been living on? I trust Mrs. Munro furnished you with a worthy kitchen allowance. These men like to eat. You, Miss Teague, may set the table."

She did. Soon enough they all sat down to a late supper of bread and melted cheese as Davey had hoped for, with just a touch of ale from a bottle dusty and languishing in the pantry that Esther didn't know about.

Mrs. Perry couldn't be convinced to join them for supper, but Esther's heart warmed at the table talk. The Rats told her of their travel to Scotland, with Avon being most impressed. "I've never stayed in an inn before," he said simply, before returning to his cheesy bread. "Did you know that the keep's servant put a warming pan in the bed? It was so comfortable."

Davey smiled at his companion, which tugged at Esther's heart. "It was even fun the next night, when we slept rough behind the stables." Davey leaned toward her, after a glance at the door, and lowered his voice. "*That* innkeeper wouldn't let Mrs. Perry share a suite with us."

"Some people aren't nice," Avon said, as matter-of-fact as if he commented on the steady drizzle outside. "But we already know that." He set down his spoon. "Davey, how can I help you tomorrow?"

"Better you help Miss Teague and Mrs. Perry," Davey said. "I will go to my old lodging and make sure I don't owe anything, then register for the term's classes." His voice hardened. "And I will continue wondering who scarpered off with my sextant, although I think I know."

"Why would someone do that?" Esther asked, shocked.

"Most people are not as nice as you are, mum," Avon said, after another brief glance at her. She was beginning to see just how much Avon took in on an average look around a room. "Davey, I could make your sextant my first skulk."

"It's probably long gone to a pawnshop."

"Never know until I skulk a bit."

It was the most ordinary-sounding conversation, except that Esther had never heard her nasty nephews mention skulking. *I am going to get an education*, she thought.

The two exchanged a glance. "Should I?" Avon asked. After a moment's thought, Davey nodded.

"I'm here for conversation," Avon said, as if he was commenting on the weather. "And more. We probably shouldn't say much, but you should know a little. The Navy Board is starting to wonder why some invalid sailors in the…the…what is it, Davey?"

"The Royal Infirmary," Davey said, "That place where the poor and indigent are treated, as well as more a middling class of people, and others who can pay well."

"It…the Royal Infirmary has an excellent reputation," Esther began, parroting what she had heard from others about the medical school and infirmary, the pride of Scotland. "It least that's what I have been told."

Davey seemed to want to placate her. "I imagine you know your town, Miss Teague."

"Certain parts of it," she told him, woefully aware how little she knew about anything beyond a lady's purview of tending to a house and going shopping in the more genteel areas. Where had she *been* all her life?

The Rats exchanged glances. "Maybe I said too much," Avon admitted.

"No, you have not," she contradicted. She took her napkin from her lap and dabbed at the corner of her mouth, not because she assumed some stray soup had lodged there, but more to gather thoughts before she spoke. Then, "P'raps I don't know my town as well as I should. Still one shouldn't expect chicanery in a world-renowned medical school."

Davey was generous in his observation. "That's part of why Avon is here, Miss Teague. It's this way: Some ill or injured tars were sent here from Oban, where the navy stations a small fleet to patrol the North Atlantic. We know they were admitted to the Royal Infirmary. They were later declared dead, but no bodies returned to their families." He gestured to Avon, who returned a sympathetic look. "Lots of blokes don't think the navy cares for its wounded and injured, or that they have families. These men did."

"Some of us don't have families," Avon added, "but many do." He brightened. "Master Six says we will have families some day and be regular members of society."

"If we can get those who think they are more fortunate than us to speak to us, and maybe not steal things," Davey said.

You are making a brave attempt, Esther thought, impressed with these young men she barely knew. "No one steals here, and we all talk to each other," she said firmly, wondering why that would raise a lump in her throat. "Maybe I need conversation, too."

Davey nodded. Avon yawned. Esther looked at the gold timepiece pinned to her bodice. "It is long past time to be sitting at table! When do you like breakfast in the morning? Will eight of the clock do for tomorrow until we know your schedule, Davey?"

He smiled. "It will do very well, Miss Teague. C'mon, Avon. Let's try out those mattresses."

They went to the door, then Avon turned back. "Miss Teague, would you mind coming upstairs in a half hour? Mrs. Six always looks in on us before light's out, and…and…we sort of like that, don't we, Davey?"

"Aye, we do," was the quiet reply.

Esther watched them go upstairs. When she turned around, Mrs. Perry stood in the doorway to the pantry. Esther observed the tall woman with the impressive bulk and the gold ring in her nose. *I defy my neighbors to have a most interesting household*, she thought.

Maybe Avon's odd skills were rubbing off on her. A quick glance had already told her everything she needed to know about Mrs. Perry. "You love them, don't you?" she asked, her voice soft, shy.

"You will, too, Miss Teague," her new housekeeper answered.

It was almost too much. *How long have I gone without conversation?* she asked herself as she smiled and nodded, already thinking how dull her life had been, up to this moment. "I'm new at this," she confessed. "Wha…what should I do or say when I go upstairs, as Avon requests?"

"I believe Mrs. Six makes sure the blankets are high around their shoulders. She usually gives them a pat."

"But they're veterans of battle!" Esther exclaimed.

"Not in their hearts. Help me with the dishes now, and we'll compose a shopping list for tomorrow."

"Can I *do* this?" Esther asked, suddenly unsure of herself, feeling fourteen instead of twice that. At the same time, she thought, *Maybe everyone needs a pat.*

"Aye, miss, you can. You're off to a famous start." The big woman laughed and returned to the kitchen. "If you don't mind a comment, how is *your* skulking?"

Chapter Sixteen

Morning came, with none the dread that Davey feared. He lay at peace, hands folded across his chest because he was used to sleeping in a hammock, which required economy of movement in a tight space. One unexpected dumping to the deck was all it took to become wary.

He missed the side-to-side rocking of a ship at sea under good sail. Pitch and yaw were another matter, but all part of the life. He glanced at Avon in the bed they had pulled over from the other room last night. Avon did make a confession last night, this fellow Rat whom Davey had discovered at Trafalgar was utterly fearless. "I really don't like a room to myself," he admitted to Davey.

"Too many years a workhouse lad," Davey said, understanding completely.

"It was best in the *Mercury*, when we were all crammed together, even t'master," Avon replied. "You can use the other room for study."

Miss Teague hadn't seemed surprised to see them sharing a room when she came upstairs. Bless her heart, she tapped on their door and stood there, too shy to come in. Davey wondered if Mrs. Perry had said something to her. Here she was, determined and brave, and her courage touched his heart.

She had done nothing more than smile at their new arrangement, then say quietly, "I used to wish I had a sister." She went to his bed first and touched his shoulder, then to Avon. Just the lightest touch, but she didn't know them at all yet. At the door again, she said, "Perhaps I need someone to talk to, as well. Goodnight."

Davey made himself savor Mrs. Perry's good breakfast, even though he wanted to gobble it down. Four years as a Gunwharf Rat with plentiful meals, except when at sea, had not erased that urgent necessity, the fear there wouldn't be enough. In a candid moment, he had admitted that to Mrs. Six. She had sniffed back her tears––such a dear lady. She had never known hunger so intense that even water seemed like a banquet. He knew he could never tell her about the time he ate grass and rose petals when the workhouse boys were sent to tidy up a cemetery. Whether she knew it or not, Mrs. Six was the one bit of normal at St. Brendan's. Maybe Miss Teague would be the same; time would tell.

He didn't know if it would help, but he felt a little braver in his dress uniform. He had dressed plainly last term in St. Brendan's black wool uniform, but there was something special about his Royal Navy uniform, authorized so recently for members of the medical corps. Equally impressive was the new leather satchel that the surgeons of Haslar had presented to him before he left for Edinburgh this time, to replace Master Six's old one he had acquired after Trafalgar.

He was never one to preen in a mirror, but he stood a moment, admiring the simple green piping on cuff and collar, and the elegant, twining caduceus on each side of his collar. It said what he was. When he pinned on the Trafalgar medal, it said even more. He shouldered the satchel.

At first, he had thought of his medical satchel as one more oddity for his fellow medical students to jeer about. He knew it was required of all Royal Navy medical personnel, even here in Edinburgh. That morning as he said goodbye to Miss Teague, who stood watching him from the front door, he decided his satchel was one more thing to remind him that medicine was his life and duty, the ocean his avenue.

In his pleasant way, Avon March included himself in the short walk to Mrs. Silsby's lodging house, located only a block from the University of Edinburgh. Davey made no comment about the rough clothing his friend wore. *Skulking clothes*, he thought to himself. *Avon, where are you bound?*

"Everything in this city is wet grey stone," Avon remarked. "This might explain the many Scottish sailors in our navy. I would want to leave, too."

"Here's another wet grey stone building," Davey said, on the other side of what in spring was probably a lovely park. "My former lodging. Former. I liked the sound of that." He knocked on the door and Mrs. Silsby opened it.

She seemed surprised to see him, but Davey knew he had said nothing about not returning. Should he ask? Why not? What could she possibly do to him now?

"Mrs. Silsby? I'm not a ghost," he said pleasantly enough. "May we come in?"

She opened the door wider, but there was no further invitation to do anything except stand there and explain himself. He glanced at Avon, who looked on with interest, as if wondering what sort of species a landlady was.

Davey had his own question. "Did someone inform you that I was not returning?"

"I overheard the lads gloating about running you off," she told him.

So that was it. His resolve had waivered every hour of his return trip, wondering at the wisdom of inflicting more punishment upon himself. It was an odd little victory, but here he was. If that was the lesson Master Six and Headmaster Ferrier wanted him to learn, he understood. *I have to show up for my life*, he thought in quiet satisfaction. *Even if that means unpleasant lodging houses.*

"As you can see, they didn't run me off," he said, handing her his room key. "I have found much better accommodations. I am part of conversations in this new place, and there is no one to steal from me. Good day, Mrs. Silsby." He turned on his heel and left her standing there with her mouth open.

"That was easy," he remarked to Avon on the sidewalk again.

"Smelt of cabbage in there," Avon commented.

"We ate a lot of cabbage and turnips," he said as they walked to the corner. "When you go to the market this morning, you might mention that I'm not overly found of either."

Now what? "I must go to the college and see to my courses and fees," Davey said.

"I have things to do," Avon said. "Was your room on that first floor?"

"Aye. Top of the landing." Davey couldn't help his sigh. "Next door to John Yerby. I suspect he stole my sextant. He denied it."

"Certainly he would," Avon agreed, sounding as cheerful as ever. Apparently even blatant thievery did not discourage him.

"I tried to jimmy his lock once, when I knew he was out. You know, just to look around." Davey couldn't help his grimace. "I am no jimmier."

"No, that was never your strong suit. I'll find my way back to Wilmer Street, and steer the ladies away from cabbage or turnips, when I accompany them to market."

"Avon, you're a friend indeed."

They parted ways. Davey knew better than to question Avon's sense of direction back to Wilmer Street. Avon always found his way about Portsmouth, even the worst hellholes.

Three more blocks – despite new confidence, Davey walked slower with each block – and here he was at the university. He stood with other students outside the financial office, studying the section of the long board labelled College of Medicine. Simple Roman numerals one through four announced, as nothing else could, the grind of four years. He waited his turn by the number two, not bothering to look around for friends, because he had none.

Those who could have helped him had made it plain last term that he did not belong amongst them. This time, he knew when he returned to Wilmer Street that Miss Teague would speak to him, with additional commentary from Mrs. Perry and Avon. He was not alone.

Ready with pad and pencil, Davey took his turn at the board to copy his classrooms and assignments. Last year, his classmates were alphabetized, except for his name, which was put at the bottom, past the W's and Y's, as if to further announce his lower-than-low status. He knew this treatment was just another dig to remind him that he would never be one of them.

He looked at the bottom, but his name was not there. Cold fear washed over him, and then for the first time, anger. How dare they bounce him entirely from the school and not inform him! The august powers-that-be might despise him and his encroaching ways, as they probably saw it, but he knew his grades were excellent. There were no charges against him.

In his anger, he looked down at his Trafalgar medal and the moment passed. No one at the University of Edinburgh had one of these. These superior people had no idea what he was capable of. He could go back to Haslar now with no qualms. Still….

Calm now, he looked at the alphabetized names this time. Good God, there he was among the others: Ten, David, right after Sterling, Richard (a pimply fellow with a perpetual sneer), and before Tompkins, John (the sneer minus the pimples).

That was a surprise, although his naturally wary mind – a workhouse imperative – warned him to be cautious. Beside his name was the list of courses for the term: more *materia medica*, anatomy and elementary dissection (students simply called it Bones), and so on. No surprises there. It was also no surprise that he was assigned to four hours every evening, four times a week, in the indigent ward of the Royal Infirmary once more. The thought that perhaps Mr. Coffin would also ward walk there suited him well enough.

He sighed at the thought of more *materia medica*, that hoary old study of pills, plasters, potions, and herbs, the mainstay of an earlier era of medicine, at times more mythical than useful. The professor was a prosy old fellow who seemed to think it beneath him, except that in Davey's experience, occasionally those old remedies were the mainstay of the profession because they worked.

But another term? He had learned *materia medica* in the Channel from Master Six and then at Haslar Hospital from seasoned pharmacist mates. Granted, he was still a most junior surgeon's assistant, but he had the credentials, and he wore the uniform now.

I could teach that course, he told himself, which released another callous from his wary heart. He looked at the two remaining courses listed by his name: the circulation of blood. Yes, yes. He had seen plenty of blood circulating at Trafalgar. He knew how to stop the flow, thanks again to Master Six and Haslar surgeons. Second year Bones followed. He liked anatomy, accompanied as it was with at least elementary dissection – a hand there, a foot here, maybe an ear. It was a place to learn bones and muscles and occasionally see them.

Trailing far after the others last term, he had attended two full dissections in Surgeons' Square near the university, where students and townsmen alike gawked from galleries as surgeons dissected, and in some cases, operated, tying down their screaming patients. He had been intensely interested, but many others were there for the spectacle only. He did not like Surgeons' Square. Dissection at college waited for the third term.

He gasped at the final course by his name. *Attendance only. Dissection 3.* Surely not. That would put him with third-year students. He already knew they were contemptuous of lower-grade students. Once they found out he was a bastard workhouse boy – if they didn't already know – they would make his life hell. He shuddered. This was an error. He would have to speak to the professor, a round, smug little fellow, who also never spoke to him in last term's Bones course, and who had favorites, not one of whom was Davey Ten. He shook his head, wondering at such a gross mistake.

"That's no error, Mr. Ten."

Startled, he turned around to see Mr. Josiah Coffin, the physician who also frequented those lowliest-of-the-lowly indigent wards at the Royal Infirmary, almost as if he had been sentenced there for some misdemeanor of his own among the medical faculty. The other students in line backed away, but not too far; Davey knew they wanted to eavesdrop.

"Sir, dissection is a third-year course. I am not eligible to attend."

"I am teaching Bones this term because of an unfortunate accident between Sir Lionel Henderson and a brewery wagon. He is yet alive but incapacitated. Ordinarily, he also assists the physician in Dissection Three."

"But…"

"I am assisting in Dissection Three as well as teaching Bones. I have requested that you attend D3."

Mr. Coffin favored him with a long look, a Master Six sort of look that always meant something more. Davey braced himself.

"I am going to name you my assistant in Bones that hour earlier."

This was worse than he thought. "Wha…what will the others in my class *say*?" Davey asked, unwilling to even consider this. He lowered his voice, aware of others straining to listen. "I know I am an object of derision to them, but not this, please."

Mr. Coffin considered the matter. "Thee is imminently qualified."

"But sir…I don't understand, Mr. Coffin."

"Thee will. Let's leave this line," he said, gesturing, and Davey followed.

"*Me*? I…I know Sir Lionel has already picked his favorite for Bones," Davey said when they were out of earshot of the others. "Do you *know* who I am? I mean, really?"

"I do. We ward-walked long enough, didn't we? Thee is also our first student ever at the College of Medicine from St. Brendan the Navigator

School, which trains up workhouse boys for the fleet." He smiled. "And I might add, trains thee well, from all indications."

"How do you know tha…"

"Our esteemed chancellor read Mrs. Munro's letter to us last year at the beginning of thy first term. He said we would admit thee whether he liked it or not, because Mrs. Munro has contributed to the College of Medicine for years, she and her family. Politics." He looked down at his well-shined shoes. "I think he meant it as a joke, but I did not laugh. I found thee most useful in that indigent ward."

Mr. Coffin looked across the corridor, as if steeling himself for more, to Davey's chagrin. "If thee wishes not to attend third-year dissection, then do not." Again that long look. "I *will* teach Bones, however, and I want thee for my assistant."

Davey looked away. All he wanted was to blend in with the other students. "Sir, please! They disliked me last year. They will hate me now, if they find I am to be your assistant!" He couldn't bring himself to look at this quiet man in black. *Now I have probably earned the enmity of Mr. Coffin,* he thought in dismay, *something I never wanted to do.* He was near tears, which would also never do. "No, please, sir. No."

"Follow me."

What could he do? He followed.

Mr. Coffin found a quiet window ledge farther away from the others and perched there. He patted the ledge and Davey sat. "Does thee recall that one time the first-year students, thee among them, were allowed into the operating theatre to watch that autopsy last term? I don't mean the spectacles in Surgeon's Square, but here in our university."

"Yes. You dissected and showed us a diseased lung, which you diagnosed as phthisis."

"All too common among the poor. Did thee see it in the workhouse?"

Davey nodded. "Aye, but I was too young to know what it was. They called it the wasting disease. Consumption, I believe."

"Aye, lad. I remember how others of thy class gasped and vomited and carried on almost theatrically." His laugh held no mirth. "No wonder we call it an operating theatre! I have seen such performances before and this was no different. Some students were shocked, to be sure, but most were showing off for each other. Thee neither winced nor faltered. Thee even leaned forward."

"It…it was interesting," Davey said, remembering the day and the odor of blood and putrefaction. Poor woman. How she must have suffered. Had she not been poor and in the lowest of circumstances, how much better her life might have been. "The poor suffer," he said. From the look Mr. Coffin gave him, he knew the quiet man understood.

"Does thee also recall the night in the indigent ward when the burned man was brought in?"

Who could forget? The man's chest, upper arms and head had been burned in an explosion in the castle's armory, his features melting together, his lungs probably still cooking. He was doomed to death, and soon. Who could forget that sight, plus the shocking odor of fear and blackened flesh? "Aye, sir, I remember," Davey said quietly.

"Thee told me thee had seen worse at Trafalgar."

Davey nodded. "It's true, sir."

"I covered him with damp towels and thee held his hand until he died."

He nodded again. "I wish we could have helped him."

"I know thee does," Mr. Coffin replied. "Again, thee did not falter or fail. I need someone of thy caliber to assist me."

"The others won't take it kindly," Davey said.

"Does thee care?" came Mr. Coffin's quiet reply. "I know how the students treat thee. It is shameful. But Davey, thee has a gift for medicine."

Davey thought of Avon and Mrs. Perry, sent to bolster him, because someone cared very much – Master Able Six. There was also the pleasant surprise of earnest Miss Teague. "My instructor at St Brendan's sent another Gunwharf Rat along to give me someone to talk to. I'm not alone now."

Mr. Coffin nodded. "Would thee believe that I am here on sufferance, too?"

Davey had heard students making fun of Mr. Thee and Thy, jeering at his odd last name, and quaking visibly when Mr. Coffin's back was turned. He was a Quaker, member of a strange sect no one seemed to respect, but no one could say why. "I would believe that, sir. May I point out that using me in this manner could be the ruin of you, too?"

It was a bold matter to question this superior man. Davey gasped inwardly at his own plain-speaking. He had spent a short lifetime saying nothing to people of power. Perhaps there really were others here on sufferance besides himself. Maybe one was talking to him now.

"I see it as a bold stroke," Mr. Coffin said. "There are some universities and hospitals that will never admit me. Here I am, on sufferance like thee, a three-year apprenticeship, so to speak. We can duck and hide, or we can stand firm. I prefer to stand firm. After all, what is the worst they can do?"

"Dismiss us?"

"Aye. The days when I would be tortured and hanged for my beliefs are long gone. I prefer a bold stroke. If I fail here, I have relatives in the United States who would find a place for me, no question. The Society of Friends is not demeaned in America, so they tell me. One of the states was even colonized by a Friend. If thee fails, or even simply chooses otherwise, thee goes to Haslar Hospital, or perhaps Stonehouse Hospital, and a ship in the Mediterranean." He smiled and looked closer. "Why is it I suspect that this is thy preference, anyway?"

"It is, but I have to prove myself *to* myself, sir."

"Aye, thee does. Every man does. Does thee have surgical aprons?"

"Aye, sir, but they're still stained from Trafalgar," Davey said. "Those stains don't come out."

"They do not. In thy case, I see them as a badge of honor. Fear no one, Mr. Ten." The long look was replaced by the smile of someone who understood. "Don't bother thyself about third year dissection. That can wait another year, if thee chooses."

Davey suddenly did something so bold that he could only credit some force outside of his body, he knew not who or what.

He held out his hand. Mr. Coffin shook it.

Chapter Seventeen

Davey quietly paid his fees and wrote down his schedule from the board, ignoring the stares of his tormentors who likely hadn't expected him to return for another year's punishment. He had larger matters on his mind. He had no doubt that he could assist Mr. Coffin in Bones, but he did wonder what new tortures his fellow students might dream up. He had spent an entire year cowering before bullies, and he was tired of it. Something about having Avon March, Mrs. Perry, and yes, Mr. Coffin on his side gave him courage.

We shall see, he thought, as he thumbed through a pharmacoepia text that appeared centuries newer than the one the pharmacist's mate at Haslar swore was the first book off Gutenberg's press. He paid for it and went into the hall again.

Oh God, they were lined up on both sides of the hall, waiting for him. He could turn around and find another exit, something he had done only last term to his shame and their hoots and catcalls. Not this time. He touched his Trafalgar medal for luck and started toward them, thinking of little Admiral Nelson charging boldly into that row of Spanish and French warships.

To his surprise, no one said anything at first. He walked between the two rows and then Richard Sterling stepped forward. His pimples were even more pronounced, and Davey had never noticed earlier that his eyes bulged a little. *Exophthalmos*, he thought. *Hmm. Such a pity there is no cure for ugly, bulgy eyes.*

He continued serenely between the twenty students, thinking about surprising these apes in Bones. Hopefully, Mr. Coffin and his superior there could find some good corpses for Dissection Three, D3. Recently dead or much mortified, he didn't care. He decided to no longer dread some memories of Trafalgar, but use them instead.

"Fancy uniform you have, Five plus Five," said John Yerby, the student Davey was nearly certain had stolen his sextant.

He stopped, looked John Yerby square in the eye, and felt some satisfaction that the Cretin appeared startled. "Aye, it is a fancy uniform, John," he said, "and my congratulations on an inventive name for me."

A few of the students laughed. To his surprise, it didn't sound like mean laughter. He knew the difference.

Perhaps a little education was in order. They could listen or not; he didn't care. He stood tall. "You like my uniform? So do I. The Navy Board has at last designated a uniform for members of the Royal Navy's medical corps, of which I am one." He laughed, meant it, and looked at John. "Add Nine to that One makes Ten. So do Eight and Two. Three and Seven. Four and Six, and your own clever Five plus Five. David Ten, tenth bastard born in the New Year of our Lord 1792."

No one laughed. Davey had the satisfaction of seeing Yerby turn away, perhaps embarrassed. The purveyor of books came into the hall to watch.

"I am a surgeon's assistant in the Royal Navy." He touched his chest. "This is my Trafalgar medal. I am required by the First Lord of the Admiralty to wear it." (He didn't know if that was strictly true, but these witless wonders wouldn't know about the First Lord.) He nodded to them, wondering where this great well of courage came from. "I will see you all tomorrow in class."

He walked the length of the silent hall, some two miles long it seemed, and found himself outside in a rare winter day with sunshine. He decided to take it as a good omen. *What did I just do?* he asked himself. Whatever it was, it felt good.

He took a deep breath of Edinburgh, and decided the walk home – yes, home – warranted more of a stroll. The hard work would begin tomorrow. He thought about sunshine in the Mediterranean, and the feel of a deck moving under his feet. Stepping off the sidewalk so as not to impede pedestrians moving with more purpose than he, Davey stopped, gave the sun a brief squint and turned until he faced south and west toward what would approximately be the Straits of Gibraltar, some distance from Scotland. He wanted to close his eyes and open them on the Rock, heralding the entrance to the Mediterranean.

"I miss you," he said softly. "I miss a heaving deck and my fellow tars depending upon me to physic them. I miss you."

There was a park close to the university. The trees were bare of leaves, and the ground soggy. No birds sang. He wiped off a park bench with his gloved hand and sat down.

He knew he should be terrified of what the enigmatic Mr. Coffin was doing to him, but he wasn't. Granted, he knew the physician only from ward-walking in the room for the lowest of the low in the Royal Infirmary. Still, he sensed a commonality. They were both on sufferance in this most esteemed of medical schools.

Another thought took him back to Trafalgar: the memory of two Royal Marine sharpshooters in the crow's nest of HMS *Gideon*. They stood back-to-back, protecting each other, as they sought their own targets on French and Spanish frigates. *Are we to be like that, Mr. Coffin?* he thought. *Perhaps I am presumptuous.*

He almost faltered when Edwin Hamilton, that fellow student he had encountered on the road home, passed the park, head down. For whatever reason, Edwin stopped and looked right at him. With no hesitation, Davey nodded to him.

Edwin nodded back and moved on. *I'll call that a victory,* Davey thought. After a few moments reflection on what to assign such a slight acknowledgment, he opened the pharmacopeia book again, happy with a text he understood. He spent an hour absorbing potions he had used, and the memories of patients both quick and dead, then ambled to Wilmer Street.

He opened the door upon wonderful aromas, a far cry from last term's dreary boiled cabbage at Mrs. Silsby's. He reminded himself that if he were aboard that putative frigate sailing through the Straits of Gibraltar, the galley smells would more likely recall Mrs. Silsby's bill of fare. Here, he could tell Mrs. Perry was in charge in her unsubtle way with navy beans and ham, and plentiful onions. He thought he smelled a top note of plum duff, little Ben's favorite sweet, after his great grandmama's crème buns.

Even better was the sight of Miss Teague, someone he knew would talk to him, and perhaps ask about his day. To both his delight and humility, she did.

"Just sling your boat cloak on the hook by the door," she told him. "Can you prop your hat on the hook, too?" He could and did.

"Dinner's ready in a short while," she said. "Come into the sitting room and tell me about your day."

Oh, bliss, except for one thing: he would never be a sitting room man. "Could we sit in the kitchen instead?" he asked. Might as well tell her why. "Kitchen people are my people, and I have to tell you: workhouse lads enjoy the sight of food."

When Miss Teague's eyes filled with tears, Davey Ten knew he had found someone that would approximate Mrs. Six. They looked nothing alike, but they shared an abundance of feeling. Maybe it was something women did. "That's the way we Rats are, ma'am."

Miss Teague could probably have said anything to that, but she told him simply, "I'll learn."

They went into the kitchen. Mrs. Perry smiled at him. "Sit yourself down," she said and he sat, knowing better than to do anything else. He didn't want to do anything else, because he knew what came next, and hoped it didn't startle Miss Teague.

The big Black woman with the gold ring in her nose plunked down his own tin cup from the *Mercury*, a prized possession. She poured in a judicious amount of hot water and added rum from what he knew had to be her own stores. He doubted Miss Teague had ever even smelled rum before.

"Thank'ee," he told her, blew on the drink, and took a small sip. Ah.

Miss Teague's eyes were as wide as saucers. Davey hoped she didn't mind. She surprised him then. "Mrs. Perry, could you give me a wee bit of that, too?" she asked.

"Aye, miss." The cook found a teacup, added hot water and a small tot of rum.

Davey smiled inside when she eyed the cup with suspicion, but picked it up and crooked her little finger, a proper lady. "What is this called?"

"Grog, ma'am," he said, then added, "Rum straight is for heroes."

She downed the contents of the cup. "A little every day?"

He laughed, feeling better than he had in many months. "Aye, ma'am. A lot after a sea action." He sobered then. "There was a lot of drinking of dead men's liquor after Trafalgar."

She grew solemn, as well, and reached out her hand to lightly touch his sleeve. "Is…is that a custom, too?"

"Aye, ma'am," he replied, not sure if he could trust himself to say more. He knew he would never tell her about the tars who tapped the admiral on the way back to Portsmouth, taking little sips of the keg of port that held the hero's small body. "We all finish off dead men's personal stores. It's a naval tradition."

"A wee bit more, Mrs. Perry, if you please. Perfect. Do you toast?"

"Aye, ma'am. That honor usually goes to the captain, but this house is your command," he said, feeling the beginning of a true connection to this thin lady trying her best to do her duty.

She raised her teacup. "To all of us here in the good ship Teague."

More callouses fell away as he drank to her toast. He didn't want the good feeling to end. Perhaps Miss Teague would be a friend, too.

"Where is that rascal Avon?" she asked. Davey heard the amusement in her voice, and it warmed him.

"He went with you to market, didn't he?" Davey asked.

"He did. Mrs. Perry came along, too. I have never been treated better by impudent merchants. She is…formidable."

"Too right," David said with a grin, pleased at her air of camaraderie, something he hadn't expected. "What's for dinner, Miss Teague?"

"Dinner is ham and beans, wheat buns and stewed apples. Mrs. Perry initiated me into the world of plum duff. I have to tell you that Avon disappeared after the market. Is..is that what he does?"

"Aye, ma'am. I never question too much."

She turned a kind look on him, then gave a little sigh of relief when the front door opened. "And here he is. Avon March, where have you been?"

"Skulking, ma'am," Avon said as he came into the kitchen. He breathed deep of the aromas. "Getting a feel for Edinburgh."

Davey felt no surprise; that was Avon's way. He was no blabber.

Miss Teague seemed to understand when to let them alone. "You two give Mrs. Perry and me a few minutes to get dinner on…on this table or in the dining room?"

Avon grinned his most cherubic smile. "Here, please. C'mon, Davey. They'll make us do the dishes, but not until later."

Davey followed Avon upstairs, thinking of the strangeness of this day. He had so much to tell Avon, and the joy was, he could tell them all.

Avon opened the door and Davey knew the strangeness was only beginning.

The missing sextant lay on his bed. His mouth dropped open in surprise. "Where? How?" was all he could say. He picked up the beautiful thing, grateful down to his stockings that no one had defaced it. At last he understood Mr. Bartleby's comment about the sextant, that even if he never used it in his whole Navy career, it was symbolic of so much more.

He ran his hands over it. "Was I right?" he asked in a whisper, almost hoping he was wrong. "John Yerby?"

Avon nodded. "I had to rifle his bureau drawers. He has a lot of smallclothes. I wonder if he pees his bed."

Davey rolled his eyes. "How did you get this?"

"There's a drainpipe between his room and yours," was all Avon said.

"No one saw you?" Davey asked, and got a sour look in return. "Certainly no one saw you," he added hastily.

The younger Rat turned serious then. "I found something else while I was, ah, rummaging."

"I would suspect John of any nefarious deed," Davey joked. "Did I tell you that he salted my breakfast tea at Mrs. Silsby's once?"

"It's worse than what you might think."

Davey's nerves went onto a high hum, a painful reminder of the last term when he was bullied and shunned. "What is?" he asked, knowing that little Avon was never prone to exaggeration. Maybe no Rat was, considering that something bad for a workhouse lad was as bad as one could imagine. Who needed to exaggerate?

"Here."

Avon reached into his shabby skulker's jacket. He held out what Davey knew was an oval plate, a shiny thing that always seemed like a taunt and come-on to the enemy, located as it was directly on the breastplate of a Royal Marine's crossed straps. A sergeant of Royal Marines would wear this, maybe a sergeant of Royal Marines sent from his station in Oban to the Royal Infirmary. Maybe a sergeant whose body was never seen again, to the sorrow of his wife and children in Portsmouth.

He looked at Avon, whose eyes locked onto his. "This is a bad business," he said, which sounded feeble and didn't begin to cover the subject. "Captain Ogilvie said it was two men, one a Royal Marine." He sat down on his bed and stared at the belt plate.

"Did you watch any dissections last term?" Avon asked.

"Two, but only from a distance." He made himself think. "One was a woman with phthisis, consumption."

Avon shuddered. "I couldn't do what you do."

"And I'd be a terrible skulker. I don't recall the other corpse, except it was a man." He closed his eyes, trying to remember that dissection, done in the afternoon with poor lighting from constant rain that even Scottish lamps could not compete with.

"Nothing more?"

"No. The other students sat lower than me," he said, remembering. "I was up higher. No one sat with me. No one invited me lower. The light was poor, and they were making gagging noises. One even pretended to faint. Sir Lionel Henderson was dissecting. Sir Lionel laughed at those fools showing no respect for human life."

Davey held out the oval plate to Avon, who put it back in his pocket. In the quick motion, he noticed the tattoo on the back of Avon's left wrist, a crude daffodil someone might find alongside the River Avon in March. Avon had proudly showed it to the other Rats on the *Mercury* once. "I did it myself," the boy said. "So I never forget."

"The corpse had a tattoo on his upper right forearm," Davey said, remembering. "I couldn't tell what it was, but who gets tattoos except our sort?"

Avon took out the belt plate and smoothed his hand across the surface in a tender gesture. "We need to tell someone."

"Who?"

Just then Miss Teague called up the stairs. "Dinner, gentlemen!"

"Her."

Chapter Eighteen

Perhaps Esther understood lads more than she thought. Her horrible nephews in Fife were nasty and opinionated like their mother, but some spark in her told her that the Gunwharf Rats who came slowly down the stairs at her call were troubled. She knew they had gone upstairs cheerfully enough. In a matter of minutes, something had changed. "Wait in the sitting room a moment. I'll help Mrs. Perry get the ham and beans on the table."

She hurried into the kitchen, wanting a word with Mrs. Perry alone. The cook was slicing a beef roast the size of Mount Matterhorn. Mrs. Perry had assured her at the butcher's that there wasn't a Rat alive who didn't crave food – good or bad – in large amounts.

"Food rules at St. Brendan's," Mrs. Perry had stated. "The workhouse cowed them in curious ways."

Better to blurt it out. "Something's wrong, Mrs. Perry. They're worried."

"Really?"

"I've certainly never been a mother," she began, as way of apology for such a declaration. "I mean…maybe I'm wrong."

Mrs. Perry hefted the beef roast as though it weighed no more than a boiled egg. "To know such things, Miss Teague, all you need to be is a woman." Her tone turned kindly. "I believe you."

The lads looked casual enough, talking to each other by the window, until Esther cleared her throat and they came to attention. If she was even right, how to play this?

"Sitting rooms used to make me wonder if I was in for a scold," she said. "My father, God rest him, was an elder in the Presbyterian Church. Sitting rooms were places to heap on burning coals."

Her plain speaking seemed to bring them out of their funk. "Miss Teague, I doubt you were ever scolded much," Avon said.

"I would wish, Avon," she said, wondering why she was unburdening herself. *Why not be honest?* she asked herself. "Let me compound my felonies. You see before you a spinster of twenty-eight. I've been called Miss Twig because I am thin."

The Rats looked at each other. She thought Davey was the natural leader, and he spoke up. "We would never call you Miss Twig."

"Thank you," she said. Why not tell them more? "Perhaps spinsters are fair game to some. Mama scolded me for arguing with young men who might or not have come to court me. Those were *my* burning coals in the sitting room of my youth." Odd that she should tell anyone of her humiliation, especially Gunwharf Rats. Maybe not so odd. They understood dashed hopes.

"I was always in trouble in the workhouse because I argued," Davey admitted. His expression brightened. "That's what got me bounced to St. Brendan's. Our late headmaster, God rest *him*, was looking for restless boys in trouble, figuring we were bored, not evil, and lacked intellectual challenge. You too, Avon?"

Avon nodded, his eyes lively. "Aye! I also picked one too many pockets of do-gooders to the workhouse. It was either St. Brendan's or Australia. T'old beadle in the workhouse even did a little jig when St. Brendan's headmaster hauled me away."

The three of them laughed together. Esther took a deep breath, hoping she wasn't wrong. "What is troubling you now?"

Silence, then, "You're hard to fool, Miss Teague," Davey said.

Mrs. Perry came to the sitting room door. "Into the kitchen," was her command. "I can't eat a whole cow by myself, and I want to hear this." No one argued.

The Rats tucked into the food. When his plate finally showed some bare spots, Davey put down his fork. Avon did the same. "It's really Avon's story, but I can start it. He, um, found my sextant. I was certain one of my lovely classmates who also roomed at Mrs. Silsby's swiped it."

"But… how did you swipe it back, Avon?"

Avon sat a little taller. "Not sayin', miss. Trade secrets."

Esther didn't know whether to laugh or look horrified. She settled on a shake of her head and a faint, "Oh, my." She looked him in the eye. "I won't ask, Avon. You're amazing."

"I know drainpipes, miss," he said. "There's more though, and it's worse." He looked at Davey, who handed her the oval piece of metal. "It's a breastplate. Royal Marines wear them smack in the middle of their chest, attached to crossed straps."

"But what…"

The Rats exchanged another glance. Davey ate some more of Mrs. Perry good dinner and Esther waited patiently. He put down his fork again. "You or me, Avon?" he asked simply.

"I'm the finder," Avon said. He leaned his elbows on the table, which earned him a loudly cleared throat from Mrs. Perry. He relocated his hands in his lap. "I'm here to keep Davey company. I'm also to do some skulking. Nothing much, mind you, at least…Well, nothing much."

"*Skulking?* I truly don't understand."

"Miss, we know a man name of Captain Ogilvie," Davey said, taking over the narrative. "He works for Trinity House. Have you heard of them, Miss?"

Esther knew she was already into something far over her head. *What a boring life have led*, she thought. Oddly enough, it seemed to energize her more than frighten her. "No, I have not."

"One of those early kings, t'one who lopped off his wives' heads, started it. Trinity teaches navigation and maintains England's lighthouses." Davy rolled his eyes. "And does what all. That's what Captain Ogilvie is involved in: the what all." He hesitated, but not for long. "People, um, disappear around Captain Ogilvie."

Avon took over. "We told you about the missing Navy man and Marine."

"You did," she said. "But this?"

Avon gave her a look of infinite patience, the look the trainer of a rambunctious puppy might use. "Mind you he's just guessing, but Captain Ogilvie thinks their bodies ended up on the dissecting table, for the education of blokes like Davey."

Mrs. Perry sat down heavily, her eyes big in her head. "Why ain't the law after them?"

Avon shrugged. He took the metal insignia from Davey. "I was snooping – that's what skulkers do – and I found this in the same drawer with Davey's sextant."

"John Yerby must be involved in something to do with the bodies," Davey said.

"There was more in that drawer," Avon added, his expression hardening. "I don't know this John, but I don't like him."

"What else did you find?" Esther asked.

Avon looked at the ceiling, as if seeing things there. "A baby's shoe, a lace glove, and a thimble."

Mrs. Perry broke the long, sad silence. "He's taking souvenirs. Where do the bodies come from? Is this legal?"

"It is, if the dead people are indigent and homeless," Davey said, recalling Sir Lionel's smug comments once at the dissection table about the poor serving their purpose. "In the indigent ward, I watched Mr. Coffin sign over unclaimed bodies to the College of Medicine. It's legal. Other bodies come from prisoners sentenced to the gallows, all unclaimed and unwanted."

Esther reached across the table and patted his hand. "Hard to imagine some people having no one, is it?" she asked softly.

"Not really." He looked at Avon, who nodded. "We saw plenty of abandoned babies."

"Some of us were those babies."

"I know nothing about such matters," Esther murmured.

"Why would you?" Davey asked. "People in the other Royal Infirmary wards usually have someone to claim them. They're better off and not homeless."

Esther wondered how it was possible to reach her age and know so little about a major part of the population. These were the people she saw begging on street corners, mostly in silence (they were Scots, after all). Week after week, she went to market and walked past them with a basket of food, paying them no mind. She looked at the Rats and writhed inside, knowing that if she saw them ragged and begging, she would have walked on by.

"John Yerby is a classmate," Davey told her. "Somehow, he is helping someone procure bodies for *my* education, which, depending, is legal." He let the thought hang. Mrs. Perry cleared the table with Avon's help, and soon the Rats were washing and drying dishes.

Esther sat down with her hook and thread in the sitting room, ready to work on a lace collar for her Sunday dress. She failed, her mind on supper's grim conversation.

Auntie Munro, what have I ever done to you that I must host Gunwharf Rats? she thought, but that sounded like whining. She went to the window and stared into the blackness, lit at intervals by streetlamps set aglow each evening by shabby men hurrying from lamp post to lamp post. Would such men end up in the ward for the poor and indigent? "There is a world I know nothing about," she whispered to the glass.

Well? she asked herself. She heard the Rats putting away the dishes. They were almost fifteen and seventeen, and had already lived harder lives than she could ever know. What right had she to tell them anything?

Every right, she decided. She went into the kitchen, where Mrs. Perry, her expression unreadable, polished silver. *I am in charge of you three*, she thought, even though the very idea made her quail inside.

"Avon, I think you should write to this Mr. Ogilvie," she said.

"I will when I know more," he replied, and glanced at Davey. "All we have now are suspicions. I mean, perhaps students like John Yerby are recruited to get the bodies to the morgue and upstairs to the operating theatre."

"Is there anyone you can trust at the school, Davey?"

"I don't really trust anyone, Miss Teague," he said, "but I might try."

"Do you have someone in mind?"

"Mr. Coffin, the Bones professor this term." He ran the dish towel through his hands, and smiled at Avon. "Maybe I can skulk a bit."

It was audacious, but she couldn't help herself. "Maybe I can learn to skulk." Why not? She had been overlooked by everyone all her life. She was a spinster and would always be a spinster.

You have no idea how invisible I am, she thought, as the Rats smiled at her. *No idea.*

Chapter Nineteen

"What will you do today?" Davey asked Avon as they lay awake in the morning, neither one inclined to leap up because the room was cold. Rain drizzling down the windows indicated an uncomfortable walk to the university.

Avon raised up on one elbow. "I'd rather be t'sea, maybe the South Pacific, where it is warm all year long." He lay back. "D'ye ever wonder why people who live in awful climates like Scotland don't move to warmer places?"

"And have you noticed how many Scots serve in the Royal Navy? They wanted to escape from chilblains and oatmeal."

Avon nodded. "I think I would like to visit the poor and indigent ward in the Royal Infirmary. You can toil in class and I will snoop. What class today?"

Davey made a face. "More *materia medica*. I think we will begin with making plasters."

"You can do that in your sleep." Avon chuckled. "In fact, I think you did that in your sleep after Trafalgar."

"I could teach it. Then I remind myself there is always more to learn, and I do." He sighed. "In the afternoon, it will be Bones." He didn't tell Avon of his meeting with Mr. Coffin, and the amazing announcement that the quiet man had chosen him as class assistant. It had to be a mistake. He lay there wondering why he could not trust even a man as well-intentioned as Mr. Coffin seemed to be.

The thought nagged at him on the way to the college of medicine, half a mile away. Bundled in his boat cloak, one of his canvas surgeon's aprons tucked under his arm, his hat shoved down to his ears, the drizzle suited his mood.

Dressed in his usual skulking clothes, Avon walked one block with him, then parted company at the corner. "We shouldn't be seen together," Avon said, as Davey pointed out the Royal Infirmary, a charitable hospital unlike any other in Europe, or so he had been informed.

"The front stairs lead directly to Ward A, where the genteel poor and those with families send their ill," Davey pointed out. "Further down the hall, you will find Ward B, better known as the indigent ward. There is a side entrance for Ward B."

"For the homeless and people like us," Avon said. He considered that a moment in his quiet way, then nodded to Davey. "Good luck today. I go a'skulking."

Luck? What is that? Davey asked himself. He felt the surgeon's apron under his boat cloak. Master Six had shoved it at him on the *Mercury*, when the little yacht, formerly owned by Captain Sir Belvedere Saint Anthony, sailed through the fighting ships at Trafalgar, searching for wounded men in the water. What else could they do? They had no cannon. After Trafalgar, other tars gave him and his fellow Rats nods of appreciation for their courage. Davey decided that courage was nothing more than ignoring fear when there was no choice. As for luck, well, please…

No one spoke to him in Materia Medica. The difference between this term and last term was that he didn't care anymore, because he had conversation in Wilmer Street. He also gave credit to his new uniform and his medal. It made him bold enough, that when the old professor called the roll and came to Davey Ten, he raised his hand and said, "I'll also answer to Davey Eight plus Two, sir." He heard some chuckles, but nothing mean, which gratified him. He silently thanked Admiral Nelson for the lesson in tackling a fight head-on.

It never failed to amuse him that after a morning of discussing and looking at scabs, carbuncles, pus, and piss, he could still be hungry at noon. He had stashed his belongings and lunch sack in his usual corner by the morgue, far away from prying eyes and light fingers and classmates bent upon mischief. Everything was precisely as he had left it, or almost so. Avon must have found his stash because the oval breastplate rested on his apron.

He looked around, wondering what magic made Avon invisible. The breastplate touched his heart. Avon must have known he needed the boost. He unwrapped the monstrous beef roast sandwich Mrs. Perry had stuck in his hands before he left this morning. He ate the sandwich and wondered how Mr. Coffin would fare in Bones, a.k.a. Anatomy and Elementary Dissection. For a small moment, fear returned. Surely there was time to intercept Mr. Coffin before class and swear off his assignment. Eyes closed, he leaned against the cold wall in his hiding place until his courage returned, then checked his timepiece, hoping to arrive to class before the others.

Bones, formerly taught by Sir Lionel Henderson who had encountered that brewery wagon, met on the college's third floor. The stairs were hard to find, and narrow, probably because for years before this more enlightened time, dissections truly were punishable by law. This was an out-of-the-way spot free from prying eyes. The small amphitheatre contained three elevated rows of chairs surrounding an operating table and a lecture stand. Front and center was a skeleton, primary target of today's anatomy class.

Bones was for second year students still trying to memorize the body's numerous bones and muscles. The operating table was for eyes, organs, muscles and whatever tidbits came their way. Davy figured those parts came from previous dissections. Nothing smelled too good, but that was medicine.

Mr. Coffin stood by the table, looking down at a man's arm. Rigor mortis had left, and the specimen lay there limp, with that peculiar color of morbidity. Poor man. The arm looked to have been wrenched out of the shoulder socket, probably a bad death. Imagine the blood loss.

Mr. Coffin wore his own apron, also stained. He looked up at Davey and invited him to the floor. "I was hoping thee would arrive early."

"Aye sir," Davey said. "I won't deny I have misgivings."

"I do not. Thy classmates may look askance and wonder why thee has this coveted position. Follow my lead. Have a seat for now." He looked into Davey's eyes. "Trust thyself."

Davey sat, his apron folded small on his lap. "What do you do when you are afraid, sir?" he blurted out, and felt his face flame. "I mean…"

"I pray. The Light directs me."

Davey sat in silence as the others trooped in, some gaping and pointing at the severed arm. He watched their faces, looking for some compassion that he felt for the rest of the body, unseen, for its owner had surely died. Of the twenty other students, only Edwin Hamilton paused a moment, then shook his head.

"Come closer," Mr. Coffin said. He looked around. "The second row gives thee some elevation." His sharp eye took them all in. "Sit next to Mr. Ten here. He has a prime seat for observation."

Davey felt his stomach contract with the old familiar fear of ostracization from last term. No, Edwin Hamilton sat next to him, not close but not far. Soon there was someone on his other side. He let out a breath he might have been holding since he left Edinburgh in despair.

Barely turning his head, Davey noticed other classmates looking around, as if wondering when Sir Lionel would materialize. They whispered among themselves. Some sat back and folded their arms, as if unwilling to even listen to this highly qualified professor.

"Thy attention, gentlemen," Mr. Coffin said. "This class is called to order. I know thee were expecting Sir Lionel to teach thee anatomy and elementary dissection. Unfortunately, he was hit by a wagon while crossing Frazer Street and cannot teach this term. I am Sir Lionel's substitute."

"Well, boil me in oil," Edwin Hamilton said under his breath. Someone else laughed in disbelief.

Others had more to say, and Mr. Coffin let them say it. After a moment, he raised his hand. Davey held his breath, hoping there would be quiet. To his relief there was silence, a resentful silence to be sure, but silence, nonetheless.

"As thee all know, it is the prerogative of the professor to choose an assistant for Bones, someone steady of hand and imperturbable." He smiled. "Said student will also do the dirty work of wiping up and disposing of rotten parts, because that is medicine, too."

Davey heard someone clearing his throat and glanced at sextant thief John Yerby, he who had carried on the longest and loudest at the dissection they witnessed last term on this fourth floor. He couldn't imagine anyone worse for a position requiring steadiness of hand and purpose, but he also knew John was a pet of Sir Lionel's. He felt the Marine breastplate in his pocket and wondered at the connection, if there was one.

"I am at liberty to choose someone this term, *not* Sir Lionel," Mr. Coffin said firmly, which stopped John, who had started to rise. "I have chosen the most qualified among thee: David Ten."

Davey closed his eyes at the shocked silence, followed by hisses and a stamping of feet. This was worse than he imagined. *I'm leaving tonight*, he thought in misery. *God help me, but I can't do this. Master Six, I need you now.*

The stamping grew louder, but something strange happened. He knew Master Six could not suddenly appear, but that didn't explain the sudden warm feeling that settled on his shoulders like a blanket. From somewhere inside his skull, he heard most distinctly, "You are equal." Euclid? Good God. Somehow, he knew better than to question the source of this sudden knowledge. It was enough to be reminded.

He looked up from staring at his shoes to see Mr. Coffin gesturing him to rise. He rose and stood beside the quiet man with oceans of courage.

"Why him, thee ask? Who in this room has debrided a burn?"

No hands went up. His tormentors' expressions remained sullen.

"Davey?"

"Twice, sir," he said, hoping his voice wouldn't suddenly vault into falsetto. It didn't. "Once in the indigent ward here, and another time on the deck of the *Mercury* at Trafalgar." How Mr. Coffin knew, he had no idea. He decided not to question.

"Does thee know how to set a bone?"

"Aye, sir, one a compound fracture. I only assisted there. The simple fracture was a greenstick break."

"Has thee ever amputated a limb?"

How could a Rat forget that? Master Six had calmly directed him on the deck of the *Mercury* in the removal of a Frenchman's arm above the elbow, as the man cursed and swore then fainted. "Aye, sir. He was a Frog, and he took exception to my fiddling with him."

"Did he live?"

"Aye, sir." Davey smiled at the memory. "He couldn't bring himself to say thankee, though."

The operating theatre was silent now. The grudging looks remained. Davey knew he was making no friends in there, but they already weren't friends, so it didn't matter.

"Thy ship, was it heaving up and down through all this?"

"Aye, sir. The deck was slippery with blood, too. We managed."

"What did thee do when the wounded men were stabilized or dead?"

Davey was silent a moment, remembering. "We threw the dead men overboard, and stashed the others here and there in our small craft." Should he? Oh, why not? "After I puked over the railing, I sat down and cried."

"How old was thee?"

"Fifteen, sir."

The silence was profound. He dared to looked around, just a quick look. The grudging looks were gone. Some few still smirked, but others were serious, maybe for the first time in an operating theatre. No theatrics here.

"How did thee feel?" Mr. Coffin asked quietly.

Davey let a long moment pass as he remembered the thick smoke, creaking and falling masts, fading whimpers of the dying, the strong odor of blood and bowel, and the sight of broken bodies of men – English, French, and Spanish – who only hours before had been alive, perhaps thinking of home and families, or wondering what Cookie had in store for supper.

"I felt immensely sad that I could not save them all," he said.

"It's a hard lesson." Mr. Coffin looked at his subdued class. "Gentlemen, come to the skeleton. Bring a pad and writing tool and look at the bones of the hand on our skinny friend. Identify those thee can. Draw them. Learn them, Davey will assist those who need help. I will prepare this arm for dissection. Davey, if thee brought an apron, put it on."

His face set, he did, looking down at the bloody stains that never came out. The others saw them, too.

No one spoke to him, but some pointed to smaller bones, and he named them. Some drew the little bones and labeled them. Edwin Hamilton hung back and puzzled a longer moment. "You helped me before," he said, his voice low.

"I can again," Davey whispered back.

Soon they gathered around the severed arm, all of them sober at last. John Yerby stood toward the back, his arms folded across his chest, the picture of petulance, angry at being no one's pet in this class, with

Sir Lionel indisposed. Edwin moved closer. "You're better at bones than I am."

"I like bones," Davey whispered back. Edwin smiled at that.

They joined the others around the arm. Mr. Coffin made a careful slit down the arm, giving a sharp look at someone who thought to gag. The student stopped. The quiet man held up a small handful of metal. "These are retractors. David, help me with these. Anyone else?"

Pimply Richard Sterling held up his hand. "Do as David does," Mr. Coffin said. "David, assist Mr. Sterling if he needs help. Ah, very good." He gestured again. "Gentlemen, come closer. Let us study the mystery of the human body through this poor man's arm."

Chapter Twenty

It never ceased to amaze Avon Marsh how easy it was to vanish in a crowd. Hard experience had taught him the skill of blending in and looking as though he belonged there, when he knew he belonged nowhere.

After leaving Davey, he had spent an hour and more walking around the University of Edinburgh, taking a measure of the place. Black-robed students hurried through the January sleet, intent upon shelter. None of that mattered to Avon. In the Bath workhouse, his best moments had come when he worked out of doors through good weather and bad. If someone had ever thought to coddle him, he wouldn't have known what to do.

Davey had pointed out the nearby building that housed the Royal Infirmary, grey stone like all the others. After luncheon *al fresco* in an alley containing ashcans stuffed with recently cast-off scraps, he found his way to the entrance and waited. He stayed near the building, alert without appearing to be so. He knew it was easy to ignore those dressed as poorly as he was without his uniform.

When there were no passersby, Avon mounted the steps quickly and went inside. He worried a moment whether someone so shabbily dressed would invite his prompt removal, then gave himself a mental slap. *Avon, me hearty*, he thought, *there is a ward here for the poor and indigent. They see people like you all the time.*

Hands in pockets, he walked down the lengthy corridor, smelling sickroom odors and wondering how Davey could do what he did. One door he passed bore a plaque stating Utility. He backed up, look around, and opened it. Perfect. He reached inside for a broom and dustpan, then found a quiet corner off the corridor where he could sweep and observe.

As he swept, he watched. As a small child he had learned to watch and be wary. Nobody noticed him as he swept and watched, not even officious-looking men, and aproned nurses with their own wary looks. He knew from years of experience that no one noticed the shabby workers who swept, mopped, emptied necessaries, and mucked out stables.

Master Six had once remarked that Avon could probably infiltrate untold inner sanctums. "You have a remarkable capacity to blend," his dear teacher told him. "Quite possibly you will be more successful on land in some way we haven't discerned yet. Something to think about."

Avon considered it now, storing information in his brain that he could commit to paper later and share with Captain Ogilvie, who knew a massive amount about skulking. *But what am I skulking for here?* he thought. *I hope I know it when I see it.*

In for a penny, in for a pound, he thought, and entered what he knew was Ward B behind an old lady wearing a ragged cloak better suited to a dustbin. This was Davey's indigent ward, with its few visitors, as if this place of suffering was meant for beggars and society's dregs. Perhaps this was where Edinburgh's prostitutes went to die, alone and unmourned. Would his own mother have died in a place like this in Bath?

Ten of the twenty beds were occupied. The old lady went to a bed with an inmate so thin as to appear skeletal. Avon swept in the shadows, watching her as she caressed the man's arm. A man in the nearest bed stared a moment, then turned away.

Avon went into the next ward, which had more beds filled: Ward A. Better dressed than the old woman in Ward B, several visitors sat here and there. Some were talking and others read out loud to patients. Two children sat on one cot as their mother took out a jam jar and bread, all from a basket at her feet. Avon smelled what must be sausage, too.

He watched as she held the jam-covered bread under the man's nose. Nothing. She waved it back and forth. No reaction. With a lift and drop of her shoulders, she looked around, then ate the morsel. She tried next with the sausage, with the same results. This time she motioned to her children to come close. She was about to divide the sausage when what must be a student in sober black and a flashy waistcoat hurried to her.

"He can't eat now," the student said. "Leave it with me. I'll see that he does it justice when he's able."

"Justice, indeed," whispered the patient in the bed closest to Avon. "Watch'em. He'll scarper off with it. Damned students." He frowned at Avon. "You're not one of them, are ye?"

"No, sir, no," Avon said. He knew just the right whining tone to use with his betters: workhouse knowledge. "I sweeps. That's all." He stretched it a little. "A student, you say?"

The patient nodded. "Vultures, more like. Sweep a little closer. I think t'aud man is dying. Wait and watch."

Avon did as he said, listening, making no eye contact, another workhouse tactic. Even now, Master Six had to remind him, "Eyes up and on me. There's no workhouse here."

"Please, sir, is he dying?" he heard the woman whisper.

The medical college student– what else could he be? – took a bored look at the chart. "Happens to all of us," he said, then amended his comment. "You could bring by some food tomorrow, though. I doubt he has entirely run his course. G'day."

"Thank ye, sir," the wife said. "Come, children."

She left the basket, even though her little ones looked at it with longing. "You watch now," the patient next to Avon said.

Sure enough, the student came back to the bedside, made a show of looking at the chart, then left with the basket. "You'll hear'em laughing in the hall," the man said. "Dreary sods." He tried to rise, but sank back. He shook his head. "I suppose he's right: it happens to all of us. Still and all…" His voice trailed off and he closed his eyes.

Disturbed, Avon swept his way out of the ward, wondering how Davey Ten could possibly get a good education in this awful place. He closed the door behind him, ready to leave, but there was the student, looking in the woman's basket with two other cronies dressed like him in black robes.

"You there!"

"Me, sir?" Avon said, falling back on his head-down cringe, cursing himself for ruining his chance to remain unnoticed. "I didn't do nuffink."

To his relief, the student came no closer. He gestured toward the indigent ward. "There's a pile of bandages in there. How'd you miss them? Are ye blind?"

"Only in one eye, sir," Avon whined.

It wouldn't have fooled a bosun for a minute, but Avon had already decided that this student was no shining example of medicine at work. "I'll move along, sir."

The student gestured to the indigent ward. "Move your sorry ass into the poor ward and take the pile of bandages to the washing room. I'll report you if you keep gawking."

What to do? Avon cringed until he nearly doubled over. "Thankee, sir. Where's t'washing room?"

The student heaved a massive put-upon sigh and looked at his companions, who by now had pulled the sausage from the basket. Avon wondered what the woman's children were eating tonight. "I ask you, where do they find dregs like this wretch?" the student asked his friends. "Down the hall to the right. Leave us."

Avon knuckled his forehead with his fist, wished them all painfully dead some day of syphilis, and scurried back to the indigent ward. He found a heaping pile of used bandages, reeking of gangrene and noxious odors he had never smelled before and hoped never to again. He was just a sweeper, after all, and an a spur-of-the-moment one, at that.

The old lady sat by her husband who lay still, barely breathing. Avon knew he could have cut and run then, with no one the wiser, but his humanity prevented it. All his life he had wondered about the woman who left him on the bank of the river Avon. Maybe his mother died alone in a ward like this one. Maybe he needed to know how awful an ending could be.

"May I help you?" he asked, knowing he could do nothing, but never a heartless person.

She shook her head. "T'physic said he was going to peg out soon, but I cannot stay." She looked down at her broken shoes. "So far to walk. It takes me time. It's cold…" Her voice trailed off. "I can't help him, me poor old jo."

She looked at Avon as though he could help her, and he almost wished he had not inquired. Angry at himself, he found a stool and joined in her vigil. He cast about for something to say, anything, and decided on, "Goodwife, d'ye have a place to bury him?" He winced at the callous sound of that, but reckoned she was someone used to hard truths.

He was right. She gave him a glance full of relief. "Aye, young laddie, I have, thanks to the nice physic." She looked around, squinting. "He was just here. He wrote it on that paper and showed it to me, even after I told him I couldna read. Said my good man would be taken to St. Luke's, potter's field for the likes of us."

Avon saw her exhaustion and her age. "Ye should go along now before darkness," he assured her. "I'll watch him." *Avon, you liar,* he thought. *You want out worse than she does.* No no, he could stay awhile. It was only midafternoon, with winter's dusk coming soon.

She sat a moment more, then bent over the old relic to kiss him, and left. Full of misgivings, Avon took her place and watched the old fellow, not certain he was even breathing and feeling far out of his league. *Davey, I could use you about now,* he thought.

Davey didn't materialize, so Avon leaned closer and listened. The man breathed but only now and then, as if it were an afterthought. Avon leaned back in the chair, happy to sit for a moment, but well aware that anyone could come into the ward, chase him out and summon the watch. Or not. The broom was his badge of work. He took it in hand, ready to rise up and sweep at a moment's notice.

He noticed the ailing man's chart on a chain at the side of his cot. He debated a moment, and decided he wanted to know this man's name at least. He doubted anyone else would remember him, because his old woman didn't appear on the rosy side of health, either.

"Thomas Perkins," he said softly, and looked closer at a birthplace in Wales, but no mention of town or birth date. He must have lived in poverty, unknown to all. Avon looked at him, his heart full. "I will remember you, Thomas Perkins," he said. "I will."

He glanced at the chart again and his heart stopped. Someone had already written in cause of death as "Incident to age," and even the time of death as "Four hours, fifteen minutes ante meridian."

If he's not dead then, will you students bludgeon him? he thought, angry at such a system of neglect. He doubted anyone would bother to inform the old man's widow. He saw no address on the paper, so how would they know where to find her?

He took heart. At least he would be buried in St. Luke's Poor Cemetery, or so the student had informed her, coffin probably nonexistent, but how would she know? He looked at the chart again and sucked in his breath. Clearly written on the chart in the spot annotated Cemetery, was *Diss.3,* the same word on his class schedule that Davey had showed him as they walked toward the university only this morning.

So much for St. Luke's Poor Cemetery. Anger filled Avon as he imagined the poor woman's distress if she were ever to know that instead of burial wrapped in an old winding sheet probably, her husband was to be cut open, his intestines unspooled and examined, his skull cracked open and his brains exposed, simply because he was too poor to bother with. Was this the same fate of the Royal Marine and carpenter's mate? Good God.

He shivered involuntarily, for a small moment wishing himself on the *Mercury* in the middle of the Trafalgar fight, something he could understand. As hard as his life had been up to his admission to St. Brendan's, that fleet action had been a fair fight. What lay before him, barely with breath in his old frame, was a man whose wife was assured a Christian burial for him, and it was all a lie. Avon's anger grew as he wondered how many other things she had been promised in her life.

He wanted to leave the building as fast as he could. He could calmly say goodnight to Miss Teague, tell Davey what he had seen, then, when the house was quiet, run away to Portsmouth. He had no money beyond a few shillings, but his instincts were good. He could find his way back to St. Brendan's.

And tell Master Six what? As he stood there, unable to take his eyes off the poor old fellow breathing now and then, Avon heard footsteps. Unwilling to be found, Avon backed into the small space holding the mound of bandages reeking of disease and mortification. He crouched down, grateful that the winter afternoon shadows were growing longer. And who came to investigate a pile of pus-filled, bloody bandages on purpose?

It was that student from the other ward, and one of his fellows more plainly dressed. As Davey watched in horror, the student poked and prodded the old fellow, who groaned, and then paused in his labored breathing, before gasping and breathing again.

"He's nearly dead," one student said. "I don't want to wait around. What say ye, John?"

Avon's eyes widened as John yanked the skinny pillow from behind the dying man's head and covered his face with it, pressing down as the man thrashed weakly, then lay still. After what seemed like forever, the student lifted the pillow and placed it behind the now-dead man's head.

"Let's go. Someone will find him." John giggled, an odd, unsavory sound, and looked at the chart. "Right-o, Mr. Perkins. We'll see you in Diss. 3 in a few days! Nitey night. Sleep tight."

Stunned, Avon crouched lower, waiting for the students to leave. When the door closed, he leaped up, ready to run. He slowed his steps by the dead man and stopped, wishing he could summon the watch and tell a constable what he had witnessed. The more cautious – cynical? – side of Avon March told him that no one would care.

He did something then that he couldn't have explained to anyone. Miss Teague had noticed after breakfast hours ago that the yarn on his watch cap had begun to unravel. "I can weave that back into your cap," she told him.

Hardly knowing what he did, but wanting to show no one but himself that someone cared for this poor man, he tugged on the navy blue yarn and bit off a length of it. He glanced around. No one in the other cots was conscious or paying attention to him. Perhaps they were already destined for Diss. 3, too. Avon tied the little length of yarn in the man's thin hair, replacing the cord that tied back his old-fashioned pigtail. He knew it was a puny gesture, but Avon wanted to assuage his own heart that the old man mattered.

He couldn't leave the infirmary fast enough.

Chapter Twenty-One

What to do? Nothing in his life had prepared Avon for what he had just witnessed. He was familiar with the hard and callous side of life – it was all he knew – but to see someone so cavalierly take a life that was going out anyway... He couldn't fathom it.

He walked slowly, unmindful of the rain because it matched his mood. He wondered that anyone inhabited Scotland. Had they no imagination? Did it never occur to Scots that there might be something better than this?

No one gave him a glance from under their umbrellas. Maybe people were eager to get home to a warm hearth and food. He trudged on, stunned by what he had witnessed, even though his life had been full of hard knocks. How could they?

He didn't know what to say, but he knew he could not remain silent at such injustice. He hadn't the courage to go up the front steps of the cheerful, well-lit house and act as if nothing had happened. He walked back and forth, feeling more alone than at any time in his life.

To his surprise, Miss Teague opened the door and peered out. "Avon," was all she said, but she opened the door wider and gestured him inside.

"Please, miss," was all Avon said, before tears came to his eyes and spilled over. It had been a terrible afternoon and now it was nearly dark.

"My goodness," she said, but she came out, not minding the rain. "Avon, what happened?"

She was looking at *him*, as if she saw something he was unaware of. To turn his dark day lighter, Miss Teague put her hand on his shoulder and pulled him close. In another moment they were both sitting on the floor in the entryway, because his legs failed him.

Why didn't this phase her? Miss Teague handed him a frilly, nearly useless handkerchief and he blew his nose.

"I hope you haven't been wandering around, wondering if I would let you inside," Miss Teague said.

He knew it wasn't a scold, but more of a kindness. To his amazement, she nudged him as they say there on the floor, a friendly gesture. "Let me get you a big towel."

"Not, not yet," he said. "Can we just sit together for another moment? It…it feels good."

Now why that should bring tears to Miss Teague's eyes, Avon had no idea. He blew his nose again.

"Certainly we may," she said promptly, which meant he had to stuff the handkerchief against his eyes after he found a clean spot. Where was all this coming from? Why was he feeling this way?

Miss Teague did something them that cemented him to her forever. She put her arm around his shoulders and said, "You can lean against me, too, Avon. It does feel good."

He wondered briefly if she had wanted someone as much as he did. Oh, but she was a calm and organized lady, living in comfort and probably never missing a meal or a night's sleep. What did she have to ruffle her days? Never mind. He could think about it later. Right now, right here, he closed his eyes in relief.

The moment passed quickly. Mrs. Perry would probably scold, if she saw all the mud he had carried in. Surely Miss Teague had noticed, and was just being kind. "I'm sorry to make a mess," he said. "This is such a nice house and I…I suppose I don't really belong here."

She could have said anything then. To his further relief, she laughed. "Avon, I don't belong here, either, but here we are. I'm pretending I know how to take care of Gunwharf Rats, and you're probably feeling out of place in stuffy Edinburgh."

"But you're in charge," he said, unused to opinions of others kindly spoken. True, the Sixes, all of them, were kindness personified, but Miss Teague had likely been informed by Mrs. Munro that she would admit two strange lads to her house on Wilmer Street and not argue about it, because she had no more standing than he did, in all likelihood. The idea gave him pause.

"Strictly speaking, it is Mrs. Munro's house," she said, then appeared to give the matter some thought. He watched her face, aware that she would never win at cards in a gaming hell. Her face was so expressive. Everyone would cheat her. She had a dimple, too, larger than Davey's.

"Mrs. Munro is a long way from here and you are in charge," he reminded her.

"So I am," she replied.

In a short life of fearsome, fraught days of deprivation, humiliation, hunger, war, death and triumph, this was the day Avon knew he would remember and treasure above all else. Something was happening to him as he sat on the floor beside a lady who had suddenly turned into someone both memorable and essential. Was this what a mother felt like? He had no real way of knowing, except that he knew he never wanted to leave her kind orbit.

This is what belonging feels like, he told himself. *I wonder if Miss Teague feels the same way.* He wanted to ask her, but he didn't even know the words.

He could try. "I hope you don't mind us here," he said.

She tightened her grip on his shoulder, he who observed and watched and skulked, almost as if he belonged to her. Would she even understand what he had to tell her? "Something awful happened this afternoon," he said. "I need to tell Davey, but I want you to know, too, because it frightened me."

"I thought something was wrong," Miss Teague said simply. "Let's figure out what to do. Whatever it is, you're not in this alone. Problems are best solved with more than one or two opinions."

Oh bliss. He wasn't going to be alone, maybe not ever again. He stood up and offered Miss Teague a hand up. She took it and they walked into the kitchen, in league with each other, united to help him do…what? He knew he had never been young. Was this what it felt like to let others do the worrying? He felt his shoulders relax for the first time in his life, and he liked the feeling.

He sat at the kitchen table, then closed his eyes and put his hands over his face, uncertain how to deal with the terror of the last few hours, followed by the equally strong feeling that his life had taken an unexpected turn. He heard Miss Teague and Mrs. Perry speaking softly, and he recognized the same gentle conversation he sometimes heard between the Master and Meridee Six, if he was really lucky. Was he eavesdropping? No, he was learning how people lived. His heart rejoiced.

His cup ran over even more when Miss Teague set a thick slice of warm bread, well buttered, in front of him. She rested her hand on his shoulder for a brief moment, then gave it a pat. "This should tide you over until Davey gets here."

"Aye, Miss Teague," he said. Another slice followed the one he finished too fast, and then another. He surprised himself again as he looked down at a third slice, equally well-buttered. A workhouse boy, no matter how full, would have gulped it down, too, since nothing in his life was guaranteed.

Miss Teague sat across from him. He wondered if she would understand. "I don't think I'm hungry now," he told her. "I think I'm full."

"They were big slices," she said.

He looked beyond her at Mrs. Perry, and saw the tears in her eyes. She understood. "I'll go wash up," he told them both, and went into the next room with its tub and basins and towels, and soap, all he wanted. Some instinct told him that Mrs. Perry would explain to Miss Teague that workhouse boys were never full, and that this moment for Avon was a memorable one. He was full.

Dash it all. He saw the tears in Miss Teague's eyes when he came from the washing room, uncertain himself how to negotiate this new way of feeling. He didn't want her pity, if that's what her tears meant, and he didn't want to cause her pain. All he could do now was mumble something about going upstairs to think about things, and wait for Davey, someone older and perhaps wiser.

He must have dozed then. When he woke, it was full dark and Davey was lying on his bed, staring at the ceiling. Avon had always been somewhat in awe of Davey Ten, a quiet and immensely capable Gunwharf Rat who had not flinched or faltered at Trafalgar, and who had endured a year of silence and more at the college of medicine.

Avon tested his new-found epiphany, telling him about the novelty of realizing that ordinary people didn't devour food because they knew there would be more. He didn't think he explained himself well, and in truth, the whole business of having enough of something *did* seem silly, childish even. "Never thought I'd see the day when two pieces of bread was enough, and a third one too much," he said, knowing how lame he sounded.

Davey laughed softly, but it was not a mean laugh. "I discovered that at Mrs. Munro's house back in Portsmouth. The Sixes took me there one evening. The matter was sirloin, and all those courses, from soup to salad to fish to venison to... oh, whatever else. I couldn't finish what was on my plate, and I wondered what was wrong with me." He sat up and poked at Avon playfully with his foot. "Damn me, Avon, but you explained that rather well. I think you should trade your skulking garb for a barrister's robes!"

They both laughed at the absurdity of that notion, but Davey turned serious, true to his nature, or so Avon had observed through their years together. "And here we are. The world is at war and I am to become a physician. What do you want to be? A skulker?"

Avon thought Davey was teasing, but then, it was hard to tell with Davey. Since everything had changed for him, he gave the matter some thought. "Someone who finds out other people's secrets like Captain Ogilvie?" Then came a wry smile. "I don't believe I want to, the same as deciding I didn't need that third slice of bread."

"D'ye think Captain Ogilvie likes what he does?" Davey asked.

Avon had never considered that, but his answer came quickly. "I wouldn't."

"I heard Master Six say once that we all dance to Napoleon's piping tune," Davey replied. "Him, Captain Ogilvie, me, you." He looked beyond Avon. "Maybe even Miss Teague, now that we have been foisted upon her. Do you think she minds?"

Avon heard Miss Teague calling them to dinner. Did she mind? He needed to know.

Davey started to rise obediently, but Avon reached out his hand to hold him in place. "I watched two students smother a dying man in the indigent ward this afternoon," he said quietly. "I'm not saying the old boy wasn't on his way out, because he was. Still, he had life in him until they snuffed it." His voice hardened; he couldn't help it. "The other one said he didn't want to be late to supper. They laughed."

Davey sat back, startled, but not surprised, Avon noticed. "They were probably your classmates."

He heard Miss Teague again. "We have to go," Davey said.

"There's more."

"Will it keep? We shouldn't keep Miss Teague waiting."

Avon nodded. "It will keep. "T'old man is past caring." He shook his head. "Maybe it shouldn't bother me. Maybe it was mercy. Except…"

"It'll keep."

"Should we tell her?" Avon said, indecisive now. What would Miss Teague think of them? Maybe there was no one they could trust with this awful turn of events.

Chapter Twenty-two

Where was this assurance coming from? Esther Teague prided herself on knowing herself pretty well. Maybe if she had been bounteous and beautiful, there wouldn't have been room in her head for intellectual musings. Ladies like her could not afford to be flibbertigibbets. Her looks were passable, but nothing special. Her chest too flat, her purse also too slim. She was cynical enough to know that a well-padded purse encouraged possible suitors to overlook other deficits, but such was not her fate.

She bided her time through dinner, settling for small talk and comments about Edinburgh, and the hope of spring eventually, all the time deeply aware that these Gunwharf Rats had somehow worked their way into her heart.

Perhaps she had been as lonely for company as Davey Ten. There was Avon, who said little but observed much. Even Mrs. Perry, capable and intimidating when it suited her, but too shy to sit at table with them. She wanted to know more about them, which meant they needed to know more about her.

"Gentlemen, we need to talk."

She sat there calmly, hands folded in her lap, back straight, the perfect lady because she was, above and beyond her spinster state and her own poverty that teetered upon the charity of relatives. With no choice in the matter, she had opened the doors of Aunt Munro's house on two uniformed young men. Nowhere had Aunt Munro or anyone ordered her to do anything except provide a safe place to live. The young men had each other to talk to, plus Mrs. Perry as a further sounding board.

Esther knew she could easily continue as the person she already was, a competent, reliable old maid who ran a well-ordered house and would do her duty. Nothing more was required of her. As she sat there, watching them exchange glances when she said they needed to talk, Esther examined her own prejudices about the very word "workhouse," and came up short in her own estimation.

What she had feared – loutish fellows with no manners, sly and sneaky – had never materialized. Davey and Avon were polite and obviously intelligent. In the single week they had been in her home, she watched the insecurities surface. They were wary around food. They somehow guarded their plates when they ate. If a pan dropped in the kitchen, or a carter's horses made noises on Wilmer Street, they flinched and started, as if ready for flight. She had no idea how much of that was from frightening and haphazard times in the workhouse before St. Brendan's, or from their experiences in fleet actions and then the deadly struggle needing only one word – Trafalgar. Perhaps all.

Watching them now, she wanted to tell them, "Trust me." She also realized the corollary: "Trust *them*, Esther."

She barely knew where to start. What had they ever been but abandoned? She wondered – and would likely never know -if they could not trust even this Master Six they spoke of. After all, he had insisted Davey leave his safe haven of Portsmouth, his fellow Gunwharf Rats, and even the naval hospital, to study where he learned a different lesson: He was not wanted. Even worse, Davey probably knew he would not be wanted.

It must end here, she decided. As she raised her eyes to theirs, a wonderful peace enveloped her. She hadn't expected any such thing, but she knew without a doubt that she cared about them, because she had been lonely, too. What became of them here mattered deeply to her; she knew that now.

She clasped her hands and leaned forward, wondering if they would believe her. "Avon, you're carrying the weight of the world on your shoulders," she said quietly. "I saw it when you walked in the door this evening." She turned her attention to Davey next, noticing his eyes were twin pools of sadness. "David, tell me how your classes went today. Be honest."

Silence. She looked from one to the other, wondering at her wisdom in confronting them even so calmly, doubting they would tell her anything. She felt doomed to failure. Where was that peace she felt only seconds ago? *Give me strength*, she thought, even as she questioned who she was asking for strength. She attended church and believed some of it, except that her life was a lonely one. So much for love thy neighbor as thyself. Piffle.

Tell them who you are, she heard from nowhere. That frightened her, until it was followed by a greater realization that the unvoiced order seemed to spring up like an early crocus in the snow.

And again from nowhere: *It's possible, Miss Esther Teague, that you need these Gunwharf Rats even more than they need you. Did you ever think of that?*

She had never considered that before, then admitted silently that she never gave the workhouse a thought, except to be grateful that she never had to go near one. The misery of the lives within such bleak walls never crossed her mind. She could imagine nothing but disappointed hopes living in workhouses, but how was that different from her own life?

"Let me tell you something more about myself," she began, taking a brave step into the unknown. "I've already told you I am twenty-eight-year-old spinster. Skinny, too. Miss Twig, remember? My neighbors think I don't know they call me that." She gulped and forged ahead. "I have never received a proposal of marriage and likely never will. I am nothing much to look at and I have no dowry. My father was a not-so-prosperous merchant who gave his two sons everything so they could succeed."

To her surprise, Avon spoke first. "You have a very fine dimple in your right cheek. It's better than Davey's."

Esther couldn't help smiling, maybe out of relief that they were paying attention.

"See? Right there," Avon said. "Davey, you're the medical man. What causes dimples?"

It was Davey's turn to grin. "A break in the zygomaticus major muscle. It runs across Miss Teague's cheek, Avon. Everyone's, in fact. Dimples are rare." He ducked his head, but his eyes looked less sad. "I like to study bones and muscles."

"I had no idea about dimples," Esther said. "Zygomaticus? Who in the world names these things?"

Somehow, everyone relaxed. She could feel it. David chuckled.

He spoke up. "If I'm not being impertinent, miss, why did your father divide his property that way?"

She has her suspicions. "I think it was because I am homely and he knew my brothers would have to take care of me. Let me live with them and tend their children." *I wonder why I did that so long*, she thought. *I could have found work as a lady's companion.*

"Did you like that?" Avon asked.

"Most decidedly not," she said firmly. "Before Aunt Munro needed me here, I had to tend my younger brother's two wretched little boys."

"Do you like us?" he persisted.

"Avon, you should be a barrister!" she declared, more enchanted than dismayed. "You've trapped me."

She thought he might take that amiss. To her relief, he laughed. "I'm not the clever Rat with words," he told her.

"I believe you are." They both regarded her with such intensity that she knew her reply mattered. She also knew these were not lads to fool with. "I will admit I was leery of this assignment. You could put into a thimble what I know about lads, and I certainly don't like my nephews."

That brought appreciative nods from both of them, so she let out a cautious breath. "I have discovered that you two are thoughtful, studious, and I suspect braver than most."

They looked at each other again. "You or me," Davey asked Avon.

"You."

David Ten looked her square in the face. "I still don't want to be here, especially after today," he said, which meant Esther had her opening.

"What happened today?" she asked, her voice quiet. She crossed her fingers, hoping he would tell her.

"Mr. Coffin, who is teaching Anatomy and Elementary Dissection, named me his assistant."

"Davey, that's wonderful!"

Avon shook his head. "Beg pardon, mum, but no, it's not. You don't want the attention, do you, Davey?"

"You know I don't," Davey replied. "I hate the stares and rude remarks to each other. All I want to do is learn, pass my oral and written exams at the end of this term, and leave."

"Not remain another two years to complete your studies?" Esther asked, keeping her voice low, and hoping he would not clam up.

"I can learn what I need to learn at Haslar Hospital from the surgeons there, who know naval medicine." He sighed. "Master Six wants me to leave on my own terms, and not slink away. That's the only reason I am here now."

"Assisting Mr. Coffin won't work?"

"I like Mr. Coffin well enough. One student in the class thought the assistantship would be his special reward for being a toady, but the professor scheduled to teach the course is incapacitated this term. That student dislikes me." He glanced at Avon. "In fact, he's the one who stole my sextant that Avon, um, retrieved."

Esther nodded, beginning to see the complexity of the matter. She had no idea what to say, except, "Avon, you've already told me you are here to skulk." *Oh, why not?* she asked herself. "I don't particularly like that idea, no matter what your leaders say."

She thought they might protest her intrusion into matters which were not her business. They did not. Could it be Avon felt the same? She also knew he would never admit it.

"They…they want a little information about those men I mentioned," he said. "The ones who went missing."

She looked at him with pity, thinking, *You're too young for this*, except she actually said it out loud. She put her hand over her mouth, ready to apologize. When Avon regarded her with bleak eyes, she knew she was right. "I mean it," she added softly. "This is a matter for a constable or a magistrate, not someone almost fifteen."

"Have we a choice in anything?" Davey asked.

She heard the force behind his words, and the resignation. *I wonder if your Master Six has any idea how you really feel*, she thought. How to say this? She picked her way carefully. "I know it is wartime, and you are in the service of king and country."

Avon opened his mouth to speak, then closed it. She saw something more in his expressive eyes. To speak or not? She, Esther Teague, was here to provide a home and conversation, nothing more. *Fiddle to that*, she thought, and stepped into the unknown.

"I may be Miss Twig and you wonder how I would know anything about anything, but I know something happened today. Tell me what it was. I see it in your eyes."

Avon looked at his fellow Rat, as if for reassurance, then at her. "In the indigent ward, I watched two students smother an old man because he wasn't dying fast enough!"

Esther gasped, and both Rats started. She let out her breath slowly, then, "My goodness, I didn't mean to startle you."

Their frowns told her there was more. "What else?" she asked, thinking, what could be worse that murder, for so it was. Or was it? She understood the complexity, if Avon was right about the old fellow already on his way out. Still, she had asked, so she waited for – and dreaded – what was next.

It exceeded her worst expectations. When Avon spoke to Davey and not her, she calmly accepted the fact that he did not entirely trust her. Why should he? "Davey, he told the old woman that her man would be buried in the poor cemetery. I think he said it was St. Luke's."

"I heard of St. Luke's last term when I ward-walked in the indigent ward." Davey shifted on the sofa, suggesting this was an unpleasant topic. "Many of the poor and homeless are buried there."

Agitated, Avon stood up and walked to the window and back. He stopped in front of Davey. "When she said she couldn't read, he showed her the chart with the words, St. Luke's, on them, so he said. Pointed it out to her."

Davey nodded. Esther saw the question in his eyes. "That's right and proper, Avon."

She felt her heart turn over at Avon's anguish. "It wasn't! I looked at his chart after the old lady and the students left. It read Diss. 3, not St. Luke's. How could she know? She couldn't read."

She heard Davey's sharp intake of breath, or maybe it was hers. "Th… that's the third year dissection class that comes after my Bones class. We meet tomorrow afternoon. I'm supposed to be there. Mr. Coffin wants me there." He turned away, shaking his head.

"He lied to her," Avon said. "Lied to an old woman."

She saw something else in Avon's eyes, something disquieting. "You think this is what might have happened to the Marine and Navy men who vanished," she added.

He nodded. "Davey, your professor might be dissecting that old gent tomorrow afternoon."

Esther glanced at Davey and saw the horror on his face. He shook his head slowly. "This is wrong."

"I know. It's nothing we can stop," Avon said. "He's dead, and would have died soon even if they hadn't smothered him, but to think there will be no burial…" He shook his head again. "He lied to her because he could, and none the wiser."

"Dissection 3 is for the third forms," Davey said. "Mr. Coffin wants me there because he knows I am more advanced than the second form students. You know, Trafalgar and all that. How will I know…."

"I bit off a section of yarn on my watch cap and tied it over his pigtail," Avon said. "If you see that, you'll know. I unraveled a length of it, bit it off, undid his little pigtail and wrapped and tied the yarn in its place. You might look for that, Davey."

What else was there to say? The three of them sat in silence. Davey spoke finally. "I will have to attend that dissection tomorrow afternoon. I must know the truth."

"Could Mr. Coffin stop the dissection?" Esther asked suddenly. "You told me he is a Quaker. True, they are a strange sect, but they have high regard for the truth, or so I have been told."

Davey shook his head. "If he did that, he might be laughed out of the College of Medicine for such an act. I could say something." He managed a chuckle that had no humor in it. "I am already held in no repute whatsoever. Who would believe me? What would this do to any other plans of St. Brendan's to help workhouse bastards find a place in society?"

The three of them were silent. "Miss Teague, I will attend that dissection tomorrow. I will ward walk that night with Mr. Coffin," Davey assured her.

"Will you say anything?" she asked, pained to put someone so firmly on the spot when she didn't even have an idea of what *she* would to. If Davey spilled the beans, the word would get out, as it always did, and his life would be even more miserable. If he did not, and if Avon said nothing, this business might continue. Who knew how many others, still living, had been sent to an early grave, and all to please a favored professor, or receive some sort of compensation for dead men's bones?

"Avon, let's go upstairs," Davey said. Esther heard all the resignation in his voice.

Maybe I need to meet this Mr. Coffin, Esther thought as she heard the door close quietly.

And what? Tell him anything of what she knew, all of which anyone with two brain cells could shoot down as pure speculation? Could she feel any more helpless? Was it even her business to betray young men who were society's pioneers, as they navigated their way to futures that could end abruptly if there was scandal attached to them?

She went into the hall when she heard the door open. Davey came to the head of the stairs. "Miss Teague, one good thing happened today."

I mustn't leap about and look like an idiot, Esther thought, even as her spirits rose a little. "And?"

"The one student who spoke to me once last term wants some help with muscles of the arms and legs. Mr. Coffin said I may help him, because that is what an assistant is to do."

"You could invite him over here," she said. "Aye, that would be good."

"P'raps I will," he said. "G'night now." He paused, and his smile was shy. "Thank'ee for listening."

"Thank'ee for talking to me," she whispered as their door closed. She stood in the doorway, disinclined to return to her everlasting crocheting. She wondered again if this peculiar assignment from Aunt Munro and Master Able Six – what sort of fellow *was* he? – was doomed to failure.

She decided to find out more about Mr. Coffin. Was he Davey's ally, or just another disappointment? She had no idea what to say to him. An icy hand seemed to grip her by the throat. How many people were carved on dissecting tables who should have gone into the earth, instead?

Now there was a poor, old, illiterate woman being duped and no one cared except two unacceptable members of society. *And me,* she thought, *and me. What about you, Mr. Coffin?*

Chapter Twenty-three

Davey was not the sort to dwell much on his life in the Saint Pancras workhouse, a place of such bleakness that he welcomed nightfall and the chance to sleep for a few hours and put away hunger and humiliation. He stopped his ears to the many tears of others after hours, because he did not cry. That human response to terror and sorrow had been beaten out of him when he was five or six. It had not returned until Trafalgar, as he admitted in Bones, when he cried because he could not save everyone that crossed the *Mercury's* deck.

He lay awake in bed that night long after Avon sighed and did his own tossing and turning, before finally succumbing to sleep. Davey recalled a workhouse sermon thundered out from the pulpit high above their heads in chapel, when the minister verbally flogged them for being a moral drain on England itself. "In a perfect world, there would be none of you to plague the rest of us," the clergyman had declared, and then pointed at the little ones terrorized in the front rows. "You, and you, and you, and you!"

As he watched in fright from a row farther back, the minister raised his eyes to the ceiling and shouted, "In a perfect world you would never exist! Do not forget that." Davey couldn't help smiling at such a preposterous statement, which earned him a beating later, one he bore with patient equanimity, because some tenderness in his heart, some sweetness, had escaped the notice of his horrible masters. He didn't understand the source of this knowledge, but it whispered to him that he was not responsible for his birth, however ignominious. It was neither logical nor kind.

He had never believed in a perfect world because he had never seen any evidence of such a thing, at least, not until he came to St. Brendan's, where no one shouted, where the word bastard was not bandied about, where teachers were firm but fair, and where he saw kindness every day. Was it perfect? No. It was many steps closer, however.

He saw kindness here at 158 Wilmer Street in the person of Miss Teague, someone oceans different from Mrs. Six, but possessing that same inclination to see matters put in their proper order and wanting, above all, for him to succeed. He did not think Miss Teague was brave enough to seek out and meet Mr. Coffin – it wasn't something ladies did – but he thought she wanted to. He knew he would never involve her in whatever happened in the college of medicine. She was too kind for that.

His last thought before he finally slept was that perhaps he could work up the nerve to talk to Mr. Coffin about what Avon had witnessed in the indigent ward. He wanted to trust the man, but was it fair to burden someone who fought battles of his own, and probably for larger stakes? He also knew Mr. Coffin needed bodies, too, for dissection, and Avon had said the old boy was on his way out, anyway.

The next day, the matter kept him silent through Materia Medica, when, after an hour of prosing over broken bones, the professor called upon one of his pets to strip down a classmate in that cold room and wrap fictional broken ribs. "Choose one among you who is stalwart," the old fellow had commanded, and pointed to Richard Sterling. "Pick someone."

With no hesitation, Sterling chose him. *Does it never end?* Davey thought, more irritated than frightened, because his mind was on whose corpse would be stretched out and awaiting them in Dissection 3.

He kept his mind blank, even as some of the indignities of Saint Pancras Workhouse began to peep and mutter in his brain. He touched his Trafalgar medal for good luck. No matter what happened in this classroom, it would never even approach the terror of that afternoon and evening, when he learned for all time how strong he was. The reminder bolstered his spirits.

Without a word, David removed his uniform jacket, blouse and under shirt. He knew they would notice the saber scar first, earned in the Mediterranean Sea not long after Trafalgar, when he and some of the other Rats were loaned out to cruisers with lesser captains than Master Six. That had been a short-lived experiment. Master Six was adamant about maintaining his own crew as a consequence of mismanagement that killed two other Gunwharf Rats from a lower class.

The older scars were from beatings at Saint Pancras, inflicted on runaways. He sat on a stool, his back to his classmates, waiting for whistles and jeers. Silence.

He glanced at Richard Sterling, one of his chief tormentors from the earlier terms, startled to see a remarkably pale face. "It's cold," Davey said conversationally, hoping to move the fellow along. If this was going to be his lot in Materia Medica this term, he might bring along a sweater to wear under his uniform.

"I've never…" Richard's voice was hesitant. Davey heard none of the usual bluster. Odd, that.

As he sat there, bare from the waist up, Davey began to take heart. Could it be that Richard Sterling had a heart, too? He looked around at the others, and saw their attention riveted on his scarred back, with no one smirking. Maybe this could be what Master Six called a teaching moment, except he usually said it in good-natured jest, after a calculus exam.

I can too, he thought. He cleared his throat. "No fears, Mr. Sterling. Be mindful of the saber scar, though. Barbary Pirates in the Mediterranean three years ago, and it's still a little tender. The older ones came from Saint Pancras Workhouse. I ran away too many times and got caught. Ten strokes with a cudgel and starvation in the cellar for three days each time. They're old injuries and don't hurt now. Go ahead, please." He waited.

His face solemn, Richard Sterling wrapped his chest. When he could speak, the professor tossed in his mite and tightened the bandage. "Firm is best, lads," was all he said, then, "For God's sake, undo him, Mr. Sterling." He returned to his desk and sat staring at the book in front of him.

For some reason, the professor dismissed them early. Davey waited until the others were gone – they seemed to take longer today – and went his usual way to the closet off the morgue. content to eat in quiet and close his eyes against the dread of Dissection 3 after Bones, and the exhaustion of a sleepless night.

He thought he heard someone in the hall and made himself small in the closet. The footsteps hesitated by the door, so he knew it wasn't Avon, who was still abed when Dave left the house, and who would have knocked and come in. The footsteps continued, and he breathed easy.

Today's Bones was a continuation of yesterday's, with more medical exploration of the arm that had been ripped away. It was in strips now, and smelled vile, so Davey knew there would probably be a new specimen to examine tomorrow.

He had nothing to say to Mr. Coffin, fearing that if he engaged in any conversation, he would blurt out the evil doings in the indigent ward that Avon had uncovered. He liked Mr. Coffin, admired him even, but reluctantly admitted to himself that he trusted him only slightly more than the other professors.

Mr. Coffin snapped him out of his gloom with a hand on his shoulder and the comment, before everyone arrived, "Something is troubling thee," he said. "Thee can tell me what it is."

No, he couldn't. He knew from last term's ward-walking in the indigent ward that Mr. Coffin had signed enough of those death certificates of unclaimed bodies. Davey knew the school of medicine needed bodies. What was another poor man to them? Or so he reasoned, until he felt that friendly hand on his shoulder. He knew his silence might mean more questions. He had to think of something.

It came easy enough because it was true. "I suppose I am wondering how this man died, whose arm we have been studying," he managed, trying to sound detached and scholarly.

"Thee is the first person to ask me such a question," Mr. Coffin said as he nodded to the arriving students and tied on his surgery apron. He looked into a distance that saw beyond the walls. "Now I am wondering if we are teaching medicine with compassion, or merely medicine."

Suddenly, Davey needed to know, not to simply take the focus off himself. "It matters to me, sir."

Mr. Coffin nodded. "And to me, although I must tell thee that I was beginning to forget."

Davey took his seat, nodding to Edwin Hamilton, who sat beside him again. Edwin spoke in the softest of whispers. "I didn't know how bad it was," he said.

Davey shook his head. "Doesn't matter," he whispered back. "I got out of Saint Pancras, and that Barbary pirate was sent to his own reward after he slashed me."

"I can tell you I have been leading a boring life," Edwin said, which made David chuckle and think this was how conversation should be.

Edwin opened his mouth to say more, but Mr. Coffin declared the class in session. "We will continue our perusal of this man's arm, concentrating on the bones of the forearm and fingers. There will be a test tomorrow."

After good-natured groans, the students got out their pads and pencils. Mr. Coffin nodded at Davey. "Please note something I should have mentioned yesterday, and will, from now on until the end of this term, as long as *I* know. This is Martin Farmer's arm. It was yanked from his body by an accident in a machine shop on Callister Street. I hope he was unconscious. If not, then he probably watched the blood spurt and then drain from his body. He probably closed his eyes in extreme exhaustion then, too deep in shock to feel pain. At least, this is my hope."

Mr. Coffin touched the mangled arm gently, which made Davey sigh. "Did he pray for release? I would. Would thee?" He spoke in a soft voice, but it carried in the room full of silent students. "I know his body was buried in God's Half Acre by the Presbyterian Church three blocks west of Princes Street. His widow kindly gave us permission to retain his arm for our studies." He spent a moment or two looking on each face, his expression resting finally on Davey's like a benediction. "Never take for granted what we do here in anatomy, because it comes at great cost, gentlemen."

It was another quiet class period. When it ended and the students filed out, Davey remained, dreading every step up the next flight of stairs that would take him to Dissection 3, where Mr. Coffin wanted him. He cleaned up the scraps and tatters of Mr. Farmer's arm, placing them in a wooden box.

"What happens to this?" he asked Mr. Coffin, hoping for an answer that would keep the heart in his body, because what happened to the arm mattered more to him at that moment than anything in his life. He had never been one to pray. Earnest and vengeful clergymen who swooped down on Saint Pancras to humiliate workhouse inmates had only convinced him that even God did not want workhouse trash, either. And yet... "I mean, it was part of Mr. Farmer."

He tensed when Mr. Coffin put his hand on his shoulder again. "Tell no one. I am supposed to carry what remains of Mr. Farmer's arm to the incinerator. What I *will* do is take it home, wrap it in a cloth and bury it in the back yard of my lodging. I have done that for several years."

Davey closed his eyes in relief. Mr. Coffin gave him a little shake. "Upstairs now. I thought I would be dissecting but I am still assisting. From his bed of pain, Sir Lionel – he doesn't like me at all – appointed another for dissections this term."

Numb with dread, he followed Mr. Coffin upstairs to the larger operating theatre. He put his hand to his mouth to see a body on the table under a white cloth. Other students had already assembled: third year students, that august body of would-be physicians who had few dealings with classes below them. They looked him over, perhaps found him wanting, then ignored him, precisely what Davey wanted.

Mr. Coffin remained beside the covered body with a short, bald fellow who was flexing his fingers, as if eager to get about the business of educational death. Davey trudged up a row beyond the students, every footstep unwilling. He sat alone. As the little professor and Mr. Coffin raised the sheet from the corpse, Davey longed for the comfortable presence of Avon March, or Master Six, or even Miss Teague, with her kind eyes and determination to do right with the Rats Aunt Munro had dumped in her lap. After seventeen years of essentially being on his own in a frightening world, he knew how much he needed someone, anyone.

Dreading what he might see, Davey looked down on the body of an old man, with a length of blue yarn tying back wispy hair. This was the man promised to St. Luke's burying ground for the poor and homeless, after a nameless student lied to an old man's widow. He looked away as the surgeon made his first incision. He covered his eyes against the great wrong that opened up before him.

Chapter Twenty-four

Miss Teague may have lived alone for three years since Aunt Munro had liberated her from her odious nephews and sent her to the comfort and ease of 158 Wilmer Street, but she remained a stickler for meals on time. Where *were* those lads?

She wanted to ask Mrs. Perry about them, but something, perhaps fear, made her hesitate. She had never met anyone like the black cook and housekeeper who towered over the rest of them. Mrs. Perry performed her duties admirably, and Esther Teague had never felt more safe in the marketplace, where ordinary folk could take liberties. *But I am ordinary folk*, Esther wanted to tell her, *and I am floundering*.

Still, it wouldn't hurt to ask Mrs. Perry. She went into the kitchen, breathing deeply of the chickens roasting in Rumford. The cook had subdued a pan of unruly, late winter tubers into a smooth mound of well-buttered mashed potatoes. Applesauce warmed on the hob, and Mrs. Perry had covered a fresh loaf of bread at the back of the hob just firm enough for slicing, but a receptacle for more butter. Esther knew she had never eaten better.

The lads were later than usual. "Mrs. Perry, where are they?" she blurted out finally, when the chicken came out of the oven with still no enthusiastic diners in sight. "All I know is there was to be a dissection this afternoon. How long does one of those *take* anyway?"

Mrs. Perry regarded Esther patiently, as though she were a little noisy dog yapping around her heels. "Maybe it takes more time than we know to slice someone open and rummage about," she said.

Someone knocked. She waited for one or the other Rat to stick his head inside then enter, but no one did. Another knock, and she opened the door.

A tall man dressed in black stood there. He wore a cloak and what looked like a beaver hat with none of the height or flare of the current style. She sighed with relief to see her Gunwharf Rats standing on each side of him.

"Heavens, it's sleeting and cold out," she scolded and opened the door wider. "Come inside."

Why did the lads hang back? She looked closer as they came inside, and the tall man closed the door. Davey's eyes were red, as if he had been crying. Avon always looked far too serious, but he seemed to carry a heavier weight, if not on his shoulders, then in his heart.

"Wh…what has happened?" she asked, expecting the worst. Was this commanding fellow a magistrate of some sort? She wanted to look closer at him, as well, but that would be rude. Still, she liked his eyes.

"Mr. Ten and Avon March told me they live here," he said. "I am Josiah Coffin, one of Mr. Ten's professors in the college of medicine."

"They do live here," Esther said. "I am Miss Teague." She bowed and he merely nodded, which she thought somewhat rude, but at least her boys were back. "Are they in trouble of some sort?" she asked, when no one seemed to have anything to say.

"They were reluctant to tell me where they lived," Mr. Coffin said. Esther watched something painful cross his face. He opened his mouth to say something, then shook his head. "I mean them no ill, and I see none here, but we have to talk."

"Could we talk over dinner?" Esther asked. "It's ready and getting cold."

"I can wait here," Mr. Coffin said. She realized then that he had a hand on each lad. She looked closer. More than a hand. He had gripped the inside of their cloaks.

"See here, sir," Esther said, disturbed by Mr. Coffin's need to grab them like fugitives. "They couldn't have been running away from you."

"This one was." Mr. Coffin let go of Avon, who gave him a tight-lipped stare. "Mr. Ten, on the other hand, was incapacitated." He released Davey, who looked away, but not before she saw the devastation in his eyes.

"There is room for you at our table, sir," Esther said. "I won't have you waiting out here for explanations. Davey, what happened?"

She asked as kindly as she could, praying that he would somehow know her heart. Aunt Munro's letters had assured her that the

Gunwharf Rats would be no trouble, and they weren't, except when she began to look closer. She took a chance then, a mighty chance, and held out her arms.

Davey was in them in a moment, Avon right beside him. She held them both, wordless, or maybe they engulfed her, until her quiet and logical mind understood that no matter how mature they appeared, part of them still suffered the damage inflicted in a workhouse.

She held them, then released them and stepped back. "Hopefully nothing is so bad that it cannot be helped by roast chicken," she told them. "Go to the washroom and scrub your faces. We'll meet you in the kitchen."

When they didn't move, her heart turned to mush. "You're not in trouble," she assured them.

They did as she said. She turned to Mr. Coffin. "Whatever you had to do to get them here, thank you," she told the tall man.

"It was the smaller one who give me thy address," Mr. Coffin said. "All Davey would say was that he didn't want thee bothered."

She hoped she wasn't being brazen, but Esther sat down after the lads went into the kitchen. After she heard the door to the washroom close, she patted the seat beside her. Mr. Coffin joined her, after removing his cloak. He looked around, noticed the hooks in the hall through the open door, and hung up his cloak and hat.

"Avon told me last night about skulking in the indigent ward and ..." She said after he sat down. "What have they told you?"

"Nothing, really. There was a dissection. When it ended and everyone left, Davey remained. It was as though he couldn't move." He took a deep breath. "I know he has seen much death at sea and he was raised in a workhouse, but he was in tears. Avon showed up and sat beside Davey in silence. Where Avon came from, I couldn't tell thee."

"Nobody can," she said calmly. "Avon is a skulker. I assume the body on the table was the selfsame man Avon said he saw in the indigent ward."

"But...what?"

Listening for the sound of the washroom door opening, she told him what Avon had witnessed. Mr. Coffin took a turn around the room when she finished, then sat down again. "My God," he said simply.

She heard the boys in the kitchen, and Mrs. Perry telling them to sit down. "Let's join them, sir."

"In a moment," he said. "Why is Avon here? Why is he snooping about in the Royal Infirmary?"

She told him about the navy man and Marine in the Royal Infirmary whose bodies were never returned to their families for burial. "Yes, Avon is here to keep Davey company – you know, give him someone to talk to. I didn't learn of the other reason until a few days ago."

"Who would give young lads such a task?" She knew Mr. Coffin was a man of no guile because his distress was obvious. Her heart warmed to him even though she knew nothing about him.

"The world is at war," she said, in her own mind thinking how foolish that sounded. Certainly, this man of medicine knew something so obvious.

"But they are so young to be involved in…whatever this is," he said. He blushed as he regarded her with apology in his eyes. "Thee is doubtless curious why someone my age is so naïve."

"Not at all," she told him. "Well, a little," she said with a smile, relieved when he chuckled. "Let's eat."

They ate in silence, Davey and Avon sneaking peaks at Mr. Coffin, who ignored them, carrying on an innocuous conversation with Esther. She knew what he told her was designed to put Davey and Avon at ease, as he spoke of his own Quaker background – "We call ourselves the Society of Friends," he explained – and the fact that the rest of the medical school faculty regarded him with some skepticism.

"I am here on sufferance, too," he concluded, and set down his fork. "Like thee, Davey, I am a specimen of some ridicule as men with power try to find ways to have me dismissed from the college of medicine because I am different."

"I didn't know," Davey said. "You and I were both ward-walking in the indigent ward because that was all we deserved?"

"Aye, lad. We don't belong."

Esther looked around the kitchen at Mrs. Perry, intimidating but perhaps more vulnerable than all of them, then the two Gunwharf Rats and Mr. Coffin. She looked inward too, at a spinster living on the sufferance of others. *None of us belong*, she thought, *except here we are together*. The notion put the heart back into her body. She wondered what Mr. Coffin would think of her opinion. It wasn't anything he would likely ever know, but she wondered.

Mr. Coffin gave her a sideways glance, almost as if seeking reassurance, which touched her heart. "Gentlemen, Miss Teague told me what Avon saw yesterday afternoon in the indigent ward. Let us have no secrets from each other, please."

Neither lad spoke for a long while, but Mr. Coffin waited with more patience than Esther felt. It was as though he had all the time in the world. The thought crossed her mind what an excellent father he would make, compared to her own, who was short-tempered and prone to jump to conclusions.

Avon spoke first, after a glance at his older friend. "That student in the poor ward lied to the old lady. The man Davey saw today is the one who is supposed to be buried in St. Luke's and not cut into little pieces." He spoke directly to Mr. Coffin. "Sir, I know students need the knowledge that dissections provide, but this isn't right."

It was Mr. Coffin's turn to hesitate. Esther sighed to see Davey look at Avon and shake his head. Mr. Coffin saw it, too. "I dislike disappointing thee, Davey," he began, slowly picking his way through what Esther suspected was a field of thorns. "I fear no one who matters would believe what Avon saw. What *I* saw and initialed, which was the chart listing time of death and designation as Dissection Three. It is the fate of many in the poor ward. No one questions it. I wouldn't have, either, had thee not told me this."

"It was a lie, sir," Avon said. "I heard what he told t'old woman. I saw the chart, which did not list a pauper's cemetery."

"I don't doubt thee," Mr. Coffin said quickly, "but…"

"…there is no justice," Avon concluded. Asking no permission, he left the table and the kitchen. With a sorrowful look, Davey followed.

"Can you trust me to somehow make it right?" Mr. Coffin said to the empty air. He leaned back in his chair, frustration etched everywhere on his expressive face. He turned to Esther. "What can I do? I have to assist at the dissection." He slapped the table in frustration. "And now I have to ward walk at the Royal Infirmary." He looked toward the door. "Davey is assigned to be there with me tonight."

"I'll remind him," Esther said, even as she hoped her two charges hadn't already abandoned the house and were heading south. Oh, but that was overly dramatic. Was it? Through some sense she could not explain –

what did she know of mothering? – she knew they were perfectly capable of doing precisely that.

Mr. Coffin must have read her mind. "Does thee think they will run away?"

"I don't know that I would blame them," she replied, honest to a fault.

He regarded her in silence for a moment. Esther looked back at him, feeling, oddly, none of her usual awkwardness. She knew how little she mattered in anyone's world, rather like a Gunwharf Rat, she thought, to her surprise. She asked herself why this earnest man didn't get up and leave, considering that there was nothing she could do. Did he see her differently?

Was this a night of plain speaking? What had she to lose? "My Aunt Mary Munro Carmichael made me caretaker of this house when she could have easily sold it. She plucked me out of an unpleasant situation as an old maiden aunt living on the mercy of others and gave me a respectable living."

"I doubt thee is a day over twenty-five," he said, which made her laugh.

"You're off by three years."

"Twenty-two then," he said. She saw the twinkle in his eyes, which made him charming.

They laughed together. He stood up. "And thee has a companionable smile," he told her. He held out his hand, an egalitarian gesture that made her hesitate, before she put her hand in his. Was this a Quaker thing?

"We're equals," he told her simply. "That's the way of Friends." He released her hand. "See if you can reason with Davey. Tell him I'll be thinking about things tonight in the indigent ward. He can think along with me, because I expect him to be there."

He paused on the front step. "I could see in thy eyes when we were introduced that I should have bowed to thee, as is common courtesy here. We Friends do not bow to anyone. Good night."

She stood at the open front door and watched him until he was out of sight. "If I were younger, I'd watch him, too," she heard Mrs. Perry say behind her. "Nice swing to his walk."

"Do be serious, Mrs. Perry."

"I am. Just you wait."

All I do is wait, and nothing has happened, she thought. She looked up the stairs. *I am good at waiting.* She went up the stairs slowly, wondering what to say to Davey Ten. She decided – audacious – to pretend he was her son, and consider what a mother might say. She knew nothing of mothering, but then, neither did Davey, she reasoned. Above all, she didn't want to know she hadn't tried everything.

Chapter Twenty-Five

"There are times, Avon, when you are exasperating."

"You're not going alone."

Davey knew that was precisely what Avon would say, and he didn't mind. Miss Teague didn't mind, either, and told him so. She had given their door a timid rap, and launched immediately into all the reasons why he still needed to ward walk that evening at the Royal Infirmary indigent ward. He heard her out, because he liked the little Scottish lady who seemed to care about them.

When she finished and stood there, hands on hips and looking militant (for her), he gave her his sunniest smile. "Miss Teague, we were planning on going together."

"Oh."

David smiled inside, the first time in a fraught day. She had obviously expected an argument. Master Six had taught him several years ago that even unpleasant tasks needed to be completed. Besides, the Quaker physician had given him food for thought. Maybe it was time he stopped thinking of himself as life's only victim.

"I could do this on my own," he said after capitulation, "but I know neither of you will rest easy."

Miss Teague smiled at that. Davey thought that her advanced age of twenty-eight probably meant no husband or children, which was a pity, because she cared. Maybe life wasn't fair to many others.

He carried that thought into the evening darkness, glad that Avon wasn't the talkative sort, either. Except tonight, he was. "It's not just you I worry about," Avon said as they trudged along, heads down against what seemed to be perpetual sleet. (Oh, why, Scotland, why?) "I'm going to sweep again in that other ward, the one with the woman and two children visiting. Why would those students hang around that bedside, as well? That patient might not be destitute, but I doubt they are wealthy."

"They could be ward-walking, same as I am," Davey said. "Walking and observing, maybe stopping to say something, or listening to a heartbeat. Or bringing over a bottle to piss in." He smiled at Avon's frown. "It's part of the duty, Avon."

"Maybe yours. Not mine."

Now was a good time to ask again. "What do you see yourself doing? I'm still curious," he asked his little friend, as they walked carefully up the front steps, mindful of ice.

Avon shrugged. "Master Six says I am fearless."

"You are," Davey replied. "You stood your ground at Trafalgar before Smitty and Master Six on the deck to make sure no sharpshooter found a target as they helmed us through the fleet."

"I don't know yet," Avon said, then grinned as he looked around and opened the first closet inside the infirmary. He came out with broom and dustpan. "You will agree that I can sweep!"

Davey let himself inside the indigent ward, bracing against the noisome stew of age and death, with a dollop of disease. Mr. Coffin sat beside a cot, head down. To disturb him, or not? Davey pulled up a stool and sat, pleased to see his professor brighten up. *I'll go first*, Davey thought. "You are only doing your job," he said, before Mr. Coffin could speak. "I'm sorry, sir. I know you have to follow through tomorrow and complete the dissection."

"Do I? I am wondering if I am straying from my own tenets. If what Avon says is true…"

"Avon doesn't lie."

"…then I assisted in the dissection of a man who was murdered against all order and reason."

"You didn't know, sir."

"I know now, and that is my dilemma." He threw up his hands. "We dissect only the homeless indigent, plus murderers and thieves, who were condemned and hanged and their bodies given to science. It is legal."

Davey didn't know what to say, after their whispered conversation. He sat beside his professor, listening to the sound of Avon sweeping. Mr.

Coffin heard it, too. He raised his head and nodded to Avon, who nodded back and continued his quiet work.

"Thee is fortunate in thy friends, Davey, even if thee has to import them from England." he said. He gestured toward the end of the ward, where someone else sat. "Maybe thee has another friend. Edwin Hamilton came earlier. I believe he wants thee to help him memorize bones and muscles." He gestured with his head. "As my assistant in Bones, thee owes him thy help."

"Very well." Davey walked to the end of the row, pausing once to listen to a man whose breathing was more labored than usual. He checked the chart, hoping not to see what Avon saw. Luckily the chart listed nothing beyond the prosaic: *In the eventuality, St. Luke's.*

Edwin looked up as he approached, and indicated a stool beside the bed of a boy with labored breathing. He sat in silence for a moment, then, "I haven't treated you any better than the others, and you have still helped me."

Davey shrugged, unsure of himself now that someone from his class seemed willing to talk.

"And…and then when I saw your scarred back …." Edwin looked away. "I am sorry for my actions."

Never before had anyone apologized to Davey for anything. He savored the moment because he was human, then said, "Apology accepted."

"I came here principally to ask if you and I could study together somewhere. The bones are vexing me."

Davey relished this little victory as well. "We can. I am here every evening, Monday through Thursday, from six to ten of the clock. Come here at half after five, and we can study."

"I was thinking perhaps at your house. It is noisy in my boarding house," Edwin said.

Davey nearly said aye, then changed his mind. Whether it was wariness, that bugaboo of all workhouse boys, or out of respect for Miss Teague, whose permission he needed, he could not have said. He shook his head, and saw a sudden flash of anger cross Edwin's face. It was gone in a moment; he had probably imagined it, considering how suspicious *he* was of others and their motives.

"I think not," he said, picking his way carefully through his own field of thorns. "I'm staying with a household where the old maid is a gorgon and fixed in her ways." (*Forgive me, Miss Teague,* he thought.) "It would be better if we meet here. Tomorrow before I ward walk. Half after five?"

What could Edwin do but agree? "Tomorrow night then?"

Davey nodded. The boy in the bed began to stir restlessly. Edwin backed away, as if afraid of the child, or perhaps afraid of his poverty. Davey looked at the chart. "Time to dose him," he said. "This won't take a moment."

Edwin backed away farther. "I wouldn't know what to do. Tomorrow." He turned and walked fast away from the thrashing child.

"And you want to be a physician?" Davey said under his breath. He measured out the laudanum and held the child in his lap as he drank the potion, cuddling the child as he had wanted to be cuddled. It wasn't so hard to do the right thing.

He looked up, feeling eyes on him. The man in the next bed watched. "Good lad," he said, and closed his eyes. When the boy slept, Davey noted his administration of laudanum on the chart and resumed his walking. Soon enough, it was time to leave. Mr. Coffin motioned to him by the door. "The evening steward is here," he said. "Where is Avon?"

He had forgotten about Avon. "He went into the other ward."

"Let's find him."

It was never easy to spot Avon, even with a broom, but there he was, sweeping down the row, blending in, becoming part of the atmosphere almost.

Davey gestured to the door. Avon gathered the sweepings into a barrel as Mr. Coffin watched, amused. "He could stay here all day and people would forget him entirely," he whispered. "He's no bumbler."

Broom in hand, Avon stopped by a bed midway down the row. They joined him. "This is the man I mentioned. His wife was here earlier, but no children. She sat a long while. She cried."

He indicated the chart and Mr. Coffin lifted it on its chain. "I see diagnosis, pharmacoepia and times administered, place of burial in the event of... Ah yes, St. Andrews Church. All respectable. All in order." He looked at Avon with a question in his eyes. "What, lad?"

"Those two students showed up as soon as the woman left," Avon said. "A third one joined them, but only briefly."

"Students other than Davey come here to ward walk," Mr. Coffin said. "This is a teaching hospital, after all."

"They wouldn't dare snuff him out and drag him to Dissection Three, would they?" Avon sighed. "Am I too suspicious?"

"Perhaps," Mr. Coffin said. "This man is safe. He has family around him. They are not rich, or he would not be here, but they are obviously respectable."

Avon looked unconvinced. "As I said, it's a teaching hospital," Mr. Coffin repeated. "Come now. It's late and Miss Teague will be missing thee."

"I go this way," Mr. Coffin said, once outside. "Please thank Miss Teague for letting me eat with thee tonight."

Avon watched Mr. Coffin walk away. "We are luckier than he is. He's lonely."

Aye, he is, Davey thought. *I wonder what he will do tomorrow at the dissection.*

Chapter Twenty-six

Josiah Coffin spent a restless night, winding himself tight his sheets until he wondered who was strangling him and why. *I wish I were not alone tonight,* he thought. *I am not liking myself particularly.*

Well, that was a silly notion. Those of the Friendly persuasion were not supposed to think about themselves overmuch. Generally, he didn't, but good Lord, what now? The thought of continuing to participate in that unhallowed dissection, even as an assistant, made his blood run in chunks.

It was one thing to dissect dead convicts and the poor and destitute who had no family. One could easily argue it was for the betterment of science and for the benefit of the living, no questions asked. He had no doubts that Thomas Perkins, the man whose identity had parted company with his remains, had been teetering upon death. Only days before, he noted the same thing, giving him only a little longer on earth. It was another matter to end any life, no matter how close to its conclusion before its actual time. This was evil, and he wanted no part of it.

He glared at the ceiling until his perhaps too-finely-honed sense of duty took over and he prepared for the day, unsure of what he would do in Dissection Three. He took heart that it was Wednesday, which meant breakfast with a friend of long standing. He wondered if he could ask the friend, a barrister, what the law might say about over-enthusiasm to end a life that was expiring anyway. He had to smile, imagining how often his friend Walt was plagued by supposed friends seeking legal advice.

Breakfast was always as the laconically named Edinburgh's Finest … Something. The inn was old and the actual name long since vanished from memory, along with the signboard. He ordered the usual – shirred eggs and too much bacon – and waited for his friend.

He heard Walt before he saw him, with his thump tap, thump tap, product of infantile paralysis that had weakened his right leg and turned his foot inward. Perhaps it was a strange friendship. Walter Scott dated him by nearly five years, Walter the limping student of law, and Josiah, the first Friend ever hired by Edinburgh University College of Medicine, and regarded with some suspicion.

He could have ordered Walt's usual breakfast for him, except that the innkeeper knew what he wanted and brought that parsimonious bowl of oatmeal as soon as Walt heaved his tall frame onto the waiting chair.

His greeting was the usual one: "Josiah, all that bacon will send you to an early grave, and you the physician."

"I wanted to order even more this morning," Josiah said, hopeful his friend would read his discomfort and offer an opening. Oh aye, here it came.

"Troubles? Did you finally find a nice Quaker girl and she won't have a man of science?"

Josiah didn't care for ribbing about his religion, except from Walt. When Walt teased him this time, Josiah thought of Miss Teague and wondered how she was faring with the Gunwharf Rats and Davey Ten's own moral dilemma.

He decided not to blurt out everything at once. "No Friendly girls around Edinburgh," he joked back. Then he couldn't wait. "Walt, thee is a judge and legal administrator," he began.

Walt raised his hand as if to shoo him away. "Not here, laddie, only in Selkirk." He peered closer at Josiah. "You look as though you did not sleep last night."

"I didn't." As Walt ate his oatmeal and washed it down with beer, Josiah laid bare Avon's declaration that a medical student had smothered an old man who was dying anyway, and falsified the record, assigning his body to the dissection table, even though they assured his wife that he would be buried in the pauper's cemetery.

Walt Scott took it in and became the barrister he was. "Any other witnesses?"

"A former workhouse lad from Portsmouth."

Walt winced at that. "No one would probably believe such a witness, should he raise the issue." He leaned forward, interested. "How are you involved??

"I am assisting in the dissection of the old fellow, and I do believe the workhouse lad."

Walt shook his head. "Unless there is another witness, or some evidence that a magistrate will consider without injuring himself in a fit of laughter, you have no recourse." He looked closer at his friend. "You don't want to continue the dissection, do you?"

"No, but Walt, I am here on sufferance. I fear I must."

Walter's tone turned from professional to personal. "No more credibility than you had in that philosophy class you told me about, because no one likes a Quaker, and they can't tell you why?"

"Thee has it." What could he say? There was another matter. "Walt, I have been wondering where these bodies come from, that we dissect. I know we get the newly hanged, or the paupers and the friendless, but this one wasn't friendless."

"Pity that." After looking around at the crowded public room, Walt leaned closer. "Don't think me macabre, but this interests me. One of your faculty makes the legal arrangements, I assume."

"Sir Lionel Henderson. I do not care for the man, but I do not see him as someone actively involved in uh, procurement."

"Josiah, you're such a babe," Walt chided. "You do not think ill of many, do you?"

"Very few. We Friends regard people as possessing the qualities of deity, if such qualities are allowed to prosper."

"As a legal administrator in Selkirk, I can tell you of grave robbers who make a living wage providing the newly dead to this very institution."

"No!" Maybe he was a babe. Josiah felt his face growing hot with embarrassment. "Thee calls them Resurrectionists. I have heard of them."

"Aye, body snatchers. We at law learn of them after the fact, although I know of a few. Slippery fellows. I have yet to see any in court." Walt pulled out his timepiece. "I must meet my father for a trip to court soon, where we will prosecute evildoers who cheat landlords and grocers." He chuckled. "The bread and butter of the law is mundane. Don't look so discouraged, friend! Perhaps be a little more suspicious if you can. You already have a hint of chicanery among medical students, if your workhouse friend is telling the truth."

Josiah laid his money on the table, adding more for Walter's oatmeal and beer. He waved off his friend's protests. "Walt, I will not be one of those friends who teases out legal advice for free. I believe thee is telling me to be wary and pay attention and not so trusting of other's motives."

"I believe I am. Oh, I do have some excellent news."

"I could use some." They walked from the public room, Josiah first, clearing a discreet path for his friend with the limp. "What is your news?"

"You're not a romantic, but my poem – I've bored you with it before - is to be published in May. If you know a sweet lady who might be interested in "The Lady of the Lake," let me know. I can sign my name to it." He gave a small salute as they parted ways. "Maybe I'll be famous someday!"

Wednesday was a slow day for Josiah until Bones, followed by that Dissection Three he did not want to attend. Because he wasn't needed until afternoon, he went to the Royal Infirmary, walking the wards, seeing order among students, nurses, and stewards that soothed his heart and mind. He nodded to other physicians taking time out from their own practices to ward walk as a community service. It gladdened his heart to know that he was employed by the finest college of medicine in Europe. Then he thought of Davey Ten, and he knew there was work to do, if all students could ever be considered equal.

Davey was waiting for him when he arrived early for class. He had already arranged the arm from yesterday, with the addition of a leg, obviously female, from some other poor person.

"I like Avon," Josiah said. "Does thee think he is interested in medicine, too?"

"Lately, I think he is more interested in justice, sir," Davey said. "Sir?"

"Aye?"

"I know you have to finish the dissection upstairs," the lad said.

"I do. I've been informed by a friend of mine, a barrister, who says we need more evidence of chicanery." He nearly told him more, but it could keep.

Class was subdued. To Josiah's relief, he saw little, if any, resentment among the students as Davey quietly went about assisting those with questions. He knew why. Before he went to his class, the Materia Medica professor had taken him aside and told him what happened yesterday when Davey Ten bared his scarred back. "I've never seen the like," the old fellow said, with a shake of his head.

To Josiah's disappointment, the professor had taken a different lesson away. "Do you think the College of Medicine is wise to admit workhouse lads? He's upsetting our students of superior background."

Josiah bit back his harsh reply, realizing, in that moment, just how much he had bitten back in the past few years, to fulfill his own ambition. The knowledge humiliated him, even as it strengthened his resolve. "Our world is changing, sir."

I am changing with it, he thought later in Dissection Three, as he stood by the dissection table, assisting as Thomas Perkins was further dismembered by the dissector. *Am I brave enough?*

He decided he was. Two Gunwharf Rats had made that amply clear to him, whether they knew it or not. When the unhallowed dissection ended, the professor dismissed his third-year class and Davey filed out with the rest, after a worried glance. Josiah gave him a reassuring smile.

"Professor McGrath, we are done with Mr. Perkins, are we not?"

"Aye, the corpse."

"Mr. Perkins," Josiah repeated. "I am claiming the body for burial."

McGrath stared at him and laughed. "Good God, man, he is in sections and pieces. He's a pauper! It's the incinerator for him."

"No. I will have him buried in St. Luke's at my expense," Josiah said, his terror gone now, because he knew – and more to the point his Inner Light knew – that this was the proper place for a man sent to an early death simply because he was poor. "I will make arrangements as soon as we finish here."

He waited for the wrath of the senior professor to descend on him. He did not wait long. McGrath pointed a crusty scalpel at him. "This is unheard of! I was going to cut off his head and send it down to you for Bones. As a favor."

"We will manage without it, Professor," he replied, "but thank thee."

"You are here for the education of students, Mr. Coffin. You forget yourself," McGrath said. "Don't think this will go unnoticed by our chancellor."

"I trust thee will inform him," he snapped back, surprised at how good it felt and keenly aware that his days at the college of medicine were now numbered. "Good day. I have arrangements to make."

It was easily done. The undertaker blanched a little when Josiah took him upstairs an hour later, but money changed hands. The man left with Mr. Perkins in a bag, and the promise to plant him in St. Luke's. Josiah only wished there was some way for the illiterate widow to know.

Lighter of purse but happier of heart, Josiah started for his modest dwelling but changed his mind. He went instead to Wilmer Street and knocked.

He thought – hoped – that Miss Teague would answer the door, and she did. He gave a slight nod and gestured for her to come out, even though Edinburgh's everlasting drizzle threatened. *I've spent my life in rain*, he thought. *I'm tired of it.*

She looked up at the same sky, then at him, and he felt better for the first time in days, maybe months. He saw the amusement in her eyes, and the fun. He had an unaccountable urge to rest his head in her lap and pour out his troubles. He kicked that thought to the curb with some reluctance. He wondered for a moment why he was even here. This was a matter between him and the college of medicine, not a kind spinster mandated to house two nautical waifs, who seemed to be enjoying what some ladies might consider an ordeal if he read her expression correctly.

"I don't mind getting wet in August, which this is not," she said. She took his hand and pulled him inside. "Davey is upstairs studying and Avon and Mrs. Perry went to the market. She left me with tea in the sitting room. I will get another cup, unless you don't mind drinking out of the saucer."

It was silly and whimsical, and he wanted more. She returned and poured him a cup. He sat back and enjoyed the moment, before thinking that she might be too busy. "If I am wasting thy time…"

"Hardly. What is the matter, sir?"

Sir seemed too formal, even though she said it in a lighthearted way. He took another sip, swallowing all his reticence along with it, and told her about Mr. Perkins's fate. "He will be buried tomorrow in St. Luke's. The remains of dissections are usually incinerated. I could not in good conscience allow that and so I told Professor McGrath. He was not pleased with my presumption."

Her eyes were so kind. She leaned forward, and he wanted her to touch him. "Excuse my atrocious cant, but is he going to have you sacked?"

"I fear my days are numbered," he told her, and in the telling felt himself relieved as never before. "We are shorthanded because Sir Lionel is indisposed, so I will perhaps be allowed to finish the term."

She folded her hands in her lap and gave him that clear-eyed gaze, the same one she fixed upon Davey and Avon that he had noticed, and if he were honest, envied. He had her whole attention. Had he been a puppy instead of a physician teetering this side of thirty-four, he would have wriggled.

He finished his tea. Why was it that tea brewed in a lovely house on Wilmer Street tasted so much better than tea in his modest quarters cluttered with books? Maybe it was the civilized use of cup *and* saucer. "I'd rather Davey and Avon didn't know."

"Why?"

"I don't want them to blame themselves for my dismissal, if it comes to that, and it likely will. I, the most junior of instructors and even worse, a Friend, should never challenge the order of things, or heaven forbid, call into question the disposal of paupers."

"But what will you do, if that is the result of what *I* would call your Christian charity to the unfortunate among us?"

"Look for employment elsewhere," he said, and stood up.

Did he see disappointment in her eyes? "I will be sorry to see you go," she said, as she walked him to the door.

"Thee barely knows me. Why?" Did he just *ask* her that? Who in the world was thinking out loud for him? He was beginning to amaze himself.

"I know a good heart, Mr. Coffin," she said. "You have one."

He walked home in amazement at his brazen behavior, looking back once at the house on Wilmer Street. Did he really, actually, kiss her cheek? He sat at his desk a long time that night, paper and pen before him, thinking to write an apology. She had stood in the doorway, hand to cheek and watched him, her eyes wide with amazement.

He thought a moment, then wrote a brief note to Walt Scott instead. It was an easy matter to find a lad on the street, hand him a shilling and ask him to deliver it. *If you are free, what about breakfast on Friday?* he scribbled. *See you in two days. I have some questions.*

Chapter Twenty-seven

Over eggs and bacon, porridge and beer two days later, Walt heard him out. "You do the kind and honorable thing, and now you fear for your position," he said, then belched quietly into his napkin.

"There was a distinct chill in Dissection Three yesterday, as we mulled over a woman dead of syphilis." It was more than that, and so he admitted it to his friend. Sir Winston had made him a figure of ridicule, asking the students, "Should we put this vile female specimen in a down-padded coffin when we're done? Mr. Coffin would perhaps agree."

Josiah shook his head, remembering. Some of the students laughed. Others seemed appalled. From his perch in the back row, Davey looked away, his expression so sad, sad enough to make Josiah wonder if the lad was thinking about his own mother, whoever she was. "I wish I could help you, Josiah," Walt said, "but I don't know how."

Josiah ate his last piece of bacon. "The thing is, I believe Avon. Last night he swept in that what I call 'The Deserving Poor Ward,' with the dying man and his family. He said the same two students were there. I know they cannot harvest this man for Dissection Three, because his family would never countenance such an atrocity. What does thee think is their aim with this poor fellow?"

Walt took another swig of beer and belched. "Best breakfast I know," he said. Josiah knew better than to interrupt the silence that followed; he knew Walt well. He sat forward when his friend's face brightened.

"Tell me something, Josiah. Have there been times when the college of medicine lacks bodies for dissection?"

"Now and then." Josiah attempted a joke that went entirely against everything he believed and regretted it instantly. What was he turning into? "Edinburgh needs more felons and criminals, I suppose. Oh, forgive that."

Walt gave him a measuring look that made Josiah cringe inside. "Josiah, are you certain you are in the right profession?"

"I have been wondering lately, not so much about medicine, but my current application of it. Aye, we sometimes lack sufficient exhibits to educate our students."

"What do you do in those cases?"

"We might dissect dogs or calves. They reveal considerable knowledge about the circulation of blood and provide practice in wielding a scalpel."

"But you need bodies."

"We do. These are modern times, and not the Middle Ages, where physicians feared for their lives if they even suggested opening up a human body."

It was Walt's turn to hesitate. "Do you, um, ever open corpses that have the whiff of formaldehyde about them? Perhaps that are even a little too tidy? Maybe you only expose their limbs to dissection?"

He didn't want to think about it. He also didn't care to remember a recent corpse on the dissecting table with hair neatly clubbed at the back of his neck in the style of the last generation. He knew without being told that the man had come from a freshly tilled grave. God help him, he knew. He also knew Walter Scot was a man of great discretion and his friend.

"We have dissected people I know were resurrected from burial grounds," he said softly, unwilling to be overheard. "Walt, what am I to do when I have a class of students eager to learn, and I pull back a sheet from someone robbed from a grave?"

"I doubt the other physicians question it," Walt said. He finished his beer. "However, I expect…"

"…better of me," Josiah concluded. He sighed and leaned back against the bench. "If it's any consolation to thee, I am certain to lose my position now because I have finally taken a feeble stand against dissecting the ill-gotten." He thought of earnest Avon March – guttersnipe bastard to some – appalled at the injustice done to an old man and his widow. He took a long look at his friend and breakfast companion. "Thee knows something, doesn't thee?"

"Aye, lad." Walt signaled for more beer, and after a questioning glance at Josiah, made that two.

"For breakfast?"

"Try it."

Josiah did, briefly considering the scruples of beer for breakfast. He took a swig when it came, knowing that beer for breakfast was still better than dissecting corpses he had no business separating from their parts.

"I do know something," Walt said, after a prim wipe of his lips. "As an officer of the petty court in Selkirk, I have heard complaints about grave-robbing. It shouldn't surprise you that some of the meeker citizens of that shire have considerable wrath directed at the college of medicine."

"I am a babe in the woods," Josiah said, thinking to himself, *Or perhaps I was happy to give the matter no thought.* That notion stung, as it should have.

"The better-heeled parishioners surround burial plots of the recently dead with iron bars," Walt said. "Some hire guards. The respectable poor cannot afford that, and must take their chances with the Resurrectionists."

Resurrectionists. Trust the Scots to give grave robbing a fitting name. He thought of the woman and children Avon had told him about in the ward he had no permission to visit, because a Quaker physician could expect no favors, being on sufferance himself. *I must find out who those students are,* he told himself, as he listened to Walt. *I can't ignore it.*

"This isn't a matter of law that interests me too much," Walt was saying, as Josiah dragged his thoughts back. "The Resurrectionists are a slippery lot, and in the favor of many on your faculty."

"I understand. What do you know?"

"I know of one I would like to send to Australia on the next convict ship – Wee Willie," Walt said.

"Singular name," Josiah commented, and took another drink. Perhaps he should order beer to accompany his eggs and bacon – tasty.

Walt laughed. "Rumor has it that he got the name from trollops and prossies who were less than impressed with his, um, manly anatomy." He rolled his eyes. "Whatever his attributes or lack thereof, Wee Willie has robbed many a grave. I'd like to see that end."

"He steals hopes and dreams, and no one's the wiser," Josiah said. "For shame."

"Can you do something about this?" Walt asked. "If your goose is already cooked, why not go out in style?" He turned solemn then, after a glance at his timepiece. "I must go. Wee Willie does something else: He takes souvenirs from the graves he robs. It's one thing to earn a dishonest living by preying on the dead. It's another to make sport of it." He rapped the table and stood up. "Keep me in touch with what you decide, my friend."

After subbing in first-year circulation of blood in Materia Medica, Josiah made his way to Bones to discover that Professor McGrath must have informed the entire college of his insistence on burying Mr. Perkins, students included. He had prepared to spend time discussing the female leg, cut open yesterday. At his suggestion, Davey was to prepare a short lecture on the bones of the feet, using the skeleton that held permanent residence in the classroom.

In its place was a turnip and four toads. Davey sat on the stool by the table, his frustration evident. No one else was in the room. Davey held out a placard. "Sir, I found this attached to the skeleton."

The placard had one word: Quaker.

Josiah took the placard and tore it in half, stuffing it in the ashcan. He took a deep breath and another, humiliated and angered at the same time. "It would seem I am to suffer for the burial of Mr. Perkins," he said when he could speak.

"Sir, you wouldn't be in this predicament if Avon and I weren't here," Davey said. "He came to skulk. What he learned is reflecting on you. We wouldn't for the world do this."

"I know thee wouldn't. It isn't thy fault, so don't blame yourself." Josiah heard students in the hall. "I think Avon has unintentionally reminded me that I have been remiss in my own conscience," he said. "I have been making a mockery of death." He gave what he hoped was a reassuring smile, praying to lessen the stricken look in Davey's eyes. "Now we will deal with frogs. I do not doubt that we can."

I am in charge here, he thought calmly as the students filed in. He could tell by the way some averted their eyes and others smirked, that they were in on the joke. Everyone, including students, must know he had seen to the burial of a pauper. He understood as never before what Davey Ten had suffered last year, simply because he was different.

Josiah gamely downed a sizeable scoop of humiliation, reminded himself that others of his faith had suffered far worse, and held up the toad by one leg.

"Gentlemen, today we will dissect these toads. As we do so, let us also consider the challenge of working in small nooks and crannies of the human body." To his relief, he saw some smiles. He set down the toad and patted it, then tossed the turnip over his shoulder. "I'll save root vegetables for some other professor. I dislike turnips."

The smiles grew wider, and he took heart. "Mr. Ten, divide us into groups, please, about four to a toad. Gentlemen, choose a leader amongst thee and pick up a scalpel." His own cheery temperament took over, something he hadn't felt in a long while. "Although these specimens have shuffled off their mortal coil, it will amaze you what happens when we touch some of their nerves and muscles."

His mood lightened. "I have it on good authority that in Louisiana in the United States of America, some people eat frog legs. Unless you are ravenous, let us forgo that culinary delight, shall we?"

His reward was good-humored laughter. A quick glance told him that two students – among them John Yerby and Richard Sterling – did not seem to get the joke. He gave each a measuring look in turn. Sterling looked away, and John glared at him.

Well, well. He held John's gaze a little longer, deriving small satisfaction when the lad finally couldn't meet his gaze. An idea formed in his mind, as Josiah wondered by what scheme he could visit Miss Teague and her Gunwharf Rats. There had to be a way that a modest man could intrude on a kind lady's domain.

Chapter Twenty-eight

Avon came on an errand from Miss Teague, or he wouldn't have been sitting in plain sight in the park just beyond the university, waiting for Davey. There he came finally, striding along the sidewalk beside the student he had helped with bones in the indigent ward. Something about the way the other student walked – maybe it was the angle of his head – seemed familiar to Avon.

Perhaps it was an overabundance of caution; more like it was the wariness born in him from his ignominious childhood. Whatever the reason, Avon eased from the bench to a spot behind a tree with significant girth, the better to see and not be seen.

Avon watched, wondering if he was losing some of his skills, stuck here in Edinburgh. He couldn't remember where he had seen the student before. No matter. He had time, and he was patient.

He joined Davey beyond the spot where the two parted. "Who is he?" Avon asked, in lieu of a greeting.

"Edwin Hamilton. He wanted to thank me for helping him pass one of Mr. Coffin's bones examinations. Muscles of the hands and feet are next week." Davey's expression turned introspective, shy almost. "He could even be a friend, p'raps." He regarded Avon. "No skulking today?"

"Only a little. Miss Teague wanted to know where Mr. Coffin lives, so you could deliver a message."

They walked more slowly toward Wilmer Street, now that Edwin had gone the other way. "Do you know where Mr. Coffin lives?"

Avon nodded; certainly he knew. "I followed him a week ago."

"Why?"

Avon shrugged, not really sure why he had done that. "Just curious. It's a modest flat on the main floor. He should close his draperies." He grinned because he was a tidy Rat. "He doesn't make his bed and there are books everywhere." Should he say more? Why not? "Miss Teague could organize him in a minute."

They both laughed. "What's her message?" Davey asked.

"She wants to invite him to dinner tonight."

"Let us deliver it. He wants cheering up, I think." Davey slowed his steps and told Avon about the humiliation of the frogs. "He turned the whole disaster into a wonderful lecture on muscle power." His frown reappeared. "Dissection Three was probably a trial for him, well, anyone with any sensibility. The professor made light of the body of a prostitute. Not a good day for our professor. I don't know what Quakers believe, but I doubt they are debauchers."

Avon was certain Davey knew as little about his own parentage as he did. *That prostitute could have been our mother,* he thought.

They crossed the park and came to a boulevard full of wagon traffic, a less cultivated area than Wilmer Street, with its stately single houses.

"I would have thought Mr. Coffin could afford more," Davey said. "His suits are good quality and he is a gentleman."

"He can afford more," Avon assured him. "I told you he should keep his draperies drawn, especially since his flat is on the ground floor."

"How did you learn that much?"

"I stole a dozen apples from a merchant and a basket, too, and told the landlord this was a delivery for Mr. Coffin, and could I leave it outside his door," Avon said. He smiled at Davey's amazement. "Davey, we *are* Gunwharf Rats. I am *not* dead to all reason. Once I knew which was his flat, I returned the apples and basket, with no one the wiser."

"Avon, you will always amaze me," Davey said. "So you either jimmied his lock or looked in his window."

"The window. It faces the back of the house. I don't know why he hasn't been robbed before. There was a very fine silver hairbrush and comb in plain sight. He even leaves pounds sterling on his desk."

"P'raps it is a Quaker sort of thing," Davey said. "I think they are supposed to lead lives with no vanity. He probably chooses to live there."

"That's it. Number Five," Avon said. Suddenly shy, he stayed back as Davey mounted the shallow steps and knocked.

Mr. Coffin came to the door in shirtsleeves and wearing slippers. "Davey, come in. I didn't know you knew where I lived."

"I didn't. Avon found you."

"And where is he?"

"Oh, around."

To Avon's surprise and odd gratification, Mr. Coffin stepped outside, looked to the alley, then back to the ashcans. He waved Avon over.

"I thought you wouldn't see me, sir," Avon said.

"I wanted to find thee," Mr. Coffin said. "Thee needn't skulk around me, lad, not ever. Come inside."

The odd feeling returned. *I would never have to ever skulk again, if I had a father like Mr. Coffin,* he thought. His delight grew as Mr. Coffin touched his shoulder. No one ever touched him except Master Six, and of course Mrs. Six, who had at one time or other enveloped all the Rats in her generous embrace. Who else? Miss Teague, hesitantly at first when she went to their room at night and tucked the blanket higher. Now she did it with no thought, as though a touch had become second nature to her, as well. He doubted she ever touched her feral nephews.

"Gentlemen, what is thy message? Sit, if thee wishes."

Say what you will about Mr. Coffin's clutter, it was mostly paper clutter, and his chairs *were* comfortable, Avon discovered. Davey held out a note for Mr. Coffin. Avon watched Mr. Coffin's face, pleased to see the frown line disappear. He looked from one to the other.

"Miss Teague has invited me to dinner tonight," he told them. "I hope she won't mind if we leave for the indigent ward directly afterward. Duty calls, Davey." To Avon's delight, he included him. "Avon, I need thee, as well. I have an idea." He tapped the note. "I wonder how Miss Teague knew I wanted to visit at Wilmer Street tonight, anyway."

"Master Six tells us Rats that women have special powers, sir," Avon said. "You will have to meet him someday, and Mrs. Six."

"I already have, Avon," Mr. Coffin said, to Davey's evident amazement. "I wanted to know thee better, Davey, and how I could help." His glance took in Avon next. "And what did I learn but that there would be two of thee? Let's not keep a kind lady waiting."

Dinner was, as Mrs. Six would say, ever so more-ish. Even though they ate in the kitchen as usual, and Mrs. Perry glared at Avon when he forgot to put his napkin in his lap right away, Miss Teague seemed to sparkle. True, she was as thin as ever, but her eyes seemed somehow softer, especially as she smiled at Mr. Coffin. Avon glanced at Davey, who winced when she stated her opinion firmly on the matter of Napoleon and his machinations. To Avon's relief, Mr. Coffin showed no disgust that a woman should have an opinion about anything. He even seemed to relish the notion. The two of them argued mildly about what the British Army should do next on the Continent, Miss Teague not giving an inch with her ideas, and Mr. Coffin holding firm with his.

If anything, they both sparkled, as if energized by good conversation, accompanied as it was by excellent food. Mrs. Perry had outdone herself. Maybe it was the softer glow of beeswax candles in silver candleholders Avon hadn't seen before, instead of tallow candles and plain sticks. Whatever it was, Miss Teague looked almost pretty.

The magic continued as they adjourned to the sitting room. Mr. Coffin laughed when Miss Teague told him that he and Davey had her total permission to sit on the carpet. "The sitting room was always my particular plague, too," she told their dinner guest. "I always wanted to sit on the floor, but my father, God rest him, was too proper. It is, after all, a sitting room."

They all laughed. Mr. Coffin held up one finger and said, "I suggest we follow suit, Miss Teague," and sat on the carpet. After a moment's delighted silence, Miss Teague did, too, declaring, "I should have done this years ago."

Mrs. Perry gave them all a great stare when she came into the sitting room with a tea tray. She took a look around, served tea, then joined them on the floor, when Mr. Coffin insisted. "We are equal," he told her. "I need to talk to all of thee, for there is something afoot."

He deferred to Miss Teague first. "If there was something particular thee needs to tell me – considering that it was thy invitation that brought me here – excuse my overreach."

"Nothing, really," she said. Avon watched with real appreciation as she rosied up with such a comment, and became, if only for a moment, almost lovely. "I am discovering, sir – p'raps the Gunwharf Rats are reminding me – that I like company."

They all looked expectantly at Mr. Coffin, who addressed himself to Miss Teague. "How much does thee know about what is going on at the college?" he asked.

"I know that you have been censured for calling the dissection of a poor man to the professor's attention, when he should have been properly buried. Then you saw to his burial." She shuddered and rubbed her arms. "I think most of us not connected to medical education probably assume that burial would always be the case."

"It is a rougher world than even I knew, when I joined the faculty here," Mr. Coffin admitted. "Professor McGrath, the dissector, as much as told me that my...my – he called it insubordination – would make this my last term here. Apparently, I am not to coddle dregs of our society, even the dead ones."

"A wretched man is Professor McGrath," she said.

Avon heard no self-pity in Mr. Coffin's conversation, only something that sounded more like apology. "I tried hard to be accepted here," he said to them all. "My grades were outstanding, and I had the ear of several academicians from other august institutions, including London University, where I matriculated, who wrote glowing references. I made no errors in an oral examination the faculty administered."

"Then you should have received the position, as you did," Miss Teague pointed out.

"Recent events have forced me to consider my motives," he said. It was Mr. Coffin's turn to rosy up. "I am ashamed to admit that I was also propelled by pride, and not just the service of mankind. I wanted to be the first person in the Society of Friends to be accepted in this august center of medicine. That is vanity to a Friend."

"Sounds like human nature to me," Miss Teague said.

He flashed her a smile, but his eyes were bleak. "I knew that some of the bodies we dissected – all for the good of scientific education, mind you – had to have been the result of grave robbing. There are obvious signs of body snatching, and I overlooked them." He put his hand on Avon's shoulder. "And thee, lad, thee was so distressed that a dying man was sent to a premature death." He looked away. "I fear I would have accepted that, too, had I not realized how much it bothered thee. I have arrived at the decision that I am not the man I should be, certainly not the Quaker. This place has changed me, and not for the better."

"I would say you are better than most of us." She said it so quietly, so kindly.

"That is quite the nicest thing anyone has told me in recent years," Josiah said. He patted Avon's shoulder. "*I* would say that Portsmouth's Gunwharf Rats have found themselves a pleasant refuge at 158 Wilmer Street."

"We have," Davey said, his voice equally quiet. "At school, some of the students are even starting to talk to me. It's a small thing, but it matters."

"As it should. Miss Teague, I know that my days here are numbered, but Davey has a bright future ahead of him. What about thee, Avon, what does thee want?"

I want to stay here with Miss Teague, Avon thought, but wisely did not say. He ventured another thought even more absurd: *I would stay with you, too, Mr. Coffin.* Another absurdity followed. *I wouldn't skulk.*

"Well?"

It was also absurd, but he could not deny it. "I would like to see justice done for Mr. Perkins."

Chapter Twenty-nine

"Let us do that, son," Mr. Coffin said. "Here is what I have in mind." Avon held his breath at the loveliness of that word. Mr. Coffin seemed not aware of what he had said. Avon knew it was a common enough endearment. He had heard the Sixes call their Gunwharf Rats sons, so he knew it was an affectionate term. Son.

"I have a friend name of Walter Scott. He is a barrister and a great student of the law, at least when he is not writing poetry. He told me a few things about grave robbing only this morning." He gave Miss Teague a deferential nod. "Are we too ghoulish for thee?"

Avon laughed when the proper Miss Teague shook her head. "If there is any way to help, count me in."

"It won't come to that," Mr. Coffin assured her. "I merely want thee to know what we are plotting. Davey and I are going ward walking in the indigent ward, as we do, of an evening. I need Avon in the other ward, sweeping and skulking, and I need Davey there, too, briefly."

"Why?"

"There are two students who show up there, perhaps the same two students who, um, did in Mr. Perkins," he said. "I want to know who they are, and Davey, you would know."

"I'm no dab hand at skulking like Avon," Davey said. Avon heard no reluctance, but the doubt was obvious.

"I don't even know when these students will appear," Mr. Coffin said, "and I could be entirely wrong about the matter. Let's give it a few days."

Davey nodded.

Miss Teague rose from the floor, too, Avon quick to notice how Mr. Coffin gave her an immediate hand up. She smoothed down her skirts and asked the logical question. "Why do you want me to know all this, sir?"

"I value thy good judgment," he said promptly, seemed to hesitate, then plunged on. "I am counting on thee for advice and opinion, for I know thee will not hesitate to give it."

Miss Teague laughed, which seemed to return them all to a comfortable place. She shook her finger at him in good fun. "My father always said I was too full of opinion, destined to drive men to distraction!" She looked at Mr. Coffin with good-natured pity. "Never tell me that Quaker men don't dodge and dart away from opinionated females!"

"I won't then," Mr. Coffin said, "even though it is true."

"You are a rare man," she told him, almost as if Avon and Davey weren't sitting there listening.

"We are all equal," Davey whispered to Avon as the two adults in the room regarded each other. "Master Six told me that." He chuckled. "And Euclid told *him*."

"Mr. Coffin and Miss Teague are, too," Avon replied, and in the saying, believed it with all his seeking heart.

Davey knew he would never be much of a skulker. After saying goodnight to Miss Teague, they walked to the Royal Infirmary just beyond the College of Medicine. "Why is it, sir, that you are not allowed to ward walk in the other ward, the one with respectable but poor people?"

"Probably for the same reason thee was shunned for an entire first year of college, and now this," Mr. Coffin said. "I am daily reminded that as a Friend, I am here on sufferance."

"I thought I was the only person so condemned," Davey said, aware that his view of the world had widened in recent weeks.

"I suspect the world is full of people like us. Maybe we should get together and form a union of some sort," Mr. Coffin joked.

I like this Mr. Coffin even more, Davey thought. *He can josh a bit. When did this happen?* He considered the matter as they walked, and decided that his professor's good humor could be dated from dinner with Miss Teague.

No matter how busy the Royal Infirmary was during the day, physicians and nurses coming and going, along with mainly upper grade students, the infirmary at night was generally a quiet place. This night was no exception. Neither was the next night, and the one following, for the rest of the week. Davey and Mr. Coffin attended the patients in the indigent ward, most of whom were fed and somnolent as night fell. Avon swept in the better ward beyond, blending into the very fabric of the walls, part of the furniture.

They decided that every hour, Davey would walk to the door of Indigent Ward B and meet Avon in the doorway of Ward A. A shrug meant nothing had changed and no one had visited Mr. Wilson – Malcolm Wilson was his name – besides his family and the physician on duty.

As much as Davey enjoyed the opportunity to learn from the quiet and ever-watchful Mr. Coffin, he looked forward to Edwin Hamilton's visit earlier each evening. Mr. Coffin had arranged for a small table and chairs in an alcove near the entrance, where he and Edwin could study together.

Davey cut stiff paper into cards, writing the names of bones or muscles on one side, and a brief description of location or other pertinent details on the back. Davey discovered soon that his fellow student's heart was not precisely in medicine. Nothing that was plainly written on the cards seemed to come easy.

One night Davey asked why, wondering if he was overstepping his bounds, but curious. What he considered so easy wasn't for Edwin, who struggled. He wasn't certain he would receive an answer. No one in his class confided in him, even though the matter of belonging bothered him less and less. There were enough students now in Bones who needed what he knew.

Edwin was silent for a while, contemplating the card. "Medical school is my father's idea," he said finally. "Not mine. My father is a printer, and he sees matriculation at this august institution…" – Davey heard the barely veiled sarcasm – "…as a step up for me." Edwin sighed and slapped down the card.

"What would you rather do?" Davey asked, even as he silently wondered why he thought Edwin had a world of choices. Maybe Edwin had no choices, either.

"I'd rather be a printer like my father," Edwin said. "I like arranging type in rows and boxes and seeing them appear on a printed page." He looked away. "My father is determined I will do better than he does, even though what he does suits me. I find the whole process of printing fascinating."

"Can't you tell him this?"

"I try. It makes him angry." He sighed. "I am to be a physician." He left the infirmary then as he always did. Davey doubted he spent any more time each night studying.

"His reluctance for medicine is my personal good fortune," Davey told Mr. Coffin and Avon as they left the infirmary that night, Mr. Coffin to go his way, and he and Avon to return to Wilmer Street and cocoa and Mrs. Perry's best biscuits, a little tradition that had begun almost with the term. "I like what I do. I wish he did."

"Medicine isn't for everyone," Mr. Coffin said. They paused at the corner. "It requires one's heart and soul." He clapped his hands. "Be ready for thy exam tomorrow in Bones. We are rapidly becoming experts in toads, mice and unfortunate dogs."

Davey watched his instructor melt into the dark night. "Avon, I think an ordinary man would bend and break under the treatment being meted out to Mr. Coffin. Here I thought I was the most put-upon specimen in the college of medicine."

Trust Avon. "What changed?"

"I did," Davey said. "I did."

The following night, everything else changed. To Davey's surprise, Avon slipped inside the indigent ward halfway through the evening and walked directly to Mr. Coffin, who bent down to listen as Avon whispered in his ear.

"Stay here, Davey," Mr. Coffin said as he followed Avon out of the ward. He returned by himself soon enough, his eyes troubled. He waited until Davey finished administering laudanum to an old wreck of a fellow with a continual cough, then took him aside.

"I must hand it to Avon. He created a minor disturbance that took everyone's attention in one direction so I could get a quick look at the students," he said. "Poor Mr. Wilson."

"You saw them?" Davey asked. "Did you recognize them?"

"Aye. There they were, John Yerby and Richard Sterling, lurking over Mr. Wilson like vultures."

"What you expected," Davey said.

"I retreated with Avon to the shadows by the door and watched them check the bedside chart but not alter it, thank God. I know they're waiting for Mr. Wilson to die. Avon's going to do us another favor, when only the patients are left in there. I need to know what that chart says."

It was a good thing they were both busy for the rest of the night, with the death of a scavenger who earned his living emptying privies and had no one to mourn him. While Davey cleaned his body, Mr. Coffin noted time of death and indicated the morgue and Dissection Three on the chart. It was completely legal, and a wise use of a body to educate physicians. He sent Davey with a note to notify the porter, who would come with a stretcher and another aide, to remove the dead man before the lights were dimmed for the night and the solitary nurse came on to knit away her night, watching occasionally.

Mr. Coffin did what he always did when someone died; Davey had seen this before and it never failed to touch his heart. Mr. Coffin sat beside the cot, his head bowed, silent for several minutes, then rested his hand on the dead man's head in a gentle farewell. *I will remember to do that, when I am back aboard ship*, Davey thought. *From the lowest seaman to the late Lord Nelson, touch matters.*

When they left the indigent ward at the end of the evening, Avon did not wait for them at the entrance of the infirmary. "Where does thee think he is?" Mr. Coffin asked, looking around.

"I don't know, sir, but he will be along," Davey replied.

"Should we worry?"

"Not yet. When he is up to something, I leave him alone."

Avon startled them both a moment later when he put his arms through theirs and tugged them away from the lamplight. Davey never doubted Avon knew what he was doing, and Mr. Coffin offered no objection.

Avon led them quickly to the corner and turned until they were out of sight of the street. "It's this," he said, and he was breathless. "I followed the students. They met with a man and the four of them stood close together on the corner."

"Four?" Davey asked. "Weren't there two students?"

"Three," Avon said. "The man must be the grave robber." He still had his arms linked through theirs and he pulled them closer. "I was standing practically behind them. The man asked when. One of the students said it would be soon. The man asked if it was still to be St. Andrew's Church and the answer was aye. Same burying ground? he asked next, and that was another aye." He took a deep breath, and another. "Then the man said, 'Let me know the funeral day, or there won't be anything for you.'"

"Payment to his young thugs, "Mr. Coffin said. "He's going to rob the grave after the burial, I am certain." He sighed, and Davey heard all the frustration. "I wish I knew a constable. Someone...."

They didn't part ways at the next corner. Mr. Coffin took a few steps toward his own flat, then turned around. "I am coming to Wilmer Street with you," he said decisively.

Miss Teague let them in the front door, surprise on her face. Since it was late, she had removed the pins from her hair, and it flowed onto her shoulders like molten gold. Davey thought Mr. Coffin spent overlong looking at her, considering the lateness of the hour. He wasn't surprised to see Miss Teague in her nightgown and robe, but he couldn't help a glance at Mr. Coffin.

Odd, that. He had the same gentle expression on his face as when he sat beside the dying man only this evening, except there was something more in his eyes, as if he looked upon a truly lovely lady and deemed it a rare privilege. Master Six looked at Mrs. Six that way. Mr. Coffin didn't need a placard strung about the neck to tell Davey this was love. He wondered if Mr. Coffin was even aware.

"I apologize for the late hour," Mr. Coffin said. "I wanted thee to be near for what I have to say."

David looked at Avon, whose face was as serious as Mr. Coffin's. There was something afoot. When both of them regarded him, Davey knew he was the target. He backed away, but Mr. Coffin rested his hands on his shoulders to hold him.

With his usual economy of words, Mr. Coffin told Miss Teague what had happened tonight. Before he was through, Mrs. Perry had joined them, standing quietly beside Avon.

"Avon noticed three students around poor Mr. Wilson's bed," Mr. Coffin finished.

"You mentioned three," Davey said. He glanced at Miss Teague, who looked as mystified as he did.

No one spoke. No one had to. Oh, surely not. "But Edwin Hamilton is my friend," Davey heard himself saying, his voice seeming high and unnatural. "He would not do something so heinous as rob a grave. He…he comes each night to study with me."

Avon shook his head, his dark eyes deep pools of sympathy. Davey closed his eyes when the tears welled up. At seventeen he knew he was too old to cry, except that he didn't feel seventeen. He felt ten, and forced into the dark punishment closet for the time he took an extra apple because he was hungry. Or even eight, when he tried to run away because his back ached from beatings, only to get more beatings as payment.

One deep breath, and another. He reminded himself that nothing about this was as terrible as Trafalgar, even though it felt much worse. "He…he didn't come to study, did he? He came to keep me occupied, so I would not go into the other ward, didn't he?"

"I assume such," Mr. Coffin said. "I hope I am wrong, but there he was, and Avon saw him. I saw him, too. Miss Teague…"

Esther Teague's arms went around him, and Davey sobbed into her shoulder. "I wanted to trust him," he cried. "I believe I did. I can't trust anyone!"

She held him close. "There are four of us in this room that you can trust," she whispered. "We will never fail you."

Mr. Coffin stepped back. Without a word, Avon started toward him, then stopped. Mrs. Perry gave him a gentle push and he found himself in the physician's arms. "I didn't want to tell Davey," he whispered. "I hate myself for what I saw."

"Kindly do not," Mr. Coffin told him. "Thee has very likely staved off the ruination of your fellow Gunwharf Rat. We do not know Edwin Hamilton's game, but we are wiser now."

He gave Davey his handkerchief. "Thine is the harder task, lad. Thee must continue to be Edwin's friend." In a moment, he clasped both Avon and Davey, as Miss Teague looked on, her face streaked with tears, too. "We want to prevent a great wrong that we know is coming to Mr. Wilson, and soon. Edwin mustn't know we are wise to the three of them."

"But what will happen to you, Mr. Coffin?" Avon asked.

"My course is already set," he replied.

"Please don't tell me you are leaving," Miss Teague said, then put her hand to her mouth, as if she spoke out of turn.

"Not until we find a little justice in all this, Esther," he replied. Avon wondered if he knew he had called the earnest and kind woman by her first name.

"All I wanted was a friend," Davey said, with so much sorrow in his voice that Avon turned his face into Mr. Coffin's waistcoat.

"Thee is richer than thee knows, Mr. David Ten. Goodnight now. Let Miss Teague tuck thee in. I hear she is good at that. Miss Teague, may I speak to thee?"

Davey and Avon stood shoulder to shoulder as Miss Teague walked their professor to the still-open door. Avon watched as they stepped beyond the door, heads close together as Mr. Coffin spoke too softly for them to hear. She nodded.

Davey didn't expect what happened next, but when Mr. Coffin kissed Miss Teague, he felt his whole body relax. "I think they are friends," Avon whispered to him, and they both smiled. "She'll probably turn really red now. See that? Let's go upstairs."

Silent, each Rat keeping his own counsel, they prepared for bed. Miss Teague was a long time coming. She rapped on the door as usual, and came inside. She sat beside Davey, her beautiful hair over one shoulder. They had seen her this way before, but there was a certain animation in her eyes that Davey saw, even by the light of a single candle.

"Hard lessons tonight," she told them.

Davey nodded. "I wanted to help Edwin," he said. "He doesn't really belong in medicine. He told me he wanted to be a printer, like his father."

"But you belong in medicine," she said.

Trust Avon. "Miss Teague, did you think we would be this much trouble?"

She laughed. "Life was getting too dull for me," she said. "Listen now. Here is what we are to do tomorrow morning. We are to meet Mr. Coffin and someone else in a café for breakfast. He gave me directions. There is a great scheme afoot."

Miss Teague patted each Rat and took the candle from the table between the beds. "Just remember," she said. "Courage."

Chapter Thirty

Courage, indeed, something easy to say at night, with a good man's arms around her, however briefly. Esther Teague did not think Josiah Coffin would actually kiss her. In fact, she had never been kissed by a man before. She had the feeling that Mr. Coffin had not intended to kiss her. He did, though, and she rejoiced. She could at least go to her grave some hopefully distant day knowing she had been kissed.

Courage in watery sunlight? Another matter. Mr. Coffin told her, when their foreheads were almost touching, that his own days at the college of medicine were definitely numbered, all because he had scruples and a conscience. Whether he knew it or not, she was involved in his life.

"I received a letter today from Chancellor McLeish to that effect," he told her. "I knew it was coming."

"You'll be leaving?" she asked, even though the answer was obvious.

Perhaps she was rude to turn away and go inside the house. Perhaps he had more to say, except she had no idea what it would be. People came into her life and left. Perhaps Mr. Coffin's removal would seem less wrenching, because she knew the Gunwharf Rats would leave, too. Early warning was either much better or far worse. She couldn't decide.

Not for the first time, Esther wondered if her life had been simpler before, when she tended her feral nephews and did whatever irritating errands her sister-in-law required, simply because she, Esther Teague, had failed in womanhood's most fundamental duty: She had never received an offer of matrimony. According to her brother, she never would.

In the solitude of her bedchamber, she asked herself just how many more years, or even months, it would have taken before she was completely cowed by her unmarried state, with its genteel poverty. In her youth, she had known such a woman, a distant relative, whom she now most closely resembled, or had, before a letter from Aunt Munro changed her life.

Now she had the comfort of a small income and the use of a pleasant house on a good street in Edinburgh. All she had to do was provide bed and board for two young men, both workhouse bastards, from St. Brendan the Navigator School in raffish, seedy Portsmouth. Providing the bed was easy, considering the extra bedchambers. Supplying the board had also become much simpler, because they came well-supplied with a cook, who subdued the kitchen in no time, and managed Esther's modest household to a fare thee well.

Davey, studious and quietly brilliant (although he would likely never admit such a thing), was mainly involved at the college. Avon was another matter. He was hers and Mrs. Perry's cheerful escort to Edinburgh's markets. He had a way of narrowing his eyes and delivering what she thought of as The Stare to merchants who put a thumb on the scale, or tried to bully her in any way, because they knew she was a spinster with no defenders.

She also knew Avon skulked, because he had been directed to find out more about the disappearance of a Marine and a carpenter's mate from the Royal Infirmary. He had begun his assignment with what she knew as his generally cheery temperament. Lately, however, he seemed to chafe at justice undelivered.

Granted, Mrs. Perry was also a force to be reckoned with, but Esther noticed that even Mrs. Perry let Avon take the lead in dealings with merchants. Their redoubtable cook also never questioned skulking because there was something intimidating about Avon that Esther Teague was hard put to define in mere words. It was almost as though Avon had quietly become the defender she always wished for.

That morning in her solitary bedroom, Esther went a step farther. She decided that she loved Avon like the son she never had. She waited for cold reason to take over, and it did, but not before giving her time for her next thought. *Surely there is more to life than the life I have been living*. She was clever with numbers. If she were a man, she could find a position in a counting house. If she were a man, she could go wherever ambition took her, perhaps even to the Caribbean sugar islands, because Scotland's bleak winters set a chill in her bones. A man could move to Barbados, or even the United States.

As the sky lightened, reason reigned triumphant again. She was a woman and dependent upon the whims of man. Thus it was, and ever would be, worlds without end, amen. This brief period in her otherwise boring existence was to be cherished and remembered, after the Gunwharf Rats returned to duties and obligations and Mr. Coffin found employment elsewhere. She was here to stay.

Esther had suffered through this argument before. Something told her that if she didn't dream bigger this time, she would never dream again. She was too old to wish upon stars. This was her life. "I want something good to happen to me," she said out loud, well aware there was no one to make anything happen.

Or was there? As she lay there, hands behind her head and staring at the ceiling, she recalled with a smile the odd circumstances that removed her tiresome housekeeper in timely fashion, and sent the Gunwharf Rats to her, all in a matter of weeks. She knew from years of Presbyterian rational thought that magic had no part in the Almighty's divine plan. What was the harm in asking for a little more? It was all silliness, but she needed a laugh.

"Listen here: Whoever you are who orchestrated the arrival of Avon March and Davey Ten, you might be done with me, but I am not done with you," she said out loud. "I am helping them. Would be it be too much to ask that I receive something in return? Something good, if you please."

Said out loud, it sounded supremely silly. In fact, she laughed and reconsidered, because she was a Scot. "If not good, then at least interesting enough to warm me all the rest of my life." Since this was a total flight of fancy, she reconsidered. "No, something good, thank you very much."

She would have returned to sleep, except there was a tap on her door. "Yes?" she asked, pulling up her blankets.

Mrs. Perry opened the door and held out a folded paper. "I don't know Mr. Coffin's handwriting, but this was stuck inside the front door."

"Goodness. I know I locked that door last night," Esther said as she got out of bed and took the note. She read, *Esther, call it a wild hare, but would thee and the Rats meet me this morning at seven at the public house with half a sign on Fortescue? It's near where I live, which Avon found by skulking last week. Someone might be able to help us. JC.*

She held it out to Mrs. Perry, who shook her head. "Never learned," she said, so Esther read it out loud. "You come, too," she told her cook. "It's a shabby part of town and there is strength in numbers."

Mrs. Perry didn't argue. By crossing the park at a half trot, they were there on time. Mr. Coffin was right about the half a sign and the generally seedy atmosphere. It was no place for a lady, Esther knew, but here she was, and ready for whatever happened, simply because she knew the next few weeks would furnish all the excitement her life would ever have.

"Mr. Walter Scott, this is Miss Teague," Mr. Coffin said, as he stood up and pulled out a chair next to him for Miss Teague. "My student Davey Ten, his friend Avon March, and Mrs. Perry, who cooks magnificently. Let me recommend the baked eggs and bacon," he concluded, then sat down.

Their orders were quickly taken, Mr. Coffin staring down the publican himself, who frowned over Mrs. Perry, then shrugged, muttering something about "serving them as is black as coal," which made Avon and Davey frown and move closer to the cook. Over coffee, which brightened Davey's eyes, Mr. Coffin wasted not a moment. "Mr. Scott here, a barrister in practice with his father, is also a magistrate in a petty court in Selkirk. Davey, he already knows what happened to Mr. Perkins in the indigent ward. I have caught him up to circumstances that make me fear grave robbers in Ward A soon."

Davey nodded. Esther glanced at Avon March, who also nodded, his expression so serious. Mr. Coffin caught her glance. "Miss Teague, hear out Mr. Scott, please."

"In the Selkirk court, I have had unfulfilled dealings with a grave robber rejoicing in the name of Wee Willie," Mr. Scott said. "Would you help me apprehend him?"

"Me?" Esther asked, hoping she didn't sound ghoulishly overenthusiastic. "Wh..why does anyone need me?"

"It's part of my idea to bring Wee Willie to justice. Once the poor man in Ward A shuffles off his mortal coil, I want you and Mr. Coffin to attend the funeral and subsequent burial." Mr. Scott rubbed his hands together, enjoying this business entirely too much, in Esther's view. "If the family decides to plant him somewhere else, it will be announced at the funeral. I have arranged for Josiah and myself to be joined by a constable, maybe two, that night in whatever cemetery it is. We'll nab Wee Willie good and proper in the act and send him on his way to a penal colony in the Antipodes."

"What about us?" Davey asked.

"You'll hang back in the cemetery," Mr. Scott told him. "No telling how many Resurrectionists Wee Willie has at his disposal. It might just be the students, but who knows?"

"And me?" Avon asked.

Mr. Scott gave him a thorough scrutiny. "I dunno, lad. These grave robbers tend to be great strapping men. You're not exactly a giant among fellows, are you now?"

Avon shook his head, obviously disappointed. Mr. Coffin clapped a hand on his shoulder. "I'll tell thee what, Avon," he said, after a glance at Esther, as if sizing her up for adventure. "Miss Teague and I will go to the cemetery as man and wife, and thee will be our son." He chuckled. "I bow to your superior knowledge of skulking. We will do what thee does: blend in and watch." He grinned at Esther. "We'll be a most harmless family. What is more innocuous?"

Esther felt her face grow warm, but she couldn't help smiling. Here she had consigned herself this morning to the kitchen midden of life. *Enjoy the adventure*, she told herself. "Why not?"

To her delight, everyone shook hands around the table, conspirators all. "I'll be in touch, Josiah," Mr. Scott said. "Do you know roughly how much longer Mr. Wilson has?"

"I have access to all medical records, even though I cannot ward walk in A," Mr. Coffin said. "I will know and contact thee accordingly, at thy father's office."

"Aye. Good day to you all."

Chapter Thirty-one

Now they waited. Avon continued sweeping in Ward A, keeping his own watch over Mr. Wilson, who grew steadily weaker. From the shadows, he observed Mrs. Wilson, a stout lady in a plain black bonnet, and her two children, who no longer sat on their father's bed, but on the floor close by but near his hand. On a good day, Mr. Wilson reached down to pat them.

He heard one conversation between husband and wife, something about eviction soon, because there was no income to pay the rent. In his own quiet way, Avon mourned that news as he wondered what would become of the family.

It troubled him all day, until Miss Teague asked him what the matter was. Of itself, that was a marvel. No one else ever divined his moods, but she seemed to know them. He debated whether to tell her about the Wilsons' troubles but he saw the sympathy in her eyes, this quiet lady who made life so comfortable at 158 Wilmer Street for him and Davey, their clothes washed and folded at the foot of their beds, her firm reminders to wash regularly, and her gentle style of management, for that was what it was.

He told her of Mrs. Wilson's burden, a soon-to-be widow with little ones to feed. Miss Teague clasped her hands together. "Find out where she lives, Avon," she said finally. "Follow her some night."

He did as she asked, always in the shadows, trailing behind the woman, a child on each side of her, the three of them trudging along, a trio against the world, where he had always been one against the world.

They walked several miles to the outskirts of Edinburgh, then stopped at a tidy row of houses, the sort of place where he wouldn't have minded living, that is, if the Royal Navy weren't part of his life now. From habit, he reached inside his shabby skulking jacket and touched his Trafalgar Medal. He couldn't decide if he did it as reassurance, or if he wanted to remember he had a greater allegiance to the crown than to Miss Teague. He memorized the address of the little row, wondering who owned it, and curious to know if it was someone kind, who might overlook late rent and never evict a widow.

Miss Teague nodded when he returned and told her. "I have an idea," was all she said. "It may come to nothing." All he knew was that later that day she sent an express letter to Portsmouth.

All week he swept, coming out of the shadows once when Mr. Wilson groaned and tried to sit up and Mrs. Wilson called out in terror. Avon dropped his broom and ran to an office in the hall where he had seen men who looked like physicians going in and out. He banged on the door, called, "Ward A!" and ducked into the broom closet. When the infirmary was quiet again, he returned to the ward, relieved to see Mr. Wilson calm again. Mrs. Wilson had pressed her head against the coverlet, her shoulders shaking. Avon's felt his heart go out to her. How to help her?

The following week was examinations at mid-term. Davey spent time in the indigent ward, coaching that perfidious Edwin Hamilton as if he were a true gentleman, and not a toady of John Yerby and Richard Sterling. In a rare moment of candor, Avon took Mr. Coffin aside – he was eating evening meals at 158 Wilmer Street now – and said if he had his way, Edwin would be a dead man.

"Then it is good thee does not have thy way," Mr. Coffin informed him, but kindly. "Edwin may be a faulty specimen, but he is also one of God's creatures, the same as thee or me."

Davey just smiled when Avon related that conversation before bed. "Trust Mr. Coffin. I decided to kill Edwin with kindness, Avon," he said before he snuffed out the candle.

"Even if he means you harm?"

"I have the feeling Edwin doesn't know what he means," Davey replied. "It's enough that I am aware I cannot trust him."

Avon thought about that, remembering the sad and shaken Davey Ten who had returned to St. Brendan's at Christmas, utterly devoid of confidence in himself. "Are the others speaking to you?" he asked.

"Generally. Master Six was right to send me to this house." He raised up on his elbow, the better to see Avon. "He insisted that you accompany me. I had thought he might send one of the younger Rats, considering how good you are at signaling and other ship to shore communications. Why you, Avon?"

He knew, in one blinding flash. "The people here, Davey," he said promptly. "I don't understand it, but I need them. Maybe Master Six knew. He's odd that way."

"And I think the people here need *you*, friend," was Davey's quiet reply.

"Captain Ogilvie wants me to skulk. He is also an assassin. I think he is training me to follow his line of work," Avon said into the darkness. "I...I don't want to."

"Then don't."

"It's my duty."

"No, it isn't."

Maybe it was that simple...and that complicated. Like Davey, he was a sworn member of the Royal Navy, and this was wartime. "I can't just leave the service willy-nilly," he said, but Davey was breathing deep now and asleep. "Or can I?" he whispered, putting actual words to his thoughts of the last week and more.

Once said out loud, he knew beyond anything that he could find a solution to a dilemma he couldn't quite put a finger on, but which was out there just beyond his reach.

How could a dying man hang on so long? That was Avon's question next week, after another excruciating turn one morning in Ward A, thank God this one not viewed by Mrs. Wilson. To his relief and surprise, Mr. Coffin ran into the ward and took charge in his quiet but firm way. "There was no one else so they sent me." He looked at the open door. "And Edwin Hamilton. He was my idea."

"It is advanced consumption, Mr. Hamilton," Mr. Coffin told the bewildered lad that Avon wanted to throttle for making Davey's life miserable. "Lend me a hand. I will show thee what to do."

Edwin did nothing of the sort, but backed out of the ward and ran. Alarmed, Avon dropped his broom and ran to the bedside, where Mr. Wilson's lifeblood was draining fast. Mr. Coffin calmly told him what to do and precisely when. In minutes, the bleeding had stopped.

"The Royal Navy is lucky to have you," Mr. Coffin said, when the crisis ended.

Avon knew he could say nothing, nod, and return to his broom, but this was Mr. Coffin, the man who, before ward walking, spent a good portion of his evenings at Wilmer Street now, no questions asked, none needed. It was only the two of them today.

"Avon?"

That was all it took. Wordless, he walked into Mr. Coffin's open arms. "I don't want to leave Wilmer Street," he managed to say, as he savored the sweetness, wondering if this was what it felt like to have a father.

"Hold that thought," was all Mr. Coffin said. Another brief hug and the quiet man left the ward in deference to another physician who bustled in and began his own survey of charts and orders. Avon retreated to the shadows, but with the heart stuffed back into his chest. Like many another Gunwharf Rat, he knew better than to hope. That morning, he made an exception for himself.

Three days later, he returned to Wilmer Street to find Miss Teague holding a letter as tears streaked her cheeks. She saw his wide-eyed stare and consternation and managed a watery laugh. She held out her hand to him and he edged closer, doubting there was a man alive, or even a growing lad, who wasn't undone by female waterworks.

It was on the tip of his tongue to ask if it was something he had done, but he didn't. He recognized that as workhouse guilt, the sort of thing that kept a body in chains only he could see.

"I did not know how fast a response could come," she told him. "I was merely hoping."

"I like hope," Avon said shyly, which made her smile, something she had been doing more and more lately, since Mr. Coffin started coming to dinner. He read the letter and gasped. It was something about a solicitor already at work on the proposal involving a block of row houses. He read, "generous offer," and "I had no idea he wanted to sell," and names of people unknown to him, and this paragraph: "Kindly assure Mrs. Wilson that there will be no eviction," and then this: "…paid for in full as long as she lives there."

He handed back the letter. "Did you…" was all he could manage.

She nodded. "I wrote Aunt Munro and told her what was going to happen. I told her I had a little money, and a little more from her would pay a few months' rent for a woman in need." She stared at the letter. "I had no idea she wanted to purchase some real estate here." Her lovely smile lifted a great weight from Avon, one he might have been carrying since birth, if he could remember that far back. "Thank you for trusting me with your burden, dear one," she told him. "We have done some good."

"Mr. Wilson still isn't going to live," Avon said when he could speak.

"No, alas. We can't do everything, but we have done something," she said. "I am going to write Mrs. Wilson. Would you see that she gets this?"

He did, placing Miss Teague's letter in the fold of Mr. Wilson's blanket before he blended into the shadows again, waiting. Mrs. Wilson came as usual, but without her children. He saw all the worry, all the sorrow, and a burden so great she seemed weighted with it.

She sat beside her dying husband's bed and noticed the letter with *Mrs. Wilson* written so large in Miss Teague's charming script. She hesitated, read it, gasped, read it again, then looked toward the ceiling. She bowed her head, covered her face with her hands, and remained that way until he could nearly feel her gratitude across the aisle and behind a stack of empty cots.

She touched the depth of his heart that Avon had not known existed when she quietly read the letter to her dying husband. "Nae fears, my jo," she said and patted his arm. "You needna worry for us." She stayed that way until Mr. Wilson breathed his last.

He looked at the chart and went to the indigent ward, waiting until Mr. Coffin finished applying a bandage to an old man's stump of a leg, assisted by Davey. Mr. Coffin knew what had happened before Avon said anything. "It was peaceful?"

Avon told Mr. Coffin about the letter Miss Teague had received that afternoon, and its result. Mr. Coffin rested his hand on Avon's shoulder and beckoned Davey closer. "We know something that no one else in Edinburgh even suspects," he said. "There is no kinder lady alive than Esther Teague. Look what she has set in motion." He looked toward the wall, almost as if he could see through it. "Now let us see if we can rid this university of body snatchers. Mr. Wilson deserves better that the fate some evildoers have planned."

Chapter Thirty-two

Josiah thought Miss Teague might shy away from his plan to include her as his wife, and Avon as their son, in his determination to attend Mr. Wilson's funeral, but she hesitated not even a little. He didn't need to launch into his elaborate reasons that they needed to be present in case the burying ground was changed. In fact, she seemed relieved.

"I thought Avon and I would have to go alone," she told him. "This is much better. We'll blend in nicely. I have a dark gray dress that shouldn't offend any Quaker sensibilities."

He could have told her that she already dressed as soberly as his own mother, but chose not to. "We will be sufficiently undistinguished. I doubt the Wilsons know anyone except modest people," he said. She pinked up anyway, which made her so attractive.

She became even more attractive to him when she laughed and leaned against his shoulder for a far-too-brief moment. "I promise not to wear my red and white striped bonnet with the red ribbons, which match my stockings," she said, then gave a whoop of laughter. "Josiah, if you could only see your face right now! I don't have anything like that, really."

"Wretched female," he teased, in turn. "Do call me Josiah. I like to hear my name and it gives me excuse to call thee Esther."

He couldn't have explained it to anyone, but when she nodded, her eyes shy, he knew this lady was perfect for him. His next thought was to hope she would overlook the fact that he was shortly to be unemployed and set adrift. He was nobody's matrimonial catch, and he knew it. "Enjoy the moment" was nowhere listed in any canon of Friend philosophy, but he planned to do precisely that. *I'm in love*, he told himself simply. He could worry later about what his fellow Friends in Edinburgh would think.

Mr. Wilson's funeral was held in Tron Kirk, not far from the Royal Infirmary, and one of Edinburgh's oldest parishes. Breakfast earlier with Walter also included two constables, neither of which planned to attend the funeral, since they would stand out like Quakers on a battlefield. Over eggs, bacon and beer, Josiah assured them he would have two Gunwharf Rats with him in the kirk graveyard.

"I'll be at the funeral, too," Walt told him, "but I cannot stay for the burial. I have a court date. I'll try to sit near you. If I see Wee Willie, I'll give you a high sign."

"And I will send a note to thee, as to where the grave is in the cemetery," he told them as he took his leave. Walt Scott nodded and raised his beer stein high.

Esther and Avon were ready for Josiah when he called at 158 Wilmer Street, both of them soberly dressed and Avon clad in his Royal Navy boat cloak. The wind was raw that morning and Josiah had no trouble keeping Esther tucked close to him as they walked to the church, Avon close on his other side. These two lovelies beside him, pretending to be family so they could observe, took away a thousand slights and pains.

The church was large, and the Wilsons probably modest parishioners, so there was no way it would be filled. Still, there were a number of simply dressed folk much like what he couldn't help thinking as the little Coffin family. They sat in a middle row, Esther on one side and Avon on the other. He saw the plain casket in front of the pulpit, with only a bit of greenery on top, but that only gave him a slight case of the shudders. Quaker services were usually conducted graveside, with no trappings or frills. Dust to dust, after all.

He did like the music and Bible readings, but he missed the silence, when friends and neighbors sat and contemplated the loss of a Friend, and what it meant to their community of believers.

"Is this anything like a Quaker funeral?" Esther whispered, her lips close to his ear. He enjoyed the sensation.

"Nay, lass," he whispered back. "I miss the silence."

"I can be silent," she said, which did strange things to his heart.

He took her hand because he wanted to, wishing neither of them wore gloves because he wanted to feel her skin. On his other side, Avon leaned against his arm. *We seem to belong together*, he thought. *I wish it could be.*

He searched the gathering, picking out Walter Scott, who looked right at him, then turned his head and pointed with his nose to a stout little fellow dressed plainly, except for an eyepopping waistcoat. The man's eyes were fixed on the coffin, giving it his full attention. *Take out a measuring tape, why don't you?* Josiah thought. Even he could tell that a grave robber worth his shovel could probably make his way into such a cheap box with little trouble, and no one the wiser. The whole matter repulsed him.

Man born of woman. Ashes to ashes, dust to dust. Where was the Quaker silence of remembrance, and then if someone so chose, a story of love and giving about the deceased? More silence, then Friends shaking hands. He glanced at Esther Teague, wondering if he dared to ask her to a Meeting.

Everyone stood as Mrs. Wilson and her two children followed the casket out the side door to the burying ground. Some of the men in the congregation left, probably to resume their ordinary employment, because Josiah suspected no one in this modest gathering of hard workers received a day off with pay, even for a funeral. Walter Scott tipped his hat to them from across the church and left for court. The older among them, Wee Willie included, followed the mourners.

"There we have it," Josiah said as the three of them clustered together, close to the wall. Josiah clapped his hand on Avon's shoulder. "I suppose we're testing a theory tonight about how evil some people can be."

There was time after Bones – whoever controlled the course had grudgingly given him a necrotic jaw to dissect – to tell Davey to take an early nap before dinner if he could. "We are meeting Mr. Scott and his constables in the Tron graveyard around eleven of the clock tonight."

"Avon, too?"

"Aye. He would probably follow us anyway, if we left him behind." They chuckled.

No one could eat dinner, even when Mrs. Perry glowered at them and threatened. She also informed them that she was coming along. No one felt brave enough to assure her that wasn't necessary. "I will have rum here when you return," Esther informed them.

"What, mum, you don't care to watch?" Avon joked.

"Not. Even. Slightly." She accompanied this with a level-eyed stare as potent as Mrs. Perry's insistence that no one was leaving *her* behind.

Esther Teague, thee could manage sons, Josiah thought, with admiration.

He decided to sit in silence in the parlor, making himself relax as he anticipated the evening's work. He closed his eyes and made himself available to his Inner Light, which, he admitted, had faltered. Medical school had provided few obstacles. He was used to teasing from others about his Quaker ways, which meant he had to study harder and graduate with a First. The dissection of bodies had given him no qualms. There was much to learn that would save lives, for the greater glory of God.

The bridge too far had been Thomas Perkins, helped to death before his time, even if his time might not have lasted another two hours, or even half a day. It gnawed at him that he had blithely dissected for years, even as he now wondered how many of those specimens had suffered Mr. Perkin's fate, simply because he was a poor man with no advocate. Mr. Wilson? Desecrating his grave was out of the question.

Perhaps he dozed then, as he had encouraged the Rats to do. He opened his eyes when his right side grew warm, and looked over to see Avon March tucked close, asleep. Esther Teague sat across the room from them, knitting. He caught her eye and she smiled. He smiled back and rested his hand gently on Avon's shoulder, deeply aware that he needed to rethink his plans, and wondering if a kind lady could overlook his upcoming dismissal from the college of medicine. Could he overlook that she was not of the Friendly persuasion? When did life become so complicated? It sounded like whining, so he stopped.

At ten-thirty, Esther waved goodbye from her front steps, and they walked to the Tron burying ground, which extended out from the back of the church toward a distant park. Walter Scott and his two constables, Mr. Bean and Mr. Turner, waited for them near the church. Mr. Bean took out his timepiece. "T'night watchman passed through here ten minutes ago," he whispered, even though no one was in sight. We wait five minutes, then follow him."

"Why not go the other direction?" Davey asked, something Josiah wanted to know, as well.

"What, laddie, and meet him coming 'round?" Mr. Turner asked. His grin showed missing teeth. "Stick to medicine, young fellow, and I'll let you lance me carbuncles someday."

Even Davey smiled at that. They set out a few minutes later, staying off the gravel path with its crunch of stones, and threading their way with the constables past mausoleums and elaborate headstones dating back one hundred years and more through Scottish history. Josiah thought of his own family's markers in Dumfries, where a brave bunch of them had allied themselves with George Fox and became quiet martyrs with a community of believers that many didn't call a church. Those graves had been desecrated. As he walked with the others, he wondered if his own ancestors had ended up on the dissector's table, since so many considered them rabble-rousing scoundrels and therefore worthy of the scalpel and bone saw, in the interest of science. *I believe I am done with dissecting*, he thought, then asked himself what else he was done with.

"There it is," he whispered finally as they came to the west wall. *Mr. Wilson's home until the Resurrection, but not these unhallowed Resurrectionists, these body snatchers*, he told himself.

Clouds settled in and dared any moonlight to penetrate, perfect conditions for graverobbing. The trees hadn't begun to bud out yet, but some of the bushes were making headway. He motioned for Avon and Davey to stay behind them, their backs against the wall. Dressed in black, Mrs. Perry was well-nigh invisible. Nearby tombstones furnished cover for the rest. Josiah idled away the hour by reading the inscription of Elizabeth McHenry, dead at twenty, twenty-five years ago. *So young*, he thought. *Maybe I could have saved her.* It was a prideful thought and he dismissed it. The earth in front of the grave marker was depressed by several inches. Perhaps she wasn't even there, but long since an uncomplaining corpse on a dissectionist's table.

The night watchman passed, after stopping to relieve himself into an empty vase at a headstone. A low *psst* from Davey at the wall took Josiah from morbid considerations. "He must feel something on the wall," Walter said, behind a neighboring tombstone. In another moment, a rope ladder snaked over, followed by that little man with the loud waistcoat, another rope over his shoulder and a shovel.

Two others followed. "Recognize them?" Walter Scott whispered.

"Aye. John Yerby and Richard Sterling."

The hidden audience remained in place. Walter Scott had told Josiah and the constables earlier that he had missed his chance with Wee Willie in his Selkirk jurisdiction when other constables had moved too slow, ending up with nothing but the sight of a clean pair of heels. "I know he runs fast, for a stout fellow," Walter told them.

Josiah watched in grim fascination as first John and then Richard took turns digging only at the end of the grave. They worked rapidly and soon created a sizeable crater in the soft earth. Josiah's unspoken question made complete sense when Wee Willie ponderously lowered himself into the pit and took his saw to the end of the coffin.

The wood was cheap. In a matter of minutes – Josiah had to give grudging respect to their efficiency – Wee Willie was aboveground again as his students in crime tugged out Mr. Wilson headfirst. With speed obviously borne of experience, John looped the rope under Mr. Wilson's armpits, and he and Richard pulled the uncomplaining man from his coffin.

"Slick," Walter whispered. "All they have to do is fill in the dirt, and who's the wiser? Damn the man."

Timing was everything and the timing was off. With a low-voiced "Now!" the constables leaped forward, followed by Josiah close behind. Quicker than sight, possibly through experience that the others lacked, John and Richard stretched the rope and tripped both constables, who went down in a heap.

They didn't stay down, but when they righted themselves, Wee Willie and Richard were over the wall and yanking up the rope ladder, leaving John Yerby, white-faced, staring up at the blank wall, trapped.

Walter came from behind the tombstone, gingerly patting his ankle. "Damned footstone," he muttered. He smiled as he saw John Yerby. "Better one than none," Walt said. Despite the smile, Josiah heard all the disappointment.

Josiah had to give John Yerby points for coolness of mind. The constables grabbed him by an arm each and stiff-walked him to Walter and Josiah, where he stood casually, a slight smile on his face. "Cheeky sort, aren't you?" Walter Scott muttered.

"He's all we need," Mr. Bean said. "You saw it all, didn't you, Mr. Coffin?"

"I did," Josiah replied.

"So did I. And I," said Davey and Mrs. Perry, nearly in unison.

"Wee Willie isn't here," Josiah pointed out.

John Yerby looked around elaborately. "Bless me, who are you talking about?"

"The body snatcher," Mr. Turner snapped.

John shrugged. "I don't see him."

Of the two constables, Mr. Turner seemed to be in charge. "We have a case," he said, glaring at John. "Mr. Scott, you saw Wee Willie, I believe."

The barrister shook his head. "It happened so fast. I tripped over the footstone at the grave and fell. When I looked up, all I saw was someone…"

"…Two someones going over a wall, and showing shoe leather," John interjected. He seemed to be enjoying himself hugely. "Maybe there were more, but *you* didn't see them."

"No, I didn't," Mr. Scott admitted, with a scowl at John.

Mr. Turner frowned and returned his attention to Josiah. "Who or what did you see, Mr. Coffin?"

"Two men going over the wall. One was Wee Willie and the other was Richard Sterling," Josiah said promptly, sure of himself. "Of this I am certain."

"You'd swear to it in a court of law," Mr. Bean added, as a matter of form.

Josiah took a sudden breath, and another. He glanced at Walter Scott, who urged him forward. "Go on, go on. We have them."

It came to this: Josiah couldn't meet Walter's eyes, or Davey's. "Mr. Bean, I am forbidden by the rules of my religion to swear any sort of oath in a court of law," he said finally. "I cannot."

"Good God, man!" Mr. Turner exclaimed, beside himself. He slapped his hat against his leg in frustration. "What is so hard about that? You would rather release those two and this sorry specimen who is enjoying himself too much? What is the matter with you?"

Josiah writhed inside, but he had no other answer beyond, "I cannot swear an oath."

"I can!" Mrs. Perry declared, as she came from the shadows. "Me and Davey here saw it all. Didn't we Davey?"

"Aye, Mrs. Perry, we did," Davey said, after giving Josiah a long look that said as clear as words: *You don't measure up.*

John started to laugh. He clapped his hands. Josiah gritted his teeth. Davey's expression turned wary, something Josiah had hoped not to see again.

"What is so damned funny?" Mr. Turner demanded. "Stop it, you fiend!"

John assumed a wounded look. He trained his eyes on the constables, tsking his tongue and shaking his head. "Come now, sirs. You don't imagine the high court or even a petty court is ever going to take the word of a workhouse bastard, for that is what Davey is, or the word of an African woman as black as coal tar?"

"Piqued, repiqued and capoted," Walter Scott said under his breath, after a long silence. "Let's go home, Josiah, and fight another day."

"I don't understand, Walter," Josiah said, feeling like his blood was about to drain away. "We have two perfectly good witnesses, even if I cannot swear an oath in court. Two of them!"

Mr. Scott lost whatever patience of his remained. "You Quakers may see them as equals. I doubt there is a court in Scotland or England that would agree with you. It's over."

Mr. Bean still wasn't having it. "Not yet. I want to at least secure this lad's name and address. I imagine we will see him again, and soon."

John laughed. "You know, sirs, if you had let me give you my name immediately – isn't that a general rule of constabulary work, anyway? – we could have cleared up this little error."

"Little error, my ass," Walter said succinctly.

"Go ahead, lad. I suppose we should do this. What is your name, if you please?" Mr. Bean said, elaborately polite.

John cleared his throat, obviously savoring his importance. *He's going to ruin me*, Josiah thought suddenly, as his mouth went dry.

"I am John Yerby, son of your own Godwin Yerby."

Josiah heard Walter Scott groan. As if on cue, Mr. Beans and Mr. Turney released John.

"*What?*" Josiah declared.

"Mr. Coffin – my, but you are well-named – my father is chief inspector of the Edinburgh metropolitan constabulary force." He glared at Mr. Bean and Mr. Turner, who lowered their batons and stepped back in sudden deference. "Good night, gentlemen. P'raps you might all pray that I develop sudden amnesia of *your* names before I get home."

He strolled away, laughing. By unspoken consent, Constables Bean and Turner gentled their silent witness, Mr. Wilson, back into his coffin and filled in the grave, taking turns with the shovel. Davey joined them and they made quick work of it.

Utterly beside himself, Josiah turned away. He knew without a doubt that word of tonight's doing would reach the college of medicine's chancellor. The decision now was to choose whether to resign in person immediately, or send a cowardly letter. He would take a post chaise to London and the sanctuary of home, where he knew his father would not scold and tell him I told thee so, but whose disapproval he would feel, nonetheless.

He glanced toward the wall, where Mrs. Perry stood. Beside her was Avon, who, for some reason, hadn't come out when the constables apprehended John Yerby. *I doubt even kind Avon wants to talk to me,* Josiah thought in perfect misery.

For the second time that night he was entirely wrong. Avon nodded to Mrs. Perry and stood beside Josiah. "Mrs. Perry didn't want me to be seen, for some reason, sir. I heard and saw everything, though."

"Thee heard John. He doesn't think much of Gunwharf Rats," Josiah told him, relieved not to see recrimination on the lad's face or in his words.

"Mr. Coffin, some people like John are natural-born bastards, and others of us had certain disadvantages of birth," Avon said. "You know that's right, Davey, don't you?"

Davey leaned on the shovel, then handed it to Mr. Turner, who patted down Mr. Wilson's resting place. "Aye, Avon. I'm sorry I was rude, Mr. Coffin."

"Thee is entitled."

"No, I am not, sir."

"Well, here we are then," Avon said, cheerful as usual.

"Avon, would thee be cheerful in a hurricane and thy ship dismasted?" Josiah asked. For no reason he could discern, he began to feel a glimmering tiny hope inside, something he never ignored as a Quaker, even a faulty, proud Quaker, as he knew himself to be. "Or on the deck of a sinking ship?"

"Trafalgar was hard, I will admit, sir," Avon said, in what Josiah figured was the understatement of the ages. "I think I have a better idea."

"About what?" Josiah said, determined not to underestimate a Gunwharf Rat ever again.

"About ridding the medical profession of John Yerby, Richard Sterling and Wee Willie," Avon said. He spoke with quiet confidence.

"What is thee thinking, lad?"

"...that we will need Miss Teague's help, and no, you cannot resign, Mr. Coffin, if that is what you are planning, at least not now." He yawned. "It's late and we are tired. I'll tell you when we're back on Wilmer Street." He strolled along with Davey. "Of course, it'll depend on Miss Teague and whether she's as game as we think."

Chapter Thirty-three

"This is out of the question, Avon. I will never permit it."

Davey was not a man to argue or question authority. *Maybe I am*, he thought, as he noted Mr. Coffin's solemn and serious expression as they sat in the parlor on Wilmer Street, Mrs. Perry in the doorway. *Maybe I am learning something more here than I could ever learn in the fleet.* He was flogged and raised to never question authority, but this was different. Mr. Coffin had to hear Avon out; now was the time to apply this valuable lesson.

"Mr. Coffin, it is a bold stroke, such as Admiral Nelson attempted at Trafalgar," Davey countered. "Avon and I were there. We saw it. Victory was ours."

"Admiral Nelson died!" Mr. Coffin said, biting off each word. "I would never endanger the life of Avon March for any vindication, so help me God."

Was it time to mutiny? Davey felt a twinge of uncertainty and glanced at Avon, his brother in arms on the deck of the yacht *Mercury*, Avon the Gunwharf Rat who ran up signals upon command of Captain Six, no questions asked. Avon, who stood fearless, protecting Smitty at the helm from sniper fire, when he knew any moment that he could be cut down by a Spaniard or a Frog with good aim. Avon, who never faltered in the face of anything.

That Avon, the one who never wavered, spoke with a certain authority that took Davey aback, until he realized that someone else had learned a similar lesson. "Then, dear sir, we will do this without your help. I will see justice done. There is no place for the likes of John Yerby around the sick, no matter that the constabulary fears running afoul of him. You know that as surely as I do."

"Aye, but…" Mr. Coffin turned toward Miss Teague, whom Davey was beginning to realize had as much strength of purpose as any Gunwharf Rat. "Esther, please agree with me."

Davey watched her expressive face, wondering how anyone could ever think her plain. He nearly smiled when the modest, quiet lady he had come to love shook her finger in Mr. Coffin's face. "Josiah, you told me that you value the opinion of women…" She stopped, and Davey could have perished on the spot from his admiration. She seemed to grow taller, even though he knew that was impossible. "Let me rephrase that: Josiah, thee told me thee values the opinion of women. I am completely in favor of this scheme, whatever thee thinks. *Now* does thee understand me?"

Davey heard Avon let out a slow breath. He put his arm around the smaller Rat as Josiah Coffin covered his face with his hands and let himself be swallowed up in Esther Teague's embrace. They clung together, and Davey knew that no matter what happened to any of them, the matter had resolved itself by love. Mr. Coffin was now officially putty in the hands of a determined woman in love, whether he knew it or not. He probably did. Mr. Coffin was nobody's fool.

"Davey, I am depending upon you to mix up the right potion," Avon said, as Mr. Coffin and Miss Teague held each other. "Those surgeons at Haslar jammed pharmacopeia down your throat for years, didn't they?"

"Aye, friend, they did," Davey said. "I can do my part."

Mr. Coffin did make another attempt. "This could be dangerous for *thee*, Esther."

Oh, but Miss Teague had a cool head. She stepped out of Mr. Coffin's embrace and sat down again with her knitting. "Josiah Coffin, if your life has been as boring as mine, I believe even *you* would dress up as a poor, illiterate woman with a dying son in the indigent ward!"

Bless the man, he kept trying. No wonder Quakers irritated some people. "Davey…"

"Mr. Coffin, I am as capable as you are to coach Avon to take those quick breaths, then long ones that show life is ebbing." He glanced at Avon, who gave them his usual, cheery smile. "When John and Richard come with their pillows to snuff out his life ahead of schedule, I am depending on Edinburgh's Finest to make an arrest that sticks."

"Witnesses? Davey, thee knows I cannot swear an oath in court."

Give up, Mr. Coffin, Davey thought. "Sir, what you need to do is somehow convince the chancellor or the vice chancellor to hide in the shadows with you. Yours is the harder task. It might be easier to enlist Walter Scott again. I trust he has not given up on you." He gestured. "Neither have we. Who's a better witness than a barrister?"

"Or a greater prevaricator, upon occasion," Miss Teague said as she began to knit.

After a moment's startled silence, everyone laughed, which cleared the air enormously. "We need cake," Mrs. Perry said. "Help me with it, Rats."

In the kitchen, Davey clapped his arm around Avon's shoulder. "How in the world did you come up with such a scheme?"

"I do a lot of thinking when I'm sweeping," he said. "But I don't know what to do about Mr. Coffin. It sounds like he won't be allowed to continue here."

"I wonder where any of us will be at the end of this term," Davey said, putting voice to his own doubts.

Avon raised his eyebrows. "And?" he coaxed.

"I don't know." He saw the disappointment in his friend's eyes, which bordered on sadness, if Davey interpreted correctly. It occurred to him that Avon didn't want to leave Edinburgh at all.

He thought about the matter in the morning, as he tamped down his own unhappiness at having to lay eyes on John Yerby again. He braced himself with the fact that his classes, which had grown smoother with bits of conversation, were probably going to get rocky once more. John and Richard would spread the word, and all would return to silence.

He waited for the familiar dread, but it did not surface. There were still people in this gray and misty city who smiled when he returned from school, and even fellow students who asked for help because he knew medicine in ways they could never understand without some coaching, which he was happy to provide. Truth to tell, he didn't really know how much sway John and Richard had over the others, anyway. There would always be Chiefs and always be Indians, an expression he heard in the corridor one afternoon when several loud American students passed him. Apparently, the new United States needed physicians, too.

Materia Medica was uncomfortable, with John whispering to his cronies while the rest of them compounded sleeping powders. True, Davey got his share of what an old foretopman called the stink eye, but more of it seemed to focus on Richard Sterling. As he concentrated on the right dose of calomel to brewer's yeast – the better to go down the gullet – Davey heard "…left me in the dust to dangle," and "…with friends like Richard, who needs foes," bandied about until the old professor, who could barely hear anyway, threw up his hands, dismissed them, and reminded them of a test on Friday.

Davey saw the division in front of his face as they left the classroom, a few loyal toadies walking with John, but more with Richard, who had sad eyes anyway, and worked them to great effect. *How blows the wind now?* Davey thought, content to walk by himself, as usual.

He wasn't alone; in fact, Edwin Hamilton startled him. "Got a minute, Davey?" he heard.

Davey knew he could have followed his wary instinct and ignored Edwin, who had cozied up to John and Richard in Ward A earlier, to his dismay. He reconsidered. Edwin probably didn't know Mr. Coffin had seen him with the other two in the ward, and made it known to Davey. What was the harm? Edwin had been the only one last term to offer even the barest kindness, even if he had sided with John and Richard. "I have a minute," he said. "Where away?"

Edwin pointed to an empty classroom. He shut the door behind him when Davey took a seat. "I owe you an apology," he said, not wasting a minute, considering that it was a Latin classroom, and Davey knew *he* didn't want to be trapped in there. "I truly do." He couldn't look Davey in the eye.

"For what?" Davey asked.

Edwin sat down next to him. "Did you know that John and Richard have been trying to recruit classmates to do a little…." He couldn't say it.

"Bodysnatching?" Davey offered.

Edwin nodded, unable to look at him. He settled on a glance over Davey's shoulder. They also wanted me to keep you busy earlier in the evening so they could have the run of Ward A and…and…"

"…check out possible candidates for Resurrection?" Davey asked gently. He doubted Edwin knew about Mr. Perkins' premature fate. No sense in making someone apologizing feel even worse. Mr. Wilson's corpse in Ward A would suffice.

Another nod, and then Edwin looked him in the eye. "I did need your help studying. That was no hum." He sighed and drummed on the desk. "They wanted my friendship to find ways to get at you."

"It happens." Davey couldn't help smiling. "I know your grades have gone up in Bones."

Edwin nodded, all seriousness. "A few days ago, they tried to talk me into helping someone rob a grave. It's not in me. I couldn't do it."

Davey felt a surge of relief. "It seems to me that things are frosty between the two of them this morning."

"You were there in the cemetery, weren't you?"

"I was. John informed the constables who nabbed him just who his father is, and they backed off as if he carried bubonic plague."

"I wish you could have captured them all. They…they're also saying that Mr. Coffin is in worse trouble now. I don't like that, either."

"Nor do I." What else was there to say? Davey looked at the wall clock. "I need to help Mr. Coffin set up in Bones."

"There is one thing more."

Davey braced himself for the worst. Edwin surprised him.

"I'm leaving the college of medicine right now. I wanted to apologize to you first, but I'm done here as of today. I have no stomach for grubbing about in people's insides. The sight of blood makes me gag."

"Blood can do that. You said your father wanted you to become a physician."

"He does." Edwin stood up and flashed a big smile. "I'll change his mind. It'll flatter him – eventually – that I prefer his line of work. Good luck to you, Davey, and thank you." He held out his hand and Davey shook it.

*

Josiah fared worse, as he knew he would. All he really wanted during the whole ordeal with the chancellor was to sit in Miss Teague's parlor and watch her knit. There was something so soothing about knitting, or maybe it was Esther Teague, herself. All he could do now was listen to Chancellor Winston McLeish rake him up and down, and think about Esther instead.

He knew he was finished here, so what did an interruption matter? "Beg pardon, sir, I assume John Yerby told thee what happened."

"He did, and he was put upon and irate, with good cause," Sir Winston snapped.

"He was also caught grave robbing," Mr. Coffin continued. "As it turned out, I was the only witness that a credible court would hear, but I cannot swear an oath, not even at law, and there the matter stands. It is against the tenets of my religion."

Sir Winston leaped to his feet. "Oh, you Quakers! It's your word against John's apparently," he shouted. "Since you refuse to swear to the matter, that suggests to me that you are not certain."

Where was his courage coming from? Josiah rose as well, but slowly. His words were measured, because he was at peace with the matter, even in this tense encounter. "What it suggests, with all due respect, is that I have not the right to condemn another of God's creatures."

Silence. McLeish seemed to have no argument to offer. Josiah felt the sudden comfort of his Inner Light, which he knew, to his everlasting shame, had begun to diminish, before this telling moment. He knew of a surety that nothing was more important to him – not country, and certainly not king. "Ultimately, sir, I have thee to thank for correcting me." There was more and he said it. "I would tell thee something else: John and Richard should never be physicians anywhere. They were partners in body snatching, sir, whether thee chooses to acknowledge it or not." He warmed to his subject again, because it felt so good to speak truth. "I will leave immediately."

To his further amazement, the chancellor held up his hand. "Not so fast, Mr. Coffin. Do you think I can replace you on a moment's notice?"

"I am certain thee can," he said. He picked up his hat and put it on his head. He never should have taken it off. It was against all he believed to bare his head to anyone, no matter his rank. That simple gesture restored something missing in his heart. "Thee will see me no more."

"Stop, Mr. Coffin," Sir Winston shouted. "Thee...dash it all! *You* can't leave. I considered it this morning after John Yerby and his father visited me in my chambers, irate and foaming – well, nearly." He held up his hands in placating gesture not lost on Josiah. "I tried to replace you, but there is no one right now. Everyone had an excuse. I don't understand that."

"Surely Sir Lionel is more able by now," Josiah said. "I have had an excellent assistant in Mr. David Ten, who will help all he can."

He touched a tender spot without knowing it. Sir Winston resumed his seat, looking older than he had minutes before. "That is a hard subject, I fear. Sir Lionel has not improved. His injured leg has never healed properly, and I am beginning to fear amputation."

"I am sorry about that," Josiah said, and meant it, to his surprise. Sir Lionel was an opinionated old professor long past his prime who never felt the need to learn new lessons. And yet… "There is no dearth of surgeons here who will do their best with him, Sir Winston."

Sir Winston closed his eyes, and Josiah felt a twinge of pity for the old fellow. It passed soon enough. How dare he not dismiss John and Richard? Then again, the world was not fair. "I will work until the end of the term, if that is what thee wishes," he said. "Now I must prepare my classroom."

The strangest sight met his eyes in Bones. The students had divided themselves evenly in half, some with Richard Sterling, and the rest with John Yerby, who smirked at him. He trained his gaze upon John, holding it steady until the student looked away. He turned to the specimen table where Davey stood, his eyes troubled.

Josiah moved closer. Someone must have jimmied the lock on his office. There, in a specimen tray, was his prized little portrait of his parents, cut into pieces. He couldn't help the groan that escaped his lips. He had no other portrait of his mother, who had passed to the Peaceable Kingdom four years ago. There she lay now, her eyes crossed out with black ink and her head cut from her body. The fiend – whoever he was – had done unspeakable things to his father's image.

He looked up at Davey, who stared back, his face pale and his eyes twin pools of misery. "This is what I found, sir," Davey managed to say, as tears coursed down his cheeks. "I could have removed it, but no."

"Thee did well to leave it alone," he said quietly to his assistant, who knew how it felt to bear the brunt of prejudice at the college of medicine. "Find me a specimen sleeve, please."

Davey opened a cabinet and took out a sleeve of heavy folded paper. In the awful silence, Josiah carefully gathered the portrait pieces together, placing them carefully, lovingly even, in the sleeve. *I am done here*, he thought. *I cannot bear this.* He bowed his head in silence in front of a classroom of students.

When he looked up finally, some of the class was gone, those fewer than he thought who supported John Yerby, as foul a specimen as Josiah hoped never to see again in his lifetime. The others sat in silence, pencils and pads ready.

The fact that most of them remained stuffed the heart back into his chest. *I can do this*, he thought, *then no more, no matter what I promised Winston McLeish only minutes ago.* He gave all credit to the fire of the Inner Light that seemed to catch and brighten until it filled him, as it must have filled the earlier martyrs of his faith, who suffered far worse. He called in silence for their strength, and opened his text.

"Here we are, nearing the conclusion of this term in Bones," he said, relieved that his voice was strong. "We have traveled from the head to the arms and fingers, through the torso and down the legs. We have reached the feet. Come closer and pay attention."

He finished the lecture an hour later, back straight, voice strong, even able to inject a little humor with "This little piggy went to market..." which made his students smile. Leaning on the table, he sent them on their way when the clock chimed its hour in the bell tower. When the last one shut the door, he dropped to his knees and stayed that way, whether in prayer or exhaustion he couldn't tell, until some force stronger than himself helped him to his feet and down the hall, back straight again, to his office, where he found all his personal books desecrated, pages ripped out and strewn around his room.

When his hands stopped shaking, he wrote a note to the chancellor, demanding that he come immediately to his office, and bring a constable. He wrote his letter of resignation on his desk, closed the door behind him and left the college of medicine forever.

"Something is wrong."

Meridee Six looked up from her rolling pin and pastry to see her husband standing in the doorway, his eyes boring into her very soul.

She took a deep breath and another. "Able? Dearest, you don't look well." Meri wiped her floury hands on her apron and took his hand, tugging him into the kitchen.

He sat. "It was all I could do to finish my calculus class," he told her, pulling her down to sit on his lap. "Something is afoot in Edinburgh."

Meri knew better than to ask how he could possibly know such a thing. He knew. "Davey?" she asked. He shook his head, which relieved her immediate anxiety. Her Gunwharf Rats were precisely that: Hers, but there were others...

"It is that kind Quaker Mr. Coffin, who visited us on his return to Edinburgh," Able said. "I cannot say what it is, except that matters have reached a terrible head."

She nestled close. "Dearest, there isn't anything you can do from this distance but trust Mr. Coffin will manage, and Davey and Avon, too." She patted his chest. "And the redoubtable Mrs. Perry."

He gave her a faint smile, and she relaxed. That selfsame smile had cajoled her through several crises already, both foreign and domestic. "You are correct, Meri, but there is someone who can help, provided I have not irked him because of my occasional protests at the way he interferes in my life."

"Euclid?" she asked, but knew it was no question.

"Aye, lass. Euclid."

Chapter Thirty-four

Thank God no one except two Gunwharf Rats knew where he lived. Josiah Coffin hurried home through an afternoon rain, the kind that reluctantly surrendered to winter only briefly, then changed into the more gentle rain of spring. Oh, Edinburgh, where is thy sting! He was quite ready to shake the dust off his feet and leave this city behind.

To his vast relief, his rooms had not been touched. At least John Yerby and whoever toadied up to him hadn't found his lodging yet. Wordless, he crammed his clothes into one portmanteau and his books and papers into another, working as rapidly as he could. He couldn't help a bleak smile when he remembered his father telling him, "Remember, dear son, never pack more than thee can carry."

He did that now, stopping long enough in the front of his lodgings to pay his landlady for another month, and to demand that she not allow anyone into his rooms for any reason. "A short trip," he lied. "I'll be back in a month." *Or never*, he added to himself. *I don't even need what is in these two bags.*

He hesitated not a moment; he knew where to go. He hailed a hackney and gave directions to 158 Wilmer Street. Outside of his head, heart and Inner Light, there was no place where he knew he would be among friends, and maybe more.

Trusting no one, he made the jarvey take a circuitous route to Wilmer Street, his head on a swivel to make sure he was not followed. Consequently, it was after dark when he knocked on the door. Her face white, her eyes wide with worry, Esther opened the door and burst into tears. Josiah came inside, dropped his bags, and held her close as she sobbed into his already wet overcoat.

In another moment, she was joined by Davey and Avon, and Mrs. Perry, who led them all into the sitting room and closed the front door, after a careful look around.

They all sat in silence. Davey stared at his shoes. Esther held his hand in her lap, wordless. Avon sat on his other side, resting his head against Josiah's arm. Mrs. Perry stood in the doorway, floured rolling pin in her hand, but tapping it with her other hand, apparently ready to defend heart and home and brain anyone who walked through that front door. *Every pacifist should have a Mrs. Perry handy,* he thought.

He must have said it out loud, because Esther sniffed back her tears and managed a watery chuckle, with a nod to the fierce black woman. He felt Avon shaking with silent laughter. Davey still looked at his shoes. Mrs. Perry glared at Josiah, then gave an elaborate wink.

He was among friends, but one of them needed bolstering. "Davey, look at me."

Davey raised troubled eyes to his. "I should have done something. I would have, but I didn't know what it could be."

"No harm and no foul, believe me," Josiah said. "Thee did precisely the right thing by sitting there, not giving an inch. I thank *thee.*"

"It was all there when I arrived in the classroom," Davey said. He gave the matter some thought. "I should have been suspicious when one of John's, um, adherents detained me after Materia Medica."

"That was the only portrait I had of my mother," Josiah said. Esther squeezed his hand. "He got into my office and destroyed my personal books."

"What chaps my hide is that John thinks he can get away with all this," Avon said. "Mr. Coffin, it is time for us to put the plan in place."

"I wish we could, but I submitted my resignation, effective immediately. I am no longer a ward walker in the Indigent Poor and Sick Ward."

"Don't give up, Mr. Coffin," Avon said, and there was no overlooking the steely glint in his eyes. "It's not Trafalgar."

No one could have said anything better.

Mrs. Perry herded the Rats into the kitchen, on some pretext about helping her with dinner. He blessed her silently for seeing his need to talk to Esther without an audience, Esther who hadn't let go of his hand. After the door closed, Josiah took a chance and put his arm around her shoulders. "I'm a fool," he said simply. "John has me over a barrel."

"Wretched little shite," she said with some feeling, which made him laugh out loud.

"Language, language," he murmured when he could speak.

"Well, he is," she asserted.

This is going to be awkward, he thought, then revised his opinion, considering that she hadn't pulled away from him or slapped his chops, even though he held her so close to him. He hadn't thought a thin woman would be soft, but she was. "I…need a place to stay, at least for a few days," he began.

"You have it here," she said promptly. "The fee is either a shilling for room and board, or a great smacking kiss."

Well, that was easy. Tenderly, he turned her face toward his and gave her a great smacking kiss.

"Quakers are frugal," she said, when she could speak, which made him laugh again, and feel that no matter what happened, things were not at their worst, as they had been earlier that afternoon. He kissed her again, feeling even better.

"I don't think anyone knows where I am," he said, as Esther cuddled closer. "I don't trust that little shite, either."

He spent a peaceful evening in the sitting room while Esther knitted and the Rats wrangled over bones and muscles in the dining room, Avon asking questions and Davey answering them promptly. The doors were open and he enjoyed their camaraderie, young men of pasts bleak beyond reason, indelibly welded together by Trafalgar and Sailing Master Able Six. The thought idly crossed his mind that Avon was learning as much as Davey about medicine.

The hardest moment came when he considered his future. He had nothing to offer Esther Teague. Frugal she might be, but she wasn't stupid. He would return to London, where his father would likely scold a bit, then suggest some course of action. When Josiah accepted the position at the college of medicine, his father had agreed, then hazarded the thought that he might write to his older brother in Massachusetts, United States. "He is doing well in his counting house, and he loves thee," was all his father said, not a man to press an issue with his sons. He trusted them. but America? Too far.

He did write a note to Walter Scott, giving him the particulars, which he sent on its way via Avon, who never seemed to forget a street or a building.

Avon set Josiah's mind at ease, too, saying that he intended to continue sweeping in the indigent ward. "I might learn more," was all he said, clinching it with, "Besides, John and Richard have never seen me before."

Mrs. Perry must have understood his low state. The breakfast she cooked – eggs, rashers of bacon, mounds of toast – went down like manna. It was all he could do not to leave for the college with Davey, feeling like a failure for allowing one wretched student to ruin his career. He thought he was not a man to cut and run, but apparently, he was.

When his thoughts reached their most unproductive by mid-morning, Esther brought him a piece of hot bread slathered with butter, which cheered him immensely. When he finished, Josiah sat at her desk in the sitting room and composed a letter to his father, or tried to.

The sitting room overlooked Wilmer Street. He had scarcely gotten beyond "Dear Father," when he saw Davey hurrying toward the house. He glanced at the clock on the mantel. It was time for Bones to begin, and here was Davey.

Esther must have seen him, too. She opened the front door and Davey practically fell inside, breathing hard. He held out a letter. "It's from Sir Winston," Davey said. "He came into Bones and pulled me out. You should have seen John smirk at that."

"Who's teaching Bones?" Josiah asked, as he took the letter.

Davey named a nonentity who always struck Josiah as terrified of students. He shrugged. He looked at the letter in his hand, thinking that if he were truly the spiteful sort, he could return it unread.

Davey must have seen that expression on Josiah's face. "Sir, he told me you had to give this matter your prompt attention."

"I don't work for him now," he reminded Davey, even as he slit the envelope open, read it, and reached for his coat, neck cloth be damned. There wasn't time.

"Sir?" Davey asked, at the same time Esther Teague handed Josiah his hat. He gave her the letter and motioned to Davey. As they hurried along, he told Davey about Sir Lionel's low state, after being struck by a brewery wagon months ago. "All this time and his leg has not healed. Davey, apparently Sir Lionel himself is demanding that I amputate." He did stop then, his hand on Davey's shoulder. "Will thee assist? The letter said he is already upstairs in Dissection Three." He shuddered. "Why me?"

They took the steps two at a time as students moved aside. "Sir Winston seemed mystified about that, too," Davey said. "He kept muttering, 'Sir Lionel is barmy,' then something about Euclid."

As he ran down the hall on the fourth floor, one side of Josiah's brain told him it was another cruel trick. The other side urged him on. "I'm a fool," he muttered again as he entered the operating theatre, then paused to see a man lying on the table, naked under a sheet, his desecration of a leg uncovered, with mottled streaks running from his ankle to just below his knee. Prosy, windy, play-favorites Sir Lionel Henderson was near death.

Sir Winston McLeish looked up from his contemplation of his old friend, his expression anguished. Gone was the superior man of yesterday, who had no qualms then about declaring Josiah a poor specimen and a meddler.

"I thought you might not come," he said. "What do you need?"

"I would like my capital knives, but they were stolen from my office yesterday," Josiah said. He turned to Davey, who was eyeing Sir Lionel's leg as well, assessing the ordeal ahead, as a good surgeon would. "What about thy knives, lad? I suspect they are clean and sharp."

"Aye, aye, sir," Davey said with a grin. "I hide mine. I don't trust this lot."

"Go get them." Josiah turned to McLeish. "I need two buckets of hot water, soap and towels."

"This man is dying!" McLeish hissed, looking over his shoulder as students entered. "We haven't time for nonsense."

"Then I am leaving," Josiah said, and started for the door after Davey, who was running down the hall.

"Very well! Very well! You're trying me," the chancellor called after him, and turned to two students, who dashed away on his command for hot water.

Josiah took a good look at Sir Lionel's leg, apologizing mentally that he had chuckled when he learned at the beginning of the term that the old windbag had been hit by a brewery wagon. No, this was a man in terrible pain who would be dead in a day if something wasn't done. Even then, he might be too late.

Feeling most unworthy, Josiah closed his eyes and prayed for the life of a man who had been one of many, whose jibes and taunts in faculty meetings were hard to forget. Never mind. Sir Lionel, boring, prosy Sir Lionel, was a son of God among the millions of sons and daughters of a God far kinder than any of them deserved, bound to each other, whether they knew it or not, by equality before the Lord. Perhaps that would remain Josiah's little secret. He considered again. It was a secret he could share with Esther Teague, because he loved her. He had to ask himself what it was about an emergency that made everything in his mind and heart so clear.

He opened his eyes to see Davey holding out his capital knives. "It's an old set that belonged to Master Six," he said. "He made sure I kept them sharp."

"Excellent. Put them in that hot water. Thee and I will wash our arms up to the elbows in the other basin."

He heard some of the students laughing as he and his assistant soaped up and washed, but he didn't care. He laughed when one of the students said loudly that he preferred to wash *after* the surgery. Fool. Josiah took out the knives and rested them on a clean towel. He wanted his surgeon's apron, but all he had was a sheet, which he ripped in half and gave the other half to Davey.

"Is thee ready?" he asked his assistant, someone he trusted with all his heart.

"Aye, sir. Nice not to work on a moving deck."

Sir Lionel appeared unconscious, but Josiah carefully opened his mouth and inserted a folded cloth to bite down on. With an efficiency born of surgery at sea, Davey had already tied down the man.

Josiah looked at the students and some physicians watching, and saw John Yerby, who rolled his eyes. *It is a good thing I am a peaceful man*, he thought. *Otherwise, I would smash him in the throat.* The idea made him smile. He looked at Richard Sterling, sitting far away from John, and so troubled in expression that Josiah felt compassion for someone too easily led. Medicine was not for Richard, either. Maybe he knew it.

No time for this. He shook his head at the grease pencil Sir Winston tried to hand him. Using the nail on his clean thumb, he marked Sir Lionel's leg beyond the ugly streaks and above the knee. "Gentlemen, of necessity, surgery must be clean and fast," he said beginning his lecture. "Amputations above the knee are always more dangerous, but we have no choice. Mr. Ten, let us begin. Someone time this. Fifteen minutes is a gold standard."

All was silent as Josiah made a sure incision. Sir Lionel's eyes opened wide. He tried to struggle, as anyone would, but he had been tied securely to the table. Josiah wrapped his arm around the wounded leg and made a circular cut in a matter of seconds.

He held out his hand and Davey gave him the saw. Several students quietly fainted at the mere sound of the saw. (No one needed to know that the sound still sent shivers up and down his spine.) His voice calm, but loud enough to carry, Josiah sawed through the muscle and bone, explaining a circular amputation. To Josiah's relief, Sir Lionel fainted. "Blessed syncope," he murmured. "Thanks be to God."

Coolly, thanking God for his serenity, Josiah described the entire surgery to his rapt, horrified audience. He paused briefly toward the end, tying off the main artery, branching arteries and veins, and looked at Davey Ten, who was destined to be as fine a surgeon as the Royal Navy ever produced. "Mr. Ten, would thee close, please?"

Davey nodded. The Gunwharf Rat, product of the workhouse, looked up when Sir Winston McLeish protested. Josiah put his bloody hand on Davey's sleeve. "Ignore him," then, "Don't disturb his concentration." How nice it was not to give a tinker's dam what the chancellor of the College of Medicine thought. He didn't work for him anymore. "Sir Winston, we know what we are doing."

They did. Josiah felt his heart soften as his mind cleared. "Time?" he asked, after Davey knotted the last stitch.

"Fifteen minutes," someone called. He heard applause.

"Good work, Davey," he said quietly, for his assistant's ears only. "I believe that the College of Medicine has nothing more to teach thee, if it ever did."

Davey stepped back as others whisked Sir Lionel away to a ward in the Royal Infirmary far superior to an indigent ward. Already, the old bore was alert and looking around. "Mr. Coffin, I would like to go back to Haslar and continue there."

"Thee would feel right doing that?" Josiah thought he knew the answer. He saw it in Davey's eyes.

"Aye, sir. I don't need to prove anything to anyone, do I?"

"Thee never did."

"But I had to know that of myself."

"Here endeth the lesson, lad," he murmured, perhaps for the last time.

Chapter Thirty-five

Josiah hated to be so uncommunicative over dinner at sweet Esther's house, but his surgeon's mind and heart were on Sir Lionel. A glance at Davey told him that his surgical assistant felt the same way. A big sigh made Esther laugh. She shook her soup spoon at him.

"You two are worthless!" she declared, but with a smile. "*My prescription is that you both go to see how that man is doing.*"

Thee would make an excellent doctor's wife, he thought, as he grinned at her. *Too bad I am unemployed and mooching off you now, as it is.* He put down his napkin and stood up. "What says thee, Davey? Shall we attempt a visit to Ward A? We might get thrown out."

Davey shrugged. "Nothing's as bad as Trafalgar," he said, and gave Avon a knowing look. "I think that is something I'd like to see stitched on a sampler."

"I have something for you first, Mr. Coffin," Avon said. "I didn't know how to tell you, because I doubt you approve of thievery. Consider it part of my background, if you would."

Josiah sat down, intrigued but not distressed. He trusted Avon. A glance at Esther suggested that she did, too. "Say on, son," he told Avon, never wincing or dodging from calling him son. It earned him a long look from Avon.

"I knew John was in Bones today, so I, uh, paid a return visit to his lodging." Avon made a face. "Davey, does she cook nothing but boiled cabbage?"

Davey nodded and laughed. "Avon, you've turned into a snob."

"Guilty as charged," Avon replied. "I climbed that drain spout by John's window again. I found this in his bureau, if you had any doubts,

223

sir." He took a paperweight from his pocket and handed it to Josiah, who turned it over in his hand to see *Dear Son* etched in the glass.

"My mother gave this to me," Josiah said, when he thought his voice might not betray him.

"I know it's not the little picture John mutilated," Avon said, "but you're lucky to have something from your mother. I wish…"

Avon paused and Josiah's heart went out to him. Should he say what he wanted to say? He had been saying plenty to people in power today. Why not say what mattered more? "Thy mother gave thee life and for this I thank her. Thee is now sharing thy life with us." He took a deep breath and committed himself. "Isn't he, Esther?"

She nodded, her eyes bright, and kissed his cheek. "I'm a guaranteed poor specimen," Josiah said only to her, as if no one else was in the room. "No employment, a Quaker, which makes me vaguely suspicious, and …"

Esther put her finger to his lips. "This can keep. We still need some justice for Mr. Perkins, don't we, Avon?"

"Aye, miss."

Esther turned her kind eyes on Josiah. "Now you and Davey need to check on your patient."

He and Davey started out at a fast walk. "Sir, call me a meddler. I don't care. I think you have fallen into Parson's Mousetrap."

Josiah laughed. "Such a novel expression! I think she cares for me, even though I have nothing to offer her."

"If you will excuse another meddling observation, I don't think that matters to her."

What could he say to that? Soon they were in the great hall of the Royal Infirmary, and not the side entrance that took them to the indigent ward. "This is where physicians specialize in diseases of the rich," he whispered to Davey, who had to cover his laugh when a matron glided by and gave him a fierce look.

"Sir! They'll throw us out," Davey whispered back.

"Not yet."

They found Lionel soon enough, his bed surrounded by fourth year students and Sir Winston. Josiah stood back deferentially, tall enough to see over most of the students. *Thee is still alive*, he thought. *Thanks be to God.*

"This is his surgeon, gentleman," Sir Winston proclaimed. "Make way."

The Red Sea parted and Josiah and Davey walked toward the bed on dry ground. Josiah motioned Davey closer and raised the sheet. "Good," he said. "Nice sutures, Mr. Ten."

"I learned from the best at Haslar," the Rat replied. "And we didn't have a slanting deck today."

"No, we didn't." Josiah leaned closer and gently shook the patient. "Sir Lionel? Is thee in there?"

The old professor's eyes fluttered open. "Aye, Mr. Coffin." He held up his hand and Josiah grasped it. "Thank you with all my heart."

"Thee is welcome. Now, thee must mind the matron and do what she says, sir. Thee will be back teaching in no time."

"Alas, no. I think it is time I retired."

Wise choice, Josiah thought. *No telling how many brewery wagons are waiting to run thee over again.* He released Sir Lionel's hand and placed it gently on his chest. "Rest now. Decisions can wait." He turned to his able assistant. "Davey, I'm satisfied. Is thee?"

Davey nodded. "I'd better get home and study some more." He seemed to stand a little taller in Josiah's eyes. "I have a term to finish. I also need to write a letter to Master Six."

They started back down the hall. "One moment, please, Mr. Coffin. I must have a word with you," Sir Winston called.

"Go on, Davey. I'll catch up," Josiah said. "If he's going to chastise me again, I'll remind him that I resigned. Yes, sir?"

"In my office."

They walked in silence to Sir Winston's office, while Josiah chafed inside. He wanted to speak to Esther, to explain himself, to do what he needed to …oh, he didn't know what to do. In all the turmoil of this year at the medical college, he hadn't thought to fall in love.

"Have a seat, Mr. Coffin. Would you like a glass of wine?"

This was a far cry from the monumental dressing-down of yesterday. "No wine, sir. What may I do for thee?"

Lo and behold, Sir Winston sat next to him, and not behind his intimidating desk that had probably frightened any number of faulty medical students into choosing another field. He didn't imagine that an apology came easily to Sir Winston, and Josiah didn't expect one. What did the man want?

"Mr. Coffin, perhaps we were both hasty. Kindly rescind your letter of resignation," he said at last. "To begin, I owe you an unpayable debt for saving Sir Lionel's life. Let us return to the way things were. What say you?"

"I remain firm in my resolve to release the college from any obligation it might owe me," Josiah said. "Now, sir, if thee will excuse me..."

"Not yet! I feel I have a debt to pay, because you saved Sir Lionel's life," Sir Winston admitted. "Surely you understand my position with a student like John Yerby, whose father is a man of marked influence. I cannot willy nilly dismiss him. What would people say?"

And here we are, Josiah thought, tired of the whole matter. He regarded his superior, who appeared sincerely troubled, but not troubled enough to commit himself, even though John had no business in medicine. It was a matter of justice for a poor man, which no one but a Quaker and two Gunwharf Rats understood...and Esther. *I need help*, he told himself.

The idea, when it came to him from some nook or cranny in his brain, struck him as audacious and unlikely. As McLeish glowered at him, Josiah gazed back with sudden serenity, as his mind cleared. All McLeish could do was say no. He had no power over Josiah Coffin. None.

"I have the ability to find you a worthy position somewhere else," McLeish said, in a wheedling tone of voice. "Nothing need be said about John Yerby."

"I can find my own position, but I thank thee," Josiah replied. He knew where that position was now, and he smiled at the audacity of it all. "I do ask something of thee, a small thing, really. Thee will never be called to account for it. It will satisfy any obligation thee thinks thee owes me for today's surgery."

"What, Mr. Coffin?"

"All I ask is that you come with me some night next week to the indigent ward and watch what happens when John Yerby ward walks there."

"Nothing will happen," McLeish snapped.

"It might not," Josiah agreed, the soul of equanimity. "If something *does*, I want you to witness the matter. If, after that, thee keeps John Yerby as a student, then the burden is on thee. I will never say anything. I don't work here anymore."

He saw doubt and irritation cross the chancellor's face. The man famed in medical circles opened his mouth several times to speak, but nothing came out.

"I, of course, can, with thy permission, continue to ward walk in the indigent ward until the end of term," Josiah said. "I know it is difficult for thee to find physicians willing to bother with the poor and homeless. They smell bad and there is a lot of pus and gangrene."

"That was another matter I wanted to discuss with you," McLeish said. He sounded tired; he sounded old. "I can get only one other physician in there. They have odd excuses. I don't know who or what they are listening to."

"I do not know precisely when John will betray himself, but it will be soon enough," Josiah said, praying silently that he was right. Wee Willie surely needed more bodies, since the graveyard fiasco had not yielded a corpse. "Thee and I will watch in the shadows. No one need ever know thee was there."

The chancellor was silent for a long moment. Josiah said nothing. Finally, "All I need to do is watch with you?" he asked.

"That is all. What thee does with what thee sees is thy business entirely."

"Well then," Winston McLeish said after a moment's thought. "My obligation to you will be paid."

"Entirely."

"Very well." The decisive Winston McLeish returned. "We'll stay in touch," he said, as he walked Josiah to the door of the Royal Infirmary.

"We will," Josiah said softly, when he was in the street again where Davey waited. They walked home. Davey had only one comment. "I hate to think that the chancellor will do nothing about John."

"It might not come to that," Josiah said. "We have another card to play, something Avon told me about, as did your Master Six. A Captain Ogilvie, who is a skulker and an assassin."

"Aye, he is."

"It might be too late to summon him. That's my only worry."

Davey laughed softly. "Avon wrote to him even before the fouled body snatching. Captain Ogilvie wants to resolve the matter of the missing Royal Navy men."

"Oh, you Rats," Josiah said, impressed. "Still, it's a long way from Portsmouth."

"He's already here." Davey had his own dimple, and it flashed now. "We didn't want to spring it on you too soon."

Chapter Thirty-six

So he was, a bit shopworn from rapid travel by post chaise. Sitting in Miss Teague's parlor, Angus Ogilvie looked somewhat like a human coiled spring.

"Do join us, Josiah," Esther said as she poured tea for Captain Ogilvie, assassin extraordinaire, or so Davey had described him on the walk home. Josiah looked on in amazement as Esther Teague, a quiet spinster coerced into caring for Gunwharf Rats, poured tea. She had blossomed into a force to be reckoned with. What a woman.

"We hope you were successful," Esther told him. "Have some tea." She turned her kind eyes on the grim man who looked like he had never suffered a fool gladly in his entire life. "Imagine this! Captain Ogilvie has been in town several days. He has been diverting us with his own skulking, up to and involving Napoleon, himself. Of course, we are all sworn to secrecy or death." She might have been discussing the weather, or whether they wanted lamb or beef roast on Sunday.

Someday, provided there is a someday, I will have to ask this darling woman if she had any idea what her life would become, he thought, as he accepted a cup and saucer and sat down.

"Tell me what you know, Mr. Coffin," the captain said, obviously not a man to waste time.

"Sir, I have convinced Winston McLeish, the chancellor of the college of medicine, to come with me to the poor and indigent ward – Ward B – at such a time as we are able to catch John Yerby in the act of smothering a patient, in this case, Avon March."

It sounded wildly absurd to Josiah, but Captain Ogilvie merely nodded, as if he heard deeds like this every day. Perhaps he did.

"Miss Teague has already shown me the shabby dress and cloak she plans to wear when Avon is admitted to the ward in a dying condition, and she his illiterate, poverty-stricken mother." He nodded to Davey. "Provided you can concoct a potion to render him, shall we say, comatose."

"I can," Davey assured him. "Mr. Coffin will check my work."

Captain Ogilvie rubbed his hands together. "My God, but you are a sterling bunch," he said. "When can we begin?"

"Tomorrow," Josiah replied, finding himself yielding to the undeniable talents of this ordinary-looking man with sharp eyes. He wanted this done. He had his own plans. "I am to continue ward walking in B. I will examine Avon's chart, noting how he seems to be failing. The students read those charts and initial them, writing their own observations. I will give it a day or two, to allow John time to plot his mayhem." He nodded to Esther. "Miss Teague, are you a great actress such as Sarah Siddons or Fanny Kemble?"

"We shall see," she replied. "More biscuits, anyone?"

"They are excellent, by the way," the captain said, sounding like an average visitor, which everyone knew he was not.

Esther blushed becomingly. "I will bring in some more."

When she left the room, Captain Ogilvie gestured them closer. "Avon and Davey have shown me that little shite's souvenir from the Royal Marine." He rubbed his hands together again and his face became more animated. "I hope that Wee Willie will be somewhere in attendance, and not just his minions. *His* career needs to end."

He must have noticed Josiah's wide eyes. "You, sir, I hear, are a Quaker, and probably no devotee of violence and murder."

Josiah shook his head, wary. Ogilvie noticed, and slapped his knee. "No fears! Your chancellor can bumble and blather about, but John might find himself on a long sea voyage. Australia might be far enough. I have other plans for Wee Willie." He stood up and stretched. "The redoubtable Miss Teague had already prepared a bedchamber for me. The hotel was wretched." He stopped in the doorway. "Mr. Coffin, don't waste a moment courting Miss Teague. I never saw another lady so in love with a man's sorry carcass as when you walked through that door. Talleyho!"

Davey clapped his arm on Avon's shoulder. "It's upstairs for us, too. G'night, sir."

Josiah stood alone in the sitting room when Esther returned with more biscuits. She looked around, surprised, and then her cheeks took on a rosy glow, competing with the sparkle in her eyes. Without a word, she held out the plate to Josiah.

He took the plate from her, set it on the table, and took her in his arms. His eyes closed in relief when she sighed and put her arms around him, standing so close that he felt amazing stirrings in his body. *This will never do*, he thought, then tossed that stupid idea aside and kissed her with all the fervency of his whole heart.

He doubted he was a good kisser, because he had almost no experience. Esther didn't seem to mind. She was no better than he. Oddly enough, together, they were wonderful kissers.

He stepped away finally because he truly was in danger of real indiscretion.

"When did all this happen?" he asked, when his mouth worked again and he pulled her down beside him on the sofa. His arm naturally seemed to circle her slim shoulders, just as she nestled close, her head against his chest. He couldn't help a little laugh. "I thought this sort of thing took a lot of time."

"Perhaps not," she said. "I'd quite given up ever meeting someone." She touched his cheek and he felt a quiet serenity fill his mind and heart. "And you?"

"Me? Medicine may have taken all my concentration. What a mistake."

Josiah knew it was time to declare himself. Surely it was past time for her to contemplate what a bad bargain he really was. He never minded silence – that was a Quaker virtue – but if Ecclesiastes was right and there was a time for every season, this was it.

All he knew was simplicity. "Esther, I love thee," he said, grateful his voice didn't crack like a lad in puberty. "I am unemployed, I am an adherent to the Society of Friends, and that will never change."

"I wouldn't expect it to," she said. "Will I be allowed to attend your church meetings?"

He felt his whole body relax with her simple question. "Most certainly." He thought briefly about offering a treatise of what such a meeting might entail, but Esther kissed his cheek and it went out of his mind entirely.

He kissed the top of her head, and ventured onto shaky ground, because he was honest. "There is this: I have absolutely no experience with women beyond medical knowledge. None."

"Well, that's two of us," she said cheerfully. She patted his arm. "I think we'll figure it out. Millions have."

She thought a moment, and he saw all her maidenly shyness. "Do you have weddings in your worship?"

"It's rudimentary, at best," he said, remembering weddings of his non-Quaker friends involving ritual supremely distasteful to him. The idea of a man insisting that a woman love, honor and obey him went against everything he believed, and he told her so.

"But what do you do?"

He took a chance, and reached for her hand. "This is what we do, my dearest." He took a deep breath and another. "If I say these words and thee replies yes, then we are married." He kissed her forehead. "We need witnesses, though, to make it binding. None here, at the moment."

He watched her expressive face, animated and intelligent. Her eyes softened as she regarded him. "Let us get through these next few days and then find witnesses." She touched his face. "There is more at stake than you or me."

He knew she was right. He pulled her up with him and kissed her cheek. "I can wait," he told her. "I might also add that though spoken vows between the two of us and witnesses is enough in the eyes of God, the government requires a marriage in at least the Registry Office."

"It will still be there when we are ready," she said. She kissed his lips, a lingering kiss that promised much, much more, and said goodnight. He watched her walk up the stairs, admiring the shape of her hips. At the top of the stairs, she squared her shoulders, then put her hand on her heart, which touched him in places he hadn't known existed.

"Soon," he said.

Chapter Thirty-seven

Esther had her doubts about Captain Ogilvie; so did Mrs. Perry. "I don't like the way that man talks to Avon," the Black woman said, after she had finished serving breakfast next morning to her Gunwharf Rats and the captain.

"What do you mean?" Esther asked, hoping she didn't sound overly suspicious, then not caring if she did.

"He speaks to Avon as though t'lad will return to Portsmouth with him and become a fulltime skulker," Mrs. Perry said. Esther saw the slow burn in her face, not an image that Captain Ogilvie would appreciate.

"And Avon?"

"He kept his eyes on his plate until he could get away," the cook told her. "Avon and Mr. Coffin left for another breakfast with Walter Scott." She made a face. "Captain Ogilvie muscled in on that."

Time to hatch the plan, Esther thought, wishing she could have gone with them. She saw Davey off to classes and spent the morning quietly fretting as she made beds and thumped pillows.

Her relief knew no bounds when the three of them returned, Josiah with his hand on Avon's shoulder, and Captain Ogilvie strolling beside them. She politely invited Ogilvie to luncheon and was happy when he shook his head. She wanted a moment with Josiah and Avon.

"When?" was all she wanted to know, when it was just the three of them.

"Tonight," Josiah told her. "Walter managed to cajole Mr. Bean and Mr. Turner into continuing on the case. Walt liberally greased their palms with a pound sterling each, the better to get their attention. You and Avon are to meet them in the park after dark. I will already be in the indigent ward, as on any other night."

"They're putting me on a stretcher then," Avon said, and she heard all his excitement. "And you will come along, sobbing and ..." He peered at her face. "Can you cry at a moment's notice?"

"I will do anything to help you, my dear," she said. "All I need to do is think how sad I will be when this adventure is over and you and Davey return to Portsmouth." The very idea brought tears to her eyes. "See there, Avon?"

Avon nodded. To her chagrin, she saw tears in his eyes, too. She touched his shoulder, which was all the encouragement he needed to open his arms to her. She held him, her eyes on Josiah, who watched them both, his face so serious.

This would never do. To her relief, Mrs. Perry came to the hall and gestured to Avon. "Luncheon is on the table," she said, and followed him into the kitchen.

"Captain Ogilvie tells me that Avon is to return with him to Portsmouth when this little adventure is done," Josiah said to Esther.

"Please no. Can you do anything?"

"I'm thinking on the matter, believe me," he said, and enveloped her in an embrace she never wanted to leave. "First things first. I will see thee tonight in Ward B. Thee doesn't know me, of course. Until tonight, then."

To her delight, he touched her hair, then rested his hand on her neck, a monumentally pleasurable feeling. He spoke quietly into her ear. "Be sure to cover thy hair. It's too beautiful and healthy-looking for a poor woman's tresses." He kissed her with some assurance, more proof that even amateurs such as they could turn adept in a short time. "I am already looking forward to brushing thy hair, some evening soon." His words put the heart in her.

That night, Esther put off her ordinary day dress and had Mrs. Perry button up the back of a ragged black dress she used to scrub floors and clean ashcans when she lived on sufferance in her brother's house. She had only hung onto it because she was a Scot and frugal.

Mrs. Perry bound her glorious hair into a tight knot and covered the beautiful mass with a dingy rag. Her housekeeper found a threadbare shawl somewhere. It smelled like unwashed bodies, so Esther pronounced it a success.

She felt the smallest glimmer of hope as she watched Avon, the quiet lad saying even less than usual over supper. When Davey made some flippant remark that the exciting life of subterfuge and mayhem would never be for him, Avon put down his fork. "It isn't for me, either," he said, his voice soft as if Captain Ogilvie could hear, even at a distance.

"I thought you liked it."

"I did until I came here." Avon left the table without a word. Davey stared after him, then shook his head. "Just when you think you know someone..."

She and Avon waited in the sitting room until full dark, holding hands. "I'm afraid," she admitted.

"That's two of us," Avon said, and gave her hand a squeeze.

They walked silently to the designated meeting place in the middle of the park, Avon's hand in hers. It was enough to hold his hand, and wish she had a son as fine as he was. A constable who introduced himself as Mr. Turner met them in the park, accompanied by a shabbily dressed Captain Ogilvie. It was not her imagination that Avon moved closer to her when the captain approached. She rested her hand protectively on his shoulder.

"Nice touch, Miss Teague," the captain said. "Everyone will see you as a desperate mother."

"It's no act, ye sleekit bampot," she muttered under her breath. Avon looked at her in surprise. "Tell you later, Avon," she said, and glowered at the captain, even though it was full dark by now and he couldn't possibly see her.

Soon Avon was prone on the stretcher, Mr. Turner carrying one end and Captain Ogilvie the other. Esther followed behind, hurrying to stay up with them. They went into the Royal Infirmary by a side door and Esther began the drama. She burst into tears, alternating between wailing and keening. She blew her nose into a disgusting handkerchief and trailed after them into a ward of twenty beds, some of them occupied, the indigent ward she had heard so much about.

Josiah watched them set Avon down where he indicated, then gently lifted the lad into the cot and covered him with a blanket. Esther noted another physician with two wide-eyed students nearly clinging to him like barnacles. They obviously knew nothing about poverty, and hung back as far as they could. Out of curiosity, Esther cried louder until she seemed on the verge of hysteria, wondering what the students would do. To her delight, one of them ran from the ward.

"Steady now .... Let me see." Josiah fumbled with his clipboard. "Ah, Mrs. March, is it?"

Esther nodded. She wiped her runny nose on her sleeve then scratched her head. The remaining student stared at her, disgust all over his face. *Pansy*, she thought, then stuck out her tongue at him. He leaped back as if she had spit on him.

"Mind thyself," Josiah growled, then turned away, because Avon started to grin.

Keeping his own distance, Josiah took Avon's medical history, or rather invented one, all within earshot of the other physician. She told him she was beside herself with worry. "I brung him in after two weeks of me dosing him," she said.

"You should have brought him in sooner," Josiah. "He looks low, which I will record on his chart."

She sniffed some more until the other physician threw up his hands in disgust and moved away. "Good show," Josiah whispered. "Even I don't like thee too much."

Avon covered his mouth with his hands to keep from laughing out loud. When Josiah could manage, he said in a carrying voice for the other physician's benefit. "He's low unto death. What'll it be when he dies? Does thee have any money?"

"None," she assured him. "It's potter's field, if it comes to that." She burst into tears again as he wrote St. Luke, Potter's Field in large script on Avon's chart. "Thee needs to leave tonight by eight of the clock," he told Esther. "Come back in the morning." He walked away, soon conferring with the other physician, who had kept his distance after his students bolted.

She stayed by Avon's cot, her hand on his arm as he pretended to sleep, and then as he slept. He woke up when the bells chimed eight and she tucked the blanket higher. When she leaned closer to tuck in the loose ends, he whispered, "I think I would have liked a mum," which made her tears fall again, not a show, but from her heart. She kissed his forehead and he sighed.

Something happened then, something she did not expect. *I am Avon*

March's mother, she thought. *I must give him a good one*. She leaned closer and spoke close to his ear. "I am your mother for as long as we are here. I wish I could always be your mother."

"I have always wondered what she was like, and why she birthed me right there on the bank of River Avon."

She had no idea, either, but something merciful nudged her and the reason was perfectly clear. "My dear Avon, I strongly suspect she wanted to make certain you were found. If she hadn't cared for you, you would have been abandoned in an out-of-the-way spot and left to die."

"Do you think so?" Avon's eyes lost their wary look and his smile… She knew she would never forget this moment.

"I know so," she replied, and she meant it with all that was in her. "She loved you. So do I."

Avon put his hands over his eyes and sobbed. Avon, the skulker, the hidden lad who swept and watched, the sailor who raised signal flags at Trafalgar and defended the helmsman with his own life. Avon, who only wanted a mother.

Esther kissed his forehead. She had no words.

She left the ward alone, wrapping her shabby shawl closer, because it was cold out, even if it was spring now, a Scottish spring with sleet. As she crossed the park toward Wilmer Street, Josiah joined her. He opened his cloak and wrapped it around her, too.

"Thee is even better than Sarah Siddons," he told her. He put his hand on her neck and pulled her closer. "We can do this," he said. "Mr. Turner remained behind to watch. I stayed long enough to see John Yerby come in and check the charts. He didn't stay long."

"I'm worried," she said.

"I am, too, but Mr. Turner's there."

"It's not that." She stopped and put her hands on his arms. "Josiah, I don't want Avon to go with Captain Ogilvie, or even back to the Royal Navy! I want him with me."

She thought he might scoff or even laugh, but he did neither. He pulled her close into an embrace that she was beginning to think was soon to become a daily requirement for her wellbeing. "This is a hard thing," she told him, unable to tell him what had passed between her and Avon in the ward. In her mind, it was almost sacred.

He was silent. What could he say? She knew they were two powerless people in a world at war, with death and disease around them, and she wanted the impossible. She had no claim on Avon March, only a deep and abiding maternal love.

"Is thee a cynic, Esther Teague?"

"I used to be," she admitted.

"Then I say to thee, dearest lady, have a little faith."

Chapter Thirty-eight

Easy to nod and say aye, but harder, alone in her bed. After considerable tossing and turning, Esther Teague decided there were two things she was certain of: She loved Josiah Coffin and Avon March. The former was the husband she always wanted, but knew, after some years and disappointments, that such a being would never materialize. The latter was the son she never had, because the former never appeared.

Everything had changed. Another surprising discovery suggested that perhaps she wasn't as homely as she had feared. It was easy to look at the Quaker physician and see a handsome man, for so he was, tall and narrow of hip with blue eyes, dark hair, and excellent shoulders. She was still too thin, but her complexion was magnificent and her brown eyes and blond hair a wonderful combination. Her mouth was still too wide, but so what? "I will do," she said out loud, and slept well.

She kept her own counsel over breakfast, grateful that Captain Ogilvie wasn't there. "He didn't say and I didn't ask," was Mrs. Perry tight-lipped comment, as to his whereabouts. Esther wondered if anyone liked the captain, and decided it wasn't someone in Scotland. He did have a wife, according to Davey. Esther assumed she was a patient woman.

No one seemed inclined to conversation; such a sober bunch they were. "I will be ward walking this afternoon and evening," Josiah said after he pushed back his plate. "I need to write some letters this morning. I will also check on Sir Lionel, our surgical patient, when I get to the Royal part of said Infirmary," which made Davey smile.

She waved goodbye to Davey from the front step and went upstairs to change into her poverty clothing. To her surprise, Josiah followed her right upstairs and into her bedchamber, which made her heart skip a beat, which she doubted was a medical possibility. He kissed her soundly, telling her to keep a close watch on everything going on in the indigent ward. When she chided him about his less-than-romantic conversation, he proved her entirely wrong. "Blood pools on the lower extremities of the dying," he murmured in a loverlike tone, and gave her a long, probing kiss that rendered her knees weak.

"We were a solemn mob this morning," he told her as she walked him to the door of her room when she thought her knees would hold her up again. "Sometimes I wonder what goes on inside that capable brain of thine."

Should she? Why not? "Over boiled eggs, I was thinking of how charming you look with a little bit of toast at the corner of your mouth."

He chuckled at that and started for the stairs. "And then by the time I got to the bacon, I was wondering how splendid you might appear with nothing on," she concluded.

He stared at her for a second, then started to laugh, a wonderful, consoling, encouraging sound that just might get them through these next few days. He staggered down a step, leaned against the stair railing and gave himself over to mirth.

"Esther, thee is either certifiable or hilarious," he said when he could speak. "I am inclined toward hilarious." He winked at her, something she hadn't thought to ever see. "I'm nothing special."

"I'll be the judge of that," she replied and went into her room to change, closing the door behind her. She heard him laughing all the way down the stairs. "We needed that," she told her red-faced image in the glass.

The day promised rain again, dreary rain. She would have used an umbrella, but Mrs. Perry told her she was too poor to own one, remember? Her cook gave her a cold tongue of beef sandwich in a packet and nothing more. "You're poor," she reminded Esther, then tucked cheese and crackers in a smaller pouch in Esther's sad excuse for a handbag.

Esther nodded her thanks. "I'm not so good at this sort of thing," she admitted. Whether she meant falling in love and wanting a man so much that she nearly ached, or attempting to help Avon and Josiah achieve well-deserved justice for a poor man who died too soon. There was also the other matter weighing so heavy on her heart, that nagging matter of Avon as her own. But here was this kind woman looking at her with sympathy. "Mrs. Perry, I am afraid."

"Afraid of what, Miss Teague?"

Esther did not hesitate. The time was over for reticence. "I fear that Captain Ogilvie will find a way to get his hooks into Avon. I don't want that." She was in tears now. "I want Avon for my son, no matter how preposterous that sounds."

Mrs. Perry hugged her. "Miss Teague, you are surrounded by capable people. Trust me. Trust all of us." She gave Esther a good-natured pat on the shoulder. "Now go watch over Avon."

Why that sounded reassuring, Esther couldn't have said to magistrate or minister. It came from a woman who, by her color, was even more powerless than she was. Still, she couldn't overlook that martial glint in those dark eyes. "Very well, Mrs. Perry, I will," she said.

"One moment."

She stopped. Mrs. Perry went into the pantry and returned with a dingy-looking sweater that surely had never taken up residence in her orderly house. "What on earth…"

"I found this is the ash can behind the house three doors down. Take it. Here are your knitting needles. Unravel this and make something for Avon. It'll keep your hands busy."

Esther took it, silently blessing Mrs. Perry. No wonder Master Six – she would have to meet the Sixes someday – had insisted she come along. Possibly Mrs. Perry was the greatest asset any dubious enterprise could have. She blew her a kiss and started for the infirmary, head down against the rain.

Davey met her at the side door of the august building. He spoke quickly, his eyes wary, well aware of his surroundings. "I gave Avon a mild draught that will render him sleepy," he whispered. "He will be too insensible to make rational comment." He grinned. "I coached him in that, too. Told him to look half dead."

Esther took a deep breath. "I will watch over him."

"You already do," he said quietly.

She made her way into Ward B, eyes down but alert. An old woman sat beside a bed at the opposite end of the hall, but there were no other visitors. She looked around, sad to see patients with no one to care for them. The unfairness of humble lives sank into her heart. She thought of the times she had passed by beggars who held out cups, and even worse, old women with the peculiar dignity that poverty gave to some, as they suffered on street corners, saying nothing. *I can do better*, she told herself. *Josiah would expect it of me.*

She sat by Avon's cot, after looking at the chart attached at the foot. *Low, and not prospering in any way*, she read. *His days are numbered.* JC followed, which she expected. Other initials followed, probably the students he mentioned. Her heart chilled to see JY and RS among them.

She blessed Mrs. Perry. The day dragged on, but she had that nasty sweater to unravel, which took time. She talked in a low voice to Avon, who mumbled semi-coherent replies, and had no trouble bursting into tears when a grand-looking fellow accompanied by Josiah Coffin came by, too.

"Any day now?" the grand fellow asked impatiently. "Hush, woman."

Josiah had the audacity to put his finger to his lips. "Quietly, Chancellor," he said. "This is poor Avon March's mother."

"Then she is lucky we have a place for the indigent."

Esther glanced at Josiah's face and loved him all the more. He said firmly but quietly, "Chancellor, there are some who are poor through no fault of their own."

"*I* don't know any," Winston McLeish huffed. "Make this quick, Coffin. I have my limits of returning a favor."

"Yesterday it was an unpayable debt, when I saved Sir Lionel's life."

To his credit, Esther thought the great man showed the smallest bit of introspection. It passed quickly. He pointed his finger at Josiah. "Tomorrow and no later," he said, and stalked off.

Josiah sat down on a stool next to the vacant cot. He looked around and took Esther's hand. "Funny, isn't it? He claims he knows no poor people who have not been pushed down into poverty through no fault of their own." He raised her hand to his lips and kissed it. "There are many kinds of poverty. All he needs to do is look in the mirror. Carry on, dear ones."

She carried on, unraveling, then beginning to knit that noisome ball of yarn. She ate her bite of sandwich, then helped a drowsy Avon sit up for awful-looking gruel. He shook his head, but she bullied him into drinking a cup of water.

The afternoon shadows were lengthening across the ward when Mr. Turner and Captain Ogilvie made their way down the aisle, bearing another stretcher. She looked up, interested and wary at the same time. Josiah followed them. She put down the knitting.

They paused at the cot next to Avon, who roused himself enough to looked around, then sink back into slumber. Esther looked closer and saw a lad, perhaps older than Avon, but wretchedly dressed. He was rail thin and coughing, with frothy foam dribbling down his chin. His eyes opened, weary eyes which looked as though they had seen every misfortune in the universe. Esther's heart went out to him. She glanced at Avon, knowing deep in her soul that this Gunwharf Rat could just as easily have found himself where this young man was.

Josiah transferred him to the cot as carefully and gently as he could. It occurred to Esther that the chancellor who had no sympathy for the poor, especially the unworthy poor in his eyes, would wonder why even this lowly specimen was given a spot in *his* Royal Infirmary. She moved her chair closer to the other cot.

"Mr. Coffin said put him here," Mr. Turner said after Josiah walked to the vacant matron's table and sat there to write. He looked at Captain Ogilvie, perfectly vile in shabby coat and trousers that smelled worse than the yarn she had unraveled. "There he was, shivering and curled up by a bank, with people stepping around him."

"We checked his pockets for any sort of identification. Nothing," the captain continued. "Nothing. Mr. Coffin wanted him by you and Avon. Dunno why."

"Perhaps because Mr. Coffin thinks I will take care of him, too," Esther said. "I will."

Josiah joined them, carrying a basin of water, soap, wash cloth and towel. He went to a nearby shelf and found a gown like the one Avon wore.

"Thank thee, gentlemen," Josiah said. "I will clean him up and assess him."

"Watcha gunna call'im, Mr. C?" Mr. Turner asked. "Master Lost N. Found?"

Josiah glared at him, and he looked away. "Sorry," he muttered. "We'll watch outside."

No words were needed. Between the two of them, they stripped the skinny lad. When Esther gagged at the odor of someone unwashed for far too long, Josiah touched her cheek. "I have a remedy," he whispered and returned to the matron's desk. He came back with a small jar of camphor. He dabbed a little under her nose. "This will help."

She breathed the bracing odor in and out. "It does."

He was so dirty that Josiah had to empty the basin several times. Pine tar soap killed the lice in his hair, which her dear man cut off close to his head.

"When do you think he ate last?" she asked, her voice hushed and horrified.

"Weeks ago. He's dying of malnutrition and probably consumption. It will be a race to see who goes first, this nameless child of God, or Avon."

"Don't say that."

He touched his forehead to hers, after another look around. "It will be a blessing. We see too many of these unwanted ones on the indigent ward, but at least they have a place to go."

Josiah tried to feed the lad some gruel, but it dribbled from the corners of his mouth. He found a sugar cube and put it between the boy's lips. He moved his lips and sucked.

"That seldom fails," Josiah told her. "Thee can give him another one." He indicated the pile of ghastly clothes. "These go to the burn pit. He'll never wear them again. I suppose that was all he had to wear during our long winter."

Esther closed her eyes and felt the tears escape anyway. "I'll watch him, too," she told the man she loved. She could not say he was unemployed, because he would always and ever be a physician, whether he was paid or not.

"I knew thee would watch."

She sat between the cots, a hand on each lad, as Josiah continued his ward walking, stopping by other cots farther away to chat, to listen and to commiserate, and to administer medicine that she hoped would do some good.

The frazzled matron returned from feeding patients to light a few lamps as darkness came. Josiah rested his hand on Esther's shoulder when he returned, and stood there looking down at one lad, then the other. He squatted down beside her.

"I am going to write on both charts. Avon's will say "Prognosis uncertain, perhaps mere days.""

"And the one we don't know?"

"Probably the same." He shook his head. "I wish he weren't nameless."

"Name him William Teague, after my father," she said impulsively. "Everyone needs a name, and that was a good one."

"Aye, miss, I will." He went to Avon's side. "Avon will stay like this all night. In the morning, I will return and write, "'The end is near. I doubt he will survive this night.'"

Esther shuddered and rubbed her arms. "Tomorrow then?"

"Tomorrow. Let us pray that Chancellor McLeish sees what he wants to see, because we have to spring the trap. His patience is wearing thin."

"How do you do what you do here?" She needed to know.

"We do God's work on earth, because He cannot be everywhere."

"You could have chosen something easier," she said, loving him with all her heart.

"And miss out on lice and gangrene?" he joked, but she heard the tenderness. He kissed the top of her head. "This is such the wrong setting, but marry me, Miss Teague. I have a powerful hankering for thee and there is no cure but matrimony."

"No witnesses here that aren't comatose," she pointed out. She knew what her answer was. "I will marry you, because I also have a powerful hankering for you, coupled with the legality of the Registry Office."

He laughed at that, and leaned closer. "Do something more, dear lady. When you leave, blend a bit into the shadows like our Avon – yes, our Avon. Thee is wearing black, and the Scots who run this place are stingy with lanterns."

"I am the skulker now?"

"I doubt John Yerby will come in here until I walk out. See what he does. See if anyone else is with him."

"I will."

He kissed her and walked slowly to the end of the hall. She breathed in the camphor still under her nose and gathered her wretched knitting. When the clock chimed, she sat another moment by Avon, assured of his even breathing. She turned then to William Teague, for so his chart now read. She watched the unsteady rising and lowering of his chest and mourned his unfortunate life. She imagined the poverty, heartbreak, starvation, disease and loneliness, and kept her hand on his shoulder.

He stirred then, and opened his eyes. Esther smiled at him. "Rest now," she whispered. "You're in a safe place." He sighed and closed his eyes, the slightest smile on his face. She patted his chest, then rose, put on her shabby shawl, and hoped it wasn't raining outside.

She walked to the nearest door then took a page from Avon's own hard life and blended into the shadows, willing herself invisible and small.

She grew impatient with the non-existent passage of time, ready to go home and get into her bed, knowing that Mrs. Perry had probably slid in a warming pan. She wondered what it would be like to put her cold feet on Josiah Coffin's legs. The pleasant thought diverted her until the moment when she heard the door open. She held her breath, suddenly fearful that whoever it was would smell the camphor and look around.

Not these two. They swaggered in, shaking off their overcoats onto several occupied cots, which made the inhabitants call out. Of their own volition, Esther's hands seemed to knot into fists.

She watched them go down the row, looking at charts, then moving on. She heard one of them mutter, "Lord, doesn't anyone *die* here anymore?" and then giggled.

She held her breath again as they stopped by Avon's bed and the newly named William Teague. "It's time for Wee Willie," she heard Giggler say. "You find him tomorrow. I'll check these charts again after Bones tomorrow."

When they left out the same side door where she stood in deep shadow, Esther waited until the bells chimed nine. She wrapped her shawl tight around her and ran through the park, not stopping for anything until she opened her own front door, where she stood panting, until her heart returned to its normal, orderly beat.

Josiah sat in the parlor, a book in his lap, his head tipped forward, asleep. She sat beside him, and rested her head on his shoulder, which roused him. His arm went around her. "Did our lovely lads show up?"

"Aye, Mr. Coffin. I don't know who they were, but one had a high-pitched giggle. I already dislike them both, because they shook their wet overcoats on some of the patients closest to the door."

"That can only be the inimitable John Yerby and some other poor sap, perhaps Richard Sterling, although they are on the outs with each other." He stood up and tugged her to her feet. "Aren't adventures fun?"

"You're the one who is certifiable," she pointed out, as they went upstairs arm in arm.

He deposited her at her door with a kiss and headed down the hall, looking back from his own door. "Miss Teague, thee is a wonder. Tomorrow will try thee. Were I a wagering man, I would bet everything I owned on thee."

She was too polite to remind him that he was unemployed and shouldn't wager large amounts. She blew him a kiss that he probably couldn't see, and went to bed, her mind and heart on Avon. She also knew her father would be touched to know that there was a young man with his borrowed name.

"I am Mrs. March for one more day," she told her ceiling. Tears gathered, but she sniffed them back. She smiled in the dark at the improbability of a physician with the surname of Coffin. Her eyes began to close as she considered the mystical strangeness of everything since she received that letter from Aunt Munro, that moment when one plodding, ordinary day after another disappeared forever.

She, Esther Teague, who had long since given up on dreams, slept like a baby.

Chapter Thirty-nine

"It happens today," Josiah said to Davey over coffee, while Mrs. Perry stirred down the porridge, ladled out two bowls and didn't spare the sugar. They ate quickly, then walked to the public house where Walter Scott waited.

Esther had already left. Josiah had watched her walk purposefully toward the college, admiring her grit, in addition to the pleasant sway of her hips in that awful rag of a dress. He thought of his own audacious plan, wondering for a moment that he had been a careful person up to now, dutifully inquiring of the Lord God Almighty if he should do thus and so, or something else. Was he losing his connection by not inquiring of the Lord?

Another thought settled gently over his heart and soul. He heard no voices; that was not something Quakers asked for. Instead, he felt the calming influence of that Inner Light, which informed him that he had not petitioned the Lord because he knew his idea was sound and needed no celestial confirmation. At that moment, he realized that he, a thirty-four-year-old physician, finally reached maturity.

During this second breakfast, Mr. Turner and Mr. Bean listened as Captain Ogilvie went over their plan, if John Yerby acted, if the chancellor didn't rescind his appearance, if Wee Willie truly did make an appearance. If if if.

"There are many moving parts to this scenario," was his only comment. Ogilvie glared at him, which set Davey's lips in a tight line.

"I hope you don't plan to back down, Mr. Coffin," Ogilvie said.

Never, Josiah thought, as he tamped down his dislike. "I will do as thee says." *Up to a point*, he was careful not to add.

Theirs was a quiet walk to the college. "It's a fine old institution," Josiah told Davey. "I made it my ambition to teach here. I suppose I am guilty of the sin of pride. I wanted to be the first Friend to do that, and now I'm unemployed."

"Wh…where do you plan to go after this?" Davey asked. He grinned. "The Royal Navy would always have you, but I know you are not an adherent of violence and war, which is our current lot."

Josiah smiled at the joke. "I'll tell thee soon. One event at a time. Study hard, my lad. Exams begin next week."

He entered the infirmary, going first to observe Sir Lionel Henderson, who was sitting up now and demanding better food. Josiah imagined the attendants were already tired of the old rip. Hopefully no one would spit in his porridge.

In the indigent ward, the sun shone onto beds for the first time in a long winter and equally dreary spring. Josiah thought over his years in this place, thinking of the quiet order he had brought to this most despised ward. His time here was over. He had walked among the dead and dying and done his best to calm fearful hearts used to life's ill treatment.

He wavered then, knowing that if he begged enough, Chancellor McLeish would keep him on, but no, his plans had changed. He found a reason to change his life.

There she sat, her concentration focused on that grubby bit of knitting. He watched with love as she stopped often, resting her hand on Avon's forehead, then doing the same to the lad in the other cot, who lay so still. The letter from Aunt Munro in Portsmouth those months ago had changed Esther Teague's life profoundly, and his as well.

Esther turned at his footsteps and set down her knitting, folding her hands in her lap. She did nothing more than smile on him, and he felt his shoulders relax and his own respirations slow. *Thee is one person out of millions*, he thought. *I'll never understand how love happens.*

The matron sat at her desk so Josiah merely nodded to Esther. For the matron's benefit, he asked how Avon did, taking his vitals – wonderfully sound, of course – and shaking his head so the matron could see his "disappointment."

"Avon is being stubborn," Esther said quietly. "He doesn't want another sleeping draught."

"Why not, lad?" he asked, curious, after looking around to make sure no one watched them.

"I can look quite dead if John Yerby and his goons attempt to smother me," Avon said. He closed his eyes. "Open my eye."

Amused, he did as Avon directed and found himself staring at a dead eye. "Such a skill," Josiah.

"It got me out of a workhouse," Avon said. He made a face. "It would have, if I hadn't sneezed."

"Don't sneeze tonight," Josiah admonished, trying not to smile, in case the matron was watching. "Do as thee chooses. I trust thee." He thought a moment. "What was thee attempting by playing dead? How old was thee?"

"I was six," Avon told him. "I knew there was something better."

Six. Josiah remembered the joy of his own childhood and he ached inside for Avon's life, even as he exulted in the lad's resilience. "Did thee find it at St. Brendan's?" He wanted to know, had to know.

"I thought I did. I may have been wrong," Avon said. He glanced at Esther. "I have another dilemma, sir."

"Be patient, Avon. That is all I ask of thee."

Josiah turned to the other cot because he had to, before his emotions betrayed him, and found another story. "How is he, Mrs. March?" he asked in a louder voice for the matron's benefit.

"Very low, Mr. Coffin," she said, in Mrs. March's rough Scots brough. "He breathes, then forgets to breathe. Dunno why I need to worry about'im, too."

"It will keep thee busy, if thee plans to sit here all day," he told Mrs. March, then lowered his voice. "Dear lady, thanks for tending to this unknown, as well."

"I told you I am calling him William Teague. He woke up last night before I left and took a little water. This morning…" She shook her head. "Water just dribbles out of his mouth." She bowed her head. "I hold his hand and he breathes better."

"I do, too," he told her, which turned her cheeks rosy. "Listen. I am going to write on Avon's chart now: *Patient is low. I doubt he will survive the night. Potter's Field.*"

"Tonight then?" Esther asked. He saw her fear, as well as her anticipation.

"Everyone will be in place. Leave here at eight as usual, Esther. Go home."

"I'd rather stay here in the shadows. Avon has indicated a prime location," she said.

He knew better than to argue the matter. She had every right to follow her own course. "As thee thinks best." He looked again at William Teague, willing him to survive the day, too.

He wrote the fateful words on Avon's chart and left the ward. He knew he had to get far away, so he returned to his old rooming house, after buying a trunk. He sorted his papers calmly, throwing away most, but keeping his precious books, the ones he had not taken to his office, where, for all he knew, they still lay in a pile, pages ripped out, urinated on.

As he sorted and packed, he realized how little of this meant anything to him. His whole heart, might and mind were centered on the two dear ones in the indigent ward. He kept the needfuls and set everything else in the close with its ashcans.

He labeled the trunk's direction, pausing a moment in homage to his own audacity at this drastic step, then summoned a carter to take him and the trunk to Wilmer Street, where all was quiet. Mrs. Perry demanded to know what was going on and he told her, knowing he could trust her.

He spent more time in the Infirmary at Sir Lionel's bedside, listening to the old windbag prose on, aware that he had no family. "Ah, laddie, I dedicated my whole life to medicine, and see where it has landed me."

"Thee has had a fine career," Josiah said, not adding that the old fellow had stopped learning anything new years ago, and was probably more of a danger than an asset to patients *and* students. Thank God the only medicine he had practiced recently was to bore a generation of students.

Josiah dropped by the indigent ward in late afternoon, hoping he would find John's initials on Avon's chart. The matron was gone. Davey walked close by, but not too close. There were others to attend to, and Davey attended.

Esther stood by the window, pressing her hands to the small of her back, obviously weary. She brightened to see him, but he went first to Avon's chart, sighing with relief to see JY. He looked at William Teague's chart, relieved to see no initials there besides his own, grateful that John Yerby was lazy and hadn't looked at both patients.

"He is no better," Esther said, coming to stand beside him. "He took a sip of water, but his eyes follow me." She leaned her head against his shoulder briefly, seeking small comfort in a place with little of that.

"Thee holds his hand?"

"All the day," she said quietly. "Josiah, why do people have to suffer?"

It was the age-old question. He had no answer beyond what he heard at a meeting in London. The Coffins had sat quietly through the hour. No one spoke. Silence was its own blessing after a tumultuous week. Finally, an old fellow rose. Even as a young boy, Josiah could see that he suffered. He looked at his mother, a question in his eyes. She whispered. "His wife passed beyond the veil last week. Pray for him."

He did silently, turning his whole eight-year-old mind and heart to the matter. The old fellow looked around, smiled, said "God is good," and sat down.

He said it to Esther. "God is good, His mercy endureth forever. Thee is here, holding his hand, doing God's work."

She nodded and sat down again, wiping the unknown lad's forehead, then taking his hand. She smiled at Josiah much as the old man had smiled, all those years ago, and he knew she knew. It was enough.

When the clock chimed its eight bells, he returned to the ward. Esther was gone or hiding in shadows, as was Davey, hiding close, Josiah was certain, because Gunwharf Rats watched over each other on land and sea. He found a hiding place of his own, hoping the others were there and ready, and prayed.

Nine o'clock, ten o'clock, eleven, then midnight. He heard, "Damn it, Mr. Coffin," and knew where Sir Winston McLeish had secreted himself. On the half hour, he heard McLeish exclaim, "You waste my time!" It was louder. Josiah covered his face with his hands.

Just then the outside door opened and two students crept inside. He could tell they were students because of the black robes. One came in quickly and the other hesitated in the doorway. *Get inside*, Josiah thought. *There is a night watchman. Hurry up, damn you!*

Instead, he heard a whispered argument. The student who hesitated left. The other one closed the door quietly and came closer. Josiah held his breath as John Yerby stopped at the matron's desk, found a blank chart on the desk and wrote on it. He tiptoed to Avon's cot, removed the official chart and substituted his own, which Josiah was certain now read Dissection, instead of Potter's Field.

He watched, seeing all the horror, as John picked up a pillow and stood over Avon. He looked around, crouched down, and covered Avon's face, pressing down hard. Josiah heard Avon gasp, struggle briefly, then go limp. John stood there with the pillow pressed down. *Please, dear Father in Heaven,* Josiah whispered. *Please, Father.*

The funny thing about plans: Sometimes nothing goes as planned. Rarely, just rarely, a plan works. This one was perfect. As Josiah watched, Mr. Turner and Mr. Bean ran from their hiding places, followed more slowly by Walter Scott, his limp slowing him down, and then Davey. With a groan, Chancellor McLeish heaved himself away from a pile of mattresses.

Mr. Turner grabbed John, that murderous student with a minor in bodysnatching, who squirmed and shrieked, "You can't do this to me!"

"Aye, we can, laddie," Mr. Turner said and gave John a good shake, like a terrier with a rat in his mouth.

Josiah ran to Avon's cot. His dear boy lay there far too still. Josiah shuddered, feeling Avon's neck, dreading the thought that John had broken it. With shaking hands, he opened one of Avon's eyes. As he stared in the low light, Avon winked the other one. Josiah hugged him. "Good job, you Gunwharf Rat," he said.

Davey gazed in admiration. "Maybe our Avon should have been on the wicked stage. He looked dead to me."

Walter strolled over and gave John Yerby a kick with his good leg, just because. He perused the altered chart and held it up for Josiah to see. "We watched him write Morgue, then Dissection."

Josiah held up both charts, the good one and John Yerby's. "What say you, Chancellor? Is this proof enough?"

Chancellor McLeish stood in front of the struggling student, who stared back, venom in his eyes. "You can't do this to me! My father will never allow it. Let me go at once."

Oh, Winston McLeish, don't. The chancellor dithered even now. "We should reconsider this…"

"I think not."

Captain Ogilvie stood in the open doorway, rubbing his hands together. "I have a better idea." He nodded to Mr. Turner, who had been joined by Mr. Bean. "Truss him up good."

"Oh, but wait, wait," the chancellor pleaded. "You can't…"

"I can," Captain Ogilvie assured him. "We will sit this evil specimen down in a quiet place with thick walls – I know just the spot – and, shall we say, encourage him to tell us what happened to a certain Royal Marine and a carpenter's mate who fell afoul of this terrible student here. I want to know his connection to someone lamentably called Wee Willie."

John stopped struggling. "You can't hurt me!"

"Aye, we can, on orders from the First Lord of the Admiralty," Ogilvie assured him. "It won't be pleasant, but the walls are thick."

Silence. A much-chastened John Yerby hung his head. "It was all Wee Willie."

Ogilvie shook his head. Josiah watched in morbid fascination at all the menace in the captain's eyes. "Who located the victims? Wee Willie already told me just outside this infirmary. He kindly volunteered the fact that he couldn't have done any of this without an inside man. You."

"You're lying," John spat back, desperation on his face.

"Mr. Turner, let him see Wee Willie. It's not a pretty sight. That way."

John dug in his heels as Mr. Turner and Mr. Bean, grinning from ear to ear, dragged him to the door. Davey held open the door elaborately, ushered them through, then followed.

Winston McLeish stared open-mouthed at Captain Ogilvie. "Who, sir, are you?"

"I am Captain Angus Ogilvie, sent by an organization around since Henry the Fifth, God and all his wives rest him, to defend and preserve the lives of Royal Navy men and anyone else that pleases King George's fancy. Wee Willie and John Yerby are mine, make no mistake." He nodded to Josiah. "We also stopped another student named Richard Sterling running away. It took barely any persuasion at all to convince him to never darken the door at the College of Medicine ever again. He even signed a paper to that effect. He mentioned something about relatives in Canada that he hasn't seen in years."

"Oh."

Josiah bit his lip to keep from laughing. Never had he heard Winston McLeish say so little that meant so much. He sat down beside Avon on the cot and put his arm around the Rat.

It was then that he noticed the stillness of the unknown lad in the next cot. He reached over and pressed gentle fingers to the thin neck. "He's gone, Avon," he said quietly.

This did, indeed, change everything.

Chapter Forty

"Mum stayed by him all day," Avon told him. "He couldn't move or speak, but he watched her all day. She sang to him and kept his face clean."

"She would do that. Mum, is it?" he inquired.

"She cried when I said it. I think that's an aye."

They waited quietly on the cot, then watched as a much-chastened John Yerby was dragged back into the infirmary, his eyes more than desperate. Chancellor McLeish made a final attempt. "Surely you can release this student," he said to Captain Ogilvie. "I am certain he will never..."

"...kill anyone again before his time like that laddie?" he asked, pointing to the cot with the unknown patient. "You're generous with your forgiveness, Chancellor," Ogilvie said. "I have a better idea. Would you like to hear it? Pay attention, John. This is what happens to scum like you."

"No, no," John begged. He tried to back away, but Mr. Turner had an amazing grip.

"You're going on a sea voyage. Here's how it begins. I've arranged for a special press gang from the Royal Navy to find you wandering in... in...what's that little place across the Firth from here?"

"Dunfermline?" Mr. Bean offered cheerfully, clearly enjoying this narrative.

"The very place. The navy keeps a smallish fleet there to guard against trouble in the Baltics. They're expecting you, Mr. Yerby." Ogilvie smiled a gallows smile that made Josiah feel his own insides turn to liquid. "And what do you know, there is a frigate in that fleet headed to Australia. Think of the fun in store for you."

"No!" John wailed. "No!"

Ogilvie looked around. "John Yerby, shame on you. You're going to wake up these poor folk who are ill. Mr. Coffin, do you have a remedy?"

"Certainly, Captain," Josiah said. The matron had a stash of bandages. It was a matter of a minute to silence John with many layers of coarse cotton. "There we are."

John glared at him and muttered something indistinct. "Thy final grade in Bones? Is that what thee wants to know? Thee probably failed. Bon voyage, John."

Mr. Turner dragged John away. Ogilvie turned his attention to the chancellor again. "No one will ever know what happened to him. I will certainly never tell." He laughed. "If you could get Mr. Coffin to swear to the matter, which he won't, no one will still ever know."

Chancellor McLeish was as chastened as John. "You mentioned someone else outside the infirmary."

"Wee Willie." Walter Scott spoke for the first time. "He's a Resurrectionist, Chancellor. A body snatcher. What did you do to him, Captain Ogilvie? Is he going on a long voyage, too?"

"Rather longer than anticipated. I happened to be holding a knife. I only had to whittle on one ear for him to tell me what happened to the Royal Marine and carpenter's mate. Davey Ten witnessed that confession." Ogilvie shook his head. "And wouldn't you know, Wee Willie turned around suddenly and ran into my knife. Poor man."

Ogilvie the Assassin turned his relentless stare on Chancellor Sir Winston McLeish, himself. "I'm certain the man was grasping at straws, Sir Winston, but he swore to me that you know him and have used his services."

"B...B...But...."

Ogilvie slapped his head. "I must have misheard him! You would, of course, never do anything as reprehensible as that."

"No, never."

"Then this is our little secret."

"Wee Willie was a bad man who will not be missed," Ogilvie assured McLeish. "I suggest we strip him, put him in the morgue, and let some professor dissect him. I recommend Mr. Coffin over there. What say you, sir?"

Chancellor McLeish moaned, threw up his hands and left the infirmary, a broken man. Ogilvie watched him go. "D'ye think he'll submit his resignation, Mr. Coffin?"

"Hopefully." Josiah regarded the captain, a man he knew he never wanted to cross. He had a relentless air about him that suggested a person might run from him, but never hide.

All he could do was ask in good faith. "Captain Ogilvie, you told me a few days ago to woo Miss Teague speedily. Or was it diligently?"

"Speedily. She is a true gem."

"I did as you suggested, and she nicely consented to marry me." Avon clapped his hands. "Thank you, Avon."

Now Captain Ogilvie looked more interested than calculating. Josiah pressed on, wearing his heart on his sleeve and not caring who saw it. "Avon informed me only minutes ago that he is already calling Miss Teague Mum. Thee sees my challenge. I have a strong feeling that I cannot have one without the other."

"Avon March is committed to the Royal Navy," Ogilvie reminded him. "I have my own plans for him."

"Avon?" Josiah asked with his whole heart, "What says *thee*?"

"Those aren't my plans, Captain Ogilvie," Avon replied with no hesitation, his voice firm, his gaze unwavering. "I can skulk, but I am no assassin, begging your pardon. I have done my duty always. I did it tonight."

"You did," Ogilvie said. "I cannot deny that I am disappointed, but…." He looked around. "Here we have you, me, Mr. Coffin and Mr. Scott over there, listening hard and trying not to show it." He was silent for a long moment, this man of fierce duty and loyalty to king and country and the Royal Navy, someone Josiah knew could hunt them down, if he chose to.

"Avon, have you ever had a choice in your life?" Ogilvie asked.

"No, Captain Ogilvie. Even the beadle at the workhouse trundled me off to St. Brandan's because I was too much trouble."

"You were valiant at Trafalgar, so I have heard from Master Six."

"We all were, sir. I was twelve years old."

Please, Joshua thought. *Please.*

He knew Captain Ogilvie would never be a soft man, or an easy man to get along with. War had probably turned him hard, war that Joshua hated with all the fervor of his peaceable heart.

"I never thought I would ask this, but what would *you* like, lad?"

Josiah closed his eyes in relief.

"Sir, I would be part of a family," Avon said. "I would decide on a vocation on my own. Right now, I am leaning toward justice."

"That is what I lean toward," the captain said, his voice much gentler now, his eyes almost soft. "Alas, the harsh kind, because we remain at war."

"Justice for people like me," Avon told him. "Aye, that is what I wish."

"How can we do that? You belong to the Royal Navy."

Avon's answer was breathtaking in its simplicity. He took the chart from his bed and put it on the unknown lad's bed, after removing the chart that read, *William Teague is not prospering.*

"We are to bury Avon March in Potter's Field?" Captain Ogilvie asked. His voice sounded strange this time, vulnerable.

Josiah let out his breath slowly. "Who is to know except us?"

"Who, indeed?" the captain asked. He took a deep breath. "Avon March, Royal Navy, gave his life for justice."

"I will pin my Trafalgar medal on him," Avon said. "That will be hard, but I'll do it."

"Where will you go from here, Mr. Coffin?" Ogilvie asked, when he had control of himself.

"America."

Clearly, Captain Ogilvie didn't expect that. He stepped back in surprise. "For a mild and quiet bloke, you can create an impact, sir! Where, might I ask?"

"I won't tell thee," Josiah said. "That way if anyone questions thee about anything or any*one*, thee has no knowledge."

He had to give the captain credit. "I know for a fact that there are many Quakers in Pennsylvania," Ogilvie said, persistent to the end.

"Aye, there are." *That's not where we are going,* Josiah thought, amused.

Ogilvie stuffed his hands in his pockets and rocked back on his heels. Avon went to his clothing hanging on a peg near the matron's desk. He turned his jacket inside out and removed his Trafalgar medal, his most prized possession. He pinned it on the now Avon March's hospital gown. He looked at it a long while. "I will name myself Adam," he said softly. "Adam Coffin."

"I have some small idea what that medal means to you, lad," Ogilvie said.

Adam shrugged. "I want a family more, sir, and I thank'ee."

Captain Ogilvie nodded to Walter Scott, who had watched the whole exchange with his mouth open. "I expect you to say nothing of this."

"Of what?" The two of them left together without a backward glance.

Only Adam, Davey, and Josiah remained in the indigent ward. While Adam dressed, Josiah ward walked, amazed that anyone could have slept through John Yerby's racket. Davey took another aisle, lantern lit and held high now, watching the patients. Josiah nodded his silent approval.

Poor John Yerby. He wanted to ask Captain Ogilvie what John's chances were of surviving to Australia, but decided he didn't want to know. They were probably on par with a garment in a hot furnace.

He found a stretcher and laid the new Avon March on it. "I would rather he were in Tron, instead of Potter's Field," Josiah told Adam, his almost-son, as they carried the body to the morgue. He left a note on the body to that effect, stating that he would return in the afternoon and finalize an appropriate funeral for Avon March, a Gunwharf Rat who swept and watched, and skulked about until he found what Captain Ogilvie wanted: the murderers of a Royal Marine and carpenter's mate. There would be money enough for a tombstone with Avon March, RN, Trafalgar Hero on it. He could probably find a way to see that it was decorated with flowers now and then. "Thee is not anonymous to the God who made us," he told the unknown lad.

"Shall we go home, Adam?" he asked the young man soon, or maybe already, his son. "I suspect that Mum has gnawed off her fingernails down to the elbow, wondering how we fared."

Adam laughed at that, and shuddered elaborately. They strolled through the park. Davey joined them. False dawn was beginning to pink the eastern sky. "I believe this will be a clear day," Josiah said. "A good day for a wedding." Adam and Davey smiled at each other.

Esther threw open the door as she heard their footsteps and grabbed them both. Since her legs wouldn't hold her, Josiah carried her into the sitting room and sat her down on the sofa, where they were joined by Mrs. Perry, wearing a nightgown of amazing proportions and flowery, to boot. Dawn truly came before they finished the whole story.

"Captain Ogilvie is going to let us go, just like that?" Esther asked, eyes wide.

Josiah nodded. "Aye, and then some. He got what he wanted – the student who killed the Royal Marine and the carpenter's mate. Alas, Avon March succumbed, but he died a hero. Somebody is going to dissect Wee Willie, but it won't be me. I think I will not dissect anyone again. What Captain Ogilvie did is proof that he is an assassin with a heart. Well, we knew that. It's anatomically impossible to wander the earth without one."

Esther rested her head against his shoulder. "I must ask: You are unemployed, my love. How do you plan to keep Av..Adam and me in yard goods and porridge?"

He could wait until they reached London, when she could see with her own eyes that his father's counting house prospered, and he had a share in it. He was still a modest man. "I have a brother on Nantucket who runs the American branch of Father's counting house. Nantucket is a small island off Massachusetts, I believe, and home to many Friends. I believe I will set up my practice there."

He turned to Davey. "Thee may choose to finish this term, then return to Portsmouth and Haslar Hospital, if that is thy wish."

"It is. Mrs. Perry and I can also close up this house and return together, if that is agreeable to her."

"Aye," Mrs. Perry said.

Josiah needed to be sure, considering his own deep regard for Davey Ten. "Davey, thee may come with us, too, if thee so chooses."

Davey's answer gratified him, heart and soul. "I have chosen medicine and the sea – chosen, mind you. It is my heart's desire, Avon, as long as I am permitted to know where you are, so I can visit in future."

"Gunwharf Rats are always Gunwharf Rats," Adam replied. "You will know."

The day had dawned. There was no point in sleeping. Mrs. Perry went into the kitchen, joined by Davey and Adam. In a short time, Josiah smelled bacon. Soon eggs would chuckle in the bacon grease. He leaned back on the sofa, and promptly fell asleep.

He woke up to bacon held under his nose by his sweet Esther, who pointed to the kitchen. Breakfast revived him. When they finished, he looked at his timepiece. "Eight of the clock. I suppose the Registry Office is open." He gazed around the table at the dearest people in his universe. "Wait here."

He easily found paper and pen in Esther's desk in the sitting room and wrote his heart. When he returned to the kitchen, he took Esther by the hand and pulled her to her feet. He took both her hands and looked into her eyes, compassionate and full of deep and abiding love for him, a most fortunate man. He cleared his throat, and read the page.

"Esther Teague, I would have thee as my wife, and equal partner in life. I cannot promise smooth sailing," he said, with a glance at the Gunwharf Rats, who nodded seriously, "but I can promise thee and our children now" – a glance at Adam – "and those to come, that I will be ever faithful and kind. What say thee, Esther Teague?"

"I say aye," she told him, her voice as resolute as his.

He kissed her. "Esther, thee is my wife, and these are our witnesses. Please sign thy names." He handed around the paper, the scratch of pen to paper music to him. In Nantucket, Massachusetts, he would frame it and give it a place of honor in their home, just as his parents' wedding pledge had a prominent place in their London home.

"Davey and Mrs. Perry, thee are invited to come to the Registry Office with us, because Scotland and England are sticklers about wedlock and probably do not trust a Quaker. Thee must join us, Avon...."

"Adam," Adam reminded.

"...Adam, since thy name will be on that certificate as my son."

Could a man be happier? He doubted it. Dressed and ready in short order, he opened the front door and stared down at the step.

There, pinned to a prescription pad, was Avon March's Trafalgar Medal, with a note that read, *This belongs to one person only. You earned it. You keep it. AO.*

Esther dabbed at her eyes. "I wouldn't call Captain Ogilvie a warm and cuddly man, but Adam, he did the right thing."

"So did I," the Gunwharf Rat said. He looked at Josiah and Esther. "I love you both." He paused. "Should I say thee?"

"In time, Adam, in time."

It became even more right that morning in the Registry Office, when the kingdom of England, Scotland and Wales through an officious clerk, deemed Josiah Coffin and Esther Teague officially united in the eyes of the nation, even though the marriage that counted took place in the kitchen at 158 Wilmer Street, witnessed by a Black housekeeper and two Gunwharf Rats.

How do these things happen? Only ten days later, after a visit to London and a counting house that left Mrs. Coffin wide-eyed and Mr. Coffin looking like he had pulled off the greatest joke of the century, the Coffins (including Adam Coffin) set sail for Boston, America, from Bristol.

The three of them stood on deck, watching England recede. Mr. Coffin had a hand on Mrs. Coffin's waist, her arm around his waist. His other hand rested lightly on the shoulder of Adam Coffin, entered in the ship's manifest as his son. Any person involved in writing family history in the distant future would probably spend frustrating time in archives trying to figure out just who that eldest son of the Coffin family really was, but did it matter?

It didn't matter to the little family, as they crossed the deck and faced west. Hopefully their descendants will content themselves with a question mark, considering that Adam Coffin, Quaker, would become a noted judge years later in the Commonwealth of Massachusetts, God save it. It's enough to know that these three hopeful immigrants were the beginning of a loving family.

That was all Avon March ever wanted.

Epilogue

S   "Providential, wasn't it, that a ship sailed at precisely the right time?"

"Able, you know perfectly well that somehow, some way, Euclid and his associates had a hand in this entire adventure."

So said Meridee Six, wisest of wives, in Able Six's opinion, and certainly the loveliest. She did have a question for her man's ears only, best delivered when they were snuggled in bed, the little ones asleep, and time theirs alone. "My love, I know we Sixes and the Gunwharf Rats have been sworn to secrecy about the actual fate of Avon March, but does it bother you that he turned his back on St. Brendan's School and the Royal Navy? I suspect the latter is an offense punishable by death."

"Aye, which is why no one outside of our small circle must ever know." Able fingered her hair. "And no, as well. I think…I know… that if you were to peel back the layers of a Gunwharf Rat like an onion, after wariness, loyalty to other Rats, and country, you would find a child always searching for his parents."

She raised up on one elbow to see him better, her curly-haired genius of a mate, and kissed him. She rested her head on his chest, pleased when his arms went around her. "You searched for your parents, too. Able, I am so sorry you didn't find them sooner."

"I found *you*, Meri. I continue to remain the luckiest man in the world." He chuckled. "Only you would believe this: I took a moment this afternoon to thank Euclid for his meddling in the Scottish matter. Avon – Adam – is where he belongs. Davey is returning here soon, now that the term is over and he has acquitted himself brilliantly. The surgeons at

Haslar can't wait to continue his education." He tickled her. "Mrs. Perry will supervise your kitchen and all of us Sixes again."

"Jamie MacGregor is third luff on a flagship, and Smitty is already a noted sailing master. Our own Nick Bonfort-Six and the other Rats are acquitting themselves on many oceans and in many ports," she added, tickling him back. "And there are new sprouts who want to become Gunwharf Rats. Good work, Durable Six."

"I could not have done it without you – or keep doing it! Go to sleep, my love. Euclid wants a word with me. I want to conserve my manly powers so we can have a romp before morning when our children wake up and the classroom beckons."

Meri kissed him so well that he almost changed his busy mind about putting off that romp until morning. She cuddled close and he took a moment to marvel that he remained the luckiest man on all seven seas and probably in the universe.

Wouldn't you agree, Euclid? Euclid? Are you bored? Asleep?

Never that. I suppose I am relieved. Able, you have been a lot of work, and will continue to be, if not you, then your little Ben. Rest your brain, my dear, unlikely master genius. Good night.

Author's Notes

This is indeed the conclusion to the St. Brendan Series. I thought I had finished the series with Book Three, *The Unlikely Heroes*, when Able Six discovered the truth of his origins. And what historical fiction writer worth her salt wouldn't like to end in the blaze of glory that was the Battle of Trafalgar?

My readers dictated otherwise. They encouraged me to write a little more about the Gunwharf Rats, those clever lads who overcame the stigma of their lowly beginnings in workhouses and proved to be of great valor and worth to a nation fighting alone against the tyranny of Napoleon Bonaparte.

Since I was sending Davey Ten off to the University of Edinburgh's famed College of Medicine, why not look into that? As a historian, I already knew a little about the College of Medicine. Digging a little deeper was gratifying. The College of Medicine in Edinburgh remains the choice of many aspiring physicians today. Guenter B. Risse's *Hospital Life in Enlightenment Scotland* was a prime source about the workings of the college, which, for the purpose of this novel, I have simplified. *Death, Dissection and the Destitute*, by Ruth Richardson, has a shocking-enough title. I found it dry as toast, but also informative.

Where did my Quaker physician come from? I got the idea for my peaceable man and delightful character from Joseph Lister, the pre-eminent physician-scientist who pioneered antiseptic surgery, saving untold lives. Specifically, *The Butchering Art*, by Lindsey Fitzharris, focuses on Dr. Lister, the father of modern-day surgery, and the child of two devout Quakers. *The Butchering Art* is a good read and I recommend it. Lister was a remarkable man.

I'll admit it: I've always been fascinated with true crime. I excuse myself by saying that historians are always intrigued by why people do what they do, and I'm sticking to that story. Reader, if you're similarly inclined, let me recommend *The Infamous Burke and Hare: Serial Killers and Resurrectionists of Nineteenth Century Edinburgh*, by R. Michael Gordon. You'll learn all you want to know about grave robbing and body snatching by these two criminal-minded Irishmen living in Edinburgh, Scotland. Burke and Hare started out in the grisly but generally legal business of procuring dead bodies for dissection and subsequent education of medical students. Unfortunately, at some point in the late 1820s, greed motivated them into killing those bodies a tad before their time, shall we say.

I did find myself in good literary company as I delved into Burke and Hare. It turns out that Walter Scott, a young barrister in Edinburgh in 1808, also found true crime fascinating, and accumulated his own research on grave robbers. I was happy to make him a friend of Mr. Josiah Coffin and let him share in this adventure with the Gunwharf Rats. Sir Walter Scott, of course, is far better known as the author of hugely popular poems such as "The Lady of the Lake," and novels such as *Ivanhoe*, the *Waverly Novels*, and my personal favorite, *The Talisman*.

Let me note this: Starting in the mid-eighteenth century, Mister was the title given to doctors who received diplomas. The title of Doctor was reserved for those who had an actual degree. Even then, Mister and Doctor were often used interchangeably. Also, certain names have been associated with adherents of the Religious Society of Friends, among them Coffin, which is why I chose it.

As I think about it, I might consider a Gunwharf Rat story or two in future Christmas anthologies. I suppose writers should never say never, and in truth, I'm as fond of the Rats as my readers.

About the Author

A veteran of romance writing, USA Today best-selling author Carla Kelly is the author of forty-six novels and three non-fiction works, as well as numerous short stories and articles. She is the recipient of two RITA Awards from Romance Writers of America for Best Regency of the Year; two Spur Awards from Western Writers of America; three Whitney Awards, 2011, 2012, and 2014; and a Career Achievement Award from Romantic Times.

Carla's interest in historical fiction is a byproduct of her scholar's study of history. Her variety of jobs include medical public relations work, feature writer and columnist for a North Dakota daily newspaper, and ranger in the National Park Service at Fort Laramie National Historic Site and Fort Union Trading Post National Historic Site. She has done contract research for the North Dakota Historical Society.

Interest in the maritime Napoleonic Wars led to novels about the British Channel Fleet. Carla has also written novels set in Wyoming, and in the early twentieth century that focus on ranching. Her books have been translated into 18 languages.

You are welcome to contact Carla at https://carlakellyauthor.com